ACT OF WILL

BOOKS BY A. J. HARTLEY

The Mask of Atreus
On the Fifth Day
What Time Devours
Act of Will

ACT
OF
WILL

A. J. HARTLEY

TOR®

A TOM DOHERTY ASSOCIATES BOOK
New York

ACT OF WILL

Edited by Liz Gorinsky

Book design by Mary A. Wirth
Maps by Jennifer Hanover

A Tor Book
Published by Tom Doherty Associates, LLC
175 Fifth Avenue
New York, NY 10010

www.tor-forge.com

Tor® is a registered trademark of Tom Doherty Associates, LLC.

Library of Congress Cataloging-in-Publication Data

Hartley, A. J. (Andrew James)
    Act of Will / A. J. Hartley—1st ed.
        p. cm.
    ISBN-13: 978-0-7653-2124-4
    ISBN-10: 0-7653-2124-6
    1. Actors—Fiction. 2. Dramatists—Fiction. I. Title.
    PR6108.A787A65 2009
    823'.92—dc22

                                                    2008038364

Printed in the United States of America

0 9 8 7 6 5 4 3 2

To Chris, my brother-in-arms.

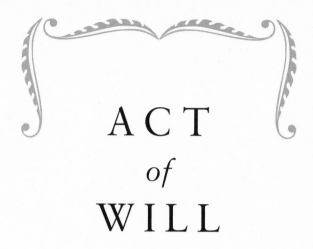

ACT
of
WILL

BY

WILLIAM HAWTHORNE

Translated from the Thrusian by

A. J. HARTLEY

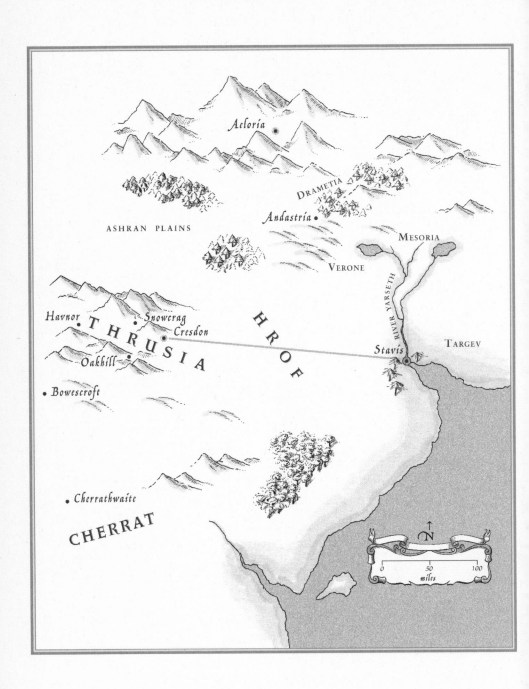

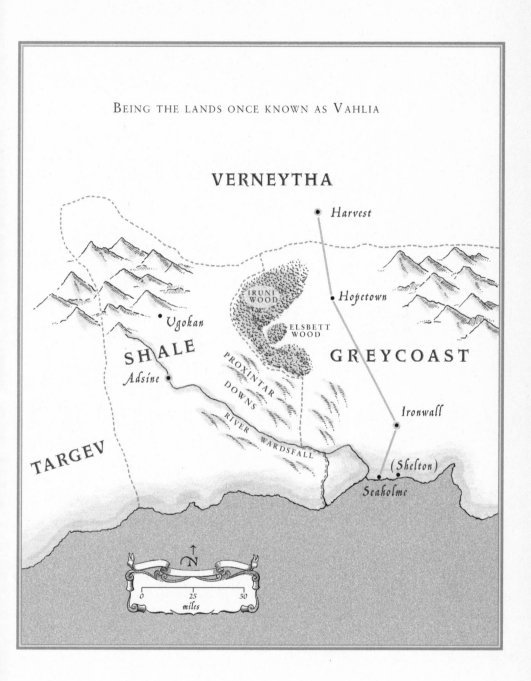

BEING THE LANDS ONCE KNOWN AS VAHLIA

VERNEYTHA

• Harvest

SHALE

• Ugokan

IRUNI WOOD

ELSBETT WOOD

GREYCOAST

• Hopetown

Adsine •

PROXINTAR DOWNS

RIVER WARDSFALL

Ironwall •

TARGEV

(Shelton)

Seaholme

↑
N

0   25   50
miles

TRANSLATOR'S PREFACE

Until a few years ago, the collection of manuscripts now known as the Hawthorne Saga had been sitting in a climate-controlled case in an obscure English library for over a century, baffling all attempts to decipher the strange language in which they were written. We knew from library records that they were once part of the Fossington collection and that they were almost lost when the east wing of Fossington House was badly damaged by fire in 1784. Parts of the second manuscript showed some light scorching, and there was moderately severe water damage to much of the first book, but how they were originally acquired and from where remains a mystery. The eighteenth-century records refer to the crate of Fossington manuscripts only as "handwritten, very old, bound in calf, in indecipherable cursive: language unknown."

Being completely unreadable, the manuscripts would have remained no more than linguistic and historical curiosities were it not for the recent discovery of certain papers located in the attic of an Elizabethan manor house in Oxfordshire, the precise location of which I am not at liberty to reveal. I was first shown these papers eight years ago. Various experts concurred that the author was none other than the famous translator Sir Thomas Henby (1542–1609). The papers were all in Elizabethan secretary hand and difficult to read, which is the only explanation I can offer for not immediately recognizing that while some of them were in plain English, others were actually transcripts of the strange language featured in the Fossington House papers. Even after I had made the connection, it was another year before I realized that the English pages were actually translations of the so-called indecipherable cursive of the Fossington manuscripts, which actually turned out to be a previously undocumented language: Thrusian. How and with what assistance, if any, Henby accessed the key to this remarkable literary find, I cannot begin to imagine, but there is no question that he did, and left both direct translations of several dozen pages and notes by which the rest might be rendered into English.*

I have made up for my slowness to realize the significance of my find by diligent work on the manuscripts ever since. Using Henby's translations and notes as a kind of Rosetta stone, I have been able to work out the grammar, diction, and tone of the Fossington House papers, which I have renamed the Hawthorne Saga for reasons that will become apparent. In the translation, I have used a modern, colloquial style in an attempt to capture—or at least echo—the uniquely sprightly and energetic Thrusian used by the author. The book in your hands, faithfully translated from the original, is the result. I only hope that you find my labor in bringing this ancient text to light to be worth the reading. If this meets with sufficient approval and I encounter no serious hurdles in the translation, I plan to complete work on the second volume of the series approximately one year from now.

—*A. J. Hartley, 2009*

---

* No identification of the place—or even the period—from which the original came has yet been made. All attempts to identify known landmarks, places, or geographical features have failed. Militarily, it lacks gunpowder and therefore seems early medieval, but the culture as presented seems later, more in accord with Renaissance Europe.

SCENE I

Show Business

The day started quietly, which, as it turned out, was not so much ironic as completely misleading. I had risen late after a long night memorizing speeches by the dodgy light of a cheap tallow candle. Mrs. Pugh—the miserable and vindictive woman who had been paid by the theatre to "look after" me since my parents died, which basically amounted to keeping me alive till my apprenticeship was done—had woken me at eleven o'clock, then forced me to eat what looked suspiciously like a bowl of fried porridge. Why anyone would do anything with porridge, let alone fry it, is a serious bloody mystery to me.

It was my eighteenth birthday, which meant that my theatre apprenticeship was officially over: now the company would either take me on as a full member, or they would cut me loose. Either way, this would be my last day in a dress. Thank God.

I'm not sure why the Empire doesn't allow women onstage. It's pretty stupid when you stop to think about it. But everyone is used to it and it keeps the likes of me in steady work, so I'm not complaining. Admittedly, most of the parts I got as a woman were comprised of simpering love poetry and vacant smiles, but once in a while I got to do a good death scene, or double as a nameless soldier in a battle, or something. That was pretty fun, and it got me out of those bloody corsets for ten minutes or so.

But none of it equaled the time I got to play a prince. I had three long speeches and a fight scene and, best of all, I got to write some of my own lines. (All actors think they're poets. Most of them aren't.) I got a standing ovation at the end of each performance. Not all the boy actors graduate to men's roles, but I was the best we had at the moment, so I figured there'd still be a job for me when I hung up my skirt for the last time. Probably. Not everyone in the company appreciated my talents, of course, least of all the really stupid ones, who—needless to say—had a lot of sway in the company. If they didn't take me in as an actor, I'd probably be able to make a living writing for them, but it wouldn't be much of a living, so I was a bit apprehensive about what they'd tell me after the show.

That was when it would happen. After the stage had been swept and the taproom closed, before they got everyone back out to rehearse the next day's show, they'd meet and vote and call me into the green room for their verdict. Then I'd be an actor, a writer, or both, or I'd be homeless with no source of income till I could cobble a play together and sell it.

I should say that being an eighteen-year-old in Cresdon means that you've been a man for at least half a decade already, even if you've made your living in a dress. I can't compare it to other places, and I'm sure there are kids my age whose comfort and happiness are still carefully engineered by other people, but unless you're gentry where I live, you pretty much have to claw your way into manhood, and there's plenty who don't make it. Kids starve, or they get beaten to death by their so-called benefactors, or they get sold into slavery. I'm not trying to shock you or convince you that I'm some kind of hero for making it this long; but I don't want you thinking you're going to get a tale about some blue-eyed tyke with a heart of gold in a world where good triumphs over evil. You're not, I'm not, and in my experience it never does.

Just so we're clear.

Anyway. I lived less than half a mile from the theatre, but one of those impromptu markets which Cresdon's residents seem so fond of had spontaneously appeared right outside the goldsmith's on Aqueduct Street. I was soon up to my armpits in goats and cheese and bales of smelly wool imported by the equally smelly herders from the Ashran Plains, north of the city. By the time I reached the backstage entrance of the Eagle Theatre, I could already hear the bugles finishing up, which meant they were halfway through what passed for a musical introduction: a florid-faced idiot called Rufus Ramsbottom and an instrument (in the loosest possible sense of the word) which he claimed was an Andastrian bagpipe but which sounded like three cats and a chicken tied together in a sack. Not that anyone took any notice. This was strictly background noise to make the paying public feel that something was starting, thus encouraging them to focus on the crucial business of buying one last pint and fighting each other for seats.

The Eagle sat at the end of a dim alley which, like all the others in the city at this time of year, was hot, muddy, and rank with the odors of wandering livestock and abandoned refuse. It was a typical Cresdon theatre: round (near enough), with a raised thrust stage, a pair of stage entrances, a balcony, a discovery space, and a trapdoor to the cellarage. The house held close to three thousand, packing eight hundred standing into the pit and seating the rest in three galleries, one on top of the other. The best view of the stage was from up top and would cost you three standard silver pieces, but you could get a good deal if you were prepared to stand down front. Some of the local aristos would pay six or seven silvers to actually sit on the stage and show off their fancy new duds, something all the actors hated with a passion. They never kept still and you were lucky if they did no more than yawn and wave to their friends. Sometimes they gave you acting notes or stopped the show to argue a plot point. Rich people always think they know best.

I got into my dress and blond wig as quickly as I could, and took a last glance over the script. We were doing a pompous tragedy called *Reynath's Revenge,* whose entire last act was a series of preposterously engineered assassinations. It wasn't just the end that was stupid. The whole play was rubbish. We'd just put it back into the repertory because a new one by the same author had opened a week or so ago over at the Blue Lion. The only audience who bothered showing up to ours had probably seen it a dozen times. It had been crap every time, but they kept coming back.

My dress was too tight around the throat because it had been made for Bob Evans, who had had the frame of a plucked chicken till he was about sixteen, when he had doubled in all possible dimensions, bursting every seam in every dress they put him in. By sheer surging hormonal bulk, combined with the timely death of old Silas Woods from the wheezing sickness, Bob attained what the kid actors all dreamed of: he had started playing men's roles.

I poured myself a small beer, lit a pipe, and joined the pre-show card game in the green room. I say "pre," but it would go on through the show, pausing only when too many of us were onstage to continue.

By the end of the second scene, the game was going badly. For me, I mean. It was going swimmingly for everyone else. I sipped my stale beer and tried to figure out how much I had lost so far.

Like most Cresdon theatres, the Eagle did double duty as a tavern and was famed for its taproom, which served beer throughout the show. When there was nothing going on onstage, cards, dice, and darts were the rule. All of these humble pastimes could be turned to advantage by a perceptive and audacious actor-cum-gambler, story-teller, and performer: namely, me. William Hawthorne, known as Will the Sharp or Quick Bill to the patrons of the Eagle Theatre and Tavern, at your service. Care to place a bet, sir, madam?

Except that it was only me who used the epithets of Quick Bill or Will the Sharp, and if your ears were good enough, you would be more likely to hear those worthy patrons announce me as Bill the Cheat, Lying Will, That Kid Who Tried to Rip Me Off, etc. etc. In fact, Bill the Incompetent might be nearer the mark, as a quick tally of today's winnings suggested.

See, the taproom was, generally speaking, fairly easy pickings. Most of the people who came to play were either regulars (who you knew to avoid) or incompetents who couldn't fork their cash over to you fast enough. But I wasn't in the taproom now; I was in the green room. Normally I played conservatively here, but today I was nerv-ous, perhaps a little too anxious to show how little I cared whether they gave me a job or not in a couple of hours. The combination had made me reckless.

The problem with the green-room games was that they were pop-ulated solely by theatre people, mainly actors. Here, the usual bluffs, prevarications, convenient fictions, and barefaced cheating would af-ford you little, because everyone there knew them of old. Rufus Rams-bottom, for example, was a lousy actor who could barely deliver a line without fumbling or dropping something, and he wasn't a particu-larly good cardplayer, but he knew a cheat when he saw one, and he was looking at one right now. He had mean little eyes and a fat pink face, producing the look of a rather slow but pathologically malevo-lent pig. Those eyes held mine, and he wasn't giving me an inch.

"Come on, Hawthorne," he said. "I have to go on."

"I doubt they'd miss you," I said. "The show's better when ac-tors do only their own lines."

This was a particular talent of Rufus's. He couldn't remember his own part if his life depended on it, but he would blurt out other people's lines constantly. It was taxing for actors and audience alike.

"Just play or fold, boy," he said, glowering so that the red bris-tles on his forehead stood on end.

"Blood and sand," I muttered as I threw my cards down, abandoning the sorry bluff. "Fold."

He grinned, raked the coins into a pile, and then marched to the stage door.

"I've counted them, Hawthorne," he said warningly before disappearing through the door. He hadn't, of course. That would have taken him, like, half an hour.

You could always tell when Rufus Ramsbottom went onstage because there wasn't a sound from the house, except maybe a few groans. Usually actors got a little patter of applause when they went on for the first time in a show, but Rufus was such a giftless swine that even the kids who only came to see the sword fights and pig's blood started shifting in their seats and muttering darkly about getting their money back.

I put my cards down and tipped my purse out onto the table. I considered the paltry pile of coins left to me, and it was like being punched in the gut by someone wearing (for reasons I can't begin to guess) very cold gloves. Rufus, however, was positively flush and getting flusher as the game wore on. He had money. I needed money— possibly a lot of it if the post-show meeting went badly. There was a certain inevitability to the whole thing, really.

The green room was momentarily deserted. Barring some clamorous fiasco in the present scene (always a possibility when Rufus trod the boards), I probably had about another thirty seconds before Jack Brundage, who had been sitting on my left, would get offstage and return to the game. I considered the pile of coins where Rufus had been sitting, took a deep breath, helped myself to two silvers, rearranged what was left, and then helped myself to another.

If I'd stopped at two, I might have got away with it. But no. Brundage emerged at the stage door just I was withdrawing my hand. I grinned and blustered and asked him what the crowd was like, but it was no good. He'd seen.

Brundage was a tall, slender man with a sardonic face that made him seem smarter than he was. He was a good minor bad guy, but didn't have the stage presence to be a real villain, and though he had a loud voice that carried well in a brassy sort of way, he delivered every line at full volume. As a man and as an actor, he had no depth, no richness or complexity. He also didn't like me very much and was a good friend of Rufus Ramsbottom.

It was thus with some trepidation that I slipped past him, avoiding his eyes as I made for the stage door. He let me go, but he was smiling that slightly twisted smile of his, like he was sucking something very sweet and very sour at the same time. He wasn't letting me off the hook; he was figuring out how best to twist it.

I listened for the cue and strode out, but my heart wasn't in it, and even the familiar patter of applause at my appearance didn't still the wobble of my stomach. This was going to get worse before it got better.

"Good day, my lord," I said on cue. "I feared I'd come too late."

I was Julia, a minor love interest in a play largely preoccupied with a series of bizarre poisonings. I'd played the part a dozen times, and though it was a smallish role by my standards, I had some speeches in the fourth act in which I whined about justice and honesty and got to rant and wail a bit. Sometimes the audience even cried.

Not today, I thought. If there was any weeping to be done, it would be me, crying over an empty purse and being drummed out of the company for dishonesty. And it might be worse. Brundage and Rufus were men of little imagination, but they usually came up with something terse and painful in the way of punishment. Once when one of the prop boys had been caught listening in on some conversation they had wanted to keep to themselves, they had cut off his right earlobe to make the point. It was as close as they came to whimsy.

Twenty lines into the scene, Rufus had an exit. Usually it was a relief to see him lumber out of sight, and the play as a whole picked up as those still onstage got to do more than navigate around his cluelessness, but not today. I knew that the moment he got off, Brundage would be waiting to tell him how I had adjusted his funds, and by the time I headed into the green room, they'd be ready to have a little word with me. Except that it wouldn't be a word. It would be something altogether different involving an oak cudgel and a bit of lead pipe. Whether or not they would hand over whatever was left to the Empire, I couldn't say, but being welcomed into the company after this seemed a long shot.

I watched him go off, my guts hollow, and it was like I'd never been onstage before. I knew I had lines, but for a moment I just stood there, my mind blank, feeling the audience starting to watch me in that too-curious way they have when they sense someone screwing up, like hyenas spotting a wounded gazelle. Rafe Jenkins glowered at me across the stage.

"So, Lady Julia," he said, completely buggering up the verse, "you already spoke to my lord Francisco?"

"What?" I said, tearing my eyes from the stage door where Brundage and Rufus were whispering just out of the audience's sightline. "Oh, right. Yes. I did."

Someone in the front row nudged her neighbor and giggled. Even in my stark, bewildered terror, a tiny part of me hated her for it.

"And," said Rafe, laboring and glaring still more pointedly, "Lord Francisco told you that—"

"That," I said quickly. "Something. Yes. He told me something."

It was like I was watching someone else, some stupid kid in a dress who had no right being onstage in public.

A ripple of mirth coursed through the entire pit and I flushed. There was a long pause and Rafe glared at me. I had no idea what my lines were. I couldn't remember the plot or who I was supposed to be. All I could see clearly was Rufus waiting for me in the green room with his cudgel. Then there was a bang at the back of the house and, for the briefest of moments, things seemed to be looking up.

The bang came from the main street entrance into the theatre. I heard shouts, and the crowd standing in the pit began to part like sheep before a dog. Probably a rowdy drunk, I thought: just the excuse I needed to slip away until things cooled down a little.

But it wasn't a drunk. It was a man on a horse, riding right into the theatre. He wore silver plate armor and a white cape. Behind him were twenty foot soldiers: Diamond Empire guards. There was a murmur of discontent, but the air smelled of unease, even panic. Nothing like this had ever happened before.

The mounted officer produced a roll of parchment and, as his horse skittered to a halt on the cobbles, started to read aloud in one of those voices that you can tell isn't used to being messed about.

"On behalf of the Diamond Empire, governors of these territories," he said, "I hereby declare this and all such theatres permanently closed as houses of rebellion and immorality. The building will be demolished by fire and the land impounded by the state. The following lewd and seditious persons are to be taken into Empire custody for their part in the playing and writing of plays and entertainments unbecoming to the dignity of an Empire territory."

I stared at him. He couldn't be serious. Close the theatres? Arrest the writers? It was madness.

The crowd thought so too. There was a surly grumbling from all over the building and a scattering of boos and hisses.

The officer nodded as if this was to be expected, and the soldiers drew their weapons. They *were* serious.

"William Hawthorne," said the officer.

"Hello?" I said guilelessly. "Yes?"

The officer paused.

"I'm reading the list," he said.

"List?"

"Of those who are to be arrested," he added with steely patience.

"Ah," I said. "William who?"

"Hawthorne," said the officer. "Isn't that you?"

"Me?" I said. "No. Never heard of him. I'm just a kid."

"That's Hawthorne, all right," said a big, booming voice from the stage-left side. It was Rufus. He took a step out onto the lip of the stage and pointed a thick finger at me. "William Hawthorne." He added, in case anyone might have missed the gist of the chat thus far, "Actor, playwright, thief, liar, and all-round snake."

It was his most flawless performance to date.

The officer considered this. Then, returning his eyes to the list, he said simply, "Take him."

SCENE II

Making an Exit

Immediately two of the foot soldiers plunged through the crowd towards the stage: I hesitated, but I had been visited by a sudden and violent conviction that being "taken" by these men would likely turn out to be a very bad thing indeed, something far beyond even Rufus's mean little imagination.

Sedition? I was an apprentice actor who had some small talent with a pen. How was that sedition?

It made no sense, but the Empire tossed that word around with fond abandon, and anyone tarred by that particular brush wouldn't see the light of day for some considerable time. Hadn't a poet in Freescroft had a hand cut off only a couple of days ago? I wasn't sure, but it suddenly seemed more than likely. And the fines! Why must authorities persist in thinking that actors have some secret treasure trove? At least if they demanded one of my hands, I could oblige. If they wanted silver, I was really screwed.

All this mental rambling took about three seconds, during which the young troopers in the pit readied themselves as if they expected some monstrous grizzly to come crashing towards them. In fact, of course, I was an adolescent in a dress—a skinny adolescent at that, whose combat skills were limited to the ability to deliver heroic battlefield speeches from old plays.

Panic set in. I had no choice but to turn myself over.

Having reached that conclusion rather reasonably, I cannot say exactly what it was that made me scale one of the pillars that supported the stage canopy and scramble over the rail onto the balcony. Maybe my simmering resentment of the Empire had finally taken over. Maybe I was standing up for the oppressed in the face of overwhelming force. Maybe I was outraged that the art of the theatre should be so demeaned by these thuggish philistines. Maybe, and this was more likely, I just hated the idea that Rufus's limited intellectual abilities should be so instrumental in bringing me to "justice." Yes, that was more like it. My pride was injured.

Stick around, I thought, *and they'll wound more than your pride.*

Two of the soldiers had unslung bows and were training them in my direction. By the time I had hauled myself onto the balcony—and try doing that in a floor-length velvet gown—one white-feathered arrow had whistled over my head and another one had slammed into the oak rail just below my hand. The crowd murmured, coming to life as if the play had picked up where it left off. I gave a startled yelp, half dumb realization of what I had begun to do, half sheer bladder-stretching terror.

I glanced down. I always loved being up here in the balcony with the music rooms behind me and a sea of faces turned up and hanging on my every word. I'd had some of my greatest actorly moments from this very spot, a suitably dramatic place to go down in a hail of arrows.

But the play wouldn't end that way. Not today. No tragedies for William. I was in strictly comic mode, which is, I suppose, why I pulled the ladder over and started shinning up to the trap in the canopy. I started up, dodged another arrow, nearly fell to a messy death on the stage below, and wrenched the trap open. As the officer below started barking more orders and the crowd began to panic, I climbed, skirts hitched round my knees.

Inside the roof canopy was what the company members mockingly called "the gods." It was from here that we lowered some poor bastard in dreadful makeup at the end of those awful the-plot-has-fallen-apart-and-only-some-ludicrously-unrealistic-device-can-cobble-together-an-ending plays. There wasn't much up there but rafters, a winch, and another ladder up onto the thatch. I was up it before you could say "death wish." The audience, those who weren't running to get out before they were held responsible for this little fiasco, applauded me. No one liked the Empire all that much.

There was a chimney stack at one part of the thatched ridge, and I flung myself at it and clung on for dear life, wondering vaguely what lunatic scheme was likely to get me out of this unskewered. The roof ran only around a part of the stage and the perimeter galleries, so I could see the chaos in the yard below quite clearly. I leaned out to look down, and another arrow shot up and came within a cricket's knee joint of finding my throat. Rufus was on the stage, shouting and pointing like the fool he was. And I was sitting on the roof in a dress being shot at by the Empire.

Oh yes. Rufus is the fool here.

Where the devil was I going? I looked around for the obligatory passing hay cart (a staple element of stories like the one I seemed to have wandered into) into which I could safely leap, but it had missed its cue. Five soldiers and the officer were on the stage now, all shooting and trying to shut Rufus up, while Brundage stood there like a sardonic angel of death, sending glances of bitter amusement up with their arrows. For the moment I was safe behind the chimney, but four of the troopers were on their way up after me.

There was still no sign of the hay cart.

There was, however, a house, its roof about ten feet away. The street was about thirty-five feet below. I released the chimney and let another arrow scud past me. Then I rose, setting one foot on each side of the sloping thatch, and began running or staggering to the far end, where I half jumped, half fell across the gap.

The edge of the neighboring roof hit me in the stomach, drove the breath from my body, and almost knocked my wig off. (Don't ask why I was still wearing it. I have no idea.) There were shouts and the sounds of running feet below. I clawed myself up, that infernal dress making it almost impossible for me to get my legs up. (*How did women move in these things?*) I hitched the skirt up around my waist and—as if they had been waiting for me to do just that—one of their arrows immediately found my thigh and stuck there like a firebrand.

I rolled myself out of sight and stared with horrified fascination at the wooden shaft that grew out of the side of my leg, wagging about as I shifted to get a better look. Any sense of pain was temporarily stifled by disbelief. This was a new dimension to my life: Bill the Moving Target, Wounded Will. I pulled at it and gasped as it slid out easily, blood seeping out in a thin trickle. Not much of a wound, I pointed out to myself, vaguely disappointed. The flat arrowhead had gone in at an acute angle, barely under the skin really, but it hurt like . . . well, like an arrow in the leg, actually, and it served to remind me of what I was doing.

I tore a strip off the hem of my dress and tried to bind it round my leg to staunch the blood, but it fell off as soon as I rose to a crouch (the bandage, not my leg). The pain, which had been dull and smoldering, suddenly reared like a small pony and kicked me irritably. For a second I just sat there, but I knew that while the wound in my leg was pretty minor, if I stayed where I was, they'd give me something to be proud of.

I started to crawl, swearing under my breath at Rufus Ramsbottom, the Empire, the patrons of the Eagle, and, without good reason, Mrs. Pugh. I passed three chimney stacks, my dress snagging constantly on the thatch, and kept going. I knew that this chain of mediocre dwellings led into one of Cresdon Town's poorer market areas, but I couldn't for the life of me remember what was at the end of the terrace. After half a dozen successful (well, reasonably successful) years as a theatrical manipulator of other people's greed and stupidity, with hardly a brush with the authorities, I was reduced to dragging my bleeding self—in a dress—through filthy, nest-filled, spider-riddled thatch, while members of the dreaded occupation force tried to put pieces of steel through my windpipe. Nice job, Will Hawthorne, you finally got what you deserve. Good old Quick Bill. Another blinding success delivered by Will the Sharp. And all for three lousy silver pieces. Not enough to cover my funeral. Curse Rufus, curse the Empire, curse me.

Then, without warning, the thatch became terra-cotta tile. Now what? I could hear geese and housewives in the street below. I lifted my head a fraction, waited for an arrow through my throat, and, when it didn't materialize, looked about me.

The town had not fared well since the Empire took control, and this was one of the poorer districts. There were puddles of stagnant, muddy water ranging from mere wheel ruts to large greenish pools across the street, all choked with refuse and buzzing with summer flies. Some of the soldiers were down there, their noses screwed up in disgust, their mud-spattered white cloaks hitched up around their thighs, but they didn't seem to know exactly where I was. I risked a glance back the way I had come and saw three more working their way across the roof. I had to get down.

I leaned out over the edge, wondering if I could survive the drop, and found myself looking upside down into an open leaded window set in the plaster and timber wall below me. An elderly woman with a bucket of God knows what poised to be dumped into the street met my gaze and held it.

Without a word she pushed the window wider and stepped back. I swung myself down and through in a single movement that only five minutes ago would have seemed impossible.

The woman silently returned to the window, caught the eye of one of the soldiers, and pointedly emptied her bucket into the over-flowing drainage ditch below. A waft of shocking stench reached us before she shut the window.

"Thank you, thank you, thank you," I babbled.

"Shut up," she muttered, "you're not safe yet. They aren't that stu-pid. Get a move on. Don't gape, you idiot, do something. What kind of a fool are you anyway, hopping around on the roof while they shoot at you?"

I looked at her with more irritation than I would have thought possible in the circumstances, and wondered vaguely if she could be related to Mrs. Pugh.

There was an open doorway that led into the house proper, a bed, a small table, and a wall of pine boards where the wing had been built out over the street so it butted up against a house on the other side.

"Got a weapon?" she asked in a businesslike tone. "Sword? Mace?"

I shook my head, temporarily dumbstruck. Of course I didn't. That would have been illegal. She tutted pointedly, a look of bored exasperation on her wrinkled features, and started rummaging in a battered armoire, from which she produced a heavy-looking felling ax. She heaved it at me haft-first and it swung madly as I struggled to control its weight.

"Go on, you idiot, go on!" she snarled, hobbling away from the swaying ax head. "Cut it down before you kill us both."

She indicated the pine-boarded wall. I stared at her, wondering if she was serious, then heard the banging and shouting of soldiers downstairs. She made an impatient gesture as if she was dealing with a mentally subnormal baboon and I, suddenly angry at her and pretty much everyone else in the world, swung the ax hard into the wood.

It was faintly satisfying to see the splinters fly. I gritted my teeth and hacked away as the old woman behind me kicked my shins and told me to get a move on. For a moment I was tempted to swing the bloody thing at her, but that desire was replaced by surprise at seeing a middle-aged man on the other side of what was left of the wall,

climbing hastily out of a tin bath and staring at me with terrified astonishment.

I turned to thank the crabby old bag but found she was already
descending to answer the door and deflect the Empire guards, clearly
the only people she hated enough to be of such dramatic assistance
to anyone. The man on the other side of the wall backed off with
disbelief in his eyes as I set to climbing through the hole. He flashed
a look of alarm at the ax, so I dropped it and made pacifying noises
that in no way helped the situation. For about the fiftieth time since
this nightmare began I wished I wasn't wearing a dress and a cas-
cade of blond curls. There was only one way out of the room, and
I took it, blundering past him onto a landing and down a staircase,
while he stood gibbering and staring as before. You couldn't really
blame him: it's not every day that a cross-dressing ax murderer
smashes his way into your bathroom. Not waiting to examine my
surroundings, I found the back door and unbolted it.

Probably the best thing to have done would have been to walk
calmly and maybe put on a coat or something, but such composure
was beyond me. I sprinted aimlessly out into the alley and down the
first street I came to, heading as far away from my lodgings as I
could and stopped.

Where was I supposed to go? Cresdon just wasn't that big, and it
was entirely walled, all gates heavily guarded. Everyone I knew
worked at the Eagle, and those who might still have offered me protection were probably busy worrying about their own necks, possibly
from the depths of some imperial dungeon. An unavoidable truth was
settling like a rock in my gut, and though I had begun the day worried
that I wouldn't get my life on the stage, I was going to end it with a
very different set of priorities. I had to get out of town, perhaps out of
Empire territory altogether. I began to run.

SCENE III

Desperate Times

I stopped running outside an inn.

It looked inviting: a board hung stiff in the still air proclaiming it, innocuously enough, the Silk Weaver's Arms. I had passed it before but never been in, which was probably a plus. I was also thirsty and had detected a comforting smell of malt and hops from the door. I had run more this morning than in the last month. My heart seemed ready to burst, my muscles ached, and my thigh hurt and was still bleeding, however unimpressively. I had to calm down and think what I was going to do next. In short, I needed a beer.

It was dark and cool inside. A handful of quiet drinkers sat at deal tables and didn't look up as I came in. I stood there sweating heavily and tried to look relaxed as I moved to the bar to order.

"Help you, er . . . miss?" said a big man in a stained leather apron. He looked like he could hump those beer barrels around on his back without losing his breath.

I scowled at him.

"Bitter," I managed. "Pint."

His eyes narrowed. I flashed a ladylike smile and straightened my wig.

"Right you are, my lady," he said, still a little uncertainly, and began to pump a tankard full. I turned away, so that I wouldn't die of thirst watching him.

"Two bits."

"Cheers," I said, pushing a couple of copper pieces across the bar at him.

"Good health, miss," he said as I drank. "Looks like you need it."

I gave a thin and lame-sounding laugh and fled into a dark corner by the fireplace.

At the next table a couple of old men were playing dominoes in absolute silence. I tried to think of nothing while my heartbeat and breathing returned to something like normal. After a couple of minutes like this I drained my glass and instantly wanted to find the toilet. Under the strain, I was amazed that my bladder had held out this long. Hell's teeth, I was a fugitive from the Empire! How could I have been so stupid? I had to get out of this dress and out of town, and perhaps a good deal farther. It was a sickening thought. For all the tales of distant lands I'd acted in, I knew nothing about life outside Cresdon, and there was a part of me that found the idea of venturing beyond the city walls almost as terrifying as what the Empire would do to me if they caught me.

Almost. I had been accused of sedition, and then resisted arrest and made the Empire—a small part of it, at least—look silly. I would be proclaimed a rebel, and after that, all bets were off. There was only one punishment for rebels. Actually there were lots of punishments for rebels, many of them inventive and colorful. They just all ended up the same way.

Well, I thought, trying to put a better face on things, putting some mileage between me and Mrs. Pugh's odious house with its cockroaches and its mice and its alarming breakfasts wouldn't be all bad. And I'd never have to listen to Rufus's bagpipe again. Bright side, see?

So, said a nasty voice in my head, *that's settled then. No problem. All you have to do is slip past the thousand armed guards who are currently looking for you specifically, and you're golden.*

Another beer seemed in order.

I got to my feet and looked toward the bar in time to see the street door kick open.

Soldiers. Three of them. I looked for a back door and started moving, wishing I had got rid of the dress and wig the moment I came in.

I made it across the room, staring ahead of me, waiting for an imperious demand to hold-it-right-there, and tried the door. It opened, but it didn't get me outside, just into a corridor lined with more doors: guest rooms, no doubt. Then there was the sound of hurried boots in the barroom coming my way, and I knew that I had about fifteen seconds.

Bolting down the corridor, I tried one of the doors, but it was

locked. The second, likewise. The third swung open and I found myself stuttering apologies and scattering pleas for help at three men
and a girl.

They were perhaps as unlikely a group as Cresdon's uncosmopolitan social milieu would ever see. The girl, who looked about my age,
was fair, pale, and slim. I had some experience of looking at pretty
girls, and there was no question that this one was a bit special. One
of the men—actually, he couldn't have been much older than the
girl—was similarly pale of complexion, though his hair was short and
brown and his eyes were green as a cat's. The other two were of foreign
stock, one black, the other of a swarthy olive complexion with dark
hair and eyes. These last two had both drawn swords as I came in.

"Help!" I squeaked.

The men peered at me. I snatched my wig off and their eyes
widened a little.

"Empire guards!" I blurted, glancing over my shoulder.

It was, apparently, the right thing to say.

For a split second they looked at me, then at each other. Then
the girl pulled one of several large trunks from the corner. Her pale
male counterpart opened it and wordlessly motioned me over.

Then they started arguing.

"Garnet, are you mad?" hissed the black man. "It could be a
trap!"

"We can't take that chance," said the girl. "We have to trust her.
Him. Whatever."

Even in my terror I managed an indignant glare.

"It isn't worth the risk," replied the black man heatedly.

"Who are you?" the olive-skinned man asked me quietly.

I thought I could hear the guards forcing the door of the first guest
room. My moments of liberty were numbered and I wanted to scream
at them. The sweat broke out on my brow and my eyes widened with
fear, but I restrained myself and gasped, "William Hawthorne. I'm an
actor. And a playwright. And," I added reluctantly, "I kind of cheated
at a card game."

"A petty criminal," said the black man, rising to his feet. He was
impressively built and in alarmingly good condition. In fact, all of
them were. He looked me up and down, his eyes lingering on the
bloodstained dress and then, as the door to the second guest room
was audibly kicked open, flashed his eyes to the olive-skinned man

who had demanded my name and who, I sensed, would have the last word.

I was right. For a second he said nothing, and then he whispered, "Get in the box. Quickly!"

The black man bundled me into the crate and sat on it.

"Oh, brilliant," I mumbled. "Put him in the box. They'll never think to look there."

The room fell silent for a second and then, muffled slightly by the wood of the crate, I heard the door open and imperious footsteps enter.

"Any of these?" demanded a soldier.

"No," replied a voice I took to be the innkeeper's.

"Has anyone been in here?"

Muffled negations and murmured inquiries as to what the problem was.

"Open those boxes!"

Blood and sand!

I heard movement and a creaking lid, then another; then I saw daylight, and the irritated face of a soldier peering in at me.

SCENE IV

A New Problem

The soldier's eyes lit up: he drew his sword swiftly and had begun to shout when something stopped him. There was a brilliant flash, yellowish, like firelight, but sudden and stark, so that everything solid went flat and pale, casting hard shadows. I think there was a sound too—a bang? Or a sudden and powerful gust of wind? I wasn't sure. And there was something else, something like falling asleep after too much beer and coming to again with a raging hangover, except that the entire process lasted no more than a few seconds. It was panic, I supposed, and some kind of weird head rush at being shoved into a crate with an Empire soldier about to drag me off to torture and execution. That had to be it.

But there was more. They were fighting. There was grunting and the unmistakable crash of metal on metal, and then a gasp of pain and the sound of a falling body.

God! I was involved in a murderous brawl with Empire guards: a capital offense if ever there was one. I clambered out of the box and started to crawl away.

Someone stepped over my back. I heard a weapon fall and then what sounded like cracking bone. I closed my eyes tighter till someone stood on my wrist and, with a yell of pain, I looked up. The pale kid who had been called Garnet faced a man who might have been the patrol officer. They had their fingers about each other's throats and were fighting for control of the soldier's shortsword. The other soldiers, astonishingly, seemed to be already dead. Or stunned, perhaps, since I could see no blood or wounds. The black man joined the last remaining fight, lending his considerable strength to wrenching the officer's sword from his hand. The officer glared furiously as his strength gave out; then the kid freed himself, hit him once, very hard, in the face, and watched him crumple to the floor.

I struggled to my feet, struck again by how light-headed and unsteady I felt. By the time I was upright the three soldiers weren't, and my barbaric saviors were busy binding the innkeeper's hands and gagging his mouth with a pillowcase. The girl was standing over the officer who had gone down the hardest with a broadsword pointed at his neck. Something in her eyes was as scary as the sword point. It was time for me to get the hell out.

The pale man with the piercing green eyes was nursing his wrist, but the group was calm, businesslike despite their earnest speed and horrifying efficiency, as if this wasn't the first time they'd dealt with Empire soldiers. I looked at the girl, half expecting to see her break down or scream hysterically, but she was as cool as the rest of them.

I coughed and muttered, "I'm dead. I may as well hang myself right now. 'Put him in the box,' they said, Your Worship. That's it. I'm dead." With a miserable whine of despair I looked at the bodies and added, with what I thought to be unmistakable sarcasm, "Great. Thanks a lot. I don't know who the devil you people are but you just did me a real favor."

The pale man looked at me with his homicidal green eyes and shrugged as if I had praised them.

"It was nothing," he said. "They were looking for you, not us. They were off their guard, their weapons were sheathed, two of them had their backs to us, and we had one extra pair of hands."

My disbelief found a new focal point. They were mad. They had to be.

The girl caught my glance and her smile slipped away, her blue eyes freezing onto mine with undisguised indignation. I swallowed and looked down.

"Time for some introductions and then a dressing of that wound," said the olive-skinned man. I gave him a look of frank incredulity and bit my tongue. These maniacs had just casually assaulted three Empire guards, and were now going to invite me over for tea and crumpets.

"You just killed three people!" I exclaimed, unable to restrain myself further. "You just bloody killed . . . I don't believe this. You just killed three people! Don't you get it? Three! Count them. Now what? Eh? Who should we kill next? The emperor? No. Here's an idea: Kill me. Please, go ahead. I'd hate to hold you up. You must have some children to massacre or something, so come on and get it over with. Save the Empire a job."

"They aren't dead," said the black man.

"What?" I muttered.

"They aren't dead," he repeated. "Any of them. Though I thought that last one was going to give us no choice."

"No choice?" I said, incredulous. "He nearly *forced* you to butcher him in cold blood? If someone says hello to you in the street, is that grounds for garroting? I mean, you must have all kinds of interesting ways of killing people who—I don't know—ask you what time it is, or offer you a piece of fruit or—"

He clapped his hand over my mouth.

Actually, I was surprised they'd let me go on as long as I had. The pale kid stepped towards me with the guard's shortsword in his hand and hatred in his emerald eyes. I struggled in the black man's grip but couldn't move. I shut my eyes and waited for the thrust of steel through my stomach. It didn't come and, after a moment of stillness, I opened my eyes.

My would-be attacker had halted and turned his back on me, muttering his fury to the girl. More anxious glances were swapped, but the apparent leader stilled them with a gesture of his hand and a stern look at me. I swallowed hard and tried to regain composure.

"This is Orgos," he said, indicating the black man, who took his big hand away from my mouth and extended it, smiling.

I stared at them in stunned silence as the introductions were concluded and my brain boiled softly. The pale savage who was no more than twenty was called Garnet, as I had already gathered, and the girl, who still hadn't quite forgotten my look of distrust, Renthrette. I gave her a friendly smile and kind of wished I'd been more impressive during the fight. Kind of.

"We do not use the names we were born with anymore, so I am taking no unnecessary risks," their swarthy leader went on. "I am Mithos, and I—"

"Mithos!" I bawled. "*The* Mithos! Oh God! Mithos the thief, bandit, cutthroat, and wholesale murderer?"

"You should know better than to trust the Empire's propaganda," he remarked grimly.

"All right," I backpedaled, knowing the terms these psychopaths preferred to be known by, "Mithos the rebel and adventurer?"

"The same," he said.

SCENE V

Things Can Always Get Worse

Adventurers" hired themselves out as investigators, guards, explorers, and specialists of various kinds, particularly if the assignment involved a balancing act between risk and profit. In effect they were burglars, thugs, murderers, and grave robbers. The Empire, in a rare moment of insight, had made the profession illegal. Adventurers were untrustworthy, and if they obeyed any laws at all, they were those of their own personal and erratic honor code. This made them dangerous people to have around and clearly a threat to the "peace" and solidity of the Diamond Empire. The Empire, moreover, had learnt that the likes of my dangerous saviors had organized much of the opposition during the initial invasion of Thrusia and continued to lead uprisings when the mood took them. "Adventurers" were rebels by any other name.

As a result, the identity of adventurers was information much sought after by the Empire's many spies and collaborators. One of the most notorious adventurers, a rebel whose name appeared on wanted lists all over Cresdon, was sitting three feet from me right now.

Reports of Mithos's physical appearance were fraught with contradictions, but I could think of half a dozen brutal attacks motivated solely by greed, the desire to eat small children, etc., that had been linked to his name. The knowledge did not make me comfortable.

I should say that I do not much like the Empire. Thrusia, the mountain region in which Cresdon is situated, fought hard against the invaders but fell the year I was born. Since then we have paid for our defiance. It seems to me that the best policy is to keep your head down and say nothing, which, until today, and despite my somewhat checkered career in the theatre, is exactly what I had done.

As ever, for those who can come to terms with the presence of an occupying force there is some profit. I have never actively collaborated with the Empire, but I have become, I must admit, a pretty passive subject. In truth I was—or assumed I was—too insignificant for them to take notice of me. I had lived like a flea on the carcass of their town and they had given me the attention a flea merits. Until about half an hour ago. And now I was sharing a room with the most wanted man in Cresdon and his conspicuously homicidal sidekicks.

To cheer myself up I tried to sit next to the girl, Renthrette, who I figured was one of their girlfriends. It seemed fairly sure that I could make her like me for my wit if not for my physique, but, for the moment at least, she was doing a pretty convincing job of ignoring me completely. I found myself sharing a box with Orgos, the one who had sneered at me for being a petty criminal and then committed about half a dozen capital offenses in as many seconds. I looked at the girl for comfort and it cheered me up a little until I felt her acid eyes upon me. I gave her my long-practiced winning smile, but she met it with a look that would have leveled a small building and turned her back on me.

God, what a fiasco.

The four of them pumped me for information about myself. I repeated what I had told them already: who I was, where I lived, why I was running from the Empire, etc. I talked, gripped as I was both by fear of the Empire showing up at any moment and by fear of what this band of cutthroats would do to me if I didn't humor them. Perhaps I could bolt for the door when they weren't looking, get out and tell the first patrol I could find that I could hand them Mithos; that would get me off whatever charges were leveled at me, wouldn't it? Orgos laid his massive sword across his knees and watched me. Absently, he tested the edge with his thumb, his eyes on mine.

I gave up the idea of running. For the moment.

After I had finished my rather meager and somewhat edited life story and declared all I owned in the world (now down to four silver pieces, a single copper coin, the clothes I stood up in, and two bits of lead), Mithos motioned us into the corridor, out of earshot of the struggling innkeeper, and addressed the group. The bar was silent and there was no sign of other soldiers.

"We have no choice but to leave. We can handle three light foot patrolmen easily enough, but they'll have a platoon of hoplites after us within the hour. We must get out of Cresdon and quickly, or else we'd have to lie low for some time. And since we have an appointment in Stavis in less than three weeks, that gives us no time to hide from the Empire here. It will take at least a week of hard traveling to reach Stavis, so I suggest we move now, before the alarm has been raised."

"What about me?" I demanded, made angry by my panic. At the moment I was caught between the devil and the deep blue sea: the grinding judicial system of the Empire and the savages I was rooming with. I couldn't decide which prospect was more terrifying.

"You will have to come with us," Mithos replied with a dissatisfied look in his dark eyes and a sigh in his voice.

"What? He's a child!" exclaimed the girl. "He will get us all killed! At best he'll slow us down and risk exposing us. And if he decides to turn us in, what then?"

"He won't," said Mithos grimly. It wasn't so much a vote of confidence as a threat, and I recognized it as such. "You need us, Master Hawthorne," he said with a half-smile. "And we can't take the chance of leaving you behind to inform on us. If that offends you, consider us your ticket out of Cresdon. Your crime is a small one, but the Empire would brand you a rebel for it, and you know how they love to make examples of rebels. How many of the bodies that hang from the basilica gibbets are rebels, and how many are shopkeepers, blacksmiths, and actors who the Empire decided were rebels?"

"I try not to concern myself with politics," I muttered, trying to stop my hands from trembling. He had a knack of saying all the things I didn't want to think about and making them sound even worse than I had thought they were.

"You are concerned with them now," said the girl bitterly. "Would that you had been concerned about them before. Though what you could have contributed to the cause I don't know."

"Renthrette," said Mithos swiftly, "we have no time for bickering. The boy will leave Cresdon under our aegis whether he likes the idea or not."

"I'm not a boy!" I exclaimed. "I'm eighteen. A man."

The girl—who couldn't have been more than a year older than me—snorted with disdain.

Mithos, ignoring my indignation, told me my options in a matter-of-fact tone: "Should you decide, once we're outside Cresdon, to ride with us to Stavis, you'll come as one who must earn his keep and keep his place. Or we can part company when we are a comfortable distance from the city. It's your choice. You will find us trustworthy unless you endanger our mission."

I nodded my agreement, anxious to go along with anything that would get me away from this inn. But as for trust, he could forget it. William Hawthorne trusted no one, and wasn't about to start with a handful of murderous rogues he knew little—all bad—about. I figured I would have them get me clear of the city. Nothing more.

My one anxiety—apart from the Empire, of course—was that they might feel obliged to do away with me to protect their precious identities before they headed for Stavis, the easternmost reach of the lands taken by the Diamond Empire armies. To seem keen to go with them might make me seem less of a security risk, though the journey itself, if it came to that, would probably kill me.

The Empire had come from the northern mountains of Aeloria, financed by the precious stones mined in their homeland. They had clad their legions in white, their pennants, banners, and cloaks overlaid with the blue diamond motif. So had they acquired their name: the Diamond Empire, wealthy, cold, hard, sharp, and smugly eternal. They had crushed the lands that bordered Aeloria and pushed south to the kingdom of Thrusia. We had fallen hard and taken the edge off the Diamond's advance for a while. Then greed set their eyes across the virtual desert plains of the Hrof wastes—a land drier than Thrusian grain whiskey or the wit of an Empire centurion—to Stavis in the east, a sickeningly prosperous port. They extended a thin finger of their force, unable to feed and water a more smothering movement in so harsh a region, took Stavis, and held it. The Hrof remained a wild place to this day, and you'd need a rollicking good reason to cross it. There was little Empire presence on the road, though the bandits, scorpions, and vultures had their own plans for you. If you make it to Stavis, you are back in proper Empire territory, but once you get through the town and head east, you are free. That might be the rollicking good reason I needed.

They probably had another.

"What is your mission?" I asked.

"That's our business," Mithos answered quietly, but with a deliberation I was not supposed to question.

"Thanks a lot," I snapped. "So you expect me to go trekking

across the bloody Hrof with you, knowing that the trip is going to be an absolute swine, and you won't even say where we're going! That's great, that is. Your name has been all over this town for months, years! But because you did me an unrequested favor and saved me from the bloody Empire, putting me right on top of its wanted list in the process, you expect me to go picnicking with you in the desert, even though it wouldn't surprise me if you put a dagger in my spine to save water. I'd be safer doing a week in the stocks."

"People die in the stocks," Garnet hissed, his green eyes flashing. I think he rather liked the idea. He was right, of course. The worthy townsfolk couldn't always be trusted to throw no more than fruit and veg at whoever was chained in the marketplace.

I went on nonetheless. "At least I wouldn't be looking over my shoulder to see whether you thugs were about to . . ."

Garnet got up. His fist was clenched round the haft of a large and mean-looking battle-ax, so I shut up quickly. He came for me anyway, grabbing a handful of dress just below my chin in a pale, strong hand and hoisting me against the wall. His eyes burned hard as emeralds and he placed the cold iron of the ax bit to my cheek. I half stood, half hung, and silently tried not to urinate. I could feel his heart racing and see the whiteness of his knuckles where they grasped the ax handle, and I braced myself for what would come next. In the end he just released me suddenly and, as I crumpled, said, "Find your own way out of Cresdon then, worm."

That put a different complexion on things.

"Sorry," I muttered. "Stressful day, you know?"

I tried a cautious smile. Whatever I thought of them, I believed they might be able to get me out, something I couldn't do by myself.

"Can I do anything to help?" I tried.

"Unlikely," said the girl.

"Can you do a Cherrat accent?" said Mithos.

"Who? Me? Are you joking?"

"No. Can you do it?"

"A little, I think," I said, doubtful as to what part this new madness was to play in my escape.

"Let's hear it," said Mithos calmly, leading us back into their room.

They checked on the innkeeper and began getting their things together, then started changing clothes. The girl turned her back first so I could see nothing worth speaking of. I caught Garnet's eye and leered towards Renthrette, hoping for a little manly understanding, but he looked murderously back. I stopped looking at her and stared disconsolately at the floor. God, what a mess.

"Sell me this shirt," continued Mithos.

"What?"

"Pretend you are a Cherrati merchant and—"

"Oh, I see. Well, er . . ." I faltered, quickly deciding that to behave like a lunatic in the company of lunatics was only reasonable. I started talking, hunching up my shoulders as I had seen the extravagant Cherratis doing in the marketplace at weekends. I was quite good at things like this, worthless though they were. I tilted my head and spoke through my nose. "You! Yes, you. Did you ever see quality like this? Feel that sleeve. That's quality, my friend. The finest . . . what?"

"Silk," he prompted.

"The finest silk you'll put your unworthy hands on this side of the great river. Purchased at great expense from the hill tribes of the North and embroidered by the twelve virgin priestesses of Cherrathwaite. And would I ask twelve silver pieces of you? No sir, not twelve. Not ten. A mere eight silver pieces. What, you cheapskate, will you ruin me? All right, all right, I'll take seven. . . ."

Shortly, Mithos smiled and told me to stop. "You have a talent, my friend," he said. "Perhaps we'll find a use for you yet. Now get rid of that dress and put the shirt on. And the trousers and boots. You'll probably need a belt with those. There's one in that box. Can you shoot a crossbow?"

"Kind of," I answered. "So long as you don't expect me to hit anything with it."

"Take this," he said. He handed me a whimsical little crossbow, one of the light, one-handed kind which was legal within the city. It probably wouldn't do much damage to anyone in armor but it was a lovely piece of work: polished russet wood inlaid with silver. It was exactly what a Cherrati would carry.

Orgos was to ride with me in a wagon full of "borrowed" trade goods whose origin I dreaded to consider. He looked good too, I must say. There are more blacks native to Cherrat than to these parts, so he didn't look at all out of place in his dark leather and crimson silks. He girded on a rapier (another weapon deemed legal because it wouldn't penetrate the plate cuirass of an Empire soldier), and completed the picture with a plumed cap.

When Renthrette turned I was disappointed to note that she was dressed in the drab, coarse, and shapeless fabrics of a peasant. She gave me a blank look and turned away. I obviously wasn't making much of an impression. She made light of a crate I could barely have lifted and my vague interest took another hit. This was unfortunate, since it was only my focus on her that was stopping me from thinking about all the terrible things I probably should have been thinking about, like where I was, who I was with, what I was doing, who was most likely to kill me, and whether they would do it this afternoon or sometime later in the week.

Orgos checked the ropes binding the innkeeper and the soldiers, all of whom were awake and frightened-looking in ways I would not have believed possible from Empire troops, and then ushered me out, heaving a box onto his shoulder and bidding me take the last bag. When only a couple of crates were left, Mithos led us into the corridor and spoke quickly. "Master Hawthorne, do as Orgos says. Speak only when you have to. I don't want you being chased across rooftops again. There is an inn called the Wheatsheaf about a mile along the Stavis road. We will meet there, hopefully, for lunch. If we are not all together by nightfall, those who have arrived should head for Stavis at dawn tomorrow. Orgos, you take the wagon through the southwestern gate. And Will?" he said, bending down to my level and speaking carefully into my face. "Don't even consider turning us in. If you do and they don't have you up on the scaffold with us, burning your entrails in front of your dying eyes, I'll make sure someone from our side does something similar. It may be less public, but it would probably feel about the same. Good luck."

We left the tavern at a moderate pace and I kept my eyes turned down. With a flick of the reins Orgos set our four Cherrati mares walking out of the inn's yard and into the streets. I fiddled with my crossbow and wondered if I should just shoot myself now and save them the trouble.

SCENE VI

❧

The Gatehouse

A light summer rain had begun to fall as we left the inn. The Cresdon streets were rapidly being churned to mud by cart wheels, horse hooves, and the shaggy, lumbering cattle they breed in these parts. Orgos steered the wagon expertly enough and, at first, said nothing, so I was free to take a last look at the city, as we hit potholes of reeking, stagnant water deep enough to drown a sheep. All in all I wasn't going to miss this place too much, even if I knew absolutely sod-all about what lay outside it.

Frequently we slowed to a virtual stop to negotiate the wagon through streets so narrow that we scraped against houses and shops on both sides. Most of them were white plaster and timber-framed ruins that tier fractionally outwards like inverted pyramids. The thatched roofs on either side of the street almost meet in the middle, but at ground level you can drive a wagon through. Just. I lost count of the number of times the street was blocked by some imbecile taking his geese or chickens to market. It took us three-quarters of an hour to cover about a mile and a half, a good ten minutes of which was spent arguing with the red-faced driver of the hay cart that was coming from the opposite direction.

I was not used to handling weapons (other than wholly ineffectual stage swords, of course, and since I had played almost nothing but girls, I didn't get to handle those much either), and the feel of the crossbow in my hands, though it was little more than a toy, excited me. As we passed the hay carter, I let him glimpse it and he stopped throwing insults at us. Orgos noticed and frowned at me.

"Sorry," I said. "I wouldn't have used it."

"You got that right," he remarked warningly. "And use your accent."

"What? Why? There's no one around."

"Get used to it now," he insisted, still using the nasal, singsong tones himself, "and you'll be more comfortable should it become essential."

"I'm shy," I answered with a coy smile that was supposed to amuse him and make him sympathetic. It didn't.

He leaned his face close to me and his black eyes fastened on to mine as he whispered, "This is not a game, boy, and there is more than just your scrawny neck on the chopping block. I am not requesting that you practice that accent, I am telling you to. Else get off my wagon."

"Right," I muttered, scared of his earnestness.

"What?" he demanded, making his point carefully.

"I mean, right you are, there, sir," I replied in the best imitation of Cherrat as I could manage. He grinned, satisfied, and his white teeth glowed impossibly in his black face. His features seemed capable of slipping from death-threatening hostility into amiable good humor without so much as a pause for thought.

I hadn't spent much time amongst black people for, in these parts, they tended to be wealthy merchants: hardly the types to frequent the Eagle. When you saw them it was usually in the marketplace, and I mean the traders' market, not the bruised-fruit-and-rancid-meat places. They were well dressed, well spoken, and accompanied by servants and occasionally "attendants" (the euphemistic term applied to bodyguards to keep them legal). These guards couldn't carry much in the way of arms in the town, of course, but they could be weighed down with plate armor and battle-axes on the roads. That was legal so long as they didn't travel in groups of more than four.

People tended to be respectful of the black merchants for their wealth and education, but you sometimes got a sense of resentment simply because they were outsiders, a resentment aggravated by the fact that our town was occupied by foreigners. I was rather fascinated by the darkness of Orgos's skin, the tight curl of his hair, and the broad features of his face. Fascinated, but not reassured. I don't suppose I'd ever been this close to a black man before, and that actually made me feel worse. I wouldn't miss this lousy town, if I got out of it, but Orgos, with his fake accent and unfamiliar appearance, reminded me of how little I knew of the outside world I was being thrown into, and I resented him for it. Whether I resented him enough to turn him over to the guards on the gate remained to be seen.

"What was that flash of light?" I said, suddenly remembering something that had been nagging at me.

"What flash of light?"

"Back at the inn," I said. "When the soldiers came in. There was a flash of light, bright like a firework. I wasn't looking right at it, but I saw the way it lit the room and then . . . I don't know. I got confused or sick or something."

"It must have been a spark from swords clashing," he said. He stared ahead of him.

"A spark that lit the whole room?" I said. "No way."

"I can't think of what else it would be," he said. "I didn't notice it."

I knew he was lying, but I had no idea why or what else it could have been, and since he was twice my size, a notorious criminal, and armed to the teeth, I said nothing.

We got stuck behind a cart containing a peasant family in bright but soiled clothes, though they were less relevant than the two underfed bullocks pulling them. We had to (I could barely believe it possible) reduce speed.

All cursing aside, we came to the gatehouse too soon for my liking. Once again, I felt the steely grasp of terror's mailed gauntlet tightening about my genitals. Around us the houses, hawkers, and wandering livestock had melted away and we found ourselves in a corner of the great sand-colored stone wall that circled the city. Fifty feet up, pairs of infantrymen walked the parapeted wall. Sentries, their white diamond-motif cloaks drawn about them against the rain, looked down upon us through the eyeholes of bright steel helms, their bows over their shoulders. I stared wide-eyed at Orgos, who made the smallest calming gesture with one hand and reined the horses.

At the angle of the two vast walls was the gatehouse, surmounted by a watchtower. The bullock cart in front of us stopped and the driver climbed down. A burly foot patrolman was asking him questions and pointing dismissively at the people in the wagon.

The dozen guards who stood alert in the gateway itself were the business end of the Empire. They too wore the white diamonded cloaks, but they bore large round shields protecting them from knee to shoulder. Iron cuirasses encased their thoraxes, and their helms were crested with white horsehair and left only their eyes uncovered.

Over their thighs and abdomens they wore skirts of white linen with metal rings sewn on. Shortswords hung at their waists, a pair of light javelins stood by their sides, and in their right hands they clasped long wooden spears tipped with fine steel. They scared the living day-lights out of me.

If I was to give myself up and turn Orgos over to the Empire, these were the men I would be assisting. Of course I had seen them before, but never had I seen them as an enemy might. They looked almost invulnerable, which, I'm sure, was the idea. They also looked like an army, like conquerors. Orgos and the rest of them scared me, but in a different way. They still seemed human, I suppose. I looked at the steel-clad guards by the gate, their weapons ready and their eyes concealed by the shade of their faceless helms, and I saw them as the myriad blades of some vast mincing machine. They stood im-maculate and motionless before us: soullessly disciplined. One glance at their iron at such close quarters illumined tracts of land, towns, and peoples ground beneath a regulated, even march. Sud-denly they didn't look like the kind of people I wanted to help. In a purely subjective moment, the decision was made.

Another pair of the foot patrolmen appeared and emptied the family out of the cart in front of us with a couple of rough orders and a poke with the butt of a short spear. They spilled out and hud-dled together. A little boy began to cry, and one of the women drew him to her and folded him into her robes: comforting and silencing in one frightened movement. The guards picked scornfully over the poor cart and then started on the people, their questions randomly mixed with insults. I felt Orgos stir fractionally as a guard pushed close to one of the women and threw some lewd remark to his com-panion. I gave Orgos a quick look and saw with horror that his right hand had strayed towards the gold basketwork hilt of his rapier. I prayed it wouldn't move any closer.

It didn't. The soldiers, bored with their harassment, contemptu-ously urged the cart through the open gate and turned to us.

"Good morning, gentlemen." Orgos beamed as we drew up to the gatehouse. From here you could see through the arch with its raised portcullis and broad outer doors, through twenty feet of city wall and past the grim, motionless infantrymen, out to the road and freedom.

The patrolmen gathered about the wagon and I tried to smile

calmly, though my face sort of froze in the process. I looked down at the crossbow in my lap and figured it was best to put it down.

In contrast to the way they had just treated the people in the bullock cart, the guards were, in their imperious way, polite: almost deferential.

"Names, identification papers, and destination, please," said the duty officer.

I looked with muted alarm at Orgos; the mechanics of our escape had not really occurred to me and we hadn't discussed such details. Orgos produced a pair of neatly rolled parchments and answered, with a Cherrati hand gesture, "I am Alberro Spirant and this is my apprentice, Geoffrey. We deal in silks, satin, velvet, cambric, lace, fine cotton, and other costly fabrics. Perhaps you'd care to see our wares?"

"We'll take a quick look in the back if you don't mind," answered the soldier patiently. Orgos drew out a small key and passed it to me.

"Show the gentlemen inside, Geoffrey," he said casually. I regarded him for a moment, my mental alarm bells clanging fiercely, and then clambered down to the wet and muddy gravel. Two soldiers followed me to the rear of the wagon. As my fingers fumbled madly at the latch on the tail flap, I could hear Orgos's precise Cherrat accent complimenting the young captain on his town and telling him of our planned route to Bowescroft via Oakhill. It sounded credible to me. I hoped they thought so.

I got the back open and stood clear as one of the guards clambered in and began poking around. There were various large boxes and crates piled high with clothes and rolls of material. He picked at a couple but obviously wasn't interested in effecting a real search.

"How's business?" said the guard at my elbow without warning. I jumped slightly and forced my voice out with an effort, only at the last second remembering to switch on that ludicrous accent.

"Not bad, my friend, not bad." I shrugged expansively. "But we're hoping for more success in—" Blood and sand, where had Orgos said we were going? "—Bowescroft and Oakhill. As you can see, there is an awful lot of merchandise to clear yet and they are rather, how might I put it, *luxurious* items. Not for just anyone, don't you know? The Cresdon folk were not as ready as we had hoped to invest in such quality."

How was that? It had sounded all right to me. I had acted myself stupid with all those arm and shoulder movements, finished with that excessive, slow Cherrati frown of thoughtful doubt, and waited for him to respond.

He merely nodded and looked away, bored. Fantastic! I was hit by a wave of elation at my success and turned to address the other guard, who was getting out of the wagon looking as apathetic as his comrade.

"Did you come across anything that caught your eye, eh, my friend? There is some fine stuff, very fine. No Thrusian cotton in there my friend, certainly not. But silk and taffeta gowns for the ladies, eh? We carry only the best. Now, you, sir, young, handsome, and strong as you are, must have some nice young lady to buy for?"

"Not today, no thanks," said the first guard, backing off. I, warming to my role, pushed him further, speaking through my nose and waggling my hands about. "But I can give you a very good price. What size would it be? We can cut and make to measure for no extra charge. The ladies love to be pampered, my friends, oh yes. Here," I said, grabbing some fabric out of the back at random and thrusting it into his hands, "feel the thickness. See how it glows with color. Notice the deep lustrous finish. Examine the detail so lovingly hand-embroidered by the twelve virgin priestesses—"

"No, really, thanks," he stammered, slightly embarrassed. The second guard was already in retreat, hands raised and mouthing polite rejections. I was about to push them still harder when Orgos called from the front.

"Geoffrey," he shouted, a definite hint of irritation showing through the blanket of his Cherrat accent. "We are ready to pass through now. Put the cloth back in the wagon, and come back here at once. You hear me, Geoffrey?"

I couldn't remember what he had called himself to the guards so I just did as he said. He seemed to be making apologies to the guards on my behalf, but they shrugged the incident off. In a minute I was back up at the front and the guards were waving us through. Then a shout from behind made me turn with panic. Hurrying along the street towards the gate was Rufus Ramsbottom with about eight patrolmen and an officer.

Now we had a problem. I flashed a glance at Orgos and he started the horses moving. I bent low in my seat as the officer came up along-side us and addressed the gate commanders.

"Trouble in the streets by C Garrison. A rebel called Hawthorne escaped from a patrol this morning. He's been concealed by sympa-thizers. Fights broke out when known rebel taverns were searched and we may have a full-scale riot on our hands in Sector Six. The high command wants no traffic in or out until the fighting is brought under control and the culprits are in custody. Close the gates."

I closed my eyes tightly and tried not to scream with frustration.

No Virtue in Almost

The gatehouse soldiers looked at each other and sighed. After the briefest of consultations, two troopers marched swiftly over to the stairway that would take them up to the mechanism used to close the immense gates. I looked back to Orgos, who was maintaining his role as Cherrati merchant, slightly exasperated by the proceedings. Glancing backwards, I could see Rufus with his back to us, waving his clumsy hands about and shouting. I turned away fast enough to break my neck and stared ahead at the infantrymen that stood in the shade of the archway, their eyes glinting through the holes in their helms.

"May we proceed, Officer?" inquired Orgos smoothly.

"We've got trouble in another sector," replied the guard. "We're going to have to close the gate. Sorry, sir."

He turned away, distracted by the sound of feet on the steps, and watched as about thirty soldiers filed down from the walls above, their shields and spears shouldered. The staircase was narrow. While the troops came down, the two men sent to close the gates had to wait at the bottom. I counted slowly to ten in my head and waited for Rufus to see me. The staircase was still jammed with descending soldiers.

"We were hoping to make Oakhill by nightfall," I ventured carefully, "and we would really prefer not to stay here with our merchandise if there is likely to be some form of civil unrest."

"Sorry," the officer said without looking at us. "No one in or out."

"Then perhaps you'd like to take another look at our wares," I said.

Orgos gave me a hard look but I ignored him.

"No," said the officer. "Thank you."

"I didn't show you the best silks," I breezed. "We keep those well out of sight. But maybe someone of your taste would appreciate them. We have damask so soft you can barely feel it against your skin. . . ."

The officer at our side glanced at the men waiting to go up to close the gates, exhaled with slow boredom and muttered, "It's time someone built another staircase up there. Go on," he said, turning to us suddenly. "Go through. Quickly."

Without further encouragement we began to move. My heart rose to my throat and I stared ahead of me, past the guards and the officer who hastily, mechanically recited the usual Empire regulations.

"If you have heavier weapons and armor you may bring them out once you are a hundred yards from the gate. Remain on the road at all times and be watchful for highwaymen. Have a successful trip, sirs," he called as we trundled through the twenty-foot-thick arch and the heavy doors. The portcullis was lowering with a heavy metallic squealing as we emerged into the light and soft drizzle. Behind us the great gates themselves began scraping and creaking until, with a deep boom, they shut tight.

For a hundred yards or so we did not speak and then, bringing the wagon to a halt in a stone-flagged space and turning to one of the boxes between us, Orgos said, "Idiot. What were you trying to do back there? Selling clothes to Empire guards! You were asking to be arrested."

He was smiling. I grinned and said, "I was just fleshing out the role a little. Giving it color."

"Idiot," he said again, but this time he laughed outright. I wanted to punch him lightly on the arm or something as a show of fellowship, but something held me back, the thought of his name dragging mine up the wanted list, perhaps. Instead I just said, "Geoffrey? You called me Geoffrey! What the pox kind of name is that?"

He gave a single bellow of laughter and opened the box. Whatever relief I was beginning to feel died as I stared at the contents: armor and weapons of the serious sort. I wasn't being allowed to forget my comrade's profession.

Orgos stood up and looked back to the massive yellowish walls of the city.

"I hate that place," he remarked, fishing a coat of ring mail out of the box and pulling it over his head.

I couldn't say much to that. I didn't really know anywhere else, though even I could see it was a bit of a sewer.

"How come they're saying I'm a rebel?" I asked. I was tiny bit pleased by the idea, even though I knew both that it was dangerous to be impressed by such things and that they were about as wrong as they could be.

"The Empire doesn't like to be humiliated," he said. "Better to be outmaneuvered by a seasoned rebel than a child actor."

The phrase irritated me, but that feeling was squashed by something rather more weighty.

"So if they catch me now . . ." I said.

"They'll charge you with more than being in a few plays they didn't like."

He gave me a shrug and a grin as he saw the effect his words had on me. "Cheer up," he said. "You're with us now."

Great.

Orgos replaced the rapier in the back of the wagon and emerged wearing a pair of the long swords he had used before, scabbarded in a harness on his back so that the hilts stood vertically up from his shoulders. I would have needed both hands to wield one of those four-foot blades, but a look at his biceps and forearms told me that he would manage just fine. He reached up to their handles, crossing his arms over his chest to see that they were in the right position, and then bade me get down and come to the back of the wagon. One of the swords, the one he had had back at the inn, had a large and irregular stone set in the pommel, amber and lustrous.

"Choose a weapon," he said. "What can you use?"

Throwing aside a few top layers of fabric, he opened a chest of armor and another two of weapons. I recalled my encouraging the Empire guards to stay and poke around the wagon a little longer. We would really have had to do some talking to explain that lot away.

I got in the back and touched some of the steel in amazed fascination. As I said earlier, I know little of weapons and I am no fighter, but just seeing this pile of purposeful and elegant arms held me spellbound. I chose.

Orgos looked at me with his mouth open and then roared with laughter, his head tipped back and his teeth showing.

"Can you even walk in that stuff?" he demanded.

I confess to having gotten a little carried away. He made me put a lot of it back. Most of it was too big for me anyway and I could hardly breathe in that helm. I could barely lift my arms and no, I couldn't really walk. I tried a corselet of light scale and swapped the two-handed great-ax I had chosen for a short sword and small shield. It was a bit of a comedown, I suppose, but I kept looking at the way the corselet sparkled in the light and it made me feel good. Actually, the sword alone was so heavy that I soon had to put the shield away too. It was a good thing I'd put that bloody ax back. It had taken all my strength to get it out of the wagon.

The rain had just about stopped, so that was one less discomfort. I drew the sword and weighed it in my hand, imagining myself a great fighter and betting Renthrette would be impressed. Next time we had some trouble they'd see a different side to Will Hawthorne. Maybe. After a couple of minutes of me waving the sword about, Orgos told me to put it away before I maimed him. Still, a moment later I saw him smile. For the first time that day I stopped worrying and relaxed enough to enjoy the ride.

The road was good thus far, paved and cambered. But as soon as the gatehouse was lost to our sight in the elms and sycamores which grew around the city, we veered off to the northeast on a series of farm tracks.

Orgos sat quietly beside me, his eyes on the trail. Maybe it was the elation of escape, the satisfaction of outwitting that moron Rufus, or just the feeling that I had done right not to run crying to the Empire, but I felt slightly better disposed to him. And whatever the dangers, I was still alive, free, and touched with something I had never felt before. It had the feel of adventure and all the anticipation that comes with it. Will the Adventurer. Hawthorne the Rebel. A childish and dangerous thought, perhaps, but there you have it. Even at the time I had a pretty good idea that it wouldn't last.

SCENE VIII

The Wheatsheaf

By about half past one, with the sun high and the rain gone, we caught sight of the inn set back from the road. I was glad of it, for the air was growing warm and humid despite the early showers and I was ready for the coolness of a shady room and a draught of beer. Or six.

The inn was a large two-storied affair of mottled grey stone with sills and lintels of varnished oak. The sign over the door showed a bunch of full, golden wheat stalks. Its roof was thatched brown and well shaped with two chimneys poking through, one of which released a thin curl of bluish wood smoke. It was all rather picturesque, like one of those cheap engravings that you sneer at in the Cresdon markets. The upstairs probably housed guests sheltering from those very markets.

After drawing the wagon up to the front, we dismounted and scraped the mud from our boots. Then Orgos tried the door and led me in.

Now, I was used to the smoky, stone-flagged, fleapit taprooms of the town from which we'd just escaped. Bars, to me, meant noise, raucous laughter, spilled beer, semifriendly gambling, and the occasional brawl. The Wheatsheaf, by contrast, dripped with class and a slightly embarrassed silence. It was obviously an eatery for merchants before they ventured into the cultural desolation of the Hrof wastelands or, for that matter, those of Cresdon. The floor was tiled with a glazed and patterned ceramic featuring the ears-and-leaves motif we had seen outside. Very fancy. There were windows of leaded glass all around the room, and as a result the entire chamber glowed, pleased with itself. There were tables set for dinner decorated with dainty vases of flowers. No dartboard. No pools of vomit and urine. No whores.

At the far end of the room by the cold hearth of a carved fireplace sat Mithos, Renthrette, and Garnet. They had changed out of their peasant clothes and wore light cotton fabrics which looked like they would breathe well, even under armor. The barman sent a boy with Orgos to tend to the horses as I hung my armor up with the rest and ordered a pint of best.

I took my mug, sauntered over to the table where the others sat, swinging the crossbow roguishly by its strap, and cast Renthrette an easy smile. She might as well have been wearing her armor, because it glanced off and fell in some dustless corner. I sat beside her anyway and made sure she noticed the sword I was wearing. I thought it made me look pretty sharp.

"Isn't it a bit early to be drinking?" she said.

"Drinking?" I repeated, momentarily baffled. "This is beer."

"It contains alcohol, doesn't it?" she said. She had a slightly prissy attitude that annoyed me.

"Not like whiskey," I said, shrugging. "But a bit, yeah. So?"

"You're a child!" she said.

"I'm eighteen," I said, straightening up. "What is it with you people?"

Mithos gave Renthrette a look.

"In the city, everyone drinks beer," he said. "All classes, all ages. It's their primary source of nutrition, which, given their markets and the condition of the water supply, is probably as well. It's liquid bread."

She wrinkled her nose at me. I framed a pointed smile and sipped my ale. It was excellent, but at three coppers a pint you would expect that.

"I still think it's disgusting," she said. "A child drinking—"

"Listen, lady, I've been working for my living since I was five," I said. "I am not a child and haven't been one for a long time. And how old are you, Grandma? Nineteen?"

"Twenty, actually."

"How incredibly ancient," I said. "I'm surprised you can still walk."

She shrugged and looked away, her face tipped slightly up as if she was trying to ignore a bad smell. I just stared at her. I didn't know what to say anyway. She annoyed me, was all. With an effort, I turned my attention to Mithos, who had been talking.

"I'm sorry, what did you say?"

He sighed pointedly and repeated the question. "How did it go?"

"How did what go?"

"Your passage out of Cresdon. Was it successful?" he concluded with a little impatience in his voice.

"No," I said flatly, "they only let me through on the condition that I would turn you in immediately. There are two platoons of Empire troops waiting outside." I grinned. "Only joking. Yes, it was successful. A piece of cake."

They looked at me silently. No one laughed. In fact they didn't seem overjoyed that I had made it out at all. There was a lengthy pause and then Orgos rejoined us. Sensing the tension around the table as he sat down, he smirked at me. Mithos looked pensively into his beer and said, "Well, Master Hawthorne, you are out of the city. We can part company here. It would take you several hours to get back to Cresdon by yourself if you wanted to inform on us, and the gates will be closed till morning anyway."

"He helped get us out of the city," said Orgos suddenly. "He's a good talker. Might prove useful."

Mithos looked thoughtfully at him, then at me. The moment felt loaded, embarrassingly so, and I was almost glad when Renthrette punctured it.

"Well, of course he's a talker," she said with a brittle smile. "He's an *actor.*"

She said it the way she might say "goatherd" or "dung beetle."

"Thank you," I said.

"So," said Mithos, still considering me like I was a fish that had fallen out of the sky. "Will you be going further with us?"

Garnet scowled across the table, daring me to say yes.

"Yes," I said simply.

"Oh, for crying out loud, Mithos," Garnet protested. "Must we carry this childish snake about with us? Why can't we leave him here?"

"Bleeding in a ditch, no doubt," I muttered.

"That wasn't what I meant," he replied testily, "though the idea has a kind of appeal."

"Oh, I'll bet it does," I shot back at him. "In fact—"

"Would you shut up for a moment," said Mithos, staring at the table. "Listen, Master Hawthorne, we don't expect thanks for saving you from the Empire, but we don't expect abuse either. Orgos thinks you might be useful and for that we will let you ride with us, but you will refrain from voicing your suspicions about our profession or character. Do I make myself clear?"

"Well, I don't know about that—"

He cut me short by banging his olive-skinned hand on the table and turning his black eyes on me. He had a firm jaw and a commanding look at all times. When he wanted to he could look very dangerous to contradict.

"Crystal," I said quickly.

"Good," he concluded.

He picked up a board with a piece of parchment listing the dishes on offer tacked to it, consulted it, and passed it round. Now, I was used to chalkboards stating the dish of the day or, more frequently, the week, so this was an unexpected benefit. I was starving, and what was on offer was a far cry from the Eagle's cheese pasties. The prices were outrageous, but I didn't have any money anyway. I figured I'd eat and worry about the bill later.

While they mulled over what they wanted I took my first decent look at them.

Renthrette was taller than me, but that wouldn't bother me if it didn't bother her. Her hair was the color of soft straw and she wore it tied back, though I had seen it breaking around her shoulders while she was getting dressed and she had looked quite the picture. Her eyes were a cool blue flecked with grey and her mouth was slim and pink. Both had a tendency to freeze up when she looked at me, but I figured I could engineer a thaw of some kind. There was a slight peach tint to her cheeks, and her nose and chin, though both thinner than the fashion, had a strength of character to them which I could have done without.

Garnet had, it suddenly struck me, something of the look of her in his own features. I remembered a play that said that lovers came to resemble each other. Maybe there was something to it. It might explain his hostility to me, his new rival. He read the menu with a kind of studied dignity, like he was about fifty-five, looking for something cheap and wholesome. His eyes were an unnervingly deep green and his hair unremarkably brownish with a slight wave to it. He wore it short but the curl was still there. He had a peppering of beard, but I'd bet he hadn't been shaving that much longer than I had. His skin was pale and would probably turn lobster pink given enough sun, hence the long-sleeved cotton shirt. Like the rest of them he was fit, but his arms were sinewy and thin despite their strength. I doubt there was an ounce of fat on him.

Mithos was the oldest of the group, though he could be no more than forty, a bit more than Orgos. I couldn't say if the darkness of his skin was just tan from the sun or it was something in his blood. The blackness of his hair (long enough to flow down to his shoulders) and eyes suggested the latter. He was the tallest of the group and stood well over six feet, his physique less obviously powerful than Orgos's, but well defined. His arms could have come off the athletic statue that stands at the entrance to the Cresdon arena. It seemed like he brooded a lot. He didn't say much, but when he did, everyone stopped what they were doing and got out their notebooks.

"While you're with us," said Mithos, "the party will cover your costs."

"What?" I said. "A party? When?"

"Give me strength," muttered Garnet. Renthrette gently rested her hand on his forearm in a soothing gesture. So, I was right! That charmless streak of thunder and rainy weather? He didn't deserve her.

"We are what I meant as 'the party,' " Mithos explained. "The group. And so long as you are with us, we will pay."

I didn't need any further explanations.

"Right. Great. Er . . . thanks, I mean. Well, then, I think I'll go for the charcoal-grilled duckling and mushrooms in garlic and black pepper sauce. Sounds good to me. And some strong blue cheese. And I'll have another pint, or perhaps a good strong cider if they have one. We'll worry about dessert later, yes?"

"Quite," said Mithos dismally. Renthrette and Garnet stared at me wide-eyed and ordered the cheese, bread, and pickle salad that was here termed the "harvester's lunch." I hadn't been able to afford to eat like this for months and hadn't actually eaten like this for rather longer. I looked around the room with interest and pretended not to notice that the price of my duckling would feed three harvesters and their children. Orgos beamed again and showed his teeth. When he smiled I forgot he was a ruthless killer, which was, I suppose, a disconcerting thought.

The "cider" came in a dusty green-glass bottle that looked like it had been ignored for a very long time. I raised it to my lips, caught the acrid vapor of strong alcohol in my nostrils, and sipped. The others, including the barman, watched with horrified curiosity while Renthrette muttered darkly about how no one should be drinking whatever it was that I was drinking. It went down like warm oil and tasted like apple syrup, crushed glass, and the kick of a Hrof ostrich. This was my kind of adventure. I finished it, wondering aloud if I should continue with more of the same or a dram from that nameless, ancient keg at the back of the shelf. The innkeeper said he thought it was one of those beers made by monks in the mountains, flavored with coriander and orange. How could I resist?

The room had begun to oscillate slightly by the time the duckling arrived, but settled down once I'd got some food inside me. I couldn't remember the last time I had so enjoyed eating. I had a sensitive palate and Mrs. Pugh's culinary horrors had been a real strain, as I told them. Renthrette paused in her lettuce chewing and made knowing eye contact with Garnet. Orgos tried some of the duck and joined in the laudation with extravagant gestures worthy of the Cherrati tradesman he had been earlier. Garnet stoically refused to sample any of it and remarked that his cheese was "really rather good."

"Consider it an inauguration then, Will," said Mithos. "We can't afford to feed you like this indefinitely."

I tried to respond but my mouth was full. Stuffed, actually.

"Also," he added, "this will be the last decent meal we get before Stavis, since I'd like to cover some mileage before nightfall. We'll be under canvas most of the week."

"Why Stavis?" I asked. I had asked before, but I felt that now that they knew I was going with them I might get an answer. Also, though it was largely due to the food and the alcohol, I was feeling better disposed to them, all things considered, and expected them to feel something similar.

"We must consult with our party leader about a job," said Orgos.

"I thought Mithos was party leader," I said.

"No," said Mithos. "And keep your voice down. The party leader went ahead to Stavis to learn the details of the mission. Our leader's identity is a closely guarded secret."

"I need another drink," I decided.

Garnet tutted as I motioned to the barman, pointing at a bottle on the back shelf. He stared, first at me and then at the bottles, and chose the wrong one. I nodded enthusiastically.

"And this job," I continued, since they were being helpful. "What is it? Assassinating an Empire officer, poisoning a garrison? What?"

"It's nothing like that," said Mithos firmly. The others seemed to be letting him do all the talking, as if to make sure they gave nothing away that he thought wasn't my business.

"It does not involve the Empire at all and will take us far out of Empire territory to the east of Stavis. More than that I cannot say."

East of Stavis? What was east of Stavis? I sipped my beer and then tried one more question. "This party leader of yours—"

"Forget it," said Garnet with a malevolent scowl. I looked to Mithos but he merely smiled softly, so I shrugged it off and finished my drink.

"Can you ride?" asked Orgos.

"Ride? Ride what?" I said.

"A horse?" suggested Garnet with lazy condescension.

"No," I replied.

"Great," he breathed heavily. "Mithos, Hawthorne can't ride."

"Then he can ride on the wagon with me," said Orgos with a smile at me and a fixed look at Garnet. We all rose to leave.

"Good," said Mithos. "Be careful how you swing that crossbow about, Will. We restrung it with gut last week. It's more powerful than you might think."

"Really?" I said, cocking it and studying the thing with apparent carelessness, allowing it to point squarely at Garnet's chest.

I didn't hear Mithos draw but I felt the edge of his broadsword against my throat.

"Humor has its place, Master Hawthorne," he whispered into my ear, "but I think you should tread a little lighter until you know the ground is firm."

I got the message and lowered the bow. Mithos sheathed his sword in a single deft motion and stood silently. I smiled as if nothing had happened, which, I suppose, it hadn't. But if I thought I would get out of it with what little dignity I had still intact, I was wrong. I didn't know how to uncock the bloody thing and as I wrestled with it I must have caught the trigger. . . .

The bolt slammed into the wall above the bar. The barman dropped a glass as he jumped back, ducked under the counter, and leapt up again, a crossbow of his own raised and aimed at my head.

"Sorry!" I called cheerfully as sweat broke out all over my body. "I'm really sorry about that. It just sort of . . . *went off.* I'm not very good with things like this and it just seemed to, well . . . you know, go off. And, er . . . sorry."

There was a moment of stillness; then Mithos, hands above his head, approached the bar as the innkeeper stared murderously. I apologized again and made soothing noises as Mithos wrenched the bolt from the wall and the rattled barman slowly lowered his weapon, looking at each of us in turn. Mithos drew some coins from his purse and put them on the bar with some quiet, friendly words. When he rejoined us he presented me with the bolt and hissed, "Learn how to use that thing before you cock it again. Orgos!" he said with a hard look at the black man. "Teach him. And, Master Hawthorne: One step out of line, just one, and you fend for yourself or worse. We are making a long and difficult trip in which we cannot afford to carry imbeciles with more pride than common sense. Not one step, Master Hawthorne. Remember."

As the boy showed us to our wagon and horses, Garnet pushed past me, shouldering me into the inn wall. He watched me regain my balance with absolute scorn, his right hand resting on the ax in his belt. I gave him a pointedly courteous bow and climbed up next to Orgos. We set off, heading east, without saying a word.

SCENE IX

The Road East

I shouldn't have had that last beer," I said, holding my stomach as the wagon rocked me from side to side.

"Renthrette will feel vindicated," Orgos laughed.

"No doubt."

He laughed again and I groaned softly to myself. She was riding twenty yards ahead of us next to Mithos, who was astride a black mare and wearing ring mail with a light helm. Renthrette looked the part too, in heavy scale and a blue-grey helm of riveted plates, which hid her hair and face completely. Garnet was riding his dappled mare behind the wagon, ax at the ready. I suppose I should have felt secure, seeing as how they were all armed to the teeth, their eyes constantly flicking around them, but this show of strength merely served to remind me that we were outlaws in dangerous country. In Cresdon the Diamond Empire's embrace was strangling, but at least it kept predators at bay. Out here we were deer in tiger country.

For the next week or so there would be few patrols, and the wolves and bandits of the Hrof country would know how to avoid them. Orgos told me that wolves never attacked people and that it was all some kind of myth. So that just left the bandits. I asked him if they were bedtime-story material as well. He didn't answer.

I started to fiddle with the small crossbow nervously. Orgos noticed and, taking the reins in one hand, showed me how to load, aim, shoot, and uncock it. I drew the slide back a dozen times until it felt like I knew what I was doing.

"Good," he said, never lifting his eyes from the road, "and that shouldn't be the only lesson you learn today. Garnet is not always an easy man to deal with, and Mithos takes self-restraint very seriously."

"I didn't notice Garnet being all that restrained," I said defensively.

"I think he suspected you were deliberately annoying him. And your sparring with his sister didn't help."

"His sister?!"

"Yes, didn't you guess? They are virtually identical."

"Perfect," I said.

"In appearance, I mean, though they share a certain . . . *earnestness.*"

"There's a euphemism if ever I heard one," I said.

"They have had hard lives," said Orgos, "and they take our profession very seriously."

"Yeah? Well, my life has been no bed of roses either. What made theirs so difficult that the rest of us have to pay them back?"

He glanced at me quickly, irritated, then looked back to the road and said, "Maybe one day I'll tell you."

Great. There wasn't a lot you could say to that.

Around us the ground looked paler, less fertile. Trees were becoming scattered and small, as if drained by the sun. It was getting hotter and the air was thick and heavy. Sweat broke out all over me but didn't evaporate, leaving me sticky and uncomfortable. We swatted at sprightly little mosquitoes that whined around our ears, drank from our forearms, and then hopped into nothingness. Little swine. Soon I could see the pinpricked pimples they left in their wake, and my temper declined. I began to mutter curses under my breath, and twice Orgos turned to me as if he thought I was talking to him. In the end, to occupy my mind, I did.

"So how did you get into this game?" I asked him.

"Another grim story," he replied, "to be saved for another day."

He stared ahead in silence and I let it go.

Since Orgos was about as entertaining as a juggler with no arms, I watched the vegetation grow still sparser and the ground more arid as the miles passed. It was pretty gripping stuff. It was also hotter than a swamp rat's armpit, which didn't help. I remember disinterestedly watching a finch tugging seeds from a thistle as we rattled past. After that, nothing.

It shouldn't be boring, being an adventurer. I knew because I was, you might say, a bit of an expert on heroic stories. My portrayal of the princess in *A King's Vengeance* had played a couple of times a month for a year and a half. There was nothing in the story about sitting around on a wagon for hours at a time.

Orgos woke me three hours later. Thanks to the quality of the road, for which I suppose we must thank the bloody Diamond Empire, we had put over thirty miles between us and Cresdon. We had passed only a couple of caravans thus far, but Orgos had woken me for a reason. Behind us was a mounted Empire patrol, closing fast.

"Get in the back," he said. "There's bolt of silk you can hide under—"

"I'm not hiding," I said.

Orgos gave me a look.

"If they stop us, they'll search the wagon, find me, and then we're done."

"You have a better idea?"

"Other than them leaving us alone? Not yet," I said. "Give me a minute."

I looked back: a full platoon of Empire troops, numbering about twenty-five with an officer riding hard. They pulled ahead of us and waved us to a halt. Then they formed a single line, circled the wagon and our outriders, and stopped, spears leveled at us.

Hiding in the back suddenly seemed like a good idea.

"We are looking for one William Hawthorne," barked the officer, "a notorious rebel. Dismount and stand clear of the wagon."

We did so, and eight soldiers climbed cautiously down from their mounts and held us at the tips of their spears while four others searched us and removed our weapons. Orgos gave me a reproachful look. No one spoke and I felt a wave of nausea washing over me. The officer, a large, tanned man with the hardened features of a soldier whose authority comes from experience in the thick of things, spoke to a younger man in the uniform of the town guard. There was a long silence and they just looked at us while someone opened the tailgate. A moment later one of the soldiers emerged from the back of the wagon and said, "Captain." He held a heavy scale tunic in one hand and a battle-ax in the other. "The vehicle is laden with weaponry, sir."

The officer turned back to me, and a thick smile spread slowly across his scarred leathery face. The Cherrati-merchant story wasn't going to cut it this time.

"Which one of you is Hawthorne?" said the officer, pleased with himself. "Or would you rather identify yourself on the rack in Cresdon?"

SCENE X

Improvisation

It's a curious thing, the way language works. You tend to presume that you form an idea and then put it into words, but this is often not the case. Words seem to have a life of their own. They start, and your brain follows like a schoolboy, trying to keep up. This was what happened here. The plan was unformed, the ideas completely undeveloped, but when I opened my mouth, words came out.

"I suggest, Captain, that you get back on your horse and return to the garrison before you make the kind of mistake that could end your career."

The officer looked momentarily knocked off balance, but then he smirked.

"Identification papers, if you please, sir," he said.

"I think that if anyone should be producing paperwork," I said, "it's you."

The smirk was still there, but his patience was thinning fast. "And why would that be, sir?" he said, leaning in so that he loomed more effectively.

"Because if I don't see something with Harveth Liefson's seal on it within the next couple of minutes, you are going to find yourself in very hot water."

Liefson's name hit him between the eyes like a half-brick.

"Commander Liefson?" he spluttered. "Why would I need Commander Liefson's signature to take you in?"

He was trying to be defiant, but there was a slightly hunted look on his face.

"That's something you're going to have to ask him, aren't you?" I said. "Or, I suppose," I added thoughtfully, "you could take it up with Section Four."

Another half-brick. The captain shrank a little and his voice went a little up in pitch and down in volume.

"Garrison intelligence?" he said. "They only handle internal operations."

"Exactly," I said. "Perhaps we should continue this conversation in private."

There was a pause, and then a light seemed to go on inside the captain's head and his mouth fell open. "But how do I know if you are really . . . ?"

I climbed down from the wagon and started walking away, and a moment later, he followed. When we reached the circle of soldiers, he gave a hurried nod and they parted for us. I kept walking away from the road till we were safely out of earshot.

"Now, just a moment," said the captain, recovering a little of his former poise. "Where do you think you're going? . . . "

"You call him Commander Liefson," I said, turning quickly and speaking urgently. "And he has a seat on the council, but you might also know that he's really Central Intelligence's witch-finder general: something the most well-informed rebels have never guessed."

That wasn't so much a half-brick as a ton of them. The captain took another step back and his mouth began to move as if he was searching for words that wouldn't come.

The captain paused, knowing that this was true and that this was far from common knowledge.

"I am William Hawthorne," I confessed. "I am also Major Johan Twiness, Section Four, Special Agent Eighty-three. You're thinking I'm young to be a special agent, I'm sure. Recruited from Homewood Prep at age twelve. You know it?"

"Yes," he said. "I didn't attend, unfortunately, but yes, I know it."

"Well," I said, moving on, "I think my cover for this mission is now well and truly shot. And Liefson is going to hit the roof when he finds out that the regular infantry have sabotaged an internal espionage mission because they didn't bother to consult with high command before turning the dogs loose."

He blinked, and I took the moment to motion him closer with a nod of my head.

"You are Seventh Infantry, yes, Captain?" I said, my voice lowered conspiratorially.

"Yes, sir. Captain J. F. Danek. Served throughout the Bowescroft campaign. Decorated for bravery in the siege of Althwaite, now placed with the Cresdon B Garrison, sir."

"Good man, Danek, outstanding," I said. "So here's the thing. I've been undercover for months. This morning some idiot corporal tried to take me in. Caused all kinds of trouble. I will have to lie low for a while so the rebels don't get suspicious. Now, it seems to me that this situation can be saved if we move along swiftly, and you keep what you have learnt to yourself. Make your way slowly back to Cresdon and—this is most important—report none of this to your superiors, whom Section Four seem to consider unreliable."

"Are you suggesting, sir, that my commanding officer may be a security leak?" said the soldier, unable to conceal the faintest hint of glee.

"Infantry man too, is he?" I asked.

"No, sir," said the soldier. "Straight from Thornbridge Staff Officer Academy, sir. Barely twenty-four. No active service."

"I see. You have my sympathy, Captain Danek. If I were you, I would lie low, say nothing, and watch your young commander like a hawk."

"I will do that, sir. Your suggestion to return, sir, is that an order?"

"Would it make life easier for you if it were?"

"I have to submit the reports on my company's actions," he said, slightly embarrassed by his predicament.

"Very well, Captain Danek. You may consider my suggestion an order."

"Yes, sir. Thank you, sir." He thought for a moment and then stood to attention, adding in his best military bark, "I shall lead my company back to Cresdon and complete my orders, sir!"

"Good man," I said. I received his salute with a superior nod and a smile of satisfaction and then marched back to the wagon, where the others were watching me silently, apprehensively.

I climbed back up onto the wagon, and the others, as if in a daze, just stared.

"What the devil did you say?" muttered Orgos.

"Does it matter?"

"Yes, actually."

"I used a little information that few people know," I said, my eyes on the soldiers as they remounted their horses.

As the soldiers walked out of earshot Garnet glared at me and said, "And how did you find out so much about Empire operations?"

"Research," I said. "I'm a writer."

"Not good enough," said Garnet. "I've never heard of this Commander Liefson. How would you know that he headed up Section Four unless—?"

"Because Harveth Liefson is a secret theatre fan and he goes to the Eagle in disguise every Saturday afternoon rain or shine," I said. "He and I have shared many a pint together and he has, once or twice, confided rather more than he probably should."

Orgos was the only one who seemed content. Mithos's eyes were cold and hard with suspicion. I smiled encouragingly but he just stared at me.

The troops had turned their horses and, with a single gesture of his hand, their captain urged them back the way they had come at a slow trot. Mithos watched them go and then laid a strong hand on my wrist. His dark face and eyes only inches from mine, he whispered, "If you turn us in or lead us into a trap, Mr. Hawthorne, I swear I'll run my sword through your heart before you can say my name."

I just sat where I was beside Orgos thinking vengefully that I should have turned them all in when I had the chance. I wasn't entirely sure why I hadn't.

⁂

It was still light, but only just. We had seen nothing more of the Empire but couldn't hope that my little ruse would hold them off for long. They might be back after us first thing in the morning, but I rather hoped old Harveth Liefson would cover for me for a few days. He had been quite a fan, and it really wasn't in his interest to reveal how I had found out so much of his professional affairs. Liefson knew I was no rebel, and he was a decent sort of guy. No: there was no doubt that the Stavis garrisons would be on the lookout for us when we got there, but I doubted we'd have much trouble from the Empire on the road through the Hrof wastes.

We pulled off the road into a glade of cedars and pines, as close to lush as we'd seen in twenty miles. We jumped down from the wagon— or rather Orgos jumped and I sort of fell—and immediately they were busy. Mithos's attitude to me had changed again. That scary, watchful suspicion had vanished, or slid under a log like a snake.

"Go and get some wood," he said. "Nothing green and nothing

too big. Just twigs and dead leaves for kindling. And don't cut any-thing live. It kills the trees and it won't burn."

"I know that. I'm not completely stupid," I told him. "I don't know why you want a fire anyway. It's roasting out here."

"We need some hot water," he answered tersely without looking up from the tent he was raising with Orgos. "Don't you want to wash? Don't you want a meal?" He paused to hammer a peg into the hard earth with a wooden mallet. "And don't you want to keep the jackals and mountain lions at a safe distance?"

He added that last one just to wind me up, as Orgos's grin con-firmed. The other two reasons would have been just fine.

"Are there mountain lions around here?" I asked, trying to sound like I didn't believe him and couldn't care less either way.

"Some," he said. "Though they tend to move closer to water. This heat can really make them irritable."

"I've heard of massive mountain lions sighted round here," Or-gos added helpfully, "even in the summer. Real monsters. I heard of a guy who was camping out here and one came right into the tent and—"

"All right, I'll get the wood," I said, and left.

By the time I had got a good armful, dropped it off by the wagon, and gone back for another, the light was going fast. I was poking around for more sticks when I saw it, just out of the corner of my eye. It reared up and its head sort of hung there in the air, its hood flared. I'm no naturalist, but I know a cobra when I see one. They turn up from time to time in the city, but this was the first time I'd seen one up close outside a street show. It watched me, its tongue flicking slightly. I wanted to call out to the others but didn't dare. Could snakes hear? I didn't even know that. I turned my head to face it and felt like I was about to pass out.

"Don't look at it."

Garnet was behind me. I hadn't heard him approach.

"They spit venom into your eyes," he said. "Look down and back off slowly."

"They spit venom?" I muttered, fear making me stupid.

"Just back away," hissed Garnet, rather like the snake.

I moved and the cobra reared another few inches and made a gasping, hostile sound like Mrs. Pugh on rent day. Garnet slipped be-tween me and it with his ax in his hand. I edged back, then scrambled away and watched Garnet staring at it. It was a good ten feet away but looked big enough to strike most of that distance. Shielding his face, he too backed off, towards me. When he reached me and the snake lowered itself to earth I spluttered, "Why didn't you kill it?"

"It wouldn't have harmed you so long as you kept your distance."

"And if it comes back?"

"We'll be sleeping," said Garnet. That was supposed to be reassuring. He added, "It can't eat anything as big as us so it will only strike at us if we threaten it. How can we threaten it if we are asleep?"

Great. So we would be sharing our camp with all manner of reptiles, which was fine so long as we didn't move and force them to kill us all.

"Snakes have worse social skills than you," I remarked. "I can't believe you didn't swing for it while you had the chance. What do you carry that ax for if you never use the bloody thing?"

"Oh," he replied menacingly, "I use it, all right."

❧

They put me on first watch. I asked what I was supposed to do and Renthrette, her lips curled with the contempt she reserved for me, said, "You watch."

That was really helpful. So I spent an hour sitting by the dying fire looking around through the night and reflected on the day. I had washed in a bucket of warm water until it was cool and brownish. I had eaten two raw carrots and some stewed mutton and potatoes flavored with the herbs Orgos found hereabouts. Not bad, but not duckling. Though I had presumed that Renthrette would do the cooking, she had left it all to Mithos and Orgos while she repaired a broken wheel spoke on the wagon, just to prove me wrong. The two men worked silently together, used to each other. How long had they been together? Ten years? More, perhaps. Ten years of tents and wagons and bloody snakes and swords. They must be out of their minds.

And I was with them. I had relieved myself in the bushes, drunk from a smelly waterskin in the wagon, and shot my little crossbow over and over until I could hit a tree at twenty paces every other time. I had been reprimanded by Mithos for bringing green wood and for shooting at live trees. I had been vaguely threatened by Garnet and ignored utterly by his good-looking sister. If things didn't change soon, I was going to make a real pig's ear out of the rest of my life.

I had watched Renthrette and her brother unpacking their stuff and laying it out. Everything was meticulously arranged: cooking pots stacked together, rope neatly coiled, horse bridles and harnesses untangled and hung up, mail corselet oiled and laid out, sword at the ready in case of emergency. Renthrette had spent much of the evening stitching some clothing, and I had watched her working with the same careful, regulated focus that typified the pair of them. I looked over to where she had bedded down in a small tent and thought about going to wish her good night, but figured she'd probably knife me as soon as I was in range.

The cicadas and crickets in the treetops buzzed and clicked smugly to themselves. Twice I heard an owl somewhere and tried to find it, wandering around the makeshift tents and trail fodder where the horses lay, but it just laughed at me invisibly. I nodded to Orgos, who lay awake inside the back of the wagon on a pile of boxes draped with the materials that had got us out of Cresdon.

"Have you done your watch?" he said, and his voice was low and hoarse.

"Not quite," I said. "There isn't much to watch, and if there was, I wouldn't see it till it had bitten my leg off. Maybe nothing's hungry. Garnet's on next but he's sleeping."

"Then leave him be. I'll do it. I can't sleep anyway." He sat up and dropped to the ground, stretching and pulling on his ring mail in an irritatingly easy motion. In the darkness he was just a shadow, save when he looked at me and I saw his eyes bright and clear. Taking one of those long swords of his he wandered over to where I had been sitting and said, "Get some sleep, Will. We have a long way to go tomorrow and we're going to have to move fast, probably off the road. Whether the Empire comes after us or not, we're in dangerous country and will be for a while. Sleep tight. *Don't let the mountain lions bite. If they do* . . . well, I guess you bleed to death."

"Funny," I said. "Thanks."

Of Gorse and Wild Thyme

I slept under the wagon in a sleeping bag of cotton so thin that I could feel every contour of the hard ground beneath me, and dreamed of the fight in the Cresdon pub when I had met the party. I was back in the chest and the soldier was opening it, seeing me, grinning . . .

And then . . . *something.*

I couldn't remember it properly, but there had been a strange amber light. . . .

When I woke, my right arm numb and my back aching, I found myself wondering how my life could have been so screwed up in only twenty-four hours. Half an hour later, Mithos told me in a confiding voice that I wasn't exactly pulling my weight as far as dismantling the camp was concerned. This was true. I started to tell Mithos that I had a bad back, but he just gave me one of those please-don't-waste-my-time looks of his and tossed me a canvas bag that felt like it had a cow in it.

So I lugged bags and boxes back into the wagon and Mithos watched and prompted me to the thrilling act of high adventure I might try next: washing the breakfast pans. I fed the horses (at arm's length). I stamped out the fire and buried the ashes. I put more stuff in the wagon. I wasn't sure I could take all this excitement.

Orgos re-dressed the wound on my leg, which showed no sign of infection and would be gone altogether soon.

"Morning, Will," said Garnet unexpectedly. "Will you be riding on the wagon again today?"

"I expect so," I said guardedly. "Why?"

"Would you mind doing me a favor?"

I regarded him steadily and waited.

"It's not a big job but my hands will be full since I'll be riding escort. Some of the armor we acquired in Cresdon needs cleaning up."

Of course: more menial labor for the party's mentally subnormal help. He handed me a coarse, heavy sack, which clanked against my legs.

"There's a wire brush, rags, some oil for the rust and the moving parts, and some polish to finish them off. Do you mind?"

I muttered that it was fine, anything to oblige, and so on, and he beamed at me, guessing how much it hurt.

"Thanks, Will," he said, his green eyes smiling brightly, "I appreciate it."

He slapped my arm good-humoredly as if to say "welcome aboard" or something similarly nauseating, and strode off to his horse. He was already in his armor, complete with helm, ax, and a leather-covered shield. He looked like an adventurer. I, however, looked like a metal polisher. I climbed onto the wagon and looked at the sack sulkily.

"Got a job?" said an irritatingly cheerful Orgos as he took his place.

"Of sorts," I muttered.

"It'll pass the time," he laughed, flashing his teeth. "You won't be wrestling cobras all the way to Stavis."

"Hilarious as ever," I said.

It was indecently early when we rejoined the road and turned towards the rising sun, with Mithos and Renthrette (who hadn't spoken to me today) riding ahead and Garnet at the rear. All around us the trees were filled with the bright, twittering songs of warblers and the shrill stutterings of sparrows. Their cheerfulness annoyed me, so I concentrated on my bits of rag and rusty armor, but within another hour the heat had kicked in and they had all shut up.

Yesterday's journey had seen us leave behind the last of the cultivated land east of Cresdon. As the patches of dry grass were replaced by parched, sand-colored earth or coarse heather and gorse, there was even less to look at. No distant houses, no grazing cattle. Nothing. The air became heavy with the aromas of wild sage, thyme, and sweat. It seemed we were leaving the humidity behind, but the temperature continued to rise. I bent over the rusty greaves and brushed them fiercely as the sweat poured down my neck.

"Drink," said Orgos, passing me a water bottle. I did so: long gasping swallows almost too earnest for my throat to take. "You have to keep drinking," he said. "By lunchtime we should have finished this

bottle between us. And you should wear a hat, Will. Even a light helmet would keep the sun off."

I grinned at his concern and went on burnishing the armor in my
lap until I could see my hot, bored face in it. I oiled it and spent several minutes trying to decide where you were supposed to wear it.
Orgos hummed tunefully to himself. I noticed when he stopped, but
I didn't look up.

"Will," he said suddenly. "How are your eyes?"

"I can see this scrap metal in my lap pretty well, why?"

"Take a look over to the left there and tell me what you see."

The very slight urgency in his lazy tone showed through, and I
turned sharply to the left.

The wagon and the horses in front were throwing up dust in a
thin ribbonlike cloud, but beyond it and the road, five hundred
yards or so over in the gorse and heather, were horsemen riding
parallel to us.

"Eight of them," I said. "Empire troops?"

Orgos shook his head.

"Get into the back of the wagon and take the crossbow," he said
carefully, with a quick flash of his eyes into mine. "Don't worry, it'll
be all right. Maybe nothing at all, but better to be safe. Go to the
back, open the top flap, and make sure Garnet knows they are there.
Then get yourself a spear and cover the rear. If you can't hold it, fas-
ten her up and come back to the front."

For a moment I just listened; then I clambered through the hatch
into the back, my heart thumping. I felt cold, but I had started to
sweat. It was becoming clear now; the moment I had climbed up the
Eagle's balcony, I had begun some unbreakable chain of events. Terror was going to follow me about like an overfriendly dog. Or maybe
a lion.

The back of the wagon was dark, hot, and bouncing erratically. I
threw the bolt on the top flap with an unsteady hand and raised it to
the roof, hooking it in place with a wooden peg. The brightness outside hurt my eyes. Garnet was riding close, his helm sparkling and his
mouth set. He had unslung his ax from the thong on his saddle and
he clasped it in his right hand. It looked huge and cruel against his
thin, sinewy arm. He saw me and nodded slightly, his eyes meeting
mine for an expressionless moment. I was conscious that we had increased speed and that Garnet's dappled mare was in a full canter

and sweating heavily. Things were slipping out of control again and my bladder seemed to have suddenly filled to bursting point.

Then I heard another horse close to the wagon, and Mithos appeared alongside Garnet. They spoke to each other briefly and he called to me over the noise of wheels and hooves, "All right, Will?"

I nodded, but my eyes were wide. My whole arm trembled as I dragged a short spear from the bundle in the dark interior and returned to my squat by the half-opened tailgate. I wondered if I should have taken an ax or sword but Orgos was right: With this I could lunge through the opening without committing myself.

Suddenly there was a flurry of movement behind the wagon and I glanced up to see Mithos and Garnet reining their horses. In the same instant, wood splintered to my right as the side of the wagon was hit by an arrow. Mithos bent his bow and loosed an arrow. Desperate to know what was going on, I leaned out and saw them coming.

The riders had split up. Three rode to the front; five charged the back. They weren't Empire. For a second I considered ducking back inside and locking myself in, but the futility of that was obvious even in my rising panic. The front was under attack, so there was no point in fleeing in that direction. I couldn't get out of the back without getting trampled to death, so I stayed where I was, spear and crossbow in hand, motionless as a cockroach that knows it's been seen but doesn't have the slightest idea what to do about it.

The wagon slowed to a halt and the air was torn by the shouts of our adversaries as they came at us. I caught a glimpse of a pinkish male face, red hair blowing back from under his helm and his eyes and mouth distorted by a roar of fury as his horse bore him into us. Garnet shrugged him off with his shield and swung his ax high as the other raised a short and heavy spear.

A man in leather and ring mail, his lance leveled murderously, was bearing down on Mithos in a full charge. Mithos waited and then, with impossible self-control, shot his bow. The arrow sped in a short horizontal path and found the bandit's shoulder. He shuddered and his horse all but threw him as he struggled to regain control. By the time the next rider had galloped in close, long yellow hair flying behind him, Mithos had dropped the bow and drawn his sword. They met and their steel rang out.

Garnet traded blow and parry with the red-haired man. He held him off but looked around in alarm when another appeared, a heavy spiked mace in one hand. I aimed my crossbow with sweating palms and without a thought in my head. Garnet tried in vain to break from his adversary and face the newcomer as the redhead raised his spear to strike. I squeezed the trigger and the bow kicked.

The bolt struck him squarely between the shoulder blades. I don't think it went all the way in, but he sort of tipped to one side and fell to the earth. Garnet looked from him to me for a split second and then heaved the bit of his ax at his new adversary. I stared.

Mithos slashed hard from above. As the blond man raised his sword to take the strike, Mithos undercut the parry and plunged the tip of his broadsword through the mail of the bandit's stomach. The wounded man went still and taut. Blood foamed at his beard and he slumped forward. At this, Garnet's assailant wheeled his horse and fled. The one Mithos had shot followed, hanging desperately around the neck of his horse, barely able to stay in the saddle. I stumbled towards the front of the wagon, but the enemy horses were charging away before I reached the hatch.

Once I got down I found another body on the road, but its face was unfamiliar. We had survived unscathed.

Suddenly, the enemy horse hooves had faded away and the empty land was utterly silent.

It hit me like a piece of pipe in a pub brawl. I dropped the crossbow, which I hadn't even remembered to reload, and found that my arms were shaking uncontrollably. My breath was coming in gasps, and my whole body was seized with shivering. I sank to my knees, fighting for air and a remnant of personal dignity. Neither was forthcoming.

The others gathered round me.

"Get him some water," said Mithos hurriedly. "Easy, Will, it's all over. No one's hurt and you did just fine."

"Yes, Will," added Garnet in a deliberately cheerful tone. "That was a nice shot. I think you saved my neck there."

Mithos and Orgos said nothing and returned their concerned gazes to me.

"Sorry," I wheezed, "I seem to be coming down with something. It must be the heat. . . ."

"Don't talk," said Mithos.

I continued to shudder convulsively. Renthrette pressed a flask of water to my lips and I drank from it, the liquid spilling around my chin as my shaking hands tried to keep it in place. I thrust it away suddenly and took a long breath as if snatched from drowning.

To my further degradation, they laid me on a blanket by the roadside. I could feel the sun beating down but couldn't convince myself that I wasn't about to freeze. Mithos emptied a canvas sack and told me to breathe into it. That was the finishing touch, of course. I sat there with a bag on my head like the hunchback in a pub joke and wondered why on earth my body wouldn't behave itself.

The sack smelled old and fusty but it somehow helped my breathing to steady. Gradually those shallow, wheezing gasps were replaced by deeper breaths that filled my lungs. I felt a weight lift from my chest and, as my temperature rose perceptibly, the shuddering and trembling eased to nothing. Orgos sat in the ditch beside me and put a strong arm about my shoulders. It was all crushingly embarrassing, and I was just considering the idea of keeping the bag in place for the rest of the day when there was a stutter of horse hooves on the road.

The redhead I had shot had dragged himself back onto his horse and kicked it into motion. They watched him go and looked back at me emerging sheepishly from my bag.

"Why didn't you stop him?" I demanded.

"Why should we?" said Orgos quietly. "What would we do with him? Take him prisoner and lug him all the way to Stavis? Execute him? We would not."

I caught a flicker of a glance between Garnet and Renthrette and wondered if they were all of the same mind. I was, for some reason, outraged. I clawed for some answer that would satisfy me.

"You could have found out who they were and why they attacked. They were probably working for the Empire," I insisted, unsure why my voice sounded so unstable.

"The Empire does its own dirty work," answered Garnet briskly. "They were bandits, no more. They keep watch for small trading caravans from Cresdon and hit them before they enter the Hrof wastes. It is not uncommon. There is no mystery about it. They just thought that attacking a couple of traders and three hired escorts would have been made worth the risk by whatever was in the wagon. It wasn't. End of story."

Close to the wagon, two horses strayed aimlessly and their riders lay on the hot road, the dusty stone beneath them stained red. I stared at them again and tried to batter the anger, depression, and exhilaration I felt into some more familiar emotion. The bearded man Mithos had killed lay on his stomach. His·helm had slipped off and his long blond hair spilled onto the road like blood. He looked quite young. I turned quickly away.

We buried them some yards off the road at my insistence, but for me it was a matter of closing the incident rather than anything to do with the dignity of the dead. Garnet said we were wasting time and Renthrette looked at me as if I was some peculiar museum piece in a case: not a very interesting or valuable piece, of course, but the kind of thing that you look at sideways and try to figure out what the hell it was used for. Mithos didn't object, and said that if Empire troops saw the graves, they might just think we were dead. It was unlikely but it couldn't do us any harm. Garnet, already forgetful of who had saved his neck, muttered that if it did do us harm, he'd know whom to thank.

We rode for an hour, until we came to a grove of shady trees, and there, in relative silence, we made lunch and rested for a while. They all thought I was still suffering from some kind of trauma. Each of them circled me warily like dogs gauging a bear. It was starting to get on my nerves.

"You did fine," said Mithos for no good reason.

"Thanks," I muttered, wishing they could find something else to talk about.

"Doing all right, Will?" asked Orgos.

"Look," I blurted suddenly, "I'm not used to being attacked or to watching people get killed, all right? Sorry. I've thrown the odd punch in my time, even the odd chair, but shooting people in the back is a new one on me. I realize that you lot have been skewering passersby since before you could walk, but some of us haven't. Most of the people I know actually get through the day without complete strangers trying to kill them. You seem to think it perfectly normal that you get attacked by bunches of homicidal maniacs. It's not! It rarely happens, except to people like you. You're some kind of disaster magnet. Everywhere you go, death and destruction alight on your wagon like a pair of bloody homing pigeons, and you don't seem to think it's odd. Let me just say it again: It *is* odd. Bloody odd, and it is likely to have rather severe effects on those who aren't used to climbing over corpses to get to the bathroom. I have, however, recovered from the experience. I am now perfectly all right and you can stop treating me like some kind of wounded horse. See? Just get on with your jolly old adventuring and next time we have to slaughter a few people you can trust me to keep my upper lip stiff as a board."

There was a momentary silence that felt particularly empty after my rather shrill explosion.

"Done?" asked Mithos, looking at the ground.

"Done," I said.

SCENE XII

The Desert

We'd chosen our lunch spot well, for I think we saw no more trees that day. The scent of wild herbs never left our nostrils but the heather disappeared, and though the gorse persisted, it seemed to get thinner, until it was just a tangled mass of brownish thorns. We were on the edge of the Hrof wastes by four o'clock and I was startled to look up and see huge vultures, grey and pink as dead flesh, the fingers of their wings spread wide as they soared their slow circles above us. I watched them to take my mind off the Empire patrol that was likely to appear on the road at any minute.

"Those things give me the willies," muttered Orgos. We had barely spoken since my last little rant. "Great winged rats," he went on. "In the morning you see them sitting in trees with their wings hanging in front of them, like dead men in rags. You can feel them waiting for you to die. They belong here in the Hrof. This is their territory."

Well, that was nice to know. The vultures drifted slowly overhead and watched us with the critical gaze of someone inspecting a forkful of pork pie whose origins had been called into question. It was disconcerting, but somehow not entirely inappropriate. The Empire, some of my old acting companions at the Eagle, and, most recently, Renthrette, had always regarded me as something resembling carrion. If I died of exposure in the next ten minutes, the world wouldn't miss me and the vultures would get a meal. I could picture the great scrawny birds squatting on my remains, spitting gristle and complaining to themselves about the poor quality of the meat coming through these days. . . .

Orgos was right. This was their land, and the only way to avoid finishing up lightly roasted and serving six was to get the hell out of here as soon as possible. The vultures circled on anyway, smugly sure that they'd be dining shortly, tucking into Bill the Succulent any day now. I shot them a defiant scowl, but riding into a desert wasn't the best way of staying alive, and given the day's events and the dubious nature of my traveling companions, I could sort of see their point.

⁂

On each day of our passage across the Hrof, the party rotated their traveling positions to ease the tedium. On one day Mithos would drive the wagon, the next he would ride at the rear, the next he would lead, and so on. Everyone would change, that is, except me. I was to sit on the front of the wagon with my crossbow, polishing armor, making idle conversation, studying maps of the area, and getting very, very hot and very, very bored.

Garnet's face was pink and peeling by the third day despite his best efforts to keep the sun off. From the morning of day four onwards he put his helm in the wagon and swathed himself from head to toe in a pair of white sheets like the swaddled corpse of some barbarian chieftain. Only his green eyes and the dark pits of his nostrils could be seen. His sunburn and his sense of how ridiculous he looked did nothing to improve his temper, so I avoided him. Most of the time he rode by himself, sulking and flaking quietly.

That said, he had warmed to me fractionally since my little meltdown with the bandits. I had been a good little apprentice, or whatever the hell they thought I was. To be honest, I had nightmares about shooting that crossbow for three nights afterwards, but I wasn't about to mention that to him. In any case, he seemed rather more content to have me around and less likely to kill me than he had before, except when he caught me looking at his sister.

Renthrette was, as you might have guessed, a very different story. She took every available opportunity to treat me with the contempt one normally reserves for bawds, tax collectors, and other social lepers. Once I had been relating some snippets of my life in Cresdon and my activities down at the Eagle. Orgos laughed at my ineptitude. Mithos complimented me on my impersonations. Even Garnet smiled and made some roughly complimentary remark about mine being an uncertain way to make a living. She looked at me with the mild revulsion you might show to a large beetle, and turned away.

One day we had to ride together. When she came to the wagon, I had already climbed aboard and extended my hand to help her. She hoisted herself up easily without my assistance and gave me a withering look. I withdrew my hand and, for a moment, withered.

"Would you like me to drive?" I tried cheerfully as she sat down.

"Did you drive yesterday?" she demanded.

"No, Garnet did," I said, thinking that that rather strengthened my position.

"And the day before?"

"Mithos drove."

"And on either occasion did you offer to drive?" she persisted.

"Er . . . no, why?" I answered guilelessly.

"Then how dare you offer today?"

"What?"

"You think I'm incapable of steering a wagon along a straight road because I am a woman?"

"No, of course not," I stammered hopelessly.

"Then what?"

"Well, I was just being civil," I suggested.

"Don't be," she said, and set us in motion with a crack of the reins.

She had stoically refused to cover her pale skin as her brother had done, because she said it impeded the movement of her sword arm. I was starting to see a lot of that stoicism and I didn't much like it.

"You really should cover up," I said. "You obviously have delicate skin. Plenty of Cresdon ladies would be jealous of it. Shame to let it burn. . . ."

"Why don't you look after your own skin?" she remarked acidly. "You've had lots of practice."

Great, Will, I told myself. *Another triumph. Will the Smooth. Debonair Bill strikes again. All right, a man can only take so much. It's time to shock her into submission with your forthrightness and straight talking. Put the pressure on. Give it to her hard and direct. Call her bluff. Here we go.* "You don't like me very much, do you?" I said with a disarming smile.

"No," she said flatly.

"Oh," I said, thrown by her candor. "Well, er . . . why not?"

"You are an ugly little worm of a man with no scruples or principles other than those that preserve your worthless hide."

She turned to me to say that, and her blue-grey eyes blazed into mine. Her voice had a strident edge to it, since she was speaking over the noise of the horses, but her tone was calm. I stared at her and tried turning on the charm.

"You don't mean that." I beamed mischievously.

"Don't bet on it."

"You can't mean, for example, that I am physically ugly! Many women—"

"I mean exactly that," she said bitterly. "Look at yourself. Skinny and with the belly of an old frog. You're what, eighteen?"

"About that."

"You have the physique of someone twice your age. Look at that!"

She poked my stomach with her index finger until it hurt. I wanted to slap her but I was too chivalrous, and didn't want the further humiliation of her beating me up.

"That's nothing a little exercise won't fix," I breathed, pushing her hand off my gut testily.

"You never do any exercise."

"I carry wood and stuff," I said in an injured tone.

"That's not exercise, that's light work," she snarled. "Call yourself a man?" she sneered. "You're an *actor*. A professional liar. You've never done a day's work in your life."

"Just because I don't use my biceps all day doesn't mean I don't work. Can't a man earn his keep with his brain instead of his arms?"

That ought to get her, I thought.

"Of course he can, if the work is honorable." She sat back, pleased with herself as if she had said something unanswerable.

"Honor!" I spat. "A fine, airy nothing to get yourself killed for. Honor, God help us! If, according to your honor, I am damned for acting on a stage, but you and your brother are praiseworthy for theft and murder, then you can keep it. Better still," I added, warming to my subject, "you can stick it right—"

"That's enough," said Mithos, who had appeared trotting at my side. "You two had better learn to live with each other for a while. And Renthrette?"

"Yes," she said, a faint pout puckering the slim pink line of her mouth.

"Mr. Hawthorne is our guest." At that her lip began to curl and he, catching her look, spoke more forcefully. "Conditions will not be good until we reach Stavis. Some degree of harmony is essential. Drink."

He indicated the cloth-covered bottle and I passed it to her. She took a long, slow mouthful and I watched her throat as she swallowed.

Passing it back to me, she caught the hard glitter of Mithos's black eyes and forced a smile.

"There you are, Mr. Hawthorne."

"Thank you ever so much, Renthrette," I said.

Mithos nodded and rode on. She watched him go and said, "In future, Mr. Hawthorne, have the dignity to fight your own battles."

I felt I had cause to protest at this, but the conversation was clearly a circular one. I fell silent and looked at the unchanging road ahead.

When we stopped to eat, Orgos caught me by the arm and beamed into my face.

"Had a romantic ride?" he asked.

"Get lost, Orgos," I replied. He gave his characteristic whoop of laughter and I grinned at him despite myself.

❧

In the second half of the week in the Hrof, I started secretly doing exercises at night, when it was cool and I was on watch. The others, Renthrette in particular, were asleep, so I could move away from the wagon and wheeze my way through some sit-ups and push-ups. There were no improvements in my physique, but I felt virtuous and that was enough at present. One night Orgos interrupted me. "You don't exactly tax yourself, do you?" He smiled.

"What's that supposed to mean?" I replied, insulted.

"You've barely broken a sweat. There are a few weights in the wagon. Want to use them?"

"Er, yes, all right," I agreed reluctantly. He went into the wagon and reappeared with a pair of small dumbbells, a four-foot bar, and a set of weights, all carried with irritating ease. In order to stave off actually having to use the bloody things, I said the first thing that came into my head.

"Would you teach me to use a sword, Orgos?"

He smiled again and said, "I'd be glad to. Though you aren't going to be a sword master this time next week, and it will take a lot to impress Renthrette."

"This is nothing to do with Renthrette," I lied. "I just need to feel safer and more useful to the party."

"Fine," he said, "but you're going to have to get yourself in shape first. I'm not sure you could manage much more than a fruit knife at present."

I shrugged off his sarcasm and made as if to go to bed.

"All right, all right, I'm sorry," he laughed, coming after me. "We'll start now if you like."

"Can I see your sword?" I asked.

He reached for the left one but I stopped him.

"The other," I said, indicating the one with the amber stone in the pommel. He seemed to hesitate for a split second and then handed it to me. It was heavy, too heavy for me to use, though not as heavy as I had expected.

"What's this?" I said, touching the stone with my fingertip.

"Nothing," said Orgos. "Decoration."

"Yeah?" I said.

"I'll get a pair of spears. Better start there."

As he got a couple of spears out of the wagon and bound their tips with cleaning rags, I wondered why I didn't believe him. Decoration? Orgos? That didn't sound right. And there was something else: a vague and unsettling memory.

A flash of light . . .

I looked at the amber gem, and, as the sun caught it, it seemed to glow with exactly the same inner fire that—crazy though it sounded— I thought had somehow incapacitated those Empire troops back in Cresdon. I considered the stone, then told myself not to be so bloody stupid and put it out of my head.

I couldn't help thinking that the spears were less glamorous than the sword I had hoped for, but Orgos assured me it was a good place to start. The spear was light and required more dexterity than strength. In my current physical state that was a good thing, as he had so penetratingly observed. I stood legs apart as he told me, and grasped the shaft with both hands.

"All right," he said, "now face me and do as I do. Grip the spear like this. Fists outwards. Your right hand a little further down. Now lunge at me. Good, but make it a smaller movement. The bigger and more obvious the lunge, the easier it is to anticipate and the harder it is for you to recover. Always get back on both feet with your weight evenly distributed like this. Right. Now try that lunge again and recover. Good."

So it went on, and I suppose I made progress, and I actually enjoyed it so much that I didn't realize how late it was getting until the minuscule wound in my thigh began to throb faintly. I also didn't notice Mithos and Garnet watching from the fireplace, or hear what they had to say. I learnt fast and my reflexes were quick, so they should have been fairly impressed. Orgos was pleasantly surprised and said so. I was flattered, even if he was just encouraging me. Still, it would take more than a bit of training to make me into the stuff of heroes. They couldn't train me in honor and bravery and the other "qualities" that would one day get them all killed.

Of Renthrette's views on the matter I heard nothing, but I strolled around the camp, spear in hand, and occasionally brought up the matter of our sparring when we were all gathered together to dine. Whenever I did so she would give me a long indifferent look as if to say that she knew she was supposed to be impressed and wasn't; then she would go back to her slow, meticulous brushing of the horses' tails or whatever the hell she was doing. But I knew her resolve was weakening. She wasn't the first to have tried to convince herself that I was some kind of repulsive and despicable rodent. I'd read the literature on such things. I'd written some of it.

Orgos, anxious to improve my other skills, encouraged me to sit on a horse, but I felt so high and ridiculously unbalanced that I could not be persuaded even to have him walk the beast round the camp. I sat on it; that was all. As far as I was concerned, that was progress enough for one day, or indeed for several. I don't trust things with more feet than me. Come to think of it, I don't trust things with fewer feet either. If it doesn't look like me, I find it suspicious, and if I ever met someone exactly like me, I would trust him still less. Trust is a highly overrated commodity, I think.

❧

By the sixth day, the wound on my leg had vanished. On the eighth day I noted a distinct weaving of grass in the hot earth, and by evening there were trees again. Earlier on in the same day I had been gratified by a glimpse of the famous Hrof ostrich. It had been a good four hundred yards from the road, but you couldn't mistake that leggy ball of feathers powering up and down the desert on those clawed, pinkish legs of tight muscle and sinew. I think I would have been disappointed if I hadn't seen one, since in my former life it was the only image that mention of the Hrof lands might have called to mind. By the late afternoon of the ninth and, somehow, longest day, we could see the distant flashes of light and color from the rooftops of Stavis. And still the Empire hadn't got me. We, and more particularly, I, had made it.

SCENE XIII

The Party Leader

On the last day of our journey I got a clearer view of Stavis and it, or rather one aspect of it, came as something of a shock.

Stavis sat astride the river Yarseth only a couple of miles from where it emptied its brown, unsightly waters into the sea. I had known this before, but being presented with the reality of the thing was a different matter. The Yarseth was merely a dark and drowsy worm, but at its mouth was the ocean, and there the sparkle was like the billion shards of some immense fractured mirror. I had never seen the sea before.

It was loathing at first sight. I'm sure there are many well-traveled and broad-minded individuals who are accustomed to the ocean and don't even recall their first glimpse of it. I, having weaseled my uneventful way into a shabby, provincial adulthood within a twenty-mile radius of the supremely shabby and provincial town of Cresdon, was neither well-traveled nor broad-minded. The sight of that near-infinite expanse of water scared the living daylights out of me, leaving me feeling not so much inadequate as nonexistent, and I found myself glancing at it furtively every few minutes to make sure it was still there. It was.

At least you could walk on the Hrof. Back in the golden age of Mrs. Pugh and her cockroach-ridden hovel, I had some nagging doubts about the very existence of the sea, as if I was preparing myself for someone to confess that the whole ludicrous "area of salty water" thing was a story to frighten children. The sea had been like magic and dragons or peace and liberty: mythically fictitious. But there it was, huge, vibrant, and glittering smugly to itself. I spent the next two days undergoing what you might call an ordeal by confrontation.

Stavis itself didn't help. The road brought us gradually into a sprawl of white-plastered buildings and a population of every racial type imaginable. Here was a Cherrati trade enclosure hanging with silk; there were the people I knew only—and quaintly—as snow folk, from farther north than any map I knew of, selling seal pelts and buying iron spear tips by the sackful. Verone herders with their smelly okanthi rubbed shoulders with Dranetian silver dealers and Mesorian glass merchants. The sea drew all races, and in Stavis they met and bartered, calculated their profit and loss in a dozen languages and a hundred dialects. And rather than feeling like one of the ingredients in this great cultural stew, I merely felt left out and longed for the familiar pettiness of Cresdon.

Our passage through the city was marked by a sudden darkening of the skies until the clouds swirled violet and cracked with electrical flashes. When the rain came I ducked into the wagon and stared out of the back as Stavis's international cross section ran for cover and the raindrops bounced eight inches high off the Empire's new-laid pavements.

The Empire had been here only eight months. In that time, Orgos assured me, little had changed, except that prices had gone up, taxes and soldiers had appeared, and the Diamond Empire was looking fat and pleased with itself. The populace adapted by marking up their cod, herring, and sailfish prices until the only people who were really any worse off were distant trade partners and, of course, the very poor. So Stavis, with the usual economic sidestep, kept everyone happy. Everyone who mattered, anyway.

We were stopped twice as we entered the city, but even I could see that such challenges were formalities and only some spectacular idiocy on my part would get us into trouble. There was nothing to suggest that even word of us had reached the laconic guards. I couldn't help being slightly offended that they had lost interest in me, but after a moment's reflection on Empire execution practices, the feeling passed. By the time Orgos had given a street name, the troops were waving us through with thinly masked apathy. That night I resolved to raise a mug of the best ale I could find and toast Commander Harveth Liefson.

Once inside the city, the party rode as a unit with its weapons stashed in the wagon. Renthrette tied her horse to the back and climbed up next to me, muttering enthusiastically about the different architectural styles and the magnificent seafood. I tried to give her the look of shriveling distaste she had thrown me every hour or so for the last week, but my heart wasn't in it. Her eyes shone as she soaked up the rain-drenched scenery or haggled for imported mangoes with basket-laden street children. The transformation was astonishing. She smiled while she talked to me and at one point actually said, "You seem to be making progress with Orgos. You learn fast, Will. If you need any help or advice, please don't hesitate to ask."

I stared at her, speechless (not a condition I often find myself in, as you will have gathered), wondering what I had done to deserve such sunny chumminess from Renthrette after our former sojourn in the frozen wastes. But it was soon clear that it wasn't just this bloody city which delighted her so much.

"She's just relaxing now," said Orgos when I pressed him on the matter. We were waiting to cross the Yarseth, swollen with seasonal rain like an overfed anaconda. Its bridges were either completely submerged or showed themselves as crazy little walkways arching in and out of the river like sea serpents. We had to be ferried across in leaky pontoon boats.

"But why is she relaxing?"

"She is comfortable here," said Orgos, "and perhaps she feels she has to—how shall I put it?—assert herself less now."

There had been a slight smile on Orgos's lips as he concluded that last sentence. He was skirting around some crucial factor.

"Fine, Orgos," I interrupted bitterly, knowing he was holding back. "Don't tell me, see if I care."

"Well," he laughed, "I think you'll figure it out for yourself when we meet the party leader tonight."

So that was it. She was practicing her charm for her big-shot lover. She didn't need to fend me off anymore, because he would do it for her. For all her posturing, she would rely on her boyfriend's sword arm after all. But all was not lost. Now, while her guard was down, I would charm my way into her heart. I would show my wit, perception, and sensitivity (the last one I would have to fake, but it had worked before), and she would fall for me. Give me a couple of days and, to Renthrette, the "party leader" would be an embarrassing, bone-crushing thug compared with the sophisticated William Hawthorne.

Still, that image of the bone-crushing thug rather slowed me down a little. I didn't particularly want to find myself chivalrously jousting some seven-foot bonehead for her hand. I toyed for a moment with the idea of turning the "leader" in to the Empire guards, but that seemed vaguely below the belt, even for me. See? After only ten days with these clowns I was already letting my judgment get clouded by their laughable principles.

Perhaps it was Renthrette's letting her hair down (literally, as it happened), and generally being amiable and gorgeous, but I was rather going off the idea of breaking company with the party here. Partly it was Orgos's broad grin, partly it was Mithos's noble tolerance of my existence, partly it was the fact that Garnet didn't ax me in my bed, and partly it was because I felt out of my depth in Stavis with its urbane, colorful populace, its Empire guards, and its immense ocean. By comparison the party felt like old friends. Well, kind of. Maybe I would travel with them until I found some placid nation of imbeciles who liked theatre and playing cards. I figured I should at least meet their "leader" and hear their plans before I decided. Who knew? Maybe there was money in this adventuring lark.

The house was in a wealthy suburb with roofs of blue slate and glass in the windows. The grey stone buildings dotted with ancient shells were as different from the lurching ruins of Cresdon as the paved, guttered streets were different from Cresdon's ratty alleys. On the corner, two men sold spidery crabs and immense lobsters. Orgos enthused about steamed lobster, but I took one look at the massive claws of one antique blue monster and wagered a few silvers on the beast taking the arm of anyone who tried to get it out of the tank.

As we stabled the horses and unloaded the wagon, Mithos said to me, "The party leader is not expecting us yet since we left Cresdon earlier than intended. I am not sure what the precise nature of the task ahead of us is, but if you wish to come further with us, I could speak on your behalf. Unless you have other ideas, of course?"

"No," I muttered uncertainly, "I have no other plans."

I wasn't actually thinking about my plans at all, because something in the reverential way Mithos and the others referred to their nameless leader was beginning to get to me. My mildly resentful disinterest was quickly being replaced by curiosity. Whatever I felt about my companions, I could not avoid the fact that they were a rather unusual group of individuals. Once I had admitted this grudging respect for them I was faced with the problem of putting a face to the leader they so clearly looked up to. When I tried to get some information out of Garnet concerning their mission east of the city, he told me that he didn't care what they were doing as long as "the leader" decided the cause was worthy. For a second he looked reflective, so I jokingly broke the mood by asking him if he would lay down his life for his precious leader.

"Unquestionably," he replied instantly.

Idiot.

The rain began again in a sudden flurry and we hurried into the house, stamping our feet and shaking our cloaks. Somewhere upstairs I heard footsteps: the party leader? My heart was beating a little faster as we entered the dim hallway, but Mithos just turned to me and said, "Will, we will meet the leader alone first and then invite you in."

I nodded dumbly and they left me standing there, listening to the rain drumming on the roof and wondering what I'd got myself into this time.

One by one they creaked their way up the wooden staircase. I pushed a door open and stepped into a bare room with a couple of chairs and waited, listening to the wordless muttering above me.

They were gone for five minutes. Maybe a little more. It felt like an hour. Then came footsteps on the stairs and Mithos appeared, beckoning to me. Instantly my heart began to patter again and I followed him up, sucking in my stomach (no mean feat) and squaring my shoulders.

At the top of the darkened stairs a door was ajar from which light and gentle conversation trickled out onto the landing. Mithos, now no more than a bulky silhouette above me, pushed the door wide and stepped inside. Before I had even crossed the threshold I heard him speak my name in introduction and, trying to look strong and silent, I glanced around.

The room was small and windowless, lit by an oil lamp that hung from the rafters and glowed yellowish, the shadows russet and amber. Garnet, Renthrette, and Orgos sat at a table looking at me, and a girl in a long dress of blue cotton stood on the other side. I caught her black eyes and, taking her to be the maid, thought vaguely that she was going to offer me a beer. I looked around for the party leader.

I turned swiftly to see if he was behind the door. He wasn't. I looked back and the girl in the blue dress spoke. "Welcome to Stavis, Will, and to our company. I am Lisha, elected leader of the group."

I stared at her aghast, and I think my mouth fell open. She

looked about fifteen. She was tiny. Smaller than me! Her hair was long, black, and straight and she had the small, elegant features and olive skin of the Far Eastern races.

But that's off the subject. What I was actually thinking as the point was pounded home like a tent peg through my skull was *No chance, mate. You have to be bloody joking. This might be your party leader's daughter or even his bit on the side, but* . . . Then I caught Renthrette's glance of knowing satisfaction and I knew that this was indeed "the leader."

She came towards me and shook my hand in a businesslike manner, ignoring absolutely the look of astonishment that gripped my face.

"Pleased to meet you, Will," she said. Her voice had no accent. I don't mean it was untainted by any special dialect; it had no accent at all. I could listen to her for hours and have no clue where she came from.

"What?" I said.

"Lisha," she prompted with a small smile.

"Right," I muttered woodenly. My eyes were starting to sting after all that staring at her, so I blinked them deliberately.

"And you are interested in joining us?" she said evenly.

For some reason this question brought a panicked chaos of uncertainty as I tried to cram this girl into the picture and then come up with a verdict.

"Well," I hazarded, "I don't know about *join,* but I may like to travel with you. Part of the way. A little distance. For a while, like."

Did I really want to entrust myself to the wishes of this diminutive female? Hardly. I could see myself enjoying a few hours of cross-cultural entertainment with her, if she was up for it, but follow her? Respect her word and put my life on the line at her command? Fat chance. Still, I couldn't have hoped for a less menacing-looking leader, and it did seem that one of my theories about Renthrette was well out of play. I cheered up.

"Well," I went on over the silence, "Mithos here said I might be able to tag along, and I reckon I could be useful. And, er, I could really do to get out of the Empire for a while, if you follow my meaning. I'm not sure I'm all that desperate to return to Cresdon. Also, Stavis. I mean it looks real nice—seafood, diverse architecture, and stuff—but it's not really my kind of town. You know what I mean, love? I'm sure you all have a ball here, but me? Too much water for a start, and . . ."

I caught Garnet's glance of shocked anger and realized that I had put my arm around Lisha's shoulders in a matey kind of way and was being, at best, casual in the way I told her my feelings on the matter. I froze and drew myself back to attention, murmuring, "But . . . er, if you don't mind me sitting in on your discussion, I would be grateful. My concern is that at present I would be more of a hindrance to you than a help. I am already in your debt for getting me this far."

That ought to do it. She smiled again—disarmingly—and asked me to sit down. I did so. Whatever she looked like, you did what she said, if only because Garnet looked ready to remove vital organs from anyone who didn't hang on her every word. At the table the lamp's ochre glow was stronger, and shooting Lisha a sidelong glance I saw, with a start, not a girl but a woman. A very young-looking woman, admittedly, but that was a feature of those Eastern females; any girl between fourteen and forty-five looked about the same age. I put her around thirty, but I had no real clue. In a short skirt and ribbons she might have passed for twelve. Except maybe for her eyes.

She did all the talking and the others sat there as if enchanted, saving their few questions till she had finished.

"The situation is a simple one, though I fancy the solution will not be," she began, unrolling a piece of mapped vellum. "Stavis is here," she said. "To its immediate east is a ninety-mile stretch of grassland and scattered hamlets. East of that the land is more fertile, but almost as sparsely populated and with few decent roads. Even traveling as the crow flies we would have to get across two hundred and forty miles of precious little. It's not hard country, but it would be very slow. I think our best bet is to sail along the coast and dock in the south of Shale. It is the count of Shale who requires our presence. He is operating on behalf of his own lands and those of Greycoast to the east and Verneytha to the north."

I shifted in my chair, and I think I made some kind of noise. Not words exactly, just a sort of grumbling sound, like the sound your stomach makes after one of Mrs. Pugh's breakfasts.

"What?" she asked. "Will, do you have something on your mind?"

"Nothing," I said. "Just . . . Those places. Shale, Greycoast, and Verneytha. I used to hear stories about them when I was a kid.

Sometimes they come up in old plays. I kind of forgot they were real."

"What kind of stories?" said Lisha seriously.

"Oh, you know," I said. "Old tales of witches and sorcerers. Kids' stuff."

"Yes," she said, as if I'd raised some important point. "The legends go some way back."

She paused for a second and looked around the table at our expectant faces. I kind of wanted to laugh at the situation, these seasoned fighters taking their orders from this little bit of skirt, talking about musty old stories of witchcraft and God knew what else. It was obviously ludicrous; so why was no one laughing?

I remembered a flash of amber light which knocked down enemy troops, a light the same color as the stone in Orgos's sword. . . .

But that made no sense. If being around these idiots was making me believe in magic, then I really should get away before I lost my mind altogether.

"The problem is simply this," she went on in the same measured, unaccented tones. "The three lands are connected by a series of vital trade routes upon which they depend for their economic survival. Recently these roads have been plagued by raiders. Not random groups of bandits such as you encountered on your way, but an organized force of trained soldiers, perhaps numbering a hundred or more. The three countries have soldiers of their own, but have been unable to track down the raiders who are slowly but surely bringing ruin to the region. Our task therefore is one of detection rather than of combat; we must determine who is responsible for these assaults and supply the baronies with the information necessary to engage and defeat the raiders.

"There is one more thing of which I think our employers are unaware. Over the last two months the Empire garrison in Stavis has almost doubled in size. Since there has not been any sign of revolt here, I fear that the Diamond Empire intends to push further east still. Shale, Greycoast, and Verneytha may prevent the Empire's advance, but only if their current situation is reversed promptly. Are you willing to take on the task?"

If that was a genuine question, no one treated it as such. They nodded with hasty nobility and only I found myself looking doubtful and chewing over details of what she had said. Details such as

240 miles by sea and an enemy of over a hundred trained soldiers. She continued deliberately, "Good. You have come a week ahead of time, which gives us longer to prepare. Will, you should speak with Orgos as to how you can best use that time. And now it is late and we must begin our preparations early tomorrow. Sleep well. It is good to be with you all again."

She smiled around at them with what seemed to be genuine affection and for a moment looked more like a mother than a daughter.

"Mithos," said Lisha, "show Will to his room, please."

I watched them grinning at each other like they were at some kind of family reunion and wondered, not for the first time, how long I could hope to last in their company.

The Hide

They were up at cockcrow. I lay in bed, a single sheet pulled up to my neck, and watched resentfully as Orgos shaved himself with the straight-bladed dagger he wore inside his tunic.

"Come on, Will," he breezed. "There's a lot to do and we are counting on you to prove yourself to Lisha."

"Why didn't you bloody tell me she was a woman?" I snarled at him.

"It's a point of security," Orgos said to the window as he parted the curtains and let the hazy morning sun fall on his face. His black skin was wet and he looked alert and energetic, curse him.

"So long as people presume the party leader is a man, she's harder to trace. I didn't want to deceive you unnecessarily, Will," he said, turning back to me and smiling, "but Lisha is invaluable to our operations."

"Why? What is so bloody special about her? She looks half my age and has a tenth of your strength. What use is she to you lot? I don't see why you even have her on board, let alone take orders from her and—"

"Easy, Will," he replied, sitting himself down on my bed so that I had to squirm to avoid getting my legs broken. "Just take it from me. She is the equal of Garnet or Renthrette in combat and can beat all of us with a spear or a rapier. Yes, even me. Her other gifts you'll see if you are around long enough."

I shrugged, something which is not easy to do horizontally with a heavy sword master sitting on you.

"She just wasn't what I expected," I muttered.

"What did you expect, Will? Some barbarian chief with a poleax and war paint?"

"No! Yes. I don't know what I expected," I protested, "just not . . ."

"A woman?"

"Yes, but that's not the point."

"You sure?"

"Of course." I rolled over and buried my face in the pillow. "I like women."

"Then there'll be no problem," he said, giving me a significant look.

⁂

I breakfasted alone on eight rashers of bacon and fried bread. I couldn't help thinking that this "operations base" wasn't really much of a place. Sure, it was in a nice area, but it was just a house, and a largely empty one at that. So why the big deal? Why keep the place at all when it was surely safer for a group of outlaws like them to stay on the move?

Garnet and Renthrette were out, probably eyeing the markets for bargains, methodically moving from stall to stall in search of a better deal, tabulating every mind-numbing detail.

"Something to show you," said Orgos, emerging from the kitchen.

He led me into a large room with a fireplace at one end, reached up, and snapped back a lamp bracket fitted to the side of the chimney breast. The entire chimney, including the dusty hearth, swung easily aside, revealing a heavy-looking door of dark wood on huge brass hinges.

"Operations base," he said simply. "We call it the Hide. Don't touch anything down here until I say you can. There are half a dozen trap devices designed by Arthen of Snowcrag. You've probably heard of him. He kept the Empire out of the mountain halls for six months virtually single-handedly. Anyway, Lisha had him defend this place for us when we brought him east."

"You got Arthen out of Snowcrag before it fell?" I asked, staring. Arthen was the stuff of legend.

"Yes, though only Mithos and I were with Lisha then. There were others, of course, but they are no longer with us."

He continued, barely missing a beat.

"In any case, there are ballistae down here that could skewer three armored men together so, like I said, touch nothing."

"Sounds good to me."

With a large steel key he opened the door, which, like the fireplace, slid easily aside despite its obvious weight. Inside I caught the acrid smell of oil lamps and found myself on a wooden landing atop a flight of stone steps spiraling into the earth. There was a lever by the doorframe. Orgos pulled it and, with a clanking of gears, the fireplace closed us in.

I moved to descend the stairs but Orgos caught my arm and held me back. Before he took another step he unhooked a lantern from the wall, turned up its flame, and groped under the wooden banister rail with his left hand. Again something clicked, and he smiled at me in the lamplight.

"Some of the stairs have special features," he said cheerfully. I gave him a nervous smile and didn't ask for details.

At the foot of the stairs was another armored door that was already open. Orgos showed me in.

"Welcome to the Hide," said Lisha, who was sitting at a table in what appeared to be a library. Mithos was with her, consulting a stack of charts. He looked up and watched me as Lisha continued, "Orgos puts a good deal of trust in you, Will, considering how long he's known you. I hope his faith is justified. You can never speak of this place to anyone. Many lives depend on us, and we cannot afford to be merciful to those who would expose us. Do I make myself clear?"

I nodded, and tried to count the number of death threats I had had since Rufus turned me in. Still, there was something slightly comic about all these grave and menacing words coming from the party's girlish "leader."

"I understand perfectly," I said, playing along, trying to match the gravity and seriousness of her tone. Orgos and Mithos looked at me with small smiles of satisfaction. The impulse to pat me on the head or feed me an apple must have been almost overwhelming.

Lisha's eyes met mine and I had the odd sensation of being somehow transparent, as if she could read my thoughts and my petty deceptions. I didn't like the feeling.

"We will leave here next Tuesday or Wednesday, depending on when we can get a ship," she said, rising to her feet and stepping lightly towards me, "so you have six days which you may use as you think best. If you need money for arms or other equipment, speak to Mithos. I suggest you do some riding, but don't bother buying yourself a horse. We'll have to get mounts in Shale. I've taken horses by ship before and it can take days for them to recover from the voyage."

Whatever you say, doll. I glanced around the racks of books. There were texts from all over the world, written in a dozen different languages, though most were in my native Thrusian and its ancient forebear, Threshalt. The collection was not so much varied as wildly diverse. Cookbooks sat next to manuals on siege techniques and indexes of poisons. I lifted down something on "dialectal oddities" and gazed at it with mild revulsion.

"What would possess anyone to write anything this tedious?" I mused.

Orgos materialized at my elbow and looked at the book.

"Can Will borrow this?" he said.

"Certainly," she said.

Orgos beamed and heaved it into my arms saying, "Something to keep you busy, Will. See what it has to say about Shale."

"Thanks a lot, Orgos," I muttered.

Mithos turned to Lisha and said, "I forgot to mention that Will has an ear for accents. Since Thrusian is the basic language of the Shale region, that may prove a useful skill."

So I did have a role. A genuine useful function for humble Will Hawthorne? Will the linguist. Bill the talker. Will Hawthorne, leading authority on the world's most boring two-foot-thick book. This was the literary equivalent of metal polishing. Still, it sounded a damned sight safer than swinging swords about, so I figured I'd go with it. I clasped the book to my chest, as if I couldn't wait to curl up with it.

Lisha's black eyes glittered at me and I felt my irritation and resentment shining through like torchlight.

"We'll find something more exciting for you later," she said.

"What?" I murmured, unconvincingly. "No, this is fine. Great. Right up my street, is this. Dialect books. Brilliant."

She just nodded and I felt stupid again.

"Perhaps you can research those old tales of the lands we are visiting," she said.

"All that magic and sorcery bollocks?" I said. "Sure. If you like."

Keep me safe and fed and I'll read whatever rubbish you like, I thought.

The next room was a gym, hewn out of the stone and running

below the foundations of the houses above. As Orgos was to demonstrate over the next hour, you could tone and strengthen every major muscle in the body with the stuff they had in there, a pretty depressing prospect for a man like me, as was the announcement that I was to "eat more healthily" from here on. No more bacon, in other words. Probably leaves, and the odd handful of seeds.

"After lunch," said Orgos, apparently unironically, "we'll see if we can get you up on a horse for a while. Bring your crossbow and you can practice that too. If we have time, we could go for a quick swim in the harbor and then have one more workout before bed."

Great. All my life I had avoided weapons, exercise, a sensible diet, horses, and water. Now they were all I had.

❧

My book on dialects was dry as a Hrof well and turgid as . . . well, something very, very turgid that I can't think of at the moment. One particularly riveting chapter was "Major Inflectional Features and Word Usage Common to Shale and Its Environs." A real corker.

It was tough to believe, but I started to prefer the prospect of perching on the back of a horse to reading. At least up in the saddle I had the challenge of controlling my bowels as the beast started to move, and as the days went by and I continued to avoid some horrible, limb-mangling accident, it became, if not actually enjoyable, then at least less nauseating. A week wasn't going to turn me into a rider (nor would it make me a weapon master) but I began to feel fractionally less terrified up there and that, Orgos assured me, was half the battle.

The swimming was a very different story. Only once in the whole week did I get out of my depth, and then I was so convinced that I was going to drown that I almost did. By the fourth day I had made no progress whatsoever and it seemed that my fear of water was actually increasing. I told Orgos that my body didn't float. I wasn't sure what the problem was but I just wasn't a buoyant kind of person.

"Right," he said unhelpfully, and pushed me off the dock. I yelled and gargled quite a bit, but when he showed no sign of coming in after me, I floated. Sort of. By the end of the week I still couldn't swim a stroke but I didn't *automatically* equate any body of water larger than a bath with certain death.

As for the Empire, things had been quiet. I was even getting used

to seeing their casual patrols, which frequented the markets and
dockyards. Down by the water there were always crowds of people
hawking and trading their wares or their favors, and you could easily
lose yourself in the crowds if panic set in. A pair of soldiers leaned
on a fishing boat one day and laughed as I flailed about in the water.
In Cresdon I might be a notorious rebel; in Stavis I was just some kid
who couldn't swim.

❧

On Monday evening we had a meeting which began with Lisha
checking off a list to see if they had missed anything. They hadn't.
Naturally. The boxes and crates and bags had been packed, trans-
ported to the harbor, and loaded aboard a light trading vessel with a
cargo of mahogany. It was bound for shores east of Greycoast but
would, for a fee already settled, deposit us in a serviceable port in
southern Shale. We were to leave at seven the next morning, and
should arrive by the end of the week, weather permitting.

They smiled and clinked their rare celebratory beer mugs with
anticipation. They were excited. I was hungry and aching and dreading the journey, but when they grinned and drank, I joined them, as
if I was one of them.

The Cormorant

The ship in which we were about to sail round 240 miles of coastline was called the *Cormorant* and was, as I should have guessed, a leaky old crate that didn't look like it would make it out of the harbor. I told Garnet that there was no way I was getting on that beat-up piece of driftwood, but he just gave a knowing smile and lugged his bag up the gangplank.

I watched him get on board and was suddenly struck by the sense of being on the threshold of a life-changing decision. I had stuck with them this long because I needed them to get me out of Cresdon and because they were useful allies in an unfamiliar and hostile world in which I knew nobody. But get on that boat, and everything would change, even if it didn't sink as soon as we hit open sea. This was the point of no return.

I turned and looked across the dockyard into the gaze of an Empire trooper, one whom I had seen in a local tavern three nights before. He was with another soldier and they were both looking at me and muttering to each other.

They couldn't have recognized me. Surely. Not now. I dropped my eyes to my bag and tried to look busy, fumbling with panic.

The boat was ready to go, but a glance told me that the guards were still watching. By the time I picked up my bag and turned to the ship, they were coming over, slowly, uncertainly, each seeming to follow the other.

"Garnet!" I called, trying to sound unconcerned. He paused in the midst of passing a crate up onto the ship and peered from me to the two soldiers, who had picked up their pace significantly. He called to Renthrette and then stooped to pick something up: a bow. I turned to the soldiers quickly.

"Everything all right, Officer?" I said, smiling blandly.

"I saw you the other night," said one of them. "I thought you looked familiar."

"Really?" I said, my heart fluttering. "Just one of those faces, I suppose."

"No," said the other, taking a step towards me. "I know you. I recognized you when I saw you the other night, but I couldn't place you."

I smiled and shrugged. "Oh?"

"Yeah," he said. "Till two months ago, I was stationed in Cresdon."

Oh, hell.

For a moment I could think of nothing to say.

"You're Rufus Ramsbottom, aren't you," he said, thrusting his hand into mine. "The actor."

He was smiling, his eyes bright, his cheeks flushed.

I blinked.

"Yes," I said, taking his hand and shaking it. "Yes, I am."

I scribbled my name—or, rather, Rufus's—on whatever they put in front of me and then sort of glided over to the *Cormorant* to find Renthrette and Garnet warily unstringing their bows, their eyes fixed on me. I wasn't sure whom they would have shot first, the soldiers or me.

I watched the soldiers from the rail, my heart still thumping. Any minute I expected them to realize that I was not the actor—and I use that term in its loosest and most degraded sense—Rufus Ramsbottom, but the actor, rebel, and fugitive for whom new torturous means of execution were being devised, Will Hawthorne. We were out of port before I relaxed enough to realize that if this had indeed been the point of no return, I had just made a career choice.

                           ❧

The captain had his eye on Renthrette from the outset. I saw the drunken half-wit leering at her as she watched Stavis fall behind us, and knew then that there would be trouble.

I passed my time fencing with Orgos on what little area of free deck there was. It wasn't easy, and I spent as much time dodging spars and deck fittings as I did his sword. Still, it kept my body moving and my mind off the amount of water under our ancient keel.

The gulls swooped infuriatingly at us for miles, convinced we were trawling. At first I felt ill, but it was more trepidation than actual seasickness, and it passed, mercifully, within a couple of hours. Oddly enough, it was Garnet who suffered most. He was greenish before the dock was out of sight and, as we cleared the sandbars that flanked the port, he began hanging over the rail with a desolate look on his face. I couldn't help feeling sorry for the poor swine.

We slept in hammocks, two to a berth, and it wasn't exactly idyllic, but the rocking of the ship actually helped me doze off. Orgos lay large and completely silent beside me. I don't think Mithos closed his eyes much, since Garnet, his berthmate, spent half the night running up to the deck to throw up. Mithos's sleeplessness turned out to be for the best when he caught one of the ratty, toothless crew pawing through our belongings. From then on, one of us kept watch.

On the morning of the second day we saw dolphins leaping off the starboard bow, apparently racing us. They flashed silver-grey into the foam of our wake like curving arrows. The sky was cloudless and we were making good time, but if there had been more to occupy the captain, things would probably have worked out better.

He was a big clumsy man with a black beard, a mouthful of gold teeth, a natty little scarlet jacket, and a penchant for heavy earrings. His voice was permanently slurred, even when he wasn't on the rum, and his tongue clicked and gurgled when he spoke. He didn't have an accent as such; you just couldn't tell what he was saying. I would just nod, laugh loudly, and say "Yes mate, exactly" a few times, until he left me alone. He spat through his beard as he talked and his eyes wandered around sparkling mischievously, so that more than once I wondered with a start of panic what it was I was agreeing to. Garnet said he looked like he had been a pirate once, and I could see his point. His face was red and leathery from the sun and salt wind, and his arms were tattooed with voluptuous women coiled around snakes and daggers. He would sidle up to you and make crude, unintelligible jokes and then slap you on the back and laugh to himself while you wondered what the hell he was going on about. He wore a short, heavy-looking cutlass with a bowl-shaped hand guard. Maybe he still was a pirate.

Renthrette was on deck waiting for the sun to go down when he made his move. I don't suppose she understood most of what he suggested, but she got enough idea to detach herself from him and head for the cabins. He'd had a skinful, however, and wasn't to be dealt with so easily. He caught her from behind, but she shrugged him off and slapped his hands away. Since Renthrette was angry but controlled, things might have been left at that had I not decided to "rescue" her.

For a moment there, it was close to perfect. I took two quick steps and caught him off balance with a punch to the jaw. He never saw it coming, and though it wasn't really much more than a slap, he slumped to the ground. Feeling pleased with myself, I turned to minister to Renthrette, who was staring at me in disbelief. I was just realizing that what I had assumed was admiration was actually outrage when I heard the captain stagger to his feet behind me, scraping his cutlass out of its rusty scabbard.

His eyes were small and full of malice, and he started to advance on me, spitting meaningless curses. I had no weapon to hand, but he was in no mood to be sporting. Renthrette closed as if to part us, making conciliatory noises, but he swung the sword at her like a club and she stepped back, giving a single unhurried shout for Orgos. The first mate appeared, ushering her out of the way, then stood there laughing. I was beginning to regret a lot of things.

On the deck, discarded from our last training session, was a blunted épée. I seized it and turned back to face the captain, who was drooling and laying about himself pointlessly with the squat and murderous-looking cutlass, his eyes locked on me.

"Perhaps we could discuss this. . . . " I ventured. He swashed wildly at me with his sword.

I instinctively raised my blunted "blade," and it almost kicked out of my hand as he made contact. He came at me again and I parried wildly, following up with a crazed lunge that didn't come close. I knew that I just had to keep him at bay until help arrived, but I couldn't manage that kind of composure. I swung like a berserker and fled from his hacking attacks, leaping rope coils and clambering over the huge racks of bound timber. He came lumbering after me, barking wordless insults and bellowing like a rabid bear. I poked at him with my (now bent) épée and hopped away again.

Orgos took him from behind, catching his sword arm and raising a dagger to his throat until he became still. As the crew roared with laughter, I scrambled to my feet and looked for somewhere to hide my embarrassment.

"My hero," said Renthrette dryly.

I tried to think of a crushing riposte that would salvage some dignity from the moment. But nothing came to mind, so I just started shouting, as one is wont to do in such situations. "Look, I was trying to help you out, right? You might show a little gratitude, for God's sake!"

"Gratitude?" she sneered. "For what? For starting, and almost losing, an unnecessary fight? Let me fight my own battles, Will."

"Right, I will," I spluttered, "And next time—"

I was interrupted by Orgos calling me from the foot of the main-mast. Lisha was with him and they looked thoroughly disenchanted.

"Oh bugger," I muttered, and went over to them, staring at the decking all the way. When I stood before them I could barely look them in the face.

"Sorry," I said in a small voice. "I just . . ."

"I know," said Orgos. His tone was soft but not without repri-mand. "Renthrette can look after herself, Will. And did you forget everything we have learned together? You looked drunker than him."

"It's different when you're fighting someone with a real sword who wants to hurt you," I replied bitterly.

"In a real fight you have to be even more composed than when you fence, because the hits are more crucial."

"Don't lecture me, all right?" I said. "I'm not a child."

"Will," said Lisha quietly.

"What?"

"There won't always be someone on hand to pull you out of trouble when you get in over your head. If only for that reason, be more cautious."

They left me to myself, and I stared over the side at the water for a while, feeling the slight sting of the salt spray on my arms and face.

SCENE XVI

Consequences

Y ou've got guts, Will, I'll give you that," said Garnet obliquely as we sat down to a supper of dry biscuits and steamed mussels. He gave me a half-smile of encouragement, and then moved to where the smell of the food didn't remind him of how awful he felt. Renthrette behaved as if the matter simply hadn't happened, which was actually a pleasant surprise. She even passed me the salt as we ate. As if we didn't have enough salt.

I saw the captain lurching around the galley in the evening and sort of smiled at him. He muttered something spiteful and gestured with his fist. I was not the *Cormorant's* most popular person.

That night it transpired that there were two meetings. The party meeting consisted of Lisha reminding us that we should "keep our heads" (directed at me) and that when we docked tomorrow we should conduct ourselves with caution and dignity (also directed at me). Mithos sat out of the lamplight, almost lost in shadow. Once he nodded solemnly, but he said nothing. Garnet ground the bit of his ax, tracing small perfect circles with a flat stone. Renthrette was rebinding her sword hilt in the same tortuous manner. Her eyes would flash from Lisha back to the weapon in her hand as she wound the thin leather thong round and round the handle, spiraling slowly and immaculately up to the pommel.

The second meeting was held in the captain's quarters, but we didn't learn of that one until the morning.

Southern Shale was in sight shortly after dawn. Though it was a lengthy stretch of coastline, there was only one convenient harbor close by, and we steered towards it under the same prevailing wind that had made our trip so swift and easy. Trouble, however, has many guises. In this case, it had a scarlet jacket and a black beard full of muffled curses.

"The captain is up to something," said Lisha as we finished breakfast. "He looks furtive."

"He always looks furtive," I said.

"But he also looks pleased with himself, and I fear he is planning to revenge himself on us for yesterday's incident."

I tried not to look guilty, but Renthrette met my eyes mercilessly. Then Garnet looked up and whispered, "Did you feel that? We're changing course. He's steering us out to sea."

He was right. A long, anxious pause followed.

"I wouldn't put it past the captain to just take us where the sharks can get us," said Mithos darkly, "and toss us overboard. Or find somewhere he could sell us."

"We'll give him a fight," added Orgos, feeling the edge of his shaving dagger.

"Could we not just grab the lifeboat and go?" Garnet suggested.

"We're too far from shore," Mithos sighed. "He could bring the ship about and plow us under."

"Then we must take the wheel," said Orgos, "and steer it in ourselves."

"There are twenty-five crewmen," said Garnet, "we couldn't hold them all off."

"Not if they were organized, we couldn't," agreed Lisha, "but we might be able to if we could somehow keep them in pockets of five or six."

She fell silently thoughtful for a moment, and then carefully, pausing between sentences, laid out a course of action.

⁂

I had crawled my way to the lifeboat unseen. The crew were still wandering around, but while they had been listless before, they were now cautious and alert. On the deck where I had "fought" the captain, two burly men, bronzed by the sun, stood with shouldered pikes, looking about them. In the stern of the ship, rising like a pulpit above the racks of bound cargo, was the castle, and in it, the helmsman. Two floors below the castle were the captain's quarters. He now shared them with five armed men, two covering the steps down to the door from the deck. I loaded my crossbow and kept as still as I could, the heat prickling on my salt-dried arms and sunburnt neck.

Lisha emerged from our cabins and fell heavily on the wet stairs. The crew watched, unimpressed. Garnet helped her to her feet, and then she ducked back inside the cabin and emerged with her spear. With this she supported herself conspicuously and hobbled out onto deck, Garnet at her side. He was wearing a dark green cloak over his tunic, and I knew what it concealed. Slowly they edged around the ship until they neared the castle.

The crew were armed with clubs, boathooks, and whatever else they could lay their hands on, but their demeanor suggested that they thought we hadn't spotted the change in course.

So much the better.

I caught a glimpse of Orgos shinning up the castle ladder only because I was watching for him. He emerged, black against the sky, his swords spinning in his hands. He dodged an advancing guard, who fell heavily onto the massive bundles of timber below, and parried the cutlass of another, turning him promptly out of the wooden turret and down onto the deck.

A cry went up immediately and the crewmen started to move at random, shielding their eyes from the sun as they looked up to where Orgos was bringing the vessel groaning back towards the coast. Lisha twirled the spear in her hands and threw off the false injury like a cloak. In a second, she stood at the foot of the castle ladder with Garnet at her side, his ax drawn and ready. As they braced themselves for the inevitable assault, Orgos started down the ladder towards them.

Through the portholes of his cabin I could see the captain shouting as he felt the *Cormorant* speeding towards mainland Shale.

Orgos took a position between Lisha and Garnet, his swords whirling about his wrists. The crew hesitated and then began to close in on them. I thought I noticed the deep green of Garnet's eyes as he flashed a look of concern from Lisha to the growing semicircle of armed men that edged closer to them, but Lisha, spreading her feet apart a little, just raised her dark spear purposefully and nodded to Orgos. As Lisha and Garnet lowered their eyes, he raised his sword, the one in his right hand, the one with the amber stone in the pommel, and there was a flash of light.

Actually, it was more than a flash. It was as if something had been dropped into a still pool, the ripples coursing out from the pommel of Orgos's sword, yellow-orange, like tongues of flame. They radiated out in a single pulse that lasted less than a second and traveled no more than a few yards from where they stood, but the crew touched by the light faltered, lowered their weapons as if stunned or unsure what they were doing. And in that second, Garnet and Lisha struck.

What the hell? . . .

Three of the enemy fell bleeding to the deck before they knew what was happening. Then Orgos was among them, his swords spinning, and two more collapsed screaming.

While I was trying to get my brain around what had just happened, Renthrette appeared from our cabin, armed with her broadsword and shield. She stalked unnoticed by the men who continued to close around the castle until she reached the captain's quarters. Mithos followed and took up a position behind the cabin door as Renthrette opened it. I sat up, crossbow at the ready, and my heart pounding fast.

Three guards exploded out of the cabin. She stepped back quickly and I had a clear shot. I followed the first one unsteadily with the bow for a split second before pulling the trigger. The weapon bucked slightly in my hands as the bolt left it. It wasn't a good shot, but it would do. My target crashed to the decking, clutching his hip. Renthrette raised sword and shield to meet the next, and Mithos engaged the third.

Renthrette's assailant crashed into her, hewing madly at her raised shield. She stood her ground, then lunged with her broadsword under the rim of her shield. The steel tip of her sword pierced his chest and, with a short-lived scream that turned every head on the ship, he crumpled at her feet. She looked absolutely controlled, even calm.

Then Mithos's man went down and he was in, flinging the captain back against the wall.

I scrambled to my feet. There was a sudden churning sensation in the pit of my stomach, and my hands were shaking like poplars in a high wind. In a few strides I was almost with Renthrette, drawing my rapier as Mithos hissed, "Call them off or you're a dead man!"

He bundled the wild-eyed captain onto the deck. I grabbed his cutlass and held on to it as the crew moved to see what was going on. Mithos showed them.

The captain had sagged against him, too frightened to hold

himself vertically. He was babbling to himself and growling. Mithos let him slip to the deck and placed the tip of his sword against the back of his neck.

"Tell them to steer us into the harbor," he hissed to the scarlet-jacketed bundle at his ankles.

The captain hesitated only a moment before following Mithos's command.

"Men like him value nothing more than their own necks," Orgos remarked. In his mouth and in that situation, the words sounded pretty scathing, but it raised an awkward question in my mind. Was I any different?

An hour and a half later, as we eased between the shipyard buildings of Shale, which rose up on each side of us, I still had no answer to that. I did have another question, though, and the moment I could get Orgos alone, I asked it.

"You going to tell me what happened there?" I demanded, nodding to where Orgos had held off the sailors. "That light. And don't bother telling me that little gem in your sword hilt is just for decoration."

Orgos frowned, hitching his equipment duffel over his shoulder. "What do you want me to say?"

"The truth," I said.

"Before he died," said Orgos, "my father used to say 'Never ask a question unless you know you can handle the answer.'"

"Very touching and profound," I said. "So. About that sword?"

"It's magic," said Orgos. "Enchanted."

"Bollocks," I said.

"All right." He shrugged.

"What am I? Five years old?" I said. "Magic? There's no such thing."

"I told you, Will. You should have listened to my father."

And that was that. He walked away and I stared after him, finally shouting, "Fine! Don't tell me."

He kept walking.

It was late afternoon by the time we got everything unloaded, and we were too tired to think or move. Finding a tavern, we settled there for the rest of the day and left the procurement of a pair of wagons to the innkeeper. I drank several pints of watery beer in big wooden mugs and followed them with a glass of what was supposed to be whiskey but tasted like paint thinner. By the time I stumbled off to my bed, the ground felt like it was undulating beneath me, coursing in great alcoholic ripples. It was, I had already decided, the closest I would ever get to being at sea again.

A Kind of Welcome

At eight o'clock that evening Orgos woke me.

"Come on, Will," he said wearily, "we're moving."

"Of course," I muttered. "After all, I've slept several hours already this week."

Downstairs, Lisha and Mithos were waiting for us, and with them was a wiry man with a thin neck and grey stubble on his chin. His hair was short, straight, and silver. His eyes were small, which, in conjunction with his thin-lipped, unsmiling mouth, made it hard to tell if he was pleased to see us.

I had half guessed who he was from the black silk robe with its tiny filigree dragon embroidery, but Mithos introduced him anyway. "This is Dathel, chancellor to the county of Shale. He and his men will escort us to the town of Adsine, in the north, where the count awaits us."

I couldn't help noticing that as Mithos made this pronouncement, Lisha became one of us, and not even a conspicuous one at that. I wasn't sure why, but I could see that this Chancellor Dathel was supposed to take Mithos to be the leader. Not that I cared one way or the other. Exhaustion and the beginnings of a slight hangover combined to make me thoroughly apathetic.

"Good evening," said our death-suited host. "My lord the count, and, indeed, all the people of Shale have awaited your coming. Your wagons are packed and I have a twenty-man cavalry escort outside. If we leave now, we should reach Adsine by dawn. Hopefully, you will be able to sleep in the wagons."

He spoke Thrusian like the rest of us but there was a lilt to it that squared with what I had gleaned from my dusty studies.

Once more I swung my pack onto my shoulders and followed them, mule-like, outside where the light was fading fast, the sky striped pink and amber.

There were two large wagons with four horses each, almost exactly like the ones we had driven across the Hrof. I clambered in, leaving whatever I was carrying where it fell. I glanced out of the back as the mounted troopers with their black dragon-pennanted lances and plumed helms drew up their formation around us. Two thoughts crossed my already-dozing mind.

First, why did anyone who could field soldiers like these need the likes of us?

Second, and more important: With such an escort, I could sleep soundly. For the first time since I left Cresdon I wouldn't have to spend an hour or more on guard, and my sleep wouldn't be scarred by fears of snakes, Empire patrols, or the murderous crew of the *Cormorant*.

I rolled myself up in two blankets, wrapped another into a kind of pillow, and, within seconds of feeling the wagon roll off, fell asleep.

❧

I woke once in the night and lay still for a while until the sense of motion and the rhythmic clop of the horses lulled me back into slumber. When I woke next, light was pouring in through the half-open tailgate, where Mithos and Orgos sat, chatting quietly, absorbing something of this new land.

I caught the familiar sounds of an early-morning market and realized we were in Adsine.

"How is it?" I asked.

"The town?" said Orgos. "Poor," he answered simply.

A few minutes later I could hear running water below us, and Mithos, consulting a map, said, "That must be the Wardsfall River. We are nearly there."

❧

A couple of minutes after that we stopped and climbed out, stretching and yawning, in the courtyard of Adsine Castle. By Empire standards it was small but solid. A perimeter wall with a single gatehouse dotted with regularly spaced turrets formed a hexagon around the courtyard, in the center of which was a single, three-storied keep. It faced south, its upper stories looking out over the perimeter wall and across the river to the town. Its foundation was cross-shaped so that its front stuck out and loomed over us, its barred windows hard and cold.

It wasn't exactly welcoming. For some time we just looked at it and said nothing while the horses were led to stables along the insides of the perimeter wall. The keep was built of a light grey stone, but it was so purposeful, so utterly lacking in whimsy or creative imagination, that it seemed dark and sinister. Even with the guards and the chancellor busying themselves around us it seemed like it might be deserted, like the ghost castles you hear tales of in pubs on winter nights.

The chancellor ordered a brace of servants to unload our wagons and carry our belongings to our rooms. He led the way and we filed dutifully after him in silence. I had slept well in the wagon, but I couldn't wait to get into a bed that didn't move on wheels, waves, or insect legs.

The doors of the keep were of oak, a good four inches thick and reinforced with huge square-headed nails. On our way upstairs we got a glimpse of the ground floor: soldiers' and domestics' quarters, kitchens and storerooms, all plain and purposeful.

Upstairs was a different tale, of carpets and tapestries and, most strikingly of all after the bustle of breakfast downstairs, silence. But if the castle had once been opulent, those days were long gone, and the place was in need of serious redecorating.

A pair of guards stood at each corner, staircase, and doorway, dressed in the black-and-silver capes worn by the cavalry who had escorted us, but armed with pikes and shortswords. They clicked their heels together and stood to attention as Chancellor Dathel passed imperiously with the smallest nod of his head.

Everything felt square and the corridors were laid out like grids. We walked fifty yards down one and came to a perpendicular gallery running from east to west, where heavy teak doors stood under guard.

"Those chambers belong to the count and his lady wife," murmured the chancellor. He indicated a line of doors in the north-facing wall.

"Your rooms," he said softly. "I expect you would like to rest, wash, and change before you do anything else, as I would."

So, whether we did or not, he intended to.

"The butler has left food and drink in the sitting room for you. I will have hot water for bathing sent along presently. Will you eat first?"

Mithos said we would, which was fortunate, because I could have eaten the inhabitants of a good-sized stable. The chancellor made a bow small enough to be a nod and glided off down the corridor like a ghost looking for somewhere to haunt. One glance at this dour old ruin said he'd already found it.

The guest rooms were diplomatically identical: clean, private, and basic. They looked out of the rear wall of the building to the scraggy hills of northern Shale.

The bar was as functional as the bedrooms. There were various old and cracked leather armchairs and some tables, scratched and discolored with age. A few sorry embroideries hung on the exposed stone of the walls, and the paint was peeling as if the ceiling had some rampant skin complaint.

"The whole place is like this," said Garnet to no one in particular. "Old money now gone. I mean, it must have cost a fortune to build, but nothing has been replaced for years."

"Cheese and ham," I announced through a mouthful of sandwich. "Not bad, but not great. Could use some pickle."

Garnet's green eyes rested on mine and narrowed. I gave him a friendly smile and went on chewing. Orgos opened his mouth to speak but changed his mind.

"Why is Mithos the leader now?" I asked as soon as I had swallowed.

Renthrette looked over her shoulder hastily as if to ensure that no one had heard my indiscretion. I laughed, and she stared at me, but Lisha spoke in her placid, even tone. "We are unsure of the social climate here. A man tends to buy more respect. That's all."

I had intended to get some satirical mileage out of this, but her frankness disarmed, as usual, and I said nothing.

Ten minutes later I was in a hot tin bath shaped like an overgrown coal scuttle, its water foaming with carbolic soap. So, here I was: a specialist, brought in at considerable expense (I hoped) to save the nation or county or whatever the hell it was. I grinned to myself and wondered whether I could get free beer at the bar. Maybe if I was really good, they'd give me a magic sword.

❦

Harsh Realities

I dozed for a couple of hours and then ate lunch with the rest of the party: cold pork salad and two slabs of brown, grainy bread. You could tell it was cheap stuff because it had that powdery taste that you get when the flour has been cut with ground chalk as a baker friend had once explained, the sacks weigh in heavier and you get a better price for inferior goods. It was pretty shoddy stuff. There didn't seem much point in being a count if you couldn't get decent bread. On top of that, dessert was a wizened apple and my first gulp of the ale told me it had been significantly watered down. I was beginning to get a sinking feeling about this place.

Then came a tour of the castle, the near-mute Chancellor Dathel steering us round the ground floor's central block of guards and infantry quarters, then into the western and eastern wings, which housed the cavalry. In each of these large white-plastered rooms of bedsteads with regulation blankets and footlockers, the reclining soldiers thundered to their feet and stood erect and silent.

One time, just to break the monotony, I started to wander around the soldiers, looking over their armor as if I was inspecting them. I picked up a burnished helmet, plumed with black horsehair, from on top of a footlocker and rapped on it with my knuckles as the soldiers stood rigid around me, eyes fixed on nothing.

"What's this made of, soldier?" I demanded of one of them.

"Iron plates riveted to leather, sir!" barked the soldier after a second's hesitation.

"And what would be harder than that?" I asked.

"Sir?" stammered the soldier.

"What's tougher than iron and leather?"

"Steel, sir."

"What else?"

"I don't know, sir."

"What are you made of, Private?"

There was a flicker of confusion in the soldier's face, and after a painful pause he said, in the same military shout, "I don't think I understand the question, sir."

"Are not the muscles and bones of a Shale trooper harder than steel, soldier?" I asked with patient dignity.

"No, sir," said the soldier.

"Oh. I mean, isn't your heart hardened with courage?"

"Er, well, sir—"

"Figuratively," I added hastily, "Private, figuratively. It's kind of a trope, a sort of poetic allusion, you see. . . ."

"Yes, sir. I see, sir."

The chancellor coughed politely, like a small beetle anxious not to offend but with the unmistakable hint that we didn't have time for this. I gave one last penetrating gaze to the assembled troops and said "At ease" to the nearest officer.

As they relaxed with a shifting of feet and a sudden rush of mutterings, Dathel caught my eye and held it. I turned to leave with as much dignity as I could salvage, but found myself face-to-face with an amused and bewildered Orgos, who pulled a what-the-hell-was-that-supposed-to-be? look, while Garnet scowled.

I really didn't care to see the bloody kitchens and meeting hall, but we marched through them all the same. Garnet and Renthrette exchanged significant looks and made penciled notes on little squares of parchment. After a while I caught Garnet's arm and asked him what the story was.

"You'd know if you'd shut your mouth and open your eyes once in a while," he muttered. "What were you doing back there?"

"Being an adventurer," I said. "I thought it was obvious. Admittedly I haven't quite got the part down yet. . . ."

"The part?"

"Yes," I explained, "you know, the *adventurer* role. The language, the mannerisms, and all that. But I'm working on it."

"It's not a role," Garnet gasped, offended. "It's a way of life!"

"Well, yes, kind of. But it's still a performance, you know? And you can help me flesh out the role by telling me what you keep writing down. . . ."

"You have no idea, have you?" he said, still aghast. "You will always just be the same lying, deceitful—"

"Oh, thanks. Keep your precious observations to yourself then."

He grabbed me by the shoulder and pushed me back against the wall, his favorite way of getting my attention, and snarled, "Just stay out of my way and don't soil our profession with your playacting."

"I'm only trying to get the adventuring, you know, the *life,* right."

"Well, start taking notice of things for yourself," he spat contemptuously. "We have just seen the living quarters of eleven hundred men," he added. "That's two hundred cavalry and seven hundred infantry for deployment in times of open conflict, without touching the two-hundred-strong guard force that holds the castle itself." He gave me an excited look, apparently forgetting his irritation.

"So?" I said.

"That's a lot of soldiers."

"Yes," I agreed, giving him the bewildered look he had given me, "it is."

Just to score a private point I sidled over to Renthrette as we ascended the stairs to the second floor behind the silent chancellor and said, "Did you happen to figure out how many servants there are here?"

"Upstairs?" she said, consulting her notes. "Twenty-three."

"Thank you." I smiled simply. It was as I had suspected; they were both as mad as each other.

"Not at all, Will." She half smiled, dubious but apparently pleased that I was showing interest. "Chancellor," she said, raising her voice slightly, "what is the male-to-female ratio amongst the kitchen and cleaning staff?"

Hell's teeth, I thought. This adventuring lark was one thrill after another.

The second floor's two northbound corridors were hung with faded tapestries, the silk plucked and moth-eaten. Semiprecious stones that had once been stitched to them had been lost or stolen, leaving only spots of less-faded color and a few hanging threads. I considered grabbing some of the ones that were left but figured that this wasn't the time.

We had returned to the dining room on the second floor and my boredom knew no bounds. The chancellor nodded to a staircase that spiraled up through this floor and beyond. "The third floor is merely ramparts and siege equipment, with a small watchtower in the center, but if you wish me to show you around—"

"No, thanks," I said hurriedly. I knew Renthrette would be looking daggers at me so I added, "You have been so kind already and I'm sure we can look over the third floor by ourselves."

His thin mouth smiled briefly, and with an "As you wish," he saw us back to our rooms. He was making his farewells when we heard a cry of panic. The chancellor wheeled and muttered, "The count's rooms!"

Mithos was the first to run, unsheathing his broadsword as he did so. Orgos drew a dagger and joined him in a couple of long, powerful strides. The others bolted after them and I followed, like a sheep who didn't want to be left alone. Over the sound of their feet I heard the crack of a heavy weapon striking timber.

It had never occurred to me that I would need a weapon, since I was sharing a fortified building with over a thousand trained soldiers. The realization that I was completely unarmed (as the others plucked knives and swords from their clothes) came too late; I had already rounded the corner.

One of the guards at the count's door was dead, his throat and shoulders slashed open. The other was slumped against the wall with a crimson-flighted arrow in his chest and blood running from his mouth. A wild-eyed man in the black cloak and heavy scale of a Shale infantryman was hacking at the count's door with a huge two-handed weapon that looked like an ax, but bigger. Scarier. As we approached, he turned on us.

Mithos advanced on him, his sword held at arm's length to parry the wide arc of that massive blade. I froze as Orgos edged closer, his knife drawn but pitifully inadequate. Mithos made to strike, but the soldier lowered his grip and swung the vast, curved ax bit at arm's length, tracing a deadly semicircle around him. Every time he swung it, you could hear the sound as it cut the air. Mithos drew back, as close to uncertain as I had ever seen him.

The man in the black cloak turned suddenly and slashed that ax at us in a great whistling sweep. I took a step back and felt the air move against my face. The others gave him a little more ground, watching his eyes for a sign of what he was going to do next. He couldn't turn back to the locked door, so unless he surrendered, he was going to try to come through us. I took another step back.

He seemed to scan our faces, as if picking the weak point of the circle that hemmed him in, and when his gaze fell on me—scared and weaponless—he seemed to decide.

Guards suddenly appeared from the main corridors, running and shouting, their spears leveled. He saw them, and his eyes grew wide and bright. With a cry of rage, he raised the ax high above his head and sprang right at me. I leapt back just as the guards arrived. At least two of their spears penetrated his chest and stomach.

As his ax fell and his roar became a fading scream I twisted my eyes away. I don't think I was the only one.

Everyone looked at each other with stunned, bewildered relief.

"Do you know him?" asked Mithos, stooping over the corpse.

Dathel muttered, "Not one of ours. I'd swear to it."

As the guards lifted him his black cloak fell open and we stared at it in silence. Stitched carefully to the inside was a lining that was clearly not regulation. There was no design or pattern on it. It was red. A crimson as deep and vivid as a new wound.

SCENE XIX

A Council Meeting

Dinner was a tense affair, to say the least. Apart from the six of us there were the count and countess of Shale, Chancellor Dathel, and the rulers of Verneytha and Greycoast and their military advisors. On each of the two doors into the dining room stood heavily armored infantrymen with swords and pikes, and the corridor guard had been doubled. They were taking no more chances.

We sat around a long mahogany table and toyed with our unexotic food, glancing round the bare walls to avoid looking at the concerned faces all around us. The beef in front of me might have been more constructively used by a cobbler but, sensing that it came from the remains of Shale's last cow, I sawed at it with my knife and chewed respectfully.

I should add that, despite the miserable castle and the lousy food, I was in reasonable spirits. I figured the situation had been exaggerated and we stood to make some easy money, and lots of it. The attack on the count's room had not seriously swayed my general optimism. Yes, the assassin would have killed me if the others hadn't been there to deal with him, but they *had* been there, and I wouldn't be going anywhere without a heavily armed escort from here on in. I was, after all, the party linguist. Mithos and the rest of them could handle the odd murderous soldier while I read books and shared pithy little observations about Shale's cultural history. It was sort of cool to have been brought in as some kind of expert, even if I wasn't really an expert in anything useful: I was a guest, a minor celebrity, even, and that was a part I could have fun with.

"In the light of today's attempt on my life," said the count, "I suggest we move rapidly to our principal business."

Count Arlest of Shale was a sinewy man in his early fifties, but he seemed exhausted, almost frail. His hair was brownish, greying; his eyes were anxious; and his cheeks hollow. He wore a monkish smock of coarse cotton, belted at the waist with brown leather, and the only sign of his office was a thin band of copper around his temples.

His wife was younger and not unattractive, despite the worry lines around her eyes. Her hair was long and reddish, her eyes a soft, foggy green, and her skin was pale as new ivory. She wore a high-collared dress of blue cambric in a slightly outmoded fashion. Her slim white hand rested on her husband's clenched knuckles through-out the meeting.

"Gentlemen," said the count, turning specifically to his fellow leaders, "this is Mithos, the group leader."

Mithos nodded to each of them and we followed suit as he gave our names. Duke Raymon of Greycoast was a robust, heavyset fel-low with a ruddy complexion, a thick russet beard, and blue eyes that sparkled amiably. He looked like a port drinker. He wore volu-minous robes of orange satin trimmed with fur and embroidered with gold thread, and heavy rings. He was the only person present who actually looked like a noble, and I rather took to him for not letting the situation get him down.

The other was an altogether different creature. He was introduced as Edwyn Treylen, governor of Verneytha. He was a small, wiry man with the sharp nose and tight, glassy eyes of a rodent, or—better still—some stoatlike predator. He clasped his thin hands and drummed his fingernails on the table very slowly, looking at us. He had a way of fixing you with his beady gaze for a minute or more as if you were an insect in a collection.

"Are they aware of the situation to date?" boomed the duke of Greycoast, his voice rolling like an empty beer barrel.

"I thought we could begin with a list of the attacks thus far," said the count softly. The somber chancellor passed him a page of spidery writing.

"Here is a chart showing the territories of our three lands," said the count. "Shale, Greycoast, and Verneytha, the last lying directly north of the other two."

He paused as if he was unsure how to proceed, and then added, "It began eighteen months ago, during the winter months, though we did not deem the matter important at that time. We received spo-radic accounts of attacks on merchant caravans between Ironwall, the capital of Greycoast, and the seaports twenty miles south. At this stage, of course, it was a purely regional affair, so I was not informed of the situation."

Here the duke of Greycoast spoke up. "It was a few inadequately reported attacks. Nothing more," he said, laying his palms on the table and leaning back with an expressive shrug. "These things happen on wealthy trade routes. There was little traffic on the road, so I just increased patrols slightly and thought no more of it."

He hesitated, and the count took the opportunity to proceed. "Duke Raymon did all he thought necessary at the time and cannot be blamed for not raising the alarm earlier," he said. Greycoast settled down, but from the quick glance he shot his neighbor from Verneytha, I got the feeling that this had been discussed less amicably before.

"Would you pass the mustard, please?" I inserted, trying to dress up the leather on my plate, having already tried some very disappointing chutney. Renthrette, who was sitting next to me, turned and gave me an incredulous look.

"What?" I whispered, slightly defensively, adding to the table at large, "Oh, sorry. I just wanted . . . you know . . . this meat . . . Sorry. Please go on."

Arlest did so, hurriedly. "The attacks continued but spread west into southern Shale, concentrating particularly around the Iruni Wood, which marks the Greycoast border. Again traders were attacked, murdered, and robbed, as were the inhabitants of some of the smaller hamlets and villages in the area. No survivors were left. The apparently random nature of the attacks prevented us from making a connection to those in Greycoast until similarities came to light almost by chance during trade discussions with the duke. In every case, the attackers were mounted and shot arrows with crimson flights."

I paused in my chewing and looked at him. I didn't like that detail about the arrows. I wasn't sure why. Maybe it just made them sound organized, but there was something else: like they wanted people to know what they were doing. Bandits didn't do that.

Arlest continued. "It was well into the spring before a survivor could confirm our fears, but by this time the assaults were widespread and had been reported as far apart as Hopetown in central Greycoast and just west of our capital, Adsine. The survivor had been taking the main trade route from Ironwall to Hopetown with a convoy of wagons

and an escort of ten men. In former days such a guard would have
been more than adequate. The road cuts straight through the Proxintar Downs, from whose hills the raiders came riding, heavily and uni-
formly armed, wearing scarlet cloaks and helms that left only their
eyes uncovered."

I looked around the room. The party was attentive. Renthrette
looked eager, almost excited. Duke Raymon was staring at the table,
though it was hard to tell if he was upset by the account of what had
happened, or embarrassed to have their dirty laundry aired for our
benefit. Edwyn Treylen sat quite still, his lips slightly parted, his eyes
roving around the room as if sizing us all up. When his eyes met
mine and held them, I turned back to Arlest.

"I am telling you this because later accounts illustrate that this is
their habitual mode of assault. Sometimes they attack with only six
or seven men. On other occasions there must have been eighty of
them or more. In each case they have just enough to ensure a comfortable victory, losing few, if any, of their own troops. As they
charge towards the caravan they shoot their bows, cutting down the
mounted resistance to nothing. They circle the wagons, shooting all
the while, often with burning arrows. Then they charge into close
quarters with their lances. If they dismount, they use a long, two-
handed axlike weapon. . . ."

He paused thoughtfully, and I saw the countess's grip on his
hand tighten encouragingly. We had seen the ax already.

"In the summer of last year the raiders reached southern Verneytha and led a series of forays into the Great Wheat Field region,
firing crops and causing immense damage to villages. Cavalry from
Verneytha went after them, but were unable to track them down. A
week later, on the trade route from Hopetown to Harvest, Verneytha's capital, a major cargo of metal goods was attacked, leaving
eight arrow-ridden wagons and a pile of corpses. Verneytha sent three
units of fifty cavalry to search the area. Two of them found nothing;
the other was destroyed utterly."

I stared first at the count and then at Treylen, the governor of
Verneytha, who was sitting as still as ever, his face blank. I'd say the
beef had turned to ashes in my mouth, but that wouldn't mean
much. What I had been thinking of as a sort of jaunt in the countryside, something a little more exciting than a picnic but of the same
basic ilk, had suddenly turned into a bona fide death trap. We were

out of our depth here. Something was very wrong, and it was the kind of something that Will Hawthorne did not wish to be part of.

As if to make me surer in my resolve, the count went on. "In October two villages close to Ugokan in northern Shale were robbed, fired, and their inhabitants brutally and methodically slain. In November some dignitaries of Greycoast and their forty-man armed escort were ambushed and executed as they crossed the Downs into Shale. Throughout the winter the attacks continued, targeting isolated, wealthy villages and trading groups in Verneytha.

"The three of us met and elected to use this castle as the base for our attempts to track and destroy the raiders. With financial support from Verneytha and Greycoast I was able to deploy my cavalry and certain units of infantry, but to no avail. I lost forty infantry in one fell swoop when their camp by the Elsbett Wood was assaulted. The cavalry spent two months pursuing red herrings and hoofprints that led nowhere.

"At that point we decided to bring in outside help. You are the third party to assist us. The first was wiped out as they escorted a vital fruit-and-vegetable convoy from Harvest. The second repaid their expenses and left. They were part of a group of fighters who hired themselves out to defend wagons leaving the Hopetown market. A huge force of what have become known as 'the crimson raiders' attacked the convoy. There were no survivors.

"Over the last month, the frequency of the raids has escalated to such a degree that we've felt obliged to close most of the major trade routes, including the vital Hopetown roads, to all traffic. The death toll of our soldiers and citizens is close to a thousand. We have lost a fortune in trade and our lands face bankruptcy and starvation. We *must* put an end to this situation."

By now there was a desperation in his voice that had not been there earlier. His eyes passed over us and they shone for a moment as if he was close to tears.

If he was, he blinked them away as Duke Raymon rocked forward and growled, "I put my men at your disposal. My seal will admit you to any building in Greycoast. We will cover all your expenses. What do you say?"

"We will help you if we can," said Mithos.

For a second I thought he was joking, but I should have remembered who I was dealing with. I was too dumbfounded to utter more than a sort of strangled gasp, which everyone seemed to associate, understandably, with the beef.

"Shale is not a wealthy land," said the count after a short smile of relief, "but we can put our soldiers and this castle at your disposal. On behalf of the three lands I can offer you one thousand silver pieces and a quarter of whatever stolen property you recover if you can put a stop to the raids. We have soldiers enough to meet them in the field, but we need to know *who* they are and *where* they are if we are to do battle on even terms. I think that is all."

The governor of Verneytha snapped his fingers and gestured brusquely to his military advisor, who placed a bag of coins on the table. The governor pushed it across to Mithos, holding him with his rat eyes. "And for a further two hundred silvers," he said, very quietly, "you will bring a progress report to my palace in Harvest, two weeks from today."

"If the count has no objection? . . . " said Mithos coolly.

"No," said Arlest, "though I expect you to keep us informed as a matter of course."

The duke of Greycoast did mind. He rubbed a pink hand over his red face and wheezed noisily. "I see no reason to pay extra for what we will all learn together," he said, eyeing Treylen frankly.

"It's my money," said Treylen. "My people's money. My lands are a little more distant. I just want to be sure I am kept properly abreast of all developments."

He said the last two words looking pointedly at Mithos. Raymon scowled but said nothing.

"Due to the widespread nature of the attacks," said Mithos, in a businesslike manner, "we will be moving around all three regions. Though the keep is a worthy and secure base for our investigations, we cannot expect to operate solely from here. When we are in Greycoast we will pass on whatever we know. Likewise in Verneytha. If there are major developments, we will ensure that word reaches all of you."

The duke of Greycoast relaxed slowly, apparently satisfied. Mithos gave him a reassuring smile and closed his hand around the bag of coins that Verneytha had given him. Treylen considered him closely, as if trying to decide whether to demand the return of the money. For whatever reason, he didn't.

The count, hesitantly, added, "My men are at your service, but you would do well to operate without them until you have the enemy's identity and whereabouts in your grasp. Frankly, I don't wish to send them out to be attacked without good reason."

"Are you suggesting," said Treylen, "that there is anything to learn about their identity? That they are not simply bandits?"

"Bandits?" scoffed Duke Raymon. "This is an army. How many cavalry units must you lose before you see that this is a tactical war with a careful and deadly enemy?"

Treylen smiled humorlessly and, speaking softly and carefully, said, "Whoever they are, they come from south of the Verneytha border."

"How dare you!" growled Greycoast, dragging his bulk up from his chair.

"If they are an army," said Verneytha, still cool, "then they belong to somebody. They aren't mine."

"Gentlemen!" said Arlest, rising to his feet with a pained look. "This is not the way. My land is too crippled by poverty and hunger for me to waste time harboring suspicions about my neighbors. We must pool our resources, not squabble amongst ourselves."

The two men fell silent, resentfully accepting the authority of their host.

"You may need each other more than you know," said Mithos. "Troops of the Diamond Empire are massing in Stavis. Whether they have some involvement in your recent troubles or not, they may soon show themselves ready to capitalize on them. That weakness can only be increased by your mutual distrust. I hope you will excuse my being so candid."

That last piece of diplomacy was instigated by a glance from Lisha.

"The Empire has always ignored us," rumbled Duke Raymon thoughtfully during the ensuing pause. "Why should that change?"

"Perhaps they have noticed your iron foundries and silver mines," said Edwyn Treylen with a hard-edged smile.

"Or your acres of crops and grazing land," returned Raymon.

"Whatever the reason," said the count, "we must bear the possibility in mind. Thank you, Mithos, for bringing it to our attention."

Mithos nodded slightly and then said, "You have said nothing of assassination attempts indoors like the one we saw today."

"It has not happened before," said the count, heavily. "The army

of Shale is the most significant force in the area, the military back-
bone of the three lands, and I am its leader. But why they should
choose this moment to strike at me, I cannot guess."

"The body of the assassin was not identified?"

"No," said the count. "A cavalryman went missing on maneu-
vers two weeks ago. It seems to be his armor, though the red cloak
and the axlike weapon are the hallmarks of the crimson raiders. The
man who used them is completely unknown to us."

"May we see the body, the cloak, and the weapons?" asked Mithos
as he rose to leave. "Unless there is more to discuss?"

That was a joke. I had been sitting there in a kind of stupor,
waiting for signs that this nightmare might show signs of improvement, but they apparently couldn't wait to ride straight into whatever portion of Hell was reserved for the very, very stupid. But there
was one more shortcut to self-destruction, and it was Duke Raymon
who brought it up.

"While you are investigating, we also expect you to try to reduce
the effectiveness of the attacks against us. In four days a major cargo
of coal is to arrive by barge in the port of Seaholme in southern Greycoast. The cargo will be loaded onto ten wagons and taken north
for the Hopetown market, where it is badly needed. It is both vulnerable and conspicuous. Some or all of you should be there to ensure its safety, though I will, of course, put a sizable force at your
command."

Mithos merely nodded, and the duke looked away, aware that he
was asking a hell of a lot.

That was my limit. I finally spoke: "Are you sure there's nothing
else we can do for you? Heal the sick and raise the dead? Move the
castle to the other side of the river? I mean, we've got a magic sword,
so I suppose anything is possible. I'll have to nip home for my fairy
dust, but . . ."

"I think," said Treylen, "that our friend is being sarcastic."

"That's the first observation in the last half hour that has made
any sense to me," I remarked.

"Will . . ." began Mithos.

"Ten wagons of coal!?" I exploded. " 'Vulnerable and conspicuous' is right! This is a fool's errand, and I'm not the fool you're looking for. There are only six of us, or hadn't you noticed? Six! What
difference—?"

I was about to go on, and in detail, when I felt the unmistakable cold of a knife blade pressed hard against the flesh of my groin. Renthrette. Her right arm was resting casually on the table, but her left had slipped under it and pushed her dagger just hard enough to pierce my breeches.

I swallowed hard, shut up, and kept very still. No one else had seen anything and they seemed to be waiting for me to finish my tirade, but I had the sneaking feeling that she had been looking forward to castrating me in the name of party dignity for some time now. I said nothing till the eyes on mine and the fractional insistence of the dagger made me mew out a few words like a startled kitten.

"Well, er . . . on second thought, it sounds quite reasonable, really. No problem at all. We'll get right on it."

When we left them, the count and his wife were still exchanging glances of weariness and bewilderment, sensations that seemed to follow me about. Renthrette never even looked at me, and none of the others seemed to guess what had happened. I kept my mouth shut, having realized in that moment, when my genitals had been hanging in the balance, so to speak, that I was sitting next to a psychopath. Had I breathed a word of this to Orgos or the others, I was pretty bloody sure that if I woke up at all the next day, I'd be greeting the dawn in falsetto.

But the situation was clearly out of control, and while Renthrette could shut me up, she couldn't change the clarity with which I saw this crimson-cloaked gateway to the underworld. If I was going to get home in one piece, I would have to come up with a new way of playing this adventurer thing, since poking holes in the script didn't seem to be helping. But, when it comes to acting, I'm nothing if not versatile.

SCENE XX

Beacons of Honor

I t doesn't look like an ax to me," I said, trying to sound interested.

The formalities over, and the dignitaries from Verneytha and
Greycoast already on their respective ways home, the party had gathered together in a cold storage room on the ground floor of the keep.
The dead assassin lay on a table, covered by a sheet. We had examined him and found nothing and, for the benefit of those who doubted
my enthusiasm—like, say, Renthrette—I had led the search. The crimson cloak was of light, commonplace wool, but the weapons were
more suggestive.

"It isn't an ax," said Garnet, touching the head of the thing with
his fingertips. It was a huge blade with a broad, sweeping edge, but
where it met the socket of the three-foot wooden haft, it was only a
couple of inches across.

Orgos spoke, his voice low and reverential, as if he was in some
dim temple surrounded by candles. "See how light it is?" he said.
"Ideal for mounted men. The edge is razor-sharp, so it slices rather
than hacks. You can see the lines and swirls where the steel has been
beaten out and reheated, over and over again, for strength, flexibility,
and a better edge than you will find on most swords: remarkable
workmanship. I saw one of these in the Cherrat lands once, many
years ago, an heirloom brought by a swordsmith from the west. He
called it a scyax."

"Is it *magic*?" I asked, innocently.

Orgos scowled at me. "Don't be stupid, Will," he said.

"Ah, I'm the one being stupid," I said, as if everything was clearer
now. "Your sword is magic, but this one isn't. Obviously. They probably messed up the—what would you call it?—enchantment? Sorcery?
Spell? I want to get this right," I explained, "because I wouldn't want
to be talking crap where magic weapons are concerned."

"What about the arrows?" said Renthrette, ignoring me pointedly.

"Finely made, but apart from the red flights, not particularly distinctive." Orgos shrugged, still glaring at me. "Their tips are of a steel hard enough to get through all but the thickest armor. They have long barbs on both flanges. You'd never get one of those out of you without making a hell of a hole. Too nasty to be a standard purchase, so probably made specially."

"Who stands to gain the most from these attacks?" Mithos asked.

"No one, really," said Lisha. "Not if we restrict our view to the three immediate lands. Incidentally, don't be deceived. They call themselves dukes and counts and governors but they owe no allegiance to any higher authority, so they are, to all intents and purposes, the kings of three small countries. They depend upon each other economically, but Shale is obviously the poor relative.

"According to the histories," she went on, "Shale relied on income from shipping for many years, and its river estuary ports in the south were very profitable. Then the sandbars shifted and the rivers silted up. Soon, it was costing more to dredge the rivers than was being made by the commerce they brought in. The ports were closed, and now, apart from the tiny harbor where we docked and a few isolated fishing villages, coastal Shale is dead.

"Combine that," Lisha continued, "with the poor soil and lack of significant mineral deposits, and you get a country with almost no resources. The only things they have here are a well-grounded reputation for horse breeding and a sizable army, by local standards at least. Shale is getting by at the moment on the money that the other two pay it to keep that army strong and ready to defend them all."

"And the others?" Mithos asked.

"Verneytha is the economic success story of the area," Lisha answered. "It is a rich nation of landowners and farmers. Growing conditions are perfect and they supply the region with the majority of its food. Closing the trade routes is hurting Verneytha, but it has also closed off Shale's and Greycoast's lifelines.

"Greycoast falls in the middle: better off than Shale, but not as wealthy as Verneytha. It produces its own barley and grazes a good deal of livestock, as well as exporting massive quantities of metal ores. Its seaports, though fewer than they were, are thriving, and produce enough for all three lands. Greycoast's biggest asset, however, is the market in Hopetown, which has, for decades, been the area's main trading site.

"So who stands to gain the most?" she said, coming back to the original question. "Nobody. They all lose, one way or another. Shale gains in that ruining the markets of its neighbors makes its own produce more valuable, and it keeps its army employed, but scarcity increases prices and Shale can hardly afford what it needs from Verneytha and Greycoast already. Shale will starve within the year. Verneytha and Greycoast are both losing badly needed trade, and no price increases will compensate for that. Economically, no one wins."

"In any case," said Mithos, "the attacks have been randomly distributed over all three countries and with equal savagery." He sighed, and then said, "I didn't want to seem unsure in front of the count, but I do think that we should move very carefully and be ready to acknowledge when the situation is beyond us. Thoughts?"

There was a moment's pause and the group looked pensive.

"We have given our word," Renthrette reminded us, a little defensively.

"That's true," I said, "and we can't tarnish our reputation."

Again Renthrette shot me an inquisitorial glance, searching for a sarcasm that was not apparently there.

"I admit," I went on thoughtfully, "that I am not truly one of you and my opinion doesn't carry much weight. But I'd like to add something. I have seen in you, all of you, something I did not believe still existed, something I'm not sure I believed had *ever* existed outside a story. I mean, valor. Honor and dignity. Virtuous intent united with courageous action. It is a remarkable sight, and I would hate to see this mission's admittedly daunting nature stifle this, what? . . . this *flame*. This beacon of principle. I know it sounds melodramatic, but that's what it is."

There was a thoughtful silence and I sensed a wave of pride in the room.

"I'm not very good at expressing myself like this," I continued, "but even at a time like this, that flame gives me courage, even if it cannot give me hope. Even as I anticipate the enemy bearing down on us in their red cloaks, I feel my strength renewed by that beacon. We will let the glow of honor illuminate the battlefield," I went on, my voice building, "however much the merciless enemy throng about us. And when they shoot us down with their barbed arrows, we will sing

our heroic defiance and the light of our beacon will shine in the
blood that pours from us. However horribly they pierce our bowels
with their spears, however savagely they mutilate us with their axes,
we will die knowing that we fell with honor. Passersby will look at
our corpses as they steam amongst the burning coal wagons from
Seaholme, and they will know that we bore the torch of valor. And
though the world will say we died in vain, that our arrow-riddled
bodies mean nothing to the vast and brutal enemy that must eventually vanquish us all, we will know differently."

There was a long silence. I waited.

It was—somewhat unexpectedly—Garnet who picked up the
gist of the thought and took the next logical step.

"But . . ." He faltered. "Don't you think? . . . "

"Garnet?" said Lisha.

"Oh, I don't know," he sighed, unsure of how much to say. "I
mean, honor is great and all, but . . . It just seems sort of futile to me.
I mean, Will's right about the valor and everything, but . . . well, how
the hell can we defend ten wagons of coal from a hundred trained
soldiers?"

"We will have an armed escort—" began Renthrette, but he cut
her off.

"I know that, but what is to say they won't just hit us with more
men still? They always win, you know? They've never been beaten
yet, did you notice? Our predecessors were valiant, weren't they? It
didn't protect them. I mean, if the valor doesn't produce results,
what's the point?"

There was a long silence. I looked at the floor. His sister just
stared at him.

"I don't know," he said with a gesture of his pale hands. "It just
seems sort of hopeless. We have nothing to go on and we could find
a hundred soldiers waiting for us as soon as we leave the castle. I say
we go back to Stavis."

Another long silence followed, cold and sharp as the ax on the
table before us.

"No," said Lisha gently but with enough conviction to show
that there would be no further debate of the matter. "Not yet, at
least. I appreciate you speaking your mind so frankly, Garnet, but we
can't say it is hopeless until we have begun our investigations. I suggest that we start with a journey to Seaholme. All of us."

Garnet fell silent, frowned, and then nodded, looking suddenly young.

So this was where the party leader pulled rank on us, I thought, as everyone made for the door and bed. The others seemed content, so I couldn't even complain that the decision wasn't democratic. I didn't know what to do or say. Even if I had wanted to go back to Stavis I wouldn't dare attempt that journey alone, and Garnet would always jump back into line when Lisha cracked her whip. For the moment I was stuck with them.

As I turned to go, Lisha caught my eye and smiled, a smile that was small and cool.

"Bravo, Will," she said, "a fine performance. And clever."

"What? What do you mean?" I stammered, but she was already leaving the room.

I slept poorly that night, partly because of my long rest in the wagon but also because my mind wouldn't stop turning the day's events over and over. Moreover, I was afraid. A touch of bluish moonlight glowed through my barred window, giving an icy hue to the castle's cold, grey stone. I lay there still and quiet, trying not to think of dukes and counts and the business we had undertaken, or those who had been hired to do the job before and now lay in shallow graves by the roads where the wagons had burned.

SCENE XXI

Stories

Over breakfast, Lisha assigned tasks. Mithos was to speak with Arlest about the logistics of our trip to Seaholme and the coal that would await us.

"Have you decided on a route yet?" he asked.

"The most direct route is also the most inconspicuous," Lisha answered. "We'll go under the southernmost tip of the Iruni Wood. If the count asks, say we haven't decided yet but we will probably take the Hopetown road."

Mithos accepted the point without comment. I think that I was the only one who was surprised at her lack of faith in our employer. Lisha turned to the rest of us, saying, "Renthrette and Garnet. We need horses and a wagon. Don't forget to get a mount for Will. Shop around a bit, because prices will be high.

"Will and Orgos, I want you to go through all our arms and armor. Find out what needs replacing and see what you can pick up. One of the crates of venom flasks got dropped when they were unloading the *Cormorant,* so look out for small vials and bottles. I will get the ingredients from an apothecary myself."

Orgos frowned, but Lisha held his eyes and he nodded.

"Don't like poisoning our enemies, huh?" I remarked as soon as she was gone.

"I would rather meet them sword-to-sword," said Orgos, looking away. "Equal terms. Their skill against mine. Their courage against mine."

"But Lisha said we should load up on venom, so I guess it's all right," I remarked. "These will be honorable poisonings. I'm beginning to see what you meant about her."

"What?"

"She's special," I said, walking away before he had chance to respond.

❧

It took us about an hour to go through the crates. The armor was all fine, but some of the leather padding inside was mildewed. We found a poorly stocked arms dealer just off Adsine's poorly stocked market, and we bought pads, two hundred arrows, a pair of ash-wood lances, and three leather-covered shields, rimmed with beaten copper. The lot cost us forty silver pieces.

"Daylight robbery," muttered Orgos contemptuously as we humped them into the back of the cart. "Remind me never to go shopping in Adsine again. Now, back to the keep?"

"Those venom flasks?" I reminded him.

"Oh," he said with a touch of irritation, "I forgot." He cracked the whip moodily and we rolled off.

"I don't know why we need to buy weapons anyway," I said, nodding at the pommel of his sword. "Couldn't you just—?"

"Drop it, Will," said Orgos warningly.

I did.

We weren't exactly surrounded by happy faces in Adsine. Sometimes children gathered around the cart and held out their thin hands for food or money. At first we gave a few pennies, but it caused such violent squabbling that we stopped, unsure of ourselves and the ethics of the moment.

"You want to hear that story still?" he said suddenly. "The one about how I became an adventurer?"

"Yes," I said. "I collect stories."

"This one is not unlike your own."

"How so?"

"I stumbled into adventurers who protected me from the Empire."

"They were after you too?" I said, pleased. "What for?"

He sighed, then said, "I killed a man. A boy, in fact."

I stared at him.

"It was an accident, of sorts," he went on. "It was many years ago. My father—who'd been a great smith—was dead, and I was forced to help out at home, trading the stuff he had made. I hated it. I wanted to make blades as he had done, so I spent hours trying to teach myself, heating, pounding, and folding the steel."

The cart creaked and he flicked the horses absently, his eyes still fixed on the road ahead or on something long ago that I couldn't see. He gave a snort of self-mockery and went on. "But I was no craftsman. So I trained with the swords I had made and couldn't sell, learned to cut and thrust and the showy tricks of swordplay. Soon I could spin a broadsword around my wrists, toss it from hand to hand, or swing it dramatically from behind my back. Spectacular and worthless. I scorned my family's pleas for help in the shop or in the fields. I was a swordsman. Swordsmen don't pick vegetables.

"Once I was taking a mule-load of pots and pans to a distant village in the hills south of Bowescroft: a rare concession to my mother. I had passed on the goods and was heading home when a storm came up. I decided to spend the night in a tavern. It was called the Brown Bear, I remember, though for years I tried to forget.

"The men in the tavern weren't used to men of my color, and presumed I was some rich kid running errands. When the first comments were made, I should have known to leave. Three men of about my age, all drunk and jealous of what they thought I had come from, began to throw insults at me. I shouted them down and one of them came at me. I knocked him down. The barman tried to calm them, but I drew and flourished my sword. One of them, a blond lad of perhaps eighteen, came for me with a bottle.

"I lunged, intending only to tear his tunic as a demonstration of my prowess," said Orgos. "Perhaps it was my anger, or the unsteadiness of my adversary, or perhaps my aim just wasn't as good as I thought. I ran him through."

I looked at him and was shocked to see revulsion in his eyes. What, I wondered, was so special about this corpse, which had begun the pile he must have accumulated since? He went on hurriedly, concluding a tale he wished he hadn't begun.

"I never went home. In Bowescroft I found my name on the wanted lists, spent three weeks in hiding, and then found my way out of the city as a guard on a trade caravan. We went north to Havnor, where I met Mithos. He gave me a new identity and a new life."

I thought for a moment. The horse hooves echoed vaguely at the back of my mind as I went through it all, scene by scene and line by line.

"Good story," I said. "Lots of moody detail and sentiment. I like it."

"It's not just a story," he said somewhat bitterly. "It's my life."

"There's no such thing as 'just' a story," I said. "They might be the most important things we have."

"When they are true," he said.

"They are usually true," I said. "In a way."

He frowned at me, so I shrugged.

"And now you are a swordsman," I said. If he thought I was questioning his remorse, he ignored it.

"I have learnt how to use my sword and, more importantly, when and for what reasons. I am no random killer, Mr. Hawthorne."

"But if someone comes at you with a sword?" I pushed.

He glanced at me and replied with the sigh of one reluctant to speak at all. "If a man, unprovoked, attacks me or wears the uniform of a sworn enemy, I will fight him. I have killed people in this line of work, but always with what I believed to be just cause. I am no mercenary, Will. I have not forgotten that young fool in the tavern all those years ago. Sometimes we act rashly or for the wrong reasons, but in these lands, at this time, the sword is the sole equalizer and, for now, I will continue to wield it."

"And when life becomes complex," I said, "people will always wish for a time like this, when skill with a weapon meant you could justly take a stand for what you thought was right and win. Another fiction, of course, a story we rehearse over and over in the hope it will come true."

"There's a big difference between fact and fiction," he said.

"Not in my book," I said. "And judging from the way you charge about like you're in a fairy tale, not in yours either."

He didn't reply, and I don't even know if he heard. That's another drawback with stories. People don't listen, or they don't listen well.

"And the sword you carry now," I added dryly, "has a magic stone in the pommel."

"Yes."

"I see," I said. "Just so long as we are rigorously maintaining this distinction between fact and fiction."

Orgos exhaled and said nothing. Indeed, there seemed to be nothing more to say. The image of a younger Orgos in a tavern turned over in my mind with the wheels of the cart, and I found myself wondering if I too would soon kill someone, and spend the rest of my life reliving the moment.

Opening Moves

We arrived back at the keep in time to hear Mithos report what he'd heard from the count.

"He has given us a tip on where we might start looking for the raiders once we have seen the coal to safety," he said, with a hard smile. "Near Ugokan just south of the Verneytha border is a complex of catacombs constructed over two hundred years ago. Apparently a few months back some children from a nearby village were playing there and never came out. A party of the villagers went in after them and was never seen again."

"Why did he not tell us this during the meeting?" said Renthrette.

"Not sure. I don't think he completely trusts the governor of Verneytha or the duke of Greycoast, but if he had any specific reason, he didn't say."

Orgos produced samples of what we had bought. Lisha looked over the glass vials and thanked him significantly. He held her gaze for a moment and then looked at the floor as Renthrette said, "You were right about the quality of the horses here. The major traders are grouped just north of the river, only a few hundred yards from here. We went to four different stables. The biggest had hundreds of fine horses but their prices were ridiculous. The other places were more reasonable. We got mounts for everyone, including a warhorse called Tarsha."

Her eyes lit up as she went on. "The warhorses were a little expensive, so we only got the one. We will have to share him. He is fully battle-trained and is in perfect condition. He is magnificent."

"How much?" interrupted Lisha.

"His coat is a glossy black that—"

"How much?" I jumped in.

"Six hundred and fifty silvers," she said quickly.

"Bloody hellfire!" I exclaimed. "That's over half the reward money!"

"That is a lot," said Lisha with a long sigh. Mithos lowered his head.

"He's a very good horse," said Garnet reassuringly.

"Does it talk?" I demanded. "Is it gold-plated? I mean, how good can a horse be? I thought you two were the meticulous and rea-sonable ones! Why does the smell of a horse turn you into squealing adolescents? Six hundred and fifty silvers! Hell's teeth, I could live for a year on that. I did! Two years!"

"He's a warhorse," Renthrette insisted. "Warhorses are expen-sive."

"Usually not that expensive," said Lisha. "I hope it is as good as you say. It's a good thing the governor of Verneytha gave us that ex-tra two hundred silvers. If the horse doesn't prove its worth, we'll sell it. I'm sure you checked it over carefully. But no more big pur-chases without consulting me first, all right?"

They demurred silently, with secret grins of joy wrinkling the corners of their thin pink lips. Lisha smiled despite herself, as if she was indulging children. Perhaps she was.

⚜

We slipped away at first light, our wheels and horses clattering across the cobbled courtyard and out through the gate of the perimeter wall as the kitchens were coming to life. In the cold, pinkish light Adsine looked peaceful and content as it sprawled by the banks of the Wards-fall. We breakfasted on bread and fruit in the saddle and said little to each other, waking privately.

We had lost sight of Adsine's hilltop castle to the slow, rolling hills of the Proxintar Downs by lunchtime. We paused and I stole a look at the stallion that Mithos now rode. It was everything and more that Renthrette had suggested, and it was only by repeating the price over and over to myself that I managed to hang on to some of my former outrage.

"Do you want to ride Tarsha for a while?" said Mithos to me sud-denly. I looked at the massive creature, its muscles rippling under its black, silky coat as it tossed its mane and flared its nostrils.

"You must be bloody joking," I said.

I rode until sunset on a bay mare, which walked calmly and easily so that I only fell off once before we camped for the night. The country had been easy—coarse fields and scattered copses—and we were on schedule. An hour or so ago we had crossed the Greycoast border, but there was no obvious change in the land as yet. North of our little camp, the edge of the Iruni Wood loomed black, and a little to the east the darkening sky was brushed with orange. I nestled close to the fire and got out one of my books from the Hide in Stavis.

It was an odd little volume which purported to be a history of the region once called Vahlia that now housed the lands of Shale, Greycoast, and Verneytha. The book itself was at least fifty years old and its pages were cracked and flaking at the edges, but the events in it were much older, many of them rooted at least as much in legend as they were in actual history. I had been reading without much enthusiasm since we left Stavis, but the book had taken an odd turn and I was suddenly fascinated.

As I said, the three lands had once been a single country divided into dozens of little principalities, each claimed by a clan or family. These clans devoted pretty much all their energies into beating each other up at every available opportunity. Usually these minifeuds had something to do with bits of scraggy grazing land that everyone treated like they were gold dust, and from time to time, certain families would get powerful enough to control most of the region. But it never lasted, and within a couple of years, the region was plunged into civil war, goatherd against fisherman, brother against uncle, farmer against merchant. The usual, in other words.

The cycle stopped about 250 years ago, and it did so in an odd way. In the middle of one of these endemic feuds, people started telling tales of how one of the clans (which clan depended on who was supplying the anecdote) had summoned a spectral force to fight on their side, a ghost army that came out of nowhere and vanished, leaving heaps of steaming corpses in its wake. Sound familiar? Of course, no one ever proved who summoned the ghost army, because it seemed to attack indiscriminately, wiping out entire families on all sides of the war. The only way the Vahlia clans survived the phantom soldiers was by bonding together into larger units, burying their differences, and joining their fighting resources. When the wars ended, just over a year later, three distinct powers had emerged. Borders were drawn up and the countries of Shale, Verneytha, and Greycoast were formed. In the next twenty years or so, the three capital cities emerged slowly from the ruined villages that had been there before, with construction on Ironwall, the most impressive and farthest east, starting first and finishing last.

I considered the ancient book and wondered what I was to make of such a yarn. There was clearly at least as much folktale here as there was history, but that is hardly unusual. The question, one I posed to the rest of the party after relaying what I had learned, was simple: Who would want to re-create some ancient legend about a ghost army and why?

"Someone who wants to scare people," suggested Orgos. "Make the raiders seem impregnable, supernatural."

"They'd have to be pretty superstitious to buy it," I said, doubtful.

"People are quick to believe the worst, however implausible, when there is no hope of victory," said Mithos, stirring the embers of the fire.

"But it's just a story," said Renthrette.

"There's a basic link between story and history," I said, beginning a lecture I had delivered many times before. But she scowled at me, so I decided to drop it.

"There was no reference to this ghost army wearing red, was there, Will?" asked Lisha.

"No," I said.

"And you don't believe in magic swords," said Orgos, "so magic armies are probably . . ."

"Nonsense," I said, "yes."

"So it's probably just a coincidence," said Garnet, as if this closed the matter.

I shrugged, but I didn't think so. I don't believe in fate, magic, or ghosts, but coincidence makes me nervous. It always leaves me feeling like the world—the rational, predictable, mundane world—is very slightly off kilter. I let it drop, but it stayed in my head, nestled there unpleasantly like a toad.

The sun had gone down, but the eastern sky was still orange, and as the darkness grew, that portion of the night seemed to have gotten brighter.

"What's that?" I said.

They turned and stared.

"A fire?" said Garnet.

"Too big for a fire," said Renthrette.

"No," said Lisha, staring at the sky and smelling the air. "It is a fire."

"We should take a look," said Orgos.

Everyone's hands slid towards their weapons. I hesitated, then followed suit.

Here we go, I thought. *Here's where it starts.*

Glimpses by Firelight

"Careful," said Lisha, taking up her helm and adjusting the chin strap, "it can't be more than half a mile around the edge of the wood."

She moved, and we followed.

It was a fire.

At first the trees and buildings were smothered in a heavy black smoke, but as we got closer we caught flashes of amber breaking through as the wind shifted. There was a village out there, and it was burning. All of it.

We tied the horses to trees and edged closer. It took me a moment to realize that we had stopped talking, that there was something over-careful about the way the others were moving. When Orgos drew his sword, I knew what was going through his mind. This was no mere forest fire. It was the work of the enemy. I wrestled awkwardly with my crossbow till it was cocked, then tugged a quarrel from its case and, with unsteady fingers, fitted it into the groove.

We saw nothing at first, since the night was upon us now and the only light came from the flames. Mithos and Lisha consulted, then divided us into threes with a wordless gesture. I moved through the smoldering bracken with Orgos in front of me and Mithos behind. When we reached the first blackened building, we paused in silence to consider our next step. I flattened myself up against the brick of the house, and it was hot. The place had obviously been ablaze for some time. Beyond the house I could see little through the smoke, and my eyes were prickling at the dry air. I was sweating, and suddenly wanted nothing more than to get out of there.

The houses were arranged on either side of a central road. In another few seconds the three of us were huddled at the corner straining our eyes to see through the black haze that filled the street. As Orgos and Mithos tried to talk over the roar of the fire, I peered out.

At the same moment, there was an explosive crack and an ominous tearing sound as half the wall above us shifted and leaned out. It was falling.

I ran forward into the road as the brickwork hurtled to the ground with a roar and a rush of sparks. Getting away from it took me across the street to a large plastered building that might have been a tavern. Its thatch smoldered and thick, greasy smoke curled from the cracks in the hot walls, suddenly enveloping me. My throat burned and I started to cough desperately as the skin of my arms pricked from the burning tinder falling from the roof. I stumbled about, rubbing my eyes, and somehow blundered out of the acrid fog and back into the burning street.

And suddenly, thirty yards in front of me, was a horseman.

He wore a helm that covered his face, and it glowed orange and yellow in the firelight. I saw the crimson cloak and the axlike scyax that hung in a leather case at his horse's neck, and then I felt his invisible eyes meet mine. The horse turned fractionally, and the head of the rider's lance dropped until it pointed at me.

For a moment, I couldn't move. Then the rider's heels tapped his horse's flanks and he was coming towards me out of the smoke and flame.

I raised my crossbow so suddenly that the bolt fell out and landed on the ground a few feet away. Pointlessly I pulled the trigger anyway and the bow twanged and kicked as I flashed my eyes up and down the row of burning houses in search of the others. They were nowhere to be seen. Horrified, I turned back to the rider.

His horse had been walking, but now he spurred it, and it leapt towards me, surging like he was riding a wave of fire. He leaned in the saddle, extending his lance arm, braced and ready for the hit. The dirt leapt up from the horse's hooves in dusty clods and the rider rocked low, scarlet cloak billowing, lance leveled at my heart.

Without taking my eyes from him and with my feet rooted to the ground I cried out, "Orgos! Mithos!"

Other riders were coming through the smoke towards me, a dozen or more of them, with their red cloaks flaring out behind them. My legs wouldn't move. Around us the flames leapt and the lancer bore down on me.

And then he stopped as if shot. He reined his horse and brought it to a stuttering halt, almost rocking out of his saddle with the effort.

The horse rose and kicked the air as the first two of the other riders drew alongside and a muffled voice called out, "What did he say?"

"Mithos," shouted another.

Then I was aware of Orgos at my side, his swords drawn. As he pulled me back into the shadows of the burning tavern, I shook off the freezing terror that had struck me and ran towards Mithos, who was standing at the corner with an arrow in his bow. He shifted as we approached, as if I was blocking his shot, and then he became very still, as if he couldn't see me at all. He drew back his bow and held it level as we ran past.

I was dashing back into the trees behind the buildings when I realized that there was no sound of pursuit. I looked back to the street and saw Mithos where we had left him, bow taut and immobile. There was no sign of the riders who had been charging me, and when I doubled back a little to look for them, I caught only a glimpse of crimson movement way over at the other end of the street before the smoke engulfed them. Then they were gone.

Questions

I was more than a little unnerved by our first real encounter with the crimson raiders, but not in the ways you might expect.

"Why did they let us go?" I demanded. We were back in our camp and trying, with no success whatsoever, to get to sleep.

"I don't know," said Mithos quietly.

"There were about fifteen of them at least," I said. "Why didn't they come after us? Why didn't they kill me when they had the chance?"

"Good question," muttered Renthrette. "Now go to sleep."

"What?" I retorted. "Doesn't this interest you? We interrupt these butchers in the middle of whatever the hell it is they do, they let us stroll away, and you don't wonder why?"

"You want to know what I wonder?" she said, leaning towards me. "I wonder why you went wandering off and then started shouting names when you were about to get what you deserved."

"I couldn't see where I was for the smoke," I protested, "and calling Mithos's name seemed to help, wouldn't you say?"

"It may have saved you," she said with another half-grin, as if that was a minor point.

"It saved all of us," I said.

She frowned thoughtfully, and looked to Lisha, who nodded.

"Will is right," she said. "For whatever reason, the name of Mithos saved us. I saw them freeze as soon as they heard it. They were turning their horses around before Will could even start to run."

"Perhaps they were afraid," I suggested, shrugging off my irritation with Renthrette.

"Of what?" asked Mithos, rising up from his place by the fire and staring out towards the orange smudge in the sky above the village. "Of a word? Of my name? No. I may have acquired a bit of a reputation in Cresdon, but nothing to make a dozen or more heavily armed

soldiers turn tail and run before they have even glimpsed me. And
here, no one knows of us."

"Then why? . . . "

"I don't know, Will," Mithos answered hastily, adding with a
touch of irritation, "Now go to sleep. We have another day's ride
ahead of us."

Since I was avoiding Orgos (having nearly got us all killed earlier
made me unwilling to deal with my combat instructor), I buried my
face in a pillow of rolled-up tunics and tried to sleep. I knew that I
would dream and I knew that there would be red-cloaked soldiers
with featureless helms riding through the fire of those dreams. There
would also be laughter and accusing fingers pointed at me. I'd been
having dreams like that ever since I met these idiots.

❧

The worst thing about sleeping outside is that you always wake at
dawn when the sun hits your face. Orgos had been on the last watch
and was now laying out a breakfast of the mediocre bits and pieces
brought from Adsine augmented by wild blackberries and stream
water which he had boiled over a tiny fire. After we had eaten we
went to the still-smoldering village. We found a few charred arrows
with traces of red flight feathers and a confused scattering of hoofprints. Mithos crawled about for a while and then said, mainly to
Orgos, "They came from the north end of the village, close to the
forest line. I'd say there were about twenty of them but it's hard to
tell. They rode up and down the street and then some of them dismounted and entered the buildings."

That, I didn't want to think about. I was dealing with things
rather better than I had expected, but I suppose that was because
last night's hellish encounter had taken place in a village full of red
light, not this blackened ruin of frames and burnt corpses. Oh yes,
there were plenty of those. I figured the count had another twenty-
five to add to his death toll, and there wasn't a hint that a single
raider had fallen.

We tracked the hooves until they came to the edge of the wood,
where the ground was too hard and cushioned with pine needles for
there to be any further trail. The sun had shone steadily by all accounts for a week now and there had been no sign of rain for longer,
so it was only the sand that the horses had kicked up that had en-

abled us to follow them this far. The horsemen had come and done what they obviously did so well, and then left without a trace.

Still, it was odd. Hard ground or no hard ground, there were tracks throughout the village, and there were occasional signs of where the raiders had come in and gone out, but a hundred yards or so beyond the village? Nothing. No sign that anyone had been there for weeks. It was as if they had just disappeared.

You'd think that this would have been a nicely ominous portent, an opportunity for the party to abandon the whole mission and slink quietly back to Stavis, but that didn't seem to occur to anyone.

Seaholme

Somehow, Greycoast was luckier than Shale. We hadn't been traveling long that day before the ground started to look greener, and we were soon crossing fields of grazing sheep.

Mithos rode Tarsha, the overpriced bundle of muscle and mane they had spent our reward on.

"Are you doing all right, Will?" he asked, apropos of nothing.

"Of course," I said. "Why wouldn't I be?"

"No reason," he said. A moment later he added, "When we get to Seaholme we will have to organize a large defensive force and be ready for anything. No more blind terror or curious solo forays, all right?"

"All right."

As if that was something I had *planned*. Has telling anyone not to panic ever helped in the slightest? No one chooses to panic. No one says, "Oh, what a good idea: panic will not achieve much in this situation, so I opt to stay calm instead."

I swear, they might be strong and courageous, but sometimes they talked like they knew nothing about anything that really mattered.

It was late afternoon when we reached Seaholme, and Duke Raymon was waiting for us.

"You have made good time," he boomed. "You have no idea how reassured I am to see you. The barges are expected around nine o'clock tomorrow evening. There's a sizable force awaiting your instructions."

"How many?" said Mithos, swinging down from his horse.

"A hundred," Raymon answered. "Sixty cavalry and forty infantry."

"Excellent," said Mithos warmly. "I had not dared to hope for so many."

"Frankly," said the duke, "I can't really spare them. But this is an important cargo and worth the extra caution."

"If the raiders are as careful as everyone suggests," added Mithos, "they will not risk an attack on so large a force."

The duke nodded, but he didn't say anything. I don't think anyone else noticed, but it bothered me.

The following day I dressed carefully and tried to carry myself with the bearing of one who knew what he was doing. It wasn't easy, partly because I didn't, and partly because Seaholme was a maze of ancient streets packed with fishermen and soldiers from the moment the sun came up. I felt almost as lost and inadequate as I had in Stavis, but this time I had to strut around and look composed. I gave it a shot, throwing my shoulders back and stalking about like a rooster. Bill the tactician. The renowned General William Hawthorne. The names didn't feel right, like I was wearing someone else's clothes and they were all too big. I remembered the riders in the burning village and, thinking that I didn't want the responsibility of arranging how we faced them, dropped the military swagger, hunched my shoulders, and tried to keep a low profile. For that part I was a natural.

The soldiers looked good in their blue tunics and capes, but their armor was light, and they lacked, even to my inexperienced eye, an air of efficiency and confidence. As we were introduced to the platoon captains I couldn't help noticing a pair of young soldiers handling two-handed spears as if they were unsure what they were supposed to do with them. Still, they looked impressive from a distance, and maybe that would be enough.

In the harbor the myriad fishing boats had been moved to clear the dock for when the barges came in. Drawn up in vast warehouses close by, ten large wagons stood empty and waiting. In fact, waiting was what we did a lot of that day. Mithos and Orgos looked over the troops and drew up plans with their leaders, but they looked less happy at the end of it than they had at the beginning.

"I don't see what more we can do," Mithos said as we sat by the docks, eating grilled fish, "but if the raiders call our bluff and attack . . ."

"What's that over there?" I said.

"What? The lighthouse?" said Orgos, squinting in the direction I was pointing, but only getting as far as the round towerlike structure that dominated the harbor. "It's used to guide ships into the port. . . ."

"No, further down the coast. It looks like another port."

It turned out that the other port had been called Shelton. I say "had been" because, according to Duke Raymon, it was now a ghost town, and had been since the bay had been closed off to sea traffic by an immense sandbar. The people had just shut up shop and moved away. It was exactly the same as what had happened to Shale, but here the fishermen had just moved a couple of miles down the coast to Seaholme.

"It's like the town here, but on a smaller scale," said the duke. "Why?"

"I was just thinking," I said, "that if the raiders were massing for an assault, they would need to do it in a place where they wouldn't be noticed—"

"Will's right," said Lisha hurriedly. "We should ride over immediately." She paused and added, for the benefit of the duke, "Don't you think, Mithos?"

❧

It took us less than ten minutes to ride over to the derelict port of Shelton. It was populated only by terns and gulls that swooped and dived at us as we walked our horses through its empty streets, fixing us with their hard, unafraid little eyes as if ensuring we were in no doubt as to who owned the place. The entire town was caked with the greenish white and grey of their droppings, and the air rang with their raucous voices.

We split up and searched the streets of silent shops. Garnet and I wandered along the harbor and poked our heads into decaying boathouses. The water had receded from the seawall and, farther out, you could see where it shallowed to nothing, barely covering a great reef of sand, dotted with the bones and split hulks of the ships that didn't get out in time. We found nothing but puffins and razorbills nesting in the boathouse walls, and air heavy with the scent of rotting seaweed. We tried the lighthouse door. It was open, and we spiraled our way up the stone tower to the open top with its wood-filled brazier and its view of Shelton. There was nothing to see but the sister lighthouse down the coast in Seaholme. I leaned disconsolately over the guano-caked side, harried by hovering terns and great, screaming gulls. The noise was giving me a headache.

It was evening before we got back to Seaholme, where the dock-hands were amassing slowly on the quay and rolling out the wagons with studied caution. I had actually thought I was being useful, for once, but since we had nothing to show for our afternoon bird-watching expedition I resigned myself to my usual role: useless Bill, Will the waste of space.

The infantry had been sent in groups of ten to hold the main roads down to the harbor. The cavalry stood close by. Everyone looked anxious and a little bored, including the horses, which chewed on their oats, waiting for something to happen.

We dined in our tavern on local cod with rice and lemon juice. Lisha gave us a last-minute summary of the situation. "Mithos, you will oversee the loading of the wagons with me. Orgos, you stay with the infantry. Garnet and Renthrette, join the cavalry. Will, you are to carry messages between all the other units."

Great. Will the errand boy. I looked out of the window, noting how quickly it had darkened. It was now half past eight and the last of the sun had disappeared ten or fifteen minutes ago. Mithos was talking: "There are two large barrels of seawater on the roof of each wagon. The raiders can't expect to get away with a cargo like this, so they will probably try to burn it on the road. We should hack the barrels open as soon as the raiders appear and drench the coal: drown it. If one of those burning arrows gets in . . . What's the matter, Will?"

"*Burning* . . ." I repeated, getting to my feet.

"What?" said Lisha.

"Garnet and I went up the lighthouse today," I said. "The one in Shelton. The brazier—"

"Had wood in it," said Garnet, getting to his feet. He looked even paler than usual.

"The town is deserted," I said, "but the lighthouse brazier is stocked with new, dry timber. The raiders aren't going to attack the wagons at all."

"They are going to lure the barges into the wrong port—" said Garnet.

"And wreck them on the sandbar," I concluded. "They aren't going to burn the coal. They are going to drown it."

The Lighthouse

T ake the horses and get over to Shelton," shouted Lisha, "except Orgos. I'll send cavalry. The barges will be in sight of the lighthouses any minute now, so move fast. If they are going to light the Shelton beacon, they'll also have to keep the Seaholme lighthouse dark. Orgos and I will deal with that."

I rode as fast as I could, but I couldn't keep up with the others. By the time I reached the foot of the lighthouse they were waiting, holding the door slightly ajar. I dismounted shakily, and Garnet nodded silently towards six horses trimmed with crimson that were tethered in the dark by the tower.

There was a sudden flare and I looked up to see the beacon atop the lighthouse ablaze. Moments later the bright orange spot of light that flickered farther up the coast, the light that was to guide the barges into Seaholme, died.

There was only one door into the tower, and we had no idea if the raiders knew we were here. There was only one way up: the tight, dark, and easily defended spiral staircase. . . .

"I wish Orgos were with us," Mithos murmured as he pushed the door open. "All right, let's go. Quick and quiet. Hand-to-hand weapons only. I'll lead, then Garnet. Then Will. Renthrette, cover the rear."

At the top the fire roared, drowning out all other sound. I looked over Garnet's shoulder into the tower and up the staircase. It was dark and narrow in there.

Mithos vaulted up the stairs and was quickly around the corner and out of sight, Garnet at his heels, his ax blade sparkling dully. Then I went. Then Renthrette. We were halfway up when I heard a door below us open, its shrunken timbers scraping on the stone floor.

Renthrette glanced up at me and gestured to keep going. I pushed into Garnet and urged him up the spiral. There was a cough from below, and a snatch of conversation resounded up the pipelike stairwell. Two of them behind us. At least.

Renthrette slapped at my legs, pushing me higher and faster as the voices began to ascend. And then we came to a halt. Above me, Mithos readied himself, touched by the yellowish light of the beacon that fell down the first four or five steps. Garnet raised his shield and huddled closer to him, the muscles of his calves taut, his knees bent and ready to spring. Below, Renthrette took one more step up and then turned her back on me, her sword arm drawn back and ready.

The first soldiers rounded the corner below at about the same moment that Mithos leapt out of the top of the stairwell. I felt Garnet pause for a moment before he followed him out with a wordless cry of fury. Below, I saw a crimson-crested helm appear in the dark as Renthrette lunged. The tip of her sword glanced off the raider's armor, and, as he hesitated, I dragged at her tunic from behind, pulling her upwards after me. If there were four of them on the top, then Mithos and Garnet would need all the help they could get. And anything was better than being trapped like a rat in the dark stairwell, enemies above and below.

I'd only gotten two steps higher when the soldier below recovered from his surprise and came after us, drawing his weapon. I took another step up and found my head in the open air, my ears suddenly filled with the roar of fire and the confusion of combat. I leapt up the last few stairs, my sword and shield extended in sudden terror. Maybe I should have stayed in the staircase after all.

One of the raiders lay crumpled by the wall, his cloak spilling out like blood. Garnet was hacking at one who was parrying with his scyax. Two others had pinned Mithos against the raging brazier. I moved towards one of them cautiously and he turned, heaving his huge axlike blade at me. I dived to the side and the weapon swung wildly, catching Mithos's other adversary in the waist. The wounded man doubled up and Mithos sprang past him, seizing the scyax-wielder by the throat.

Garnet made a feint attack with his ax and then cut at his enemy's shoulder, but the raider dodged and struck out with his scyax. It caught Garnet's forearm and opened up a long gash that made him cry out and drop his ax. Renthrette, who was emerging from the stairwell backwards, wheeled and released a shout of anguish.

Her brother had raised his shield in front of him and was sheltering behind it, agony contorting his features. The raider cut at him again with the scyax, and Garnet, taking all the weight of the strike on his shield, shuddered and fell back towards the crackling brazier. I was with him in two strides. The raider sensed my approach and turned to face me.

I lunged, and, as he pulled his scyax across his chest, ready to swing, something Orgos had taught me kicked in. I dropped the tip of my blade under his parry and it connected. It was a weak strike, nothing like enough to pierce his breastplate, but as the sword kicked in my hand I lost my balance and fell forwards. Suddenly my face was inches from his helm and I could see blue eyes through the eye slits and a misty stone like an opal set into the bronze between them, glowing orange in the firelight.

I saw the panicked look in his eyes. He tried to wield the scyax against me, but it was too big and I was too close. I fell upon him and my sword point slid up his cuirass and found the soft flesh of his throat. My body weight carried me forwards. I couldn't have stopped myself if I'd wanted to.

Then there was a scream, a long, slow cry that stopped abruptly. One of the raiders had fallen from the tower as he struggled with Mithos. Blood streaming from a broad slash in his cheek, Mithos ran for the stairs, where Renthrette was holding off the last two.

"The fire! Put the fire out!" he shouted.

Without another word he flung himself down the steps, sword aloft.

I tore two of the scarlet cloaks from the dead raiders, plunged them into a bucket of seawater by the brazier, and pulled Garnet to his feet. His arm was bleeding heavily but he said nothing as he seized the edge of the cloaks. We stretched them taut over the brazier as the flames jagged out from underneath. The heat was almost unbearable, but just before I released the steaming fabric, the light died and smoke began pouring out. It was done.

The last of the raiders fled, seized his horse, and galloped away before Renthrette or Mithos could give chase. I grasped the stone of the tower to hold myself up and inhaled the sea air deeply, staring out into the darkness until the shock and nausea subsided. I was covered in blood, but it wasn't mine.

The four of us stood together, wheezing, staring west, waiting. It was almost a minute before we saw the brightening spark of the Sea-holme lighthouse flare up to guide the barges in.

The Convoy

We moved off at first light, a column of dark wagons bristling with spears and escorted by sixty horsemen in royal blue cloaks and silver helms. We looked ready for anything and, suspecting that we weren't, I hoped that appearances would do the trick. I didn't know what Mithos had told the duke about how close his precious cargo had been to the bottom of the ocean thanks to a mere handful of the raiders. I had always known they could outnumber us, but I had presumed we could outthink them, like in the stories. I was pretty pleased with myself for figuring out the lighthouse ruse, but I also knew that if we hadn't caught them off-guard in a space too small for them to swing those bloody ax things, the evening would have gone rather differently.

We sent some of the infantry to recover the corpses of the raiders so we could inspect them, but they couldn't find them, or they lost them, or something.

"How is that possible?" I yelled at the young officer in charge of the detail. "They were at the lighthouse. Did you find the lighthouse?"

"They weren't there," he said. "Not when we got there. Somebody must have taken them."

Great. I doubt we would have discovered anything from them, but it was disheartening to have missed the opportunity of learning *something* from our brush with death.

"I hear you did your part at the lighthouse," said Orgos.

"I guess," I said, uncertain whether I was proud of the fact or not. The whole thing had unnerved me rather.

"You guess what?" said Renthrette, appearing at my elbow.

"Nothing," I said, hoping she wouldn't pursue it.

"Sounds like Will was quite the warrior," said Orgos.

Her slim mouth frowned.

"I didn't see," she said flatly. "I think he helped."

Orgos shrugged uncertainly and carried on what he was doing. That was it: Will the conquering hero risking his life for his comrades, for her miserable brother, no less, wading courageously into the fray, saving the day with his finely honed skills, and all she could come up with was an "I think he helped." Great.

Lisha and Garnet supervised the loading of the wagons and I wandered the streets, ready to relay messages from our stationed guards. That was the official story, anyway. In fact, I was sick of hanging around the harbor and being asked for advice by adolescent infantrymen who couldn't figure out a way to get a barrowload of coal into the back of a wagon without tipping it all over the dockside. So I excused myself, grabbed a few bottles of beer, and tried to impress some local women with tales of my heroic exploits. Another failure.

❧

I slept for the first ten miles or so, slouched over the tailgate of the third wagon with my crossbow beside me. When I woke there was a thin sea mist rolling about us, so that the horses and wagons a few yards away were pale and indistinct. Lisha ordered that we close up, and soon the horses behind us had their noses to our wheels. I patted them awkwardly and offered them apples on the end of my shortsword.

Duke Raymon had gone on ahead, casting politic smiles of confidence and, more significantly, pouches of silver in his wake: ten silver pieces for each of the party "for expenses." All things considered, I supposed, I wasn't doing too badly: unless, of course, the raiders tried smashing our convoy and its poxy escort of schoolboy soldiers. Then I would be doing very badly indeed.

Garnet was riding alongside a handsome young cavalry officer with blond hair trailing from beneath his helmet. I couldn't catch what they were saying, but they seemed to have connected somehow. Once, the officer threw back his head and laughed loudly, flourishing his lance in a strong right hand. Garnet nodded enthusiastically and showed off his ax. They wanted something to happen: could hardly wait. Even their horses seemed to be tapping out dance steps on the road, as if eager to gallop away from the wagons and into the fray.

Close by, a pair of the officer's men (they couldn't have been more than my age) swapped nervous smiles and lies about past experience, glancing around the countryside with studied carelessness. I was still watching them when the cry went up from the back of the column, "Raiders! Raiders to the rear!"

Instant confusion. All around me the faces of the escort soldiers were torn with panic. Their horses snorted and kicked their front hooves. At least one soldier was unseated and thrown to the road, his mount bolting off into the mist. Mithos passed me, spurring his horse to the rear of the column and shouting, "How many of them are there? Where's the infantry commander?"

The wagons collided as some increased their speed and some stopped outright. The horses caught between them neighed and stamped furiously. I scrambled out and up to the roof where two young infantrymen were shouting at each other.

"Douse the coal," I said, starting to tip one of the huge water barrels. "Soak it."

They did so in stunned silence and then stood there, waiting for me to tell them all was well, or what to do to make it so. I primed my crossbow and looked out over the backwards snake of the misty wagons. They were all still now, and clogging the roadway so that the cavalry were spilling out at random and gathering in aimless huddles around the tail of the convoy. The fog was still too thick to see properly, but I could hear the officers shouting for word of the attackers. God willing, it was a false alarm.

Mithos and Lisha had dismounted and were urging the infantry into a protective line against the wagons, the heads of their long spears extended to keep the invisible horsemen at bay. But the cavalry had no idea what they were doing, and as their commanders yelled, the force split, some inside the defensive spear wall and some out. I saw Garnet charging amongst them, trying to draw them together, his ax and shield raised. At his elbow rode the blond officer, cloak flying out behind him as he spurred his horse towards the rear. He had drawn his saber and held it aloft in a clean, white-gauntleted hand, so that it flashed in the soft morning light. He looked at me, or rather at something in my direction, and I saw his earnest, commanding features. Garnet joined him, his face lost in the shadow of his horned helm, and they cantered out of sight.

There was a moment of stillness. Then it started.

Chaos

We heard the raiders before we saw them: They came charging in through the mist, loosing arrows that flashed out of nowhere and streaked like sparks into the open wagons. They appeared only for a moment, their crimson cloaks whipping about them, their faceless, bronze helms crested with scarlet horsehair. Their bows were drawn again almost as soon as the first arrows left their hands. They aimed and shot in a single motion as their horses pounded the earth beneath them. Our soldiers fell back with terror as the crimson specters materialized, loosed their arrows, and wheeled away. Then there was a moment of stillness, a shocked hole in the morning.

The silence was filled by the groans of the injured or dying. Officers cried out to regroup or extinguish the flames, and the panic-stricken infantry shot bows and crossbows blindly into the mist, hitting nothing. Then came the drumming of hooves and the cry of realization as they came again, the scarlet soldiers shooting their flaming arrows.

They never came within more than thirty or forty feet of the spear line, but by the end of their second assault I could see seven or eight of our men dead or close to it and one wagon already well ablaze. Mithos was screaming for crossbowmen and lining them up behind the kneeling rank of spears. Renthrette joined him and they stood at either end of the line, their bows drawn back and ready.

There could be no more than a couple of dozen raiders attacking, but their skill and training made each of their men worth several of ours. Mithos ordered our cavalry back and out of danger. The blond officer protested angrily, then wheeled his horse with contempt and rode it back to the blue-cloaked horsemen. I heard him calling to them, saw the light on his raised saber again, and thought vaguely about how noble and courageous he seemed. Mithos was crouching with the archers. I think I called something encouraging out to the cavalry officer, but I'm not sure.

They came as before and their arrows rattled into the wagons like burning hail. Two more infantrymen fell before Mithos gave the order to shoot.

The heavy crossbows jolted in the inexpert hands of the infantry and several bolts flew wide, but there was also a staggered smack as some found their targets, and two of the crimson-cloaked horsemen fell. A great chestnut stallion, a jet of blood shooting from where a bolt had pierced its neck, stumbled and crashed down, casting its rider over its head and pinning him to the earth. The others reined their mounts and turned them about, their order momentarily broken. A shout of triumph rose up from the spear line.

The young cavalry officer roared something at Mithos and spurred his horse through the spears, his sword lifted high above his head. Without waiting to see who followed him, he galloped after the raiders. About thirty horsemen went after him, through the ruptured spear line, vengeful elation in their raised voices and lowered lance heads. Mithos, his arms spread wide, shouting incoherently, tried to bar their path, but they brushed him aside and he fell into the ditch. I was running towards the infantry, who now stood cheering their comrades on, when I saw the fear in Mithos's eyes as he stumbled to his feet. Dimly, I realized that he was listening.

I stopped running as all about me fell simultaneously still. There were horses coming from the north. A lot of them.

Through the mist we could just make out the blue and silver of the cavalry as the raiders they chased slowed and turned to face them. Then we saw the others, fifty or more of them, their scarlet and bronze blurring through the fog as they bore down on the Greycoast cavalry. The raiders hit them side-on at unbearable speed. I doubt that the young officer knew they were there till he felt the tip of a lance tear through his side.

I was close to Mithos now and I saw him wince as the two forces clashed, the blue swept aside by the crimson. He watched, unflinchingly, trying to piece together the carnage that the mist veiled. Then came a sound from our ranks: slow, horrified disbelief, like the gasp that ripples round a theatre audience, stupidly amazed.

Lisha appeared among us.

"Where's Garnet?" she demanded. Mithos didn't respond, so she seized his arm and shook him.

"Where's Garnet? Mithos! Did he go with them?"

In a dazed tone, his eyes still staring towards the sounds of clashing steel and shouts of pain, he said softly, "Yes. Yes, I think so. I didn't see him go, but I think he did."

Lisha turned away and shouted, "Renthrette! Get the rest of the cavalry together and take them to the rear of the column. The raiders will come back and I want what's left of the cavalry to hit their flank. Orgos, get that spear line together. Now! Will, get down here and make sure every crossbow is loaded and ready. Then help me get these archers into a line behind them. Shoot over the top and bring the horses down. If we hold out against the first wave, I want the spear line to advance and deal with the fallen enemy. Orgos, are you listening?"

She turned back to Mithos and he nodded once and began calling orders to the spear company. Orgos threaded himself through the line, hurriedly repositioning hand grips and adjusting shield straps. Lisha watched Mithos for a split second and then leapt onto her horse.

"Will," she said, "take care of the archers and crossbowmen."

"Me?"

She kicked at the stallion's flanks so that it shuddered away. I turned to the frightened archers and waved them into a line behind the spears. The crossbowmen bent double over their weapons, drawing back the slides and fitting bolts with their free fingers. They were about ready when the sound of hooves set us staring into the soft, dreadful greyness ahead.

Before the riders emerged it was clear that there weren't many of them. There were in fact four, in ragged blue cloaks, with their weapons shattered and their eyes mad. Garnet was with them. He tore the helm from his head and gasped the air as he rode. His shield was splintered and the left side of his face was covered with blood. He raised his ax for us to see but there was no pride or joy in his eyes. He looked numb with shock, almost lifeless. Afraid.

The infantry watched them as if they were ghosts. Close by, somebody began to weep. The four cavalrymen stopped and stared about them, unsure of what to do next.

"Join the cavalry at the back," shouted Mithos. They passed

outside the spear line to where Renthrette and Lisha were silently walking the remaining horsemen away from the caravan, into the misty field. Mithos turned, and for a moment, his eyes met mine. No expression showed in his face. I smiled despite myself and longed to be elsewhere.

"Stand firm, Will," said Orgos darkly as he passed, reading my thoughts.

For a minute or two there was silence. The soldiers around me shifted uncomfortably, their nervousness increasing. Then Mithos called, "They are coming! Crossbows to the front."

I pushed forward through the double ranks of spears and the others followed me. We found ourselves on the front line at the edge of the road, nothing between us and the lines of shadowy crimson horsemen. I turned to Mithos in alarm. "We're all going to die," I whispered.

The words just came out: Honest. Scared.

"Quiet, Will," he answered, quickly, without looking at me. "They will charge any moment now: try to break the line by hitting us directly. When they are in range, shoot. Then drop into the ditch and let the spearmen advance over you."

I think he was going to say more, but the mist suddenly thinned and a gasp of dismay slid out of our troops. The enemy were trotting towards us, no more than 150 yards away now, in a long, tight line. Their horses were calm and massive, their lances raised like a thicket of steel. Even at this range you could see their uniform bronze-faced helms: a true army.

I looked for the remains of our cavalry but they were nowhere to be seen. The line of crimson-cloaked soldiers kept coming. God, there were a lot of them. Seventy or more. Half of our sixty cavalry were dead and the rest were gone with Lisha and Renthrette. I stood with seven other crossbowmen in front of about sixteen spearmen and nine or ten archers. We didn't have a chance, but the raiders weren't going to give us an option.

And I think it was then that I noticed that one of the raiders was different from the rest. His bloodred helm was topped with a pair of horns, and his cloak looked heavy, like it was made of fur lined with crimson silk. He carried something that might have been a spear or a staff of some kind, and he never moved at all.

With a breath of quiet resolve they surged towards us. Mithos yelled the order and there was a thin swish of bows from behind me. Still they came on, their steeds churning the grass as they galloped on. None fell to the arrows. I held up my hand. A second pattering of arrows flew overhead and fell harmlessly behind them. In four or five seconds they had halved the distance between us.

Wait. Wait.

"Shoot!" I shouted. I shot for the neck of a white charger with a cloak of crimson over its leather barding. It shuddered as the bolt struck home and dropped to its knees, but the rider slid easily from the saddle and drew out his scyax. Mithos grabbed my shoulder and thrust me to the earth. I didn't even see how many we'd brought down. Not many, I think. We fell on our faces in the drainage ditch and the spearmen stepped over us.

My hands fumbled for the crossbow slide and began tugging it back. The sound of the horses grew deafening. Through the legs of the spearmen I saw their speed break as they hit the embankment and a couple of them stumbled. The horses lurched up the grassy slope and, refusing to go further, boiled around the spear line. I saw one horse, unable to halt its advance, lunge and spit itself upon a spear, falling only a couple of feet away from where I crouched. The spearman in front of me suddenly cried out and fell heavily, blood gurgling from his lips. He wasn't the only one.

The raiders pulled back. I suppose the order to advance was given before they realized how large a hole gaped in our poor defenses. I think six or seven of our spearmen had fallen and the line no longer really existed. As the raiders drew away I could see the vast hulks of their dead horses. We had killed only two of the raiders themselves.

"Draw your swords," shouted Mithos. The enemy were dismounting, unwilling to force their reluctant mounts on our meager spear line. They were coming on foot, grimly, deliberately, with their huge, cruel-headed scyaxes sparkling coldly in their hands. There were so many of them, it seemed madness to resist but, knowing what would surely happen if we attempted to surrender, I finished cocking my crossbow and struggled to my feet.

Vaguely I smelled the sour smoke of two wagons blazing at the front of the convoy and, with a defiant cry, aimed and shot at the advancing line. The bolt struck one of them in the head, rang out sharply, and glanced away. He paused for a second and came on. Terrified, I reached for my sword.

Orgos was beside me, his twin swords with their fine long blades held out before him. On my left a soldier dropped his spear and fled, crying bitterly. With murderous calm the enemy clambered up the embankment to where we waited. When the first man reached the top, Orgos cried out and fell on him. Mithos followed suit and a handful of others lunged and slashed inexpertly with their swords. More raiders pressed around us. I stabbed at one and he parried it easily. A young infantryman fell to a scyax beside me and his hot blood splashed across my arms.

That was enough for me.

I moved back from the fray as Orgos's inspired blades swept a bronze head from its shoulders and then turned to fend off the strokes which fell upon him from all sides. I ran, turning to watch only when I was safe behind the heavy wheel of one of the wagons. My hands shaking worse, I fumbled with my crossbow and wondered if I could catch one of the stray horses and make a run for it.

Then out of the mist came the remnants of our cavalry with Garnet at the head, Lisha and Renthrette on the flanks. The Greycoast lancers hit the dismounted raiders in the flank, stunning them with the impetus of the wild charge. For a moment the tide changed and several of the enemy fell. But the advantage was lost as soon as the enemy got over the surprise. Then they turned to face the cavalry, some of them hacking at the horses to stop the advance while the rest retreated to their mounts.

What was left of our spear line broke rank and plunged down the embankment after them. There was a familiar flash of amber light, and the raiders seemed to slow, unsure of where they were or what they were doing. And out among them, leading the charge, was the source of the fiery flash, Orgos. He was a demon. Of the dozen or so men the raiders lost that day, I think Orgos killed half of them. Mithos ran with him and Garnet harried them from the saddle, his ax tracing wide and brutal arcs. I crept out from behind the wagon and stood up to watch.

It couldn't last. The raiders shrugged off our inexperienced infantry and, by sheer weight of numbers, put us on the defensive again. A crossbowman was hacked down beside Mithos and the last of the spearmen turned tail and fled towards the wagons. The raiders went after them, though they shied away from Mithos and Orgos, the only ones still standing firm.

"Fight me, damn you!" roared Orgos.

He leapt into the mass of bronze-and-crimson warriors with Mithos at his heels. Garnet's horse ploughed into the enemy and he leapt from it, swinging his ax as he dived. I caught a glimpse of Renthrette trading blows with two of them. There were dozens more. Absolute victory was theirs, but the party fought them still.

Then I saw Lisha. She stood apart, watching as the last of our men fell to the scyaxes. There were only two or three of our escort still fighting and the muddy earth was thick with corpses swathed in royal blue cloaks. Still, Lisha dug her heels into the glossy flanks of the black warhorse called Tarsha and crashed into the throng of the enemy.

"No!" I shouted.

The battle was lost. She heard me and for a split second her eyes found me out, oblivious to the plunging and stamping of her battle-trained stallion. Then she raised her black-shafted spear and struck downwards. There was a bluish spark like a small lightning storm, and a thunderous roar. I stared, astonished. Two raiders fell before her, and Tarsha's hooves rained down upon them. The rest of them parted before her in confused panic as she made her way to where the remainder of our company stood: Orgos and Mithos with their blades outstretched daring the enemy to attack, Garnet and Renthrette bleeding but angrily defiant, and two or three tattered soldiers from Greycoast, the last of our hundred-man escort. They gathered about Tarsha's steaming sides, and Lisha, her black hair spilling from her helm, looked sternly about her. I was pretty sure that sixty or more of the enemy remained, but only a couple of dozen were visible. The others had melted away in the mist, and that could mean only one thing: They were about to attack again.

It was now or never.

I slipped between the wagons and started to head in the opposite direction, hoping to lose myself in the misty fields till it was over. Then I could get a horse and head north. My adventuring days were done.

"Where shall we stand, sir?"

It was one of the Greycoast spearmen, who had recognized me. He had retreated to the wagons, to hide, probably, but now he had regained his laughable courage. He wasn't alone, either. There were five or six others, one with a horse and a couple with bows, all clinging to the shelter of the wagons but now watching me expectantly.

"Do what you like," I muttered, clambering over a dead horse to the far side of the road.

"Sir?" said the soldier.

"Be heroic," I muttered sarcastically. "Charge!"

"That way, sir?" said the bewildered soldier, squinting out into the misty emptiness where I was heading and then glancing back to where Mithos and the rest stood, squared for the final, inevitable assault on the other side.

"Oh, yes," I said. "Definitely this way, if you value your skins."

With that I started to run into the mist where it was densest, getting as far away from the wagons and the battle as I could. The few remaining stragglers ran after me, though God alone knew what they thought they were doing. Distantly I heard Orgos shouting at the enemy back there, but I ran on, gasping for breath, my heart thudding against my ribs, no thought in my head but escape.

Then the wind gusted, and everything changed.

The mist ahead shifted. It rippled clear for a moment and I saw the scarlet cloaks of forty men no more than ten yards away. They were dismounted, getting ready for a quiet attack on the rear that would wipe out the survivors. I would have sworn they hadn't been there only seconds before, but they were there now, and I had run right into them.

I froze. The heavy mist was coursing back into place all around us. They obviously hadn't seen me, and with care I might still slip by them and make a run for it. I was considering how I might do this when one of the infantrymen who had "fled" with me ran blindly into my back. I fell forward with a startled cry and, as I hit the ground, my temperamental crossbow went off. There was a shout of pain as one of the raiders twisted to the ground clutching his abdomen, and then a stuttering and scattered shout as the half-dozen men who had followed me pitched their spears and shot their bows.

The raiders were, of course, in no real danger. They were, however—perhaps for the first time in their savage career—taken completely off-guard. They weren't ready to fight and they didn't know whom they were fighting, where the enemy were, or how many they numbered. One horse fell, maybe more, and one of the Grey-coast troops got in close enough to lunge his spear into the stomach of one of the unwary raiders. No more than shadow figures in the thick mist, the raiders stumbled about in the confusion, trying to get back into their saddles, calling out to each other and nervously watching for their equally shadowy attackers. A few more arrows fell amongst them and I heard another shout of pain. I don't know if they lost any others, but I do know that in seconds they were gone: mounted and fled.

"Brilliant!" said one of the spearmen, wheezing heavily.

"What?" I gasped, still lying on the damp ground.

"That was a stroke of tactical genius," he said as the others gathered about us, exhausted and beaming. "And real courage," he went on. "It's an honor to serve under you, sir."

With that commendation and a grin of triumph, they hurried back to the wagons for more. I sat there in the mud for a moment and then, very slowly, followed.

By the time I found my way back to the road the survivors had gathered with the party. The raiders stood a hundred yards away, regrouped and orderly, though somehow you could tell that there was to be no final attack. I slipped in amongst the party, hoping that as Mithos's name had saved me in the burning village, so his presence would now. We stayed where we were, conscious of the wagons smoking behind us but staring at the crimson, faceless line.

And then the raider with the horned helm and the staff finally moved, raising his arms in some grand gesture. The staff traced a slow circle in the air and, as the raiders began to walk their mounts away, I had the odd impression that the mist was getting thicker around them. Only a solitary officer, distinguishable by the lateral plume across his helm, paused and looked back at us before he too pulled his horse around and rode slowly away into the mist. He seemed to fade as the fog thickened, and then they were gone.

The Fallen

Though many have fallen," called Orgos from atop one of the wagons, "we ride in triumph to Ironwall. We owe much, even our very lives, to each other and to those who didn't make it through. But we owe the most to one man whose courage and ingenuity saved the lives of many, perhaps of the convoy itself. When we reach Ironwall, we will celebrate, but for now let us simply cry, 'Three cheers for Will Hawthorne!' Hip hip, hoorah. Hip, hip . . ."

This came as something of a surprise to me, and for a split second I thought it was an unpleasant joke at my expense. But they cheered loudly and gripped my shoulder and shook my hand and said I was a good fellow and a dashed fine general. And since their saying so seemed to make everyone forget what a fiasco the whole thing had been, I took my praise modestly.

I caught Renthrette watching me thoughtfully. Our eyes locked and I couldn't think of anything to say. She tried to smile in an encouraging sort of way, but she still looked shocked and exhausted from the battle. I nodded quickly and looked away.

This was where I got off. I had seen enough and had decided that staying to be massacred with the rest of them was not my idea of a fun day out. I hadn't told them yet, but I was done.

Funnily enough, it was Orgos who had made me realize that this was no place for me. In his little post-slaughter speech he had said in his proud, warrior voice, "We leave the field honorably, and had they charged us at the end, they would have learnt to their cost that valor permits no surrender." He meant it, too. What I had intended as a prompt to get them to see the futility of what they were doing, he was echoing without a trace of irony.

Well, speak for yourself, mate. The road was littered with bodies.

We had been inches away from being a huddle of corpses beside a few burning wagons, another failed defense against the raiders; but we would have died honorably and that made it all right. No. Honor is just the carrot that leads donkeys like Orgos to pointless deaths, leaving the downtrodden without a champion and the tyrants secure as before. Call me pragmatic, call me cynical, but I didn't get it and I wasn't about to die for it.

Despite Orgos's words of honor and triumph, I detected a glimmer of panic amongst the party as they looked over the casualties. I suppose we are brought up to believe that the good guys always win in the end, though they might take a few tear-jerking losses along the way. Sooner or later the enemies are brought low by that superior skill, or that extra spark of intelligence, or that flash of magical power too mysterious for the narrator to have to justify it. Well, we hadn't seen any of that. They had wiped our force out and toyed with the survivors. I'd seen some more of that strange light from Orgos's sword, and something similar from Lisha's spear, but whatever such things were, they clearly weren't enough. For once, Lisha's party didn't have the edge, and—however much they tried to keep it to themselves—it shocked them like a spear in the side.

Before we set off I saw Mithos and Lisha standing together. He loomed over her in his stained armor and she talked up to him. Though I don't know what was said, it was a while before they parted. When he caught my gaze I thought he faltered for a moment before he spoke. "Give them a hand putting that fire out, Will. Then help Lisha collect the dead for burial."

I did, but I'm not going to talk about that.

⚜

There was something else as well, the icing on the whole horrible cake. We hadn't killed any of the raiders. Not one. There wasn't a single corpse on the battlefield wearing the scarlet and bronze of the enemy. This was troubling on several levels.

I had seen several of the raiders go down. I would have sworn that we had killed maybe a dozen—not a huge dent in their force, of course, but enough to prove they were mortal. I wandered the battlefield when the fog lifted, but there were none.

"The mist was thick," said Garnet. "They must have come back and taken away their dead while we were tending to our survivors."

"And the tracks?" said Renthrette, gazing out over the fields. "There are hoofprints on the battlefield itself. They radiate out for a couple of hundred yards. But beyond that, nothing. How did they get here? Where did they go?"

SCENE XXX

Ironwall

It was evening by the time we reached the city. A slight buzz of excitement rose up from the wagons as the citadel's towering walls and turrets came into view. In other circumstances I might have been impressed too, since it far outshone anything I'd ever seen in the Empire lands, but I was having a bad day. It seemed like I'd had a lot of bad days lately. Since I blamed my companions for that, I ignored their vaguely awestruck whispers about the scale of the fortifications and glowered at the Greycoast capital.

Ironwall looked like it had emerged from the earth. It was completely contained by its perimeter wall—no straggling inns and houses overspilling the city proper—and only the road we were on showed signs of civilization beyond its massive battlements. It breathed unassailable authority from its granite bulk. I shifted uneasily in my saddle as the thing got closer, filling the horizon and looming over us like storm clouds.

Renthrette had raised the beaver of her helm by the time we approached the huge gatehouse, but her face gave so little away that she might as well have kept it down. She had been like that since the battle: quiet, watchful, uncertain. It was weird and a little scary. If the raiders could leave her unsure of herself, then their powers had no limits.

She had ridden ahead to announce our coming, since it took about ten minutes to get the massive porticullis open, and by the time we got there, soldiers and townsfolk had gathered along the walls to watch our entry. I think they were cheering. I dismounted, tethered my horse to the back of the wagon, and climbed inside, where I felt less exposed. Garnet rode out to the front looking brave and stalwart.

An expensive-looking wagon bearing a silversmith's arms was stuck in the roadway, trying to get out of the city and head north.

The old man driving it paused to cheer us on. He wore a silver pendant at his throat shaped like a sun disk with a huge blue stone in the center. The cheering increased, muting only slightly as the corpse wagons passed over the bridge and into the city.

Duke Raymon had left his litter and stood before us, shaking Mithos by the hand and beaming conspicuously to the crowd. He was dressed in turquoise silk with a fur mantle and looked regally impressive. There was a touch of swagger in his gait, which may once have merely been his size but was now part of his politician's confidence. On either side of him stood Arlest, count of Shale, and Edwyn Treylen, governor of Verneytha. In a voice meant to be heard throughout the region, he said, "Welcome, thrice-noble Mithos and your honorable companions. Today you have shown the people of Greycoast that there is yet hope. The ruthless enemy of our people, the enemy indeed of the free world, will be vanquished. This cargo is of great import to us, but more so is this victory over the crimson tyrants who rape our land. Together we have shown them that we will not submit to their barbarism. Greycoast and its allies stand firm and will give no quarter to those who persecute the innocent. We will sorrow for those who fell, but we will also celebrate the dignity of their ends, for their blood has been turned to gold by the service they have performed for their country. We salute you all for your stand against evil."

The crowd exulted and waved their Greycoast flags. They threw flowers and their petals fell about us like snow. The injured remnants of our escort smiled proudly and shouted back words of triumph and determination. God help them.

❧

Only when we reached the palace did the duke's smile slip away. He began to scowl at us irritably before finally slamming his fist on the great walnut table before him and roaring, "Sixty-five dead and thirty injured? Three wagons destroyed and the contents of one other all but burnt up? You incompetent fools!"

I stared at him in astonishment as he released the chain clasp at his throat and shook off his fur mantle, his face red and ugly with sudden anger. Arlest was watching uncertainly, his features drawn and his eyes weary. The weaselish Treylen looked out of the window, as if stepping out of the room.

Mithos said, in a deliberately measured tone, "We brought the majority of the cargo to Ironwall as requested. The casualties we sustained were . . . regrettable, but apparently unavoidable."

"Unavoidable?" bellowed the duke, his mouth wide through his beard, the fat in his cheeks quivering. We were in his throne room, a large stone chamber surrounded by guarded archways from which his words echoed.

"Now, Raymon," said Arlest, conciliating. "I'm sure the party did what it could—"

The duke cut him off, continuing to berate us as if the count weren't really there. "You are professionals," he snorted, his voice full of derision, "but you can't protect a few wagons with a hundred men? How is it possible that you could have lost so heavily? And how is it possible that you pathetic mercenaries emerged unscathed?"

At these random insults and queries I saw Garnet, his green eyes suddenly lit with fury, lay his hand to the haft of his ax. Lisha also saw and touched his wrist gently with her fingertips. He froze. Mithos answered, "The men you gave us were untrained and inadequately equipped to deal with such an adversary."

"So you sent them in to protect your worthless hides?" shouted the duke.

"We stood in the front line," persisted Mithos, his voice still restrained, but with an increasing edge of bitterness. "We fought alongside them and organized them as best we could. Ask them. The enemy was vastly superior to our force, something we were unprepared for."

"Unprepared for?" the duke responded. "You were warned—"

"You gave us raw recruits!" Mithos inserted. "What did you expect?"

There was a frosty pause, and Treylen turned back from the window, as if he thought that what happened next might be interesting. Greycoast stepped up to Mithos's chest and whispered hoarsely into his face,

"How dare you interrupt me and toss me this abuse! You are in Ironwall now, friend, and I have great power here. Absolute power. If you do not learn some respect for your superiors, it will be beaten into you. Henceforth you will address me as 'sir' and speak only when you are asked to. Is that clear?"

Mithos looked at him silently, his fists clenched so that the olive skin of his knuckles whitened. By the heavy entrance door a pair of guards exchanged swift glances and swung the heads of their pikes round towards us. Treylen raised one eyebrow, curious to see how Mithos would respond.

"Is that clear?" repeated the duke of Greycoast, leaning closer still to Mithos.

"Yes," said Mithos slowly, adding, after a pause, "sir."

"Good," said the duke with an unpleasant smile of satisfaction. "Now—"

I couldn't take it anymore. "No, it's not good, and I'll respect my superiors when I meet them."

This was probably not the best thing I could have said, but I figured I was out of this farce for good, so what the hell. I continued, "I'm sure that Your Most Excellent Majesty was grieved that you couldn't be with us when the convoy was attacked, and I for one wish you had been around to enlighten us with your brilliant military mind, but you weren't. You see," I said, starting to feel good about myself for the first time in weeks, "I know it *sounds* like child's play, defending ten wagons of coal with a hundred soldiers who are waiting for their voices to break, but that's because you wouldn't know a battle plan if it bit you in your massive ass."

Lisha stirred but I cut her off before she could say anything.

"No," I said quickly, with a look in her direction, "it doesn't matter anymore, so I'll say what I like. Now, Your Royal Immensity, judging from your speech to the ignorant masses earlier, you either have no grasp on reality or choose to ignore it when it suits your political career."

I couldn't stop. I was enjoying myself, and he wasn't the only one who needed someone to blame. I pointed my finger squarely at him and went on. "You spoke of their dignified deaths. What do you know about death? I was there and there was no dignity. Not that you care. I'll bet the armed escort that brought you home from Seaholme was a sight better trained than the boy soldiers you left with us. But then, what's a hundred boys compared to a duke? You probably eat close to that at a sitting."

I sat down.

"Are you finished?" he murmured, with the kind of cold reserve that you know is going to explode any second.

"For the moment," I said cheerily.

"Did you know that throughout Greycoast, treachery is punishable by death, the traitors being hanged, drawn, and quartered?"

"No, I didn't know that."

"And do you know how we define treachery here?" asked the duke.

I thought for a moment and said, "Calling you a fat, self-important bastard would probably do it."

"Guards!" he called, lashing out with one heavily braceleted fist. They came at me with their pikes and rapiers. His knuckles caught me just under the chin, and I felt my head lurch up and back so that the room spun for a second. I whirled away from him, barely retaining consciousness as my teeth slammed together. The guards descended on me like hawks. They pinned my arms behind my back and, at the duke's cursory command of "Get him out of my sight," they marched me out. One guard gestured to Garnet in a way that suggested the misguided nature of any intervention on his part. They had to virtually carry me out of the room.

SCENE XXXI

More Consequences

I came to my senses (if you can call them that) as I was pitched headlong into mud, total darkness, and appalling stench. I was lying facedown in the slime of a dungeon floor, my legs chained together. The dampness and cold suggested that I was underground, in the palace basement, perhaps: the lowest point of the citadel in more ways than one. I rolled over and tried to spit the filth from my mouth. I tried to sit up, but the mud squirmed beneath me and I fell back into it. The odor of excrement and decay was overpowering. A thin line of pale light showed under the door. Sliding up to it, hands sunk to the wrists in the ooze, I began to kick and shout.

My face was right up against the door when the jailer on the other side kicked it and sent me sprawling on my back.

"Shut up," he shouted without looking in, "or I'll come in and break your legs. Both. Several times." Someone laughed, impressed with this display of wit.

Miserably I floundered across to the far wall—the cell was only about ten feet square—and sat against it trying to believe that they couldn't keep me here long. Such thoughts led rather inevitably to the question of what would happen to me when they brought me out.

I went over the incident with the duke and replayed the scene in my mind a dozen times with a few more incisive remarks assigned to yours truly. I soon had a tidy little plot in which straight-from-the-shoulder Will scared the cruel despot into gross abuse of his power, but even as I was reflecting on how it would bring the house down, I knew it was false. Here was no honor, only misery and shame. But why should a lack of honor bother me, of all people? What was really bothering me was how stupidly pointless my outburst had been. It could never have gotten me anywhere other than here, something I had known before I started talking, but I started anyway. I enjoyed

making speeches, but I had a sneaking suspicion that there had been
something righteous in my motivation, something distressingly principled. Or, at the very least, something like guilt for the pretty
shameful circumstances that had the people of Ironwall thinking of
me as a hero. It was an alarming notion.

The time passed slowly. I called out for water, suspecting that
beer wasn't on the menu, but only got more abuse and distant laughter from the less hopeful inmates of other cells. I had to go to the
bathroom and did so in a corner, then sat as far away from it as possible with my back against the scummy wall. Thick, foul-smelling
liquid coursed down the mossy rock. It soaked my back and made
me shudder with cold and a sense of contamination.

In another part of the subterranean jail someone was being
whipped. Long, slow lashes rang out and cracked into agonized
gasps. I thought I saw a rat slide in under the door but I never saw it
leave. I wanted to block off the crack with my soiled shirt to keep
them out, but if they were already in with me, then that would make
the problem worse. I listened and heard their thin voices. One time I
put my hand down on warm, matted fur and pulled myself away
screaming as the creature's thin, fibrous tail slipped through my fingers. I got to my feet and stood quite still. Hours passed.

When the door was abruptly kicked open, I leapt through it and
sprawled into the relative light of a circular stone chamber. The jailer
kicked me once with a heavy leather boot and then put his weight on
the small of my back, making me gasp and splutter through the
muddy straw in my face. Seizing me by the hair, he wrenched my head
up into the light of a torch, and I caught its pitchy scent with something like relief.

"This one?" he said brusquely. I heard a murmur of assent from
close by but could see nothing but the blinding flare of the torch.
"Get out," said the jailer. He kicked me squarely in the rear and
added, "And get a wash." The guard laughed like it was the funniest
thing he'd heard for days.

The irons were stripped roughly from my legs, and a sack was tied
over my head. I was dragged up a flight of steps by two men. A third
followed, a spear point pressed against my spine. We passed through
long, echoing corridors of cold stone and then, as I was steeling myself for whatever verbal reprimand I was about to get, we stepped out
into the open air. I was flung hard onto a wooden platform of some

kind and then, with sudden and terrified panic, I heard it: the familiar bustle of an expectant crowd. As the bag was dragged from my head I saw a sea of upturned faces and the chill shadow of a gallows.

You have got to be kidding, I thought.

They weren't.

There was Duke Raymon, large and impassive, flanked by his counterparts from Shale and Verneytha, watching me from a throne ten yards away. He met my gaze and then bade the shirtless, hooded executioner begin. Two guards dragged me forward and forced my head through the noose as I struggled and kicked, tying my hands behind me as they did so. Arlest, the only one I could see showing any kind of concern, was muttering earnestly to Raymon, who ignored him, then said something to Treylen, who just smiled thinly and shrugged. When the count of Shale continued to talk, the duke turned and shook his head once, glaring and final. Whatever Arlest had been trying to do to stop this brutal farce, the duke was having none of it.

Arlest looked across the crowd and shook his head fractionally. I followed his gaze and saw Mithos watching. He looked down, then straightened up and began pressing his way through the people, making for where the duke was sitting. I wanted to see what happened, but there was a man in a black hood who had other plans.

The executioner took the slack out of the rope and stood before me, a viciously curved and jagged knife in his hands. I should have known that a simple hanging was too much to hope for. The brazier for my intestines was brought forward and, as the executioner began to unfasten my filthy shirt, a great hush descended on the crowd. Whatever Mithos was doing, it didn't seem to be slowing things down.

I stood on my toes as they began to hoist me up, but in a second I felt all my weight on the rope which cut into my throat. My feet flailed for some purchase on the ground, but it was too late. I hung there for a long, sickening moment, and then dropped, gasping and retching on the floor. The executioner gave me a few seconds, and then hitched me up again. I looked up as the rope started to tighten and saw Duke Raymon.

He had left his throne and now stood next to me, center stage, as it were, switching his eyes from me to the crowd and back. Mithos— unarmed—was hovering behind him. Then he held up his hand and the world fell silent.

"Perhaps you would like to say something, Mr. Hawthorne?" he said, loud enough for everyone to hear. I thought quickly, and for a split second Mithos's eyes met mine. This was one of those key performances when you had to get the lines just right.

"I throw myself upon your gracious mercy, Lord Duke," I managed.

A ripple went through the crowd and the duke's lip twitched fractionally. This was what he had wanted. "Is that all?" he said indulgently, his voice louder. I gasped for breath and swallowed.

"I humbly beg pardon for offending your royal personage and can only plead unfamiliarity with the customs of your land and the great authority you so rightly hold. I throw myself upon your merciful generosity and—"

"Enough!" he shouted, and it was a call to the executioner and to the crowd. As the one cut me free, the other cheered rapturously, lauding the duke's spontaneous and benign wisdom. He gestured expansively as they carried me away, and the audience—for that was what it was—applauded wildly.

But if he had emerged as the benevolent and omnipotent ruler, I had at least emerged, and that was more than I had hoped for. It took some time for the horror of it all to subside. I would never know how much of the outcome had been planned in advance or whether my apology had made any difference. Well, I thought, as I scrubbed myself down and chose a clean shirt, I had lost nothing by making it. After all, they were only words.

The only real catch was that my decision to leave the party had been temporarily stymied. The duke had cut off our expenses after my little outburst, and though he had forgiven me for my "treason," he hadn't renewed our funds. Mithos came to see me and made things clear: The party figured I owed them. I told him that I was the one who had talked my neck out of the noose, but he said he had been trying to talk Raymon round since the moment I was arrested, and that he had also got Count Arlest to petition on my behalf. Without his intercession, he said, I would not have been allowed to "talk my neck out of the noose."

I wanted to argue because I didn't want to feel dependent on him or the party, but he clearly had a point. So I shrugged and muttered a thank-you, and said I would stick around, help out, and so on. However, Mithos, who was apparently prepared for me to make conciliatory noises, was not to be fobbed off with platitudes. He announced that I could start by earning some money. How was up to me.

I grinned. War, honor, political decorum: these things were beyond me. But sing for my supper? That, I could do. And I knew just the song.

SCENE XXXII

The Elixir of Sensenon

It was midmorning. The sun was warm as I passed out of the palace gates and wandered down towards the market, strolling along the fortifications whose towers bore the decomposing heads of traitors and murderers. It was good to be free and breathe the clear air again. I whistled as I went about my business, stowing the flasks I had prepared in a leather satchel.

The Ironwall market was a delight. I glanced around and got an idea where the guards were, assessed the general affluence of the townsfolk, borrowed a box from a copper worker, and set it up in the middle of the square. Getting onto it, I took a deep breath and began the show. "Gather round, ladies and gentleman. Yes, madam, you too. Gather round to hear of something that will change your life. No sir, I am no priest, prophet, or preacher. I am an apprentice to the sage priests of the Ottorian dragon herders who has seen marvels now told only in the tales of children."

A couple going though a selection of pots and pans at a nearby stall stopped to listen, shading their eyes against the sun. A cluster of merchants beside them turned my way as well. It was starting.

"I have ridden the northwinds astride the ice wyverns," I announced, in a full hit-the-back-wall voice. "I have crossed the Southern Ocean with Arrulf the pirate, who paints his toes with the blood of virgins and eats gold at every meal. I passed a year with the lizardmen in caves east of the Grey Forest, and dined with trolls in the fiery chasms of the western volcanoes. I resided four winters in the Library of Lore (ancient and modern) under the tutelage of Erelthor, high mage of the Council of Light. And after these my wanderings, I have come to your humble market, and I bring you life."

There was quite a crowd gathering now. I could see the skeptics on the outside smiling and nudging their friends, but that was no matter. There are always enough fools, and besides, I was good at this. If the skeptics wound up paying out with the rest of them, it wouldn't be the first time.

"Good people of Greycoast! Worthy residents of Ironwall! I bring you the elixir of Sensenon! After years of study and penitent worship, the council has permitted me to sell a small amount of the elixir to the world, the place commanded by divination and the drawing of numbers. You, proud Ironwall in the land of Greycoast, have been selected!

"Oh, Sensenon, after these long centuries your people will finally be satisfied! No more will they suffer the chills of winter or the fevers of summer. No more will their skin age and their eyes fail! Lo, it says in the book of Onthrast: 'Their cheeks shall be as babes and they shall see ants on the horizon and count their legs.'

"It will build your muscle and lose your fat. See the results in less than a week! It will make you potent and fertile, witty and intelligent. Yes, madam, it cures piles. Certainly, it straightens bones, enlarges the brain, strengthens nails, gives sheen and body to hair, beautifies complexion, and richens eye color. Ladies, apply it your skin and body hair falls away. Gentlemen, do likewise for a full and lusty beard. Can you afford to turn away?

"Across continents I have searched for the ingredients and measured them out as Sensenon prescribed. For each vial, a blend of badger bile and seven hairs from the snout of a grizzly bear are added to the ground beak of a Hrof ostrich, a sliver of the bamboo found only in the rain forest of the Xeltark, and a pinch of the moss that grows above the snow line on Mount Valten. These are simmered for three years in a special distillation of Thrusian brandy and Stavissian hemlock, and into them are stirred powdered pearls and emeralds. The whole is seasoned with bee urine and shaken in a cup of purest gold lined with leaves of the screaming mandrake. It is brought to a boil for exactly thirty-seven seconds in the dragon-breath furnace of Salhayazim, and stirred with the fibula of a ruby-throated leaping wombat as the secret words of completion are breathed into it. At last, it is ready and I present it to you, Sensenon's all-natural elixir— yours, for a limited time only, for just two gold pieces."

That last part was true, at least, for I always drop the price by half after five minutes, once the real morons have gone home satisfied. Ten minutes after that I'd drop it by half again. In a country village I might go lower, but in a worldly-wise hub of commerce like this place, they won't buy if you go too cheap. They figure that expensive means good.

The party arrived halfway through. I ignored them and sold my wares, figuring their speeches about truth and virtue and how naughty it was to tell fibs would be shorter and easier to ignore if I'd made them a potful of money. This turned out to be right.

But as I was packing up, having made a tidy twenty-eight gold pieces and a handful of change, Garnet said, "Have you got any left?"

"Any what?"

"Any of the elixir."

I gave him an odd look. "Why?"

"Well," he said, "if it does only half the things you said it does, then—"

"It doesn't," I said quickly, with something like shock. "Why should it?"

"Well," he said guilelessly, "your learning, and the special ingredients . . ."

"Learning have I none," I said, smiling. "As for the ingredients, well, it's mainly puddle water, clay, and something a little special of my own that you don't want to hear about. There are a few flower petals in there, but not enough to make it palatable."

Garnet looked at me in silence. I'd just sold the last bottle to one of the guards, who now leaned against a gibbet holding a corpse labeled CUTPURSE. I shrugged and slid the gold through my fingers into Lisha's bag.

"Well done, Will," she said.

"My pleasure," I replied honestly.

Romance

In the Eagle, tales of adventuring had always been stuffed full of colossal dragons, all insatiable greed, murderous fury, and breath that would singe your eyebrows at four hundred yards: absolute evil in physical form. I'd never *believed* that rubbish, of course—nobody did—but even a hard-line realist like me would like to be proved wrong from time to time. Not too often, mind. I don't know what I'd do if I met some hulking troll in a dark alley. A smallish goblin would be all right, I suppose: something I could kill without too much effort or qualms of conscience. That had always seemed the core attraction of life wearing a sword in stories: You could hack and slay all day and then put the pile of corpses down to honor, the triumph of goodness, the protection of puppies, and so on.

It didn't seem to work like that in reality, though I wasn't sure Garnet and Renthrette had figured that out yet. For them, there was always a line drawn, and they were on the side of truth, justice, and sunshine. There were a lot of people on the other side of the line, and once you were over there you could very easily became ax meat. This was disturbing for someone like me, who frequently wandered from one side of the line to the other without even realizing it.

Lately I'd been on fractionally better terms with Renthrette, though that wasn't saying much, and even that limited progress had less to do with her feeling more comfortable with me and more to do with feeling less comfortable with the mission, if you see what I mean. She had made her disdain for my moral status clear after my conciliatory words to the duke (the fact that he had been ready to execute me did not strike her as relevant) and had referred to my money-raising methods as "snakish and deceitful," so we weren't exactly ready for candlelit dinners, but she called me stupid less often and always seemed to be weighing the things in my character that nauseated her (most of them) against my undeniable, if erratic, usefulness to the party. Whenever I did something right she would give me a long look of muted surprise, as if she were watching a camel say the alphabet at high speed: unexpectedly praiseworthy but somehow suspect. I'd bought her a drink a few nights before and she gave me that very look when I didn't try to weasel my way into her affections and/or underwear. Even I wasn't certain what I was doing, since I'd pretty much given up hope of progress in that direction. Pretty much.

I hadn't met many women lately, because the party members always seemed to be watching me like the vultures we'd seen in the Hrof, their faces heavy with sermons on virtue or equality. I watched keenly for signs of romantic goings-on amongst the group, but everything seemed cerebral and professional, curse them. I had thought people went into adventuring for romance (sex) and excitement (sex). It was just my luck to hitch up with the only celibate mercenaries in Thrusia. I started saying what a good physique Lisha had to Garnet, but his green eyes started to get that cold, homicidal look, so I dropped it. I said nothing of Renthrette, fearful that Mithos or Orgos would show interest and then I'd really be screwed. Or, rather, I wouldn't. I liked to pretend I had a chance, even if she was only just getting over the impulse to put a dagger through my windpipe every time she saw me.

A sample piece of recent dialogue: "You have beautiful eyes," I said to her, very smooth over the top of my tankard. We were sitting in a tavern waiting for the others to join us and she was drinking tea (for God's sake!).

"Oh right," she said with the smallest of smiles that turned into something grimmer around the edges. "I'm supposed to be flattered. You can compliment me on my eyes because that's classy, whereas to refer to my breasts would be crude."

"But your eyes, er . . . show your personality," I faltered.

"I might not know the theatre, but I've seen the poetry, Will. Eyes are just part of the catalogue. Eyes like crystal, isn't it? Ruby lips and ivory skin. Then ankles, thighs, and so on, down the list. The composite woman. A collection of parts for your pleasure."

"It's not as if I'm not attracted to you as a person," I said.

"Meaning what, Will? I pour nothing but derision on you all day, but if I came to your bed at night, you'd be all over me like sauce on one of your succulent entrees."

"Well, I don't know about that," I lied.

"Oh, please."

"Well, all right. Maybe so," I confessed, trying to smile in a winningly flirtatious way. "So what?"

"So 'as a person' doesn't extend beyond this body, which happens to fit all your little criteria?"

"Most of them," I muttered.

"What?"

"Your nose is a little . . ."

"Thanks, Will." (That was sarcastic, in case you missed it.) "But at least you're being honest, for once. Fortunately, I am feeling charitable and will refrain from going through the list of ways in which you, physically, don't make the grade."

That stung.

"What is your problem, exactly?" I said irritably. "What is it that got so stuck up you that you can't get it out?"

"How apt." She smiled. "I must have something stuck up me because it isn't you. How like a man."

I was, for once, speechless. She was quite calm, even amused, which was new for her. The worst part was that she was right. A million times I'd heard some oaf lumber back to his barroom mates and tell them that the girl who had just blown him off was "a right bitch" or "not that pretty when you got close" and I had always smiled knowingly to myself. Now I was the oaf, and there was no dark corner and group of friends to bring me solace. I felt like the fox scowling up at the grapes he couldn't reach. What a bitch.

The upside, however, had been the ease—even the enjoyment—with which she had rejected my oafish advances. There had been no vitriolic screaming, no threats of evisceration, no torrents of frosty contempt, and when I had abandoned the chase she had actually smiled, as if it had been a kind of game we were playing and she had won a round. Later, when the others did show up to make plans for whatever new madness we were to embark upon, I caught her looking at me. When I turned my sulky face towards her, her grin had been so open and knowing that I found myself returning it.

Since we would learn nothing in the palace, we had decided to split the party and stay in inns scattered about the city. Lisha and Orgos would be in the Silversmith's Arms, an upmarket place for traders and the local gentry. Garnet and Renthrette went to a middle-class tavern called the Bear's Paw. I got the cheap end of town (surprise, surprise), and would spend the next night in the dubiously titled Swan with Two Necks, dodging cutthroats and pickpockets. The fact that I was sharing a room with Mithos didn't especially cheer me up, since he tended to be a sort of portable storm cloud: largely dark and silent, occasionally brightening up to flash lightning and thunder at you. Still, maybe I'd get a game of cards.

Just before I left with Mithos, I made a point of examining Lisha's black-shafted spear. I hadn't forgotten that odd blue lightning flash. I was unsurprised to find that the silver metal of the spear's ferrule, where the shaft fit into the tip, was set with a large irregularly shaped blue stone. It didn't make me feel any better.

SCENE XXXIV

The Ritual

M ithos and I walked our horses down to the eastern edge of the city. Much of the second level, below the palace and public buildings, was a walled enclosure of public grazing land and private crop fields that were designed to keep the citadel going in times of hardship. Since the majority of the region's agricultural produce came from Verneytha by road, this was going to be one of those times. Below the cobbled, narrow, and spiraling streets were vast water cisterns, cut out of the rock and fed by springs. If need be, this place could close its gates for a very long time.

The citadel made up in fortifications what it lost in military presence. Soldiers patrolled the walls, but there weren't many of them for a city this size: just four hundred. Garnet and Renthrette had it all penciled out: half infantry, half local militia. The latter were mainly city police and would not be called upon in the event of a military confrontation. That was what Shale was for. Still, with fortifications like this, Greycoast didn't need much to defend the place.

Our tavern lay up against the far eastern wall of the citadel in a maze of narrow streets with butchers' shops on every corner. Greying meat was laid out on stone slabs in the sun where old women fanned at flies as they haggled over prices. Rabbits were suspended from poles, and cow heads, as yet unskinned or de-eyed, watched us from the gloomy interiors.

The Swan with Two Necks was the kind of hole you might have expected it to be, so I won't waste time telling you about its various surprisingly unpleasant aromas and their close relationship with the clientele. It was the kind of place you went armed to and carried only as much as you intended to spend. Its menu was miserable but it had, as a house special, a dish intriguingly named after the tavern itself. We ordered this with cheerful expectation, but the "swan with two necks" turned out to be a scrawny chicken with two hopefully positioned blood sausages. Delightful.

"How long do we have to stay in this dump?" I wanted to know.

"A night or two," said Mithos, pulling gristle balls from his teeth and pushing them to the side of his plate. "No more. We just have to ask around. See if anyone can tell us anything interesting."

"Is that likely?" I asked, regarding the bar's dodgy-looking patrons.

"No," said Mithos shortly, "though I expect everyone has a theory."

"Well, we'll see," I said, cheerfully producing a pack of cards.

Mithos gave me a look and said, "Be careful, Will. There aren't enough of us to bail you out tonight."

"Come now, Mithos," I said, "Cautious Will?"

☙❧

We spent the next two hours moving around the tavern individually, asking leading questions about raider attacks. Not subtle, I confess, but fairly safe, since it seemed that the inn was holding a Village Idiot convention. An eager young man told me that the raiders were a fiction created by a top-level group of conspirators whose motives were obliquely linked to a suppression of the lower social orders. The barmaid had it on good authority that they were ghost riders who vanished at dawn. One genius produced a matchbox from an inside pocket and confided that he only let the raiders out when his wife beat him for coming home drunk. . . .

The less hopelessly moronic people that I spoke to presumed I was an adventurer wanting to hire myself out as a guard. A fur trader offered me fifty silvers to ride with him to the Hopetown market. I tried to get him to pay me in advance but he wasn't that stupid. I made friends with a couple of young ladies and introduced one of them to Mithos. He just shook his head and moved away. The ladies, irritated at his lack of interest, doubled their prices, and that was my night blown.

Close to midnight the room was starting to empty. All around us people were pushing clubs and daggers into conspicuous scabbards to deter attackers in the dark streets. Only then did the barman come over and tell us we had a guest. He was sitting by the empty fireplace, a heavy and moth-eaten cloak drawn about him. We approached and he rapped on a pair of chairs with a stick. We sat and listened.

"Been asking about the raiders? Not adventurers neither, else you'd have taken up with the fur man. So, different interest. Like me."

He looked at us suddenly and his face was sweaty and scarred, ugly in the lamplight. His eyes had a mad, sightless look.

"Yes," said Mithos simply, leaning closer to him. I had begun to notice something about him that I didn't like, a smell not unlike the rancid butchers we had passed earlier. Dirt and blood, caked and drying. Foul.

"You want to taste the power," he rasped. His voice had a thick, sluggish quality that made me faintly nauseated. Mithos nodded and drank from his mug.

"Drink," said the man significantly. "Drink ale till you can get something better."

I stared hard at Mithos. I had a very bad feeling about this.

"Drink of the destroyer and you'll never be destroyed," rasped the voice. "I know where it is, if you want it. Though it will cost you."

"How much?" said Mithos mechanically.

"A little gold." He shrugged. "Maybe more. But you know it's worth it."

"What is it?" Mithos asked, and I saw a tension in his shadowed face.

"The ritual," he answered, "the blood charm. The life of a raider engorged with the lives of his victims. Yours for the drinking. Yours for life."

He leaned close to me and smiled. Something black and coagulated stuck between his rotten teeth. His breath smelled like decaying flesh. I turned away, suppressing the bile in my throat.

"Take us there," said Mithos, rising.

The stranger rose and lurched towards the door, swaying strangely, his dark, decrepit cloak trailing through the sawdust. We followed.

He led us through the streets, through alleys I wouldn't have dared to pass at this time of night in other circumstances, though I was too focused on the shambling figure in front of us to worry about anything as mundane as a mugging.

"What are we doing?" I whispered to Mithos.

"I'm not sure," he replied, "probably nothing of any use. Still, we've nothing better to do."

I could think of a hell of a lot of things that were better than wandering the lightless streets with this foul-smelling maniac, but I said nothing.

All of a sudden we came to an unmarked doorway. He led us inside and up a narrow, creaking stairway. I put a hand into my cloak and gripped the hilt of my shortsword. At the top of the stairs was a big man with a shaved head and a spiked mace. I let go of my sword. Behind him was a curtain of wooden beads, and as our guide muttered to him, he stepped aside and we passed through.

On the other side we found ourselves in a small room dimly lit with thick candles that made the walls flicker madly. The bead curtain rattled behind me and I felt eyes turn upon us. There were people arranged in a circle around what looked like an altar stone. The stone was at least six feet long and on it rested the body of a headless man. He was naked, and a similarly naked but ancient woman was chanting over his corpse, opening his veins with a large knife. There was blood all over her.

"Oh, this is great," I hissed at Mithos, "I just love black-magic rituals. They're so *rational*. And they attract such nice people." I tugged desperately at his sleeve, whispering, "Let's get the hell out of here. Now."

Silently he nodded at the corpse's feet, where clothes and armor were piled. I saw the folded scarlet cloak and the bronze cuirass. There was no helm, but since there was no head, that wasn't surprising. I looked at Mithos again for explanation but he was staring at the naked priestess or whatever she was. Her tired flesh hung in ripples and bags, which the candlelight caught and emphasized.

She was collecting the corpse's thickened blood in a goblet, mixing it with some strong-smelling alcohol to make it fluid, and heating it over a candle, all the while chanting something inaudible under her breath. The air was heavy with the scent of blood and hot wax. It stuck in my throat. The woman pushed her hand into the corpse and there was a sucking sound. I looked away at this, but Mithos pressed a coin into the hand of our guide, who was leering at us with gruesome satisfaction, and started whispering to him. "Where did you get the body?"

"North, towards Hopetown. They attacked a wagon of silver

traders. Killed them all. Only this one of the raiders fell. We have his blood, his life. Now it is time to drink."

"Actually," I muttered, "now that you mention it, I think I'll pass after all. I'm sure it's delicious, but I had a really big dinner. . . ." I stopped as the priestess took a long gulp from the chalice and some of the thick liquid dribbled down her chin. I could bear no more.

Blundering out, down the stairs and into the street, I spat and gasped and waited for Mithos to follow.

He didn't. Ten minutes passed before he emerged, wiping his face and marching me swiftly along the narrow street back towards the Swan.

"What happened?" I gasped.

He didn't reply, just kept walking. I repeated the question but he muttered, "Nothing. Come on. This is a dangerous area."

He didn't relax till we were back at the inn. He threw himself onto his bed and sighed up at the ceiling.

"Such a pleasant evening," I said.

"Yes."

"And worthless."

"No," he said, "it wasn't." Fishing in his pocket, he produced a small leather purse. "This was taken from round the raider's neck."

He emptied it onto the floor and I pulled the lamp closer to see. Some small coins rolled out and under the bed. A square of stiff paper fell to the ground. It was a pass to the Hopetown market dated three days ago. The blank spaces on the printed card had been filled out by a strong hand in black ink. "Permission given to a group of six under the name of Mr. Joseph (trade party leader) to trade in the Hopetown market for the date of 7.7." Three days ago.

"Which means what?" I said.

"It means we head north at first light," said Mithos. "Better get some sleep."

He blew out the candle and I lay there in the dark, trying not to think about the blood ritual, or what Mithos might have done to get his information.

The Hopetown Road

By nine o'clock we had gathered the party and were making for Hopetown. They were right about that portcullis. It was still closing almost ten minutes after we'd gone through it. Of course, you could see for miles from the walls and towers, so there was no danger of an army catching them with their pants down.

The dangers of the road notwithstanding, I was glad to leave Ironwall, with its self-important duke and its blood-drinking inhabitants. A couple of times I spoke to Mithos about that night, but he didn't seem to want to talk about it. After a while, neither did I. We had our clue and I chose to forget how we'd got it.

We traveled incognito, you might say, most of our armor concealed by voluminous cloaks and hoods. Orgos, being the most easily recognizable in these uncosmopolitan parts, rode inside the wagon with me. I sat at the tailgate, cradled my crossbow in my lap, and prayed I wouldn't have to use it.

I didn't. We'll never know if some scout of the raiders watched from the distant hills and decided we weren't worth attacking, but that suited me. We reached Hopetown shortly after sundown, rented rooms at the Bricklayer's Arms under the name of Morgan, and unloaded crates of iron and copperware that we had hurriedly purchased in Ironwall. We dined on fat-basted potatoes and roast pork with lots of bristly crackling. Garnet and Renthrette had a salad.

"Tell us a story, Will," said Mithos, his eyes closed and his head back.

Orgos caught my eye and nodded. I thought of something suited to my audience, took a long breath, and began:

> "Unto the court of Sardis came a knight,
>   Whose name the scribes of legend have set down
>   As Helthor, mightiest soldier of the line

Whose gleaming sword full many a man has slain.
He longed to lead proud Sardis into war
And vanquish cities with its valiant host,
As if he meant to torch the universe,
Or grind its stars to powder 'neath his heel."

And so it went on. It lasted close to an hour and they were silent throughout. At the end, when Helthor finally gets his just deserts and the stage (it was my own adaptation of an old play) is strewn with bodies, there was a long, satisfied pause. Garnet, who had listened with great attentiveness asked, "And how did Helthor's child rule Sardis?"

I gave him a long, silent look. There was something in his voice that said he thought the story was true, like I had known this mythical psychopath personally. I knew he was neither joking nor stupid, but this was one of his curious blind spots. Renthrette tried to give me a hostile look but she looked faintly confused. I had to say something to Garnet, but the question was all wrong. The story was over and Helthor's son ceased to exist as soon as I concluded the epilogue. The son was closure, the restoration of order and promise of better things to come, nothing more. I answered him carefully.

"He lived long and happily, ruled his country well, and was accounted a great king and a good man."

Garnet watched me thoughtfully for a moment. Everyone was silent.

"Good," he said simply. And I suppose it was. Hadn't I said all tales were true once told? They form a kind of reality, even if it's one we can't live in.

Having said that, of course, reality—my reality—had gotten rather odd of late. Aside from the horrors of being an adventurer, whatever that was supposed to be, I was still struggling with some key details that didn't fit my pragmatic worldview. First there was Orgos's sword and Lisha's spear. Then there was the raiders' ability to appear and disappear without leaving the slightest trace.

I started with Orgos.

"Are you ready to hear the answer this time?" he said.

I nodded. It was a lie, but I didn't actually say anything, so it was only kind of a lie, right?

"The sword is an artifact of power," he said. "It was a gift from

Arthen of Snowcrag. I believe he found it, though he never said where. You've heard of such things, surely?"

"In stories," I sneered, and then stopped myself and said simply, "Yes."

"The stories are true," he said, equally simply. "The artifacts are rare, most of them are very old, and most people who have one either don't recognize what it is or don't know how to use it, but they are real."

"And you have one," I said.

"And know how to use it," he replied. It wasn't a boast, just a statement of fact.

"And Lisha's?" I ventured.

He gave me a quick look. He didn't know I'd seen it.

"Yes," he said. "Lisha has one too. Its power is a little different from mine, more versatile. I don't know all it can do."

"Are there any others I should know about?" I asked, trying not to sound snide. "I mean, if Renthrette has a magic bottle opener or something . . ."

"We have no others," he said.

"How do they work?" I asked. "I mean, I know . . . *magic,* and all," I said, trying not to sound like an idiot, though saying that word with a straight face made you sound like an idiot all by itself, "but how, exactly?"

"The crystal is what gives the artifact its power and character," said Orgos, "though using it requires something of the wielder as well."

"Like what?"

"It depends on the artifact, though they all need tremendous mental focus and a sense of purpose from anyone trying to use them."

"So I couldn't use it," I said, grinning.

"No," he answered. "I can use mine, that's all. I couldn't use Lisha's if I tried, and I doubt she could use mine. They are very . . . *individual* items. Mine requires a total faith in the righteousness of my cause."

"Naturally," I said.

"You wanted to know about it," he said, a tad defensive.

"Let me try."

I was kidding, really, but he drew it and passed it to me without a second thought. I took it and felt its weight in my hand. Then I stood up, threw back my shoulders, and held the sword above my head. I shut my eyes and focused. Nothing happened.

"Is there a magic word or something?" I said, squinting at Orgos with one eye.

"No magic word," he said, smiling.

I shut my eyes and concentrated as hard as I could for about a minute; then I gave it back to him.

"I think it's broken," I said.

He grinned and sheathed it.

And did I believe any of it? I'm really not sure. I had seen things I couldn't explain. This explained them. Kind of. I remembered how the sight of the sea had alarmed me in Stavis because it had shown me how out of my element I was. I wasn't sure what "my element" meant anymore, especially since the Empire had shut the theatres down and tried to string me up as a rebel, but magic swords? Come on. If they didn't exist, I was screwed, because my life depended on people who thought they did, and if they did exist, I was screwed, because . . . well, just because. How could I even live in a world where the words "magic sword" weren't a kind of joke?

It was as if Mithos had been listening in on my thoughts and had devised a way to make me feel that, if I wasn't exactly in my element, I could at least function usefully. The innkeeper, he said, had told us where we could get permits for the market. Since it was close by, he said we should take a pitch-covered torch and go right away.

It was late by the time we reached the office, but light showed under the door, so Mithos knocked loudly, then turned to me and whispered, "Take over, Will."

"What?" I gasped, caught off-guard.

"Do what you do," he said. "Talk."

"It's after eleven o'clock!" shouted a voice inside. "Come back tomorrow."

I waited for a second, but Mithos just shrank into the shadows and stood there in silence.

"Er . . . open up," I ventured, knocking louder, "we need to see you now."

"Why?" demanded the voice, irritably. There was movement inside and I heard a woman giggle.

"We need to check your records from the Saturday market."

"You can't, they're not public property. You need a warrant, or something. Can't see them. Good night."

Mithos tapped me on the arm with Duke Raymon's seal. Ignoring it, my face pressed to the door, I spoke again, my voice officious. "I'm from the inspection office. Come on, come on. I haven't got all night. I have to have the documents updated by tomorrow morning." Mithos's tap with the seal became more insistent.

"You'd better have all the proper papers," said the voice inside, "or I'm not showing you anything."

"I just want a look at one day's entries," I said, trying to sound official. "Though I could go back to the duke, get the paperwork which is so dear to your heart, and proceed to check every single market permit you have issued this year to make sure that number agrees precisely with your total commission." There was a sudden silence and I knew I had the old chiseler. If this was anything like Cresdon, he would be issuing fake permits to account for the income he made from bribes. "Just show me the ledger and I'll take care of the paperwork," I concluded. "No questions asked."

There followed muffled curses, a pensive silence, and then the sound of a couple of bolts being snapped back. Mithos, after one last poke with the seal I wasn't going to use, stepped out of sight.

A middle-aged man with a potbelly, a robe thrown around him and belted with cord, stuck his head round the door.

"Is this really necessary?"

"Just get the ledger, will you, sir?" I said in the bored and superior tone of the petty bureaucrat. "It won't take but a second, and you'll still be employed in the morning. There now," I added with the sarcastic condescension I had heard from Empire patrols a thousand times, "won't that be nice?"

"I live here, you know," said the man. "It's not just an office. It's my home. No privacy."

"I'm deeply moved," I said.

"What do you need?" muttered the man, resignedly.

"Market permits applicable to last Saturday," I said, starting to follow him through the doorway. Potbelly turned on me with quick embarrassment, shielding the room's interior and its sniggering inhabitant with his body.

"Just wait there, if you please," he said, glancing over his shoulder. "I'll bring you what you want. Last Saturday? Right."

He shuffled off, whispering to his girlfriend or whore, who was hissing like a bag of vipers. He clumped around and returned to the doorway's rectangle of light with a heavy ledger in his hands.

"Can I use your table, or something?" I asked, taking the book brusquely.

"I'd rather you didn't," said the man, awkwardly shifting his feet. "Someone not paying market taxes?" he added to fill the silence.

"Among other things," said I, without looking up. "Thank you for your assistance. Have a good evening."

I heard the woman giggle again as the door closed and figured that he would.

I joined the others in the shadows outside.

"There were five parties registered under the name of Joseph on Saturday," I said as soon as we were out of earshot, "but only three of them were six-man groups. We have addresses for all of them."

"Are you going to explain that little performance?" asked Mithos.

"What's to explain?" I said innocently.

"We have the seal! We don't need to take chances with stories!"

"Well, don't ask me to do the talking, then!" I said, stopping and facing him. "If you don't like what I do, don't ask for my help. This is what I do," I said. "It's my thing, my oeuvre, my . . . *element*. And besides, what happened to keeping a low profile? Flashing that seal around is as close to shouting 'here we are' as makes no difference."

Mithos glanced at Lisha and then back at me. "You're right," he said, "my apologies. And you could memorize the addresses, just by glancing at them?" he asked.

"Well, yes," I said.

"Impressive," said Mithos.

"Hardly," I answered as we headed back to the inn. "Try learning the lines for the female lead of a new play two days before you open. That's impressive."

Investigations

We spent the morning staring at a map marked with the location of each raider attack. Right in the middle, just on the Greycoast side of the Shale border, was the mark of a small castle.

"What's that?" said Lisha.

"I'll find out," said Mithos. "The raiders must have an operations base in the area. Maybe that's it."

"Track down the three Joseph addresses," said Lisha to Orgos. "See if any of them looks big enough to house troops or stolen property."

The Hopetown marketplace was a very different kettle of fish from the one in Ironwall: professional hard selling everywhere you looked. You could have bought anything you wanted there, and a lot of stuff you didn't. The stall keepers shouted, intimidated, and just plain lied to make a sale, gracelessly thrusting coins into a chest before the customers could change their minds. The barefaced economics of it all just wasn't my style. I was glad to see Orgos strolling over to speak to me.

"We have found all three of the 'Joseph' houses," he said. "Renthrette and Garnet have spent the morning checking out the addresses and they think one of them is empty. We're going now."

"You mean, breaking in?"

"Yes. Just to look around."

"You're sure it's empty?"

"Positive."

"And we'll be in absolutely no danger?"

"None at all."

"I'm your man."

Mithos told us to be very careful, and made some not wholly complimentary remarks about my being wiry and thus well suited to housebreaking. I don't think he believed I hadn't done it before.

The house belonging to Mr. Brineth Joseph was in a poor suburb of town. It was made of timbers that had warped and splintered away from their rusty nails like the scales on a rotting fish. By now it would probably have been cheaper to torch the place and start over. We found a downstairs window unlocked and clambered in; not exactly maximum security, but then, as we quickly discovered, there was bugger-all worth stealing.

There were two bedrooms upstairs and a little kitchen-bakery on the ground floor. They obviously sold bread in the market. The furniture was basic, and the clothes were few and threadbare. Several of the interior doors were missing, probably burned when the weather turned cold.

"Palatial," I muttered. "If they are bandits, they're really bad at it."

Orgos picked up a tiny pair of boy's shoes whose heels were worn to nothing. He just looked at them and said nothing. I sighed, a little irritated that these people's poverty should take the edge off our adventure. The bakery was clean but poorly stocked, and the flour was coarse and cut with chalk in fine old Cresdon style. There was no sign of anything remotely suspicious.

"Ah, the thrifty lower classes," I said sardonically as we slipped out. "Salt of the earth."

"Don't make light of poverty," said Orgos. "It kills more than the raiders ever will."

"Really?" I said. "How interesting. Having been destitute most of my life I never would have known that."

Orgos didn't reply. Sentimental idiot.

Mithos was pleased with our report.

"Well, we can cross that one off the list," he said.

We would have to watch the other two houses closely. I suggested breaking in by night, but this was generally considered an extraordinarily bad idea, even by my standards.

"So we just sit around and wait?" I said.

"Until we get a better lead," said Mithos.

And, right on cue, we got a better lead. Orgos burst into Lisha's room, where the rest of us had gathered, and tossed a curved knife on the bed.

"Look at that," he exclaimed. "Familiar?"

"Not to me," I muttered, wondering why I felt a thrill of alarm whenever Orgos got excited about weapons.

"It's kind of like the scyax that we looked at," said Garnet, picking it up and holding it up to the light.

"The same steel," said Orgos triumphantly. "The same workmanship."

"Where did you get it?" asked Lisha.

"I was stocking our weapons chest in the marketplace and came upon a stall that sold nothing but this stuff. The stall keeper was reluctant to tell me where he got his material, but I persuaded him. He is supplied exclusively by a weapons dealer known locally as the Razor. He pays certain traders in town well above the average for the best ores and sells his exclusive wares to whoever can afford them."

We were about to ask more when Mithos came in hurriedly. He pointed to the center of the map again.

"That building in the middle of the map?" he said. "It's a keep. A fortification belonging to one Eric Thurlhelm, known as the Razor."

⁂

We were dining in the same tavern we'd been at since we reached Hopetown. Renthrette was watching one of the Joseph houses and Orgos had returned to the market for supplies, but I was eating steak and kidney pie and swilling it down with a dark, mellow beer, half bitter, half mild. Mithos took a forkful of steak and told me what he knew.

"I spoke to a garrison officer," he said. "Thurlhelm, the Razor, moved here from Thrusia shortly after it fell to the Empire. He is rich. He pays his taxes and keeps himself to himself. The duke doesn't ask about his past operations, where he gets his money from, or how he amuses himself at present. The keep is larger than his requirements, since he lives alone save for a few friends, various female companions, and a sizable staff of servants. He has a resident defense unit of about thirty men. I think it's time we checked him out—cautiously. The Razor runs his house as he pleases and we can expect rough justice from him if we get on his nerves. We can also expect trouble from the duke, who won't want to lose the tax revenue unless it's absolutely necessary."

"What a prince," I said, dark memories of the scaffold in Ironwall haunting me briefly.

"Quite."

"Has anybody given any thought," I said, figuring it was time we addressed this, "to how the raiders are able to get from wherever they are to the site of an attack without anybody seeing them and without . . ."

Mithos was staring across the room, oblivious to me. By the empty fireplace a man was sitting at a table. He had his back to us but his head was turned slightly in the way people do when they are trying to listen in on someone else's conversation. Mithos was motionless except for his left hand, which was moving silently for the small crossbow on the floor by my chair.

I watched in confusion as he pulled the weapon onto his lap and cocked it with one deft motion, his eyes still fixed on the stranger. Then he opened his left palm and extended it towards me.

"What?" I murmured.

"A bolt," he breathed, barely audibly.

I reached behind me uncertainly, took hold of the feathered end of a quarrel, and drew it out of the bag. But my eyes were on Mithos and as I passed it to him, another one slid out and clattered to the stone floor.

Suddenly the man leapt to his feet and spun around, raising a pair of small crossbows, one in each hand and pointed directly at us. His eyes were dark and cold, his mouth set, and I knew that he meant to kill us.

Mithos turned the table over, sending the crockery crashing to the ground and pulling me down behind it with him. There was a slight swish and one bolt cracked into the tabletop as the other slammed into the wall behind us. I felt the wind in my hair as it passed.

Mithos dived to the right, rolled once, and aimed the crossbow. Our would-be assassin had fled. Mithos went after him, but the streets were a maze. He could have gone anywhere.

Or he could have just vanished like the raiders always did, even when they were dead.

Mithos returned, breathing hard, and plucked the crossbow bolt from the tabletop. It was flighted with crimson feathers.

SCENE XXXVII

Time for a Beer

My intention to abandon the party had been only temporarily suspended, but this new attempt on my life put a slightly different complexion on things. It bore thinking about.

On the one hand, of course, it made my desire to get away from the party and the arrowheads, lance tips, fire, and death that seemed to follow them about stronger still, but it also made life without the likes of Mithos at my side rather less appealing. And painfully brief. Without him, I would have been snuffed out like a candle, and not a particularly bright candle at that. Scattering crossbow bolts on the ground in a moment that called for absolute silence hadn't been too bright, and it had been an act of unprecedented mercy that Mithos hadn't killed me himself. His glower on returning from the empty street softened into a resigned sigh and the muttered remark that it "could have happened to anyone." Perhaps so, but it had happened to me, and, to my mind, it usually did. The idea of running from the party, top though they were on someone's unpopularity list, was, for someone with my combat skills, roughly equivalent to going swimming with three or four large rocks chained to my legs. I wondered absently if the party members thought of me as the rock chained to their legs. I made a mental note to be a little nicer to them, in case they should decide that this rock-lugging bit wasn't worth the effort. If I was cut free of the party, I would sink. Fast.

"I wonder," said Mithos in the voice of a man who had been hunted before, "whose idea that was."

"The raiders', obviously," I said.

"You think so?" he asked pensively. "It takes more than a few red feathers to make a crimson raider. And until now they've seemed almost anxious to keep us alive."

Mithos left me to think this over and I took out the map we had been looking at earlier.

"Hi, Will!" said Garnet enthusiastically. "I heard about the attack. We must be making progress."

That was Garnet logic for you.

"I see you've got the map there," he said, keen as mustard. "Considering tactics?"

"Er, yeah," I answered, wondering what I had been doing and realizing with muted shock that he was sort of right. I had been having those Adventurer Thoughts again. In the circumstances, that was odd.

"So," he said, sitting down.

"So?"

"Here we are," he said, pleased again, "in a pub."

"That's right," I answered, conscious of the way he was putting me on my guard again.

"Two mates out for a beer," he concluded.

I thought "mates" was a bit strong, but I let it go. There was a pause and I sat back in my chair as he looked hopefully about him and then back to me.

"Garnet, is there something on your mind?"

"No," he answered emphatically. "Not at all."

"You want to talk about the guy who shot at us? . . . " I guessed, reluctantly.

"No," he said with a little gesture of defiance. "Let's not talk work."

So that's what it is, I thought, *when someone tries to skewer your jugular with a crossbow bolt: work.*

"I just thought," he went on, "that we could, you know, do what ordinary people do."

"I'm an expert on that," I said.

"I thought you would be. So what do they do? Ordinary people, I mean."

"They drink, they talk, they play games, they pick up women . . . " I said.

"Games?" he asked.

"You know, cards, darts, dominoes, or something."

"Let's play cards," he said with an enthusiasm that said it was going to be a long night.

"What can you play?"

"Nothing," he said, slightly frenetic now, "but you can teach me, right?"

This was getting seriously strange. But I watched the slightly hunted way he seemed to be looking around, the shifty nervousness, like a kid about to be deliberately naughty, and it made a kind of sense to me. Garnet had been with the party for years. In that time he had gone from child to dignified warrior with his ax and his honor code, and he had never had a second to sit back and be an ordinary kid, make a fool of himself, get a little wild, and have a good time without worrying if he was being noble or righteous. Now I was here, representing all he had missed, all he didn't know of the ordinary world, and he was cautiously ready to give it a shot.

Fair enough, I thought. Endearing, really.

Time to educate him in some of life's simple pleasures. We ordered beer, or, rather, I ordered it for him. He had no preferences.

We got six pints: a selection of ales, a lager, a wheat, and a milk stout. He gulped down one of the ales and was halfway through the lager when, with a sudden sense of alarm, it occurred to me that he had never drunk beer before. Even in those party meetings, I wasn't sure I had ever seen him take more than a sip at a toast. The fact that he had finished one of the ales, the lager, and had made serious headway on the stout by the time the thought had fully registered confirmed both my suspicions and my panic.

"Let's take it easy, shall we?" I said, grasping the beer in his hand and pushing it back down onto the table.

"This is great," he said, apparently unaffected. "Let's get some more. I didn't know it would be this much fun, just sitting in a bar."

I grinned and sat back as he got to work on another ale. I supposed I was overreacting. Things didn't look so grim after all. I went to the outhouse and, on my way back, walked into Renthrette. She smiled at me rather warmly and I knew that I had somehow gained masculine adventurer points by nearly getting killed again. She was wearing a light summer dress and had let her hair down. It took about thirty seconds for things to get grim.

"I heard you were with Garnet and thought I'd join you." She smiled, her eyes meeting mine. This rash of goodwill was a veritable epidemic. "I hope you're looking after him," she said coyly.

I chuckled and said, "He's over—"

I had started to point to our table, which she had her back to, when I saw Garnet, sprawled across the table in a pool of spilt beer. He had drunk at least two pints in the time I had urinated away one.

"Er, I think he just left," I spluttered. "Yes. You can probably catch him if you leave quickly."

"You can come with me, then."

"Yes. Yes, I mean, I could do that," I said, thinking desperately. "But, well. But I have to settle the bill."

"I'll wait," she said, nicer—damn her—than she had ever been before.

"Well, it could take a while. We had some, er . . . complicated drinks and—"

"Complicated?"

"Yes."

"How?"

"Well, you know. Complicated. Complex."

She gave me a blank look.

"Mixed!" I exclaimed. "They were mixed drinks and it always takes a while for the barman to figure out how much they cost."

"Oh," she said. "I'll sit down then."

She turned, took a few steps towards the table where Garnet was now dragging himself upright with a bleary, vacant look in his eyes, and froze.

Then, very slowly, she turned and there was the look I knew so well: cold, cynical, murderous, and reserved entirely for me.

"He drank too quickly . . . " I began.

"This is your fault," she muttered in a voice like dripping acid.

"Renthrette?" said Garnet distantly. "I don't feel well."

As his sister turned to him, he seemed to reconsider this statement and amended it.

"I feel *really* bad," he said, clearly surprised.

I made a run for it, slamming a few coins on the bar as I left. I could handle a lot of things, but Renthrette protecting her cub from the evil Mr. Hawthorne wasn't one of them. I had reached the door when I heard the guttural surge and splash of vomit, followed by Renthrette's imperious yell:

"William Hawthorne, come back here!"

No chance. No chance whatsoever.

SCENE XXXVIII

The Razor's Edge

Garnet had stayed in bed late, groaning. Renthrette had banged on my door, and while I lay still, pretending not to be there, it occurred to me that this was the first time she had actually wanted to come in. The irony was almost unbearable.

It was going to take three people to maintain surveillance on the remaining two Joseph houses. That meant only half of the party could be spared to investigate the Razor's keep, but since even Lisha's little band wasn't stupid enough to go storming a castle with a small army inside, numbers didn't matter too much. We just had to decide who was going where.

Garnet and Renthrette were tired of surveillance and thought this Razor thing sounded like action. They put their names forward, which would count me out; after the previous evening, I didn't want to be anywhere near them. I figured I'd just stay where I was and let Mithos chaperone the dismal duo.

I should have guessed that things wouldn't be decided so democratically. That night I was told to get my stuff together. Orgos and Lisha and I were going to see Mr. Razor and his boys. Garnet and Renthrette, though pleased to see the back of me, must have been livid.

"Will, do you want to ride Tarsha?" asked Lisha as we saddled up.

"Nope," I said with a slight shudder.

"Why not?" she asked as she launched herself into the saddle.

"Because I value my life," I answered, "as if you didn't know. Where's the wagon?"

"We aren't taking the wagon," Orgos beamed. "Too slow. Just fill your saddlebags and we'll go as we are. Hopefully we'll be back in a couple of days."

"By about three or four o'clock we should come to an inn," said Lisha. "The Sherwood. That's less than a mile from the keep. We can stay there."

Six hours on horseback, I thought, clambering awkwardly into the saddle. *Wonderful.*

Orgos grinned at me. I told him to go away, or words to that effect, and he spurred ahead, laughing. My horse started slightly at the movement and I fell off. It was going to be a long day.

The tracks we followed took us directly west towards Shale through meadows of long, sweet-smelling grass, hedged fields of barley, and clustered fruit trees. We went at a canter, occasionally walking the horses to let them get their breath back. Whenever we started to move faster again, I gripped the reins and the beast's thick mane as tightly as I could until the panic subsided.

We ate our lunch of cold chicken, goat cheese, and coarse-ground oat bread by a clear stream where dragonflies hovered. Orgos chilled a bottle of plum wine in the stream and we shared it among us. Lisha preferred the water. She told us the names of the plants that grew by the stream and their uses, and then I watched her entice a red-and-black butterfly into her fingers and study it carefully, tenderly, before it flew away. I was going to remark that this was a bit odd for the grim party leader, but something in her glance told me not to.

The sun was hot as we rode the rest of the day, so we took it slower than before. I had a very slight headache from the wine, but I was also getting more relaxed and at ease on horseback and the miles passed surprisingly quickly. Orgos told me more tales of ancient battles and heroes, and I recited parts of the banned Thrusian history plays. Orgos lapped it up. It almost felt like I had something in common with this principled swordsman and his artifact of power. Weird.

The sun was still high when we rounded a bend in the hedged track and saw the Sherwood set back from the road, its chimneys placidly curling smoke. I was sweating a little and was glad of the shady porch where we could take our boots off while the stable boy dealt cautiously with Tarsha. The kid looked awestruck and terrified at the same time, which I could relate to.

The innkeeper was glad to see us. He introduced himself and offered us cold roast pheasant for supper. We bathed, changed, and came down to eat as the sun set. Apart from two blokes at the bar, we had the place to ourselves.

"Innkeeper!" I called, trying out the local dialect with fair success. "This is the best piece of roast pheasant I've ever had. Do you know that? I mean it."

The innkeeper smiled with genuine pleasure. The two men at the bar had turned around and were nodding agreement. They were big, athletic types with thick sculptured biceps and suntans. Probably laborers.

"Trapped 'em in the woods myself yonder, sir, I did," said the innkeeper.

"Remarkable," I said. "Just the right gamy flavor without being too sharp, and moist but not greasy. This is a tribute to the bird. Remarkable. I expect it is much in demand round these parts?"

"To tell you the truth, sir," he said, "there aren't many people around here. The farmers just come in for a pint in the evening."

"What about that castle up the road there?" I asked him smoothly. A cloud passed over his face.

"Aye, sir," he muttered, starting to turn away, "I supply them."

"Not good customers?" I ventured.

"Depends what you mean by good, doesn't it?" he said.

Seizing our beer jug, he shuffled off to the bar.

"Interesting," said Lisha. "But don't be too obvious."

"Me, obvious?" I asked, faintly offended. "Subtle Will? Please."

"So," I said as the innkeeper came back, "gives you a hard time, does he?"

"Who?"

"Whatsisname," I said, pretending to fumble for it. "The Razor."

"You know him?" the innkeeper asked, suddenly uneasy.

"Only by repute," inserted Orgos.

"Very wealthy man is Mr. Thurlhelm," said the innkeeper. "Gets anything he wants. Servants, women, entertainers, the best food and drink around; you name it."

"How did he make his money?"

"He was an arms dealer in the West," he confided. "Thrusia.

Sold to the rebels for years until he realized they were going to lose. Then sold to the Empire. Never comes in here himself, of course, but his people do."

"Are there a lot of people at the keep?" I asked.

"Not usually," he said. "But they get visitors. Big groups of them. The servants talk about them, but only when they think no one's listening, if you know what I mean. Not popular, Mr. Razor's guests. But they never leave the castle, so that's all right."

"You've never seen them?" I asked, trying not to grin with excitement.

"No one does," he said. "We only know they're there when they send their food and drink orders."

"More than usual, is it?"

"Three, four times as much," he said. "No one leaves the castle while it lasts. Then things go back to normal."

"And you've never seen these guests arrive?" I said, as if this was a minor curiosity.

"I've never even heard their horses on the road."

We thought for a moment and there was silence. The men at the bar had stopped talking. They had their backs to us. I wondered how much they had heard and whether it mattered. I had no idea whether we had been talking loudly, but suspected we had.

"How often does this happen?" Lisha asked.

"Once a month or so, sometimes more."

We sat around and nothing happened, save that the two men from the bar drank up and left a couple of minutes after our talk with the innkeeper. Lisha and Orgos exchanged significant glances. I looked up and muttered, "Well, at least the raiders eat." The others gave me a blank look. "I mean, they appear out of nowhere and their corpses don't stay put. It's good to know they actually have to have food sent to them. It means they're human."

❧

It was dark outside the Razor's keep. Nights were short at this time of year and I figured it would be dawn soon. We had ridden past the fort and tethered our horses just under the lees of the Elsbett Wood, a hundred yards or so to the west. The castle was square and surrounded by a wall topped with a gatehouse flanked by a pair of turrets. In daylight it probably looked like a toy: a rich man's whimsy.

At night it was rather more forbidding, despite the glowing windows. We nestled amongst the trees and watched the silhouettes of sentries moving between the parapets. There was a faint sound of music and laughter drifting from within like smoke.

I yawned and stretched. We had rested for a few hours before we left the inn, but my body still told me I should be asleep. I thought about Garnet sitting in Hopetown sullenly grinding his ax blade with slow circles of his whetstone, and Renthrette watching over his shoulder in case he missed a bit. I couldn't help feeling sorry for Mithos having to babysit those two little rays of sunshine. The thought made sitting out here in the middle of the night slightly more appealing.

I wandered into the trees a little way off to relieve myself—too much beer, as usual. I had just about finished when I noticed that the quality of the darkness had changed: it was getting misty. In seconds the mist was a thick fog pooling among the trees. It was odd the way it just seemed to come out of nowhere, and, though the night had been warm, the temperature seemed to drop dramatically. And there was a strange quality to the mist. It reminded me of something. . . .

The convoy from Ironwall. The scarlet cloaks flashing through the dense, grey air . . .

I felt the prickling of the hair on the back of my neck. I was still, holding my breath.

And then there was a sound in the mist. The soft clop of hooves. Horses. A lot of them, walking towards me.

I forced myself to move, running back to the others, tripping over roots I couldn't see and glancing off tree trunks.

"Horsemen!" I hissed at Lisha and Orgos. "Raiders, I think. Coming towards us through the forest from the west."

"Quickly?" gasped Orgos.

"No, walking."

"How many?"

"I didn't count," I said. "A lot. This might be a good time to leave."

"Where did they come from?" asked Orgos.

"I don't know," I said. "The woods."

But that wasn't strictly true, was it? I had been in the woods, and I had been pretty sure that I had been alone. And then it got misty and they were there. But I didn't want to think about that.

We shifted quickly, shying away from the keep and sticking to

the tree line. We checked over our shoulders as we moved, not speaking. The forest hung with an aura of dread. Something bad was going to happen. You could feel it. Whether we would be part of it, I
couldn't say.

Moments later the dark outlines of the horsemen appeared.
They traced a broad arc along the edge of the woods only yards
from where we had been waiting. There were perhaps sixty of them,
silent and controlled, moving ominously forwards, rolling slowly
down towards the keep. But they didn't go in, not yet. A rider wearing the horned helm I had noticed during the raiders' attack on the
coal trotted over the bridge, and we heard the muffled voice of a sen-
try. Then the doors swung open and the raiders moved en masse. But
there was no slow, measured caution now. They were charging.

"What is going on?" I whispered.

In seconds they were across the narrow bridge and through the
gatehouse. Cries of confusion quickly replaced the music and mer-
rymaking in the fort. Then screams, an occasional clash of metal,
and then nothing. Less than five minutes later the raiders rode out
two abreast, turned towards the mile-wide gap between the Elsbett
and Iruni woods to the southwest, and rode away. A heavy mist was
gathering about them before they were completely out of sight,
and I knew we wouldn't be finding any telltale hoofprints in the
morning.

Ten minutes later, as the birds were beginning to sing in the
woods and crows had begun to gather on the turrets of the little castle, we went in. We scurried from wall to wall, whispering and glancing about us constantly, but there was no one left to raise any kind of
alarm. There were bodies transfixed with red-feathered arrows
slouched across the parapets or sprawled on the stairways to the
walls, and our fear slipped away from us. In its place came only revulsion mixed with a shoddy relief. The raiders wouldn't be coming
back, though why they had turned on the man who seemed to have
been their ally, we had no idea.

We entered the banquet hall and found the revelers lying amidst
pools of spilled wine and overturned plates of venison and suckling
pig. It had been a sumptuous feast. The Razor had been a large,
cruel-looking man. He was sprawled out on the table, his flesh still
glistening like a dish ready for the carving. There was blood everywhere. It collected in pools on the floor, soaked the fine silks of the

dead, and ran into the golden goblets that had fallen with them. A banquet for the dead, I thought to myself. It looked like the final scene of a play.

It was the stuff nightmares are made of, of course, but I was still alive, and the Razor had probably got no more than he deserved. These days it seemed I took my comfort where I could get it.

It was less easy to keep things at arm's length when we got back to what was left of the inn. The innkeeper was dead, and the stable boy could tell us nothing that we hadn't guessed. The raiders had asked for us by name before they ransacked the place and set it on fire. The crossbowman in the Hopetown tavern had been no random guest. For whatever reason, the Razor's honeymoon with the raiders had ended abruptly, as had ours. Whatever purpose we had served had come to an end. They were looking for us, and we could expect no mercy from them now.

SCENE XXXIX

Watching

I slept most of the afternoon in the Bricklayer's Arms, back in Hopetown, while Lisha passed on what we'd learnt to the others. It didn't seem to me like we had much to report, apart from the knowledge that we would probably be dead by lunchtime.

The Joseph groups, it seemed, had been keeping a low profile over the last couple of days, tending their stalls in the market and having no mysterious visitors or secret meetings. We were no nearer even to determining *which* group might be connected to the raiders, let alone explaining what that connection was or how we might exploit it. Another blind alley?

Garnet appeared as soon as I woke up, but I was in no mood to defend myself for the state he had been in when I left.

"Don't start," I grunted into the pillow. "How was I supposed to know you didn't drink?"

"Never mind that," he said hurriedly with a slight twitch. He wanted to know every detail of my experiences at the Razor's keep. He listened too attentively, and kept asking about what Lisha had done or said or thought. For the first time, I wondered what his feelings for her really were. It probably should have occurred to me ages ago.

"How's the market?" I asked, changing the subject.

"Tedious," he said, suddenly gloomy.

"With all that hustle and bustle and trading and sales talk and gold," I exclaimed, "surely not. Let's go. Maybe we could get a beer."

He gave me a pained look.

"Listen, Will," he began, "about that night. I'd rather you didn't talk about it in front of the others. About my getting, you know, a bit tipsy."

"Tipsy?" I said. "No, mate. My grandmother, if I had one, would get 'tipsy' on a glass of sweet sherry before dinner. You, on the other

hand, got *wrecked*. Steaming, roaring drunk. Plastered. Blotto. Rat-
ted. You might have been tipsy for a moment three sips into your first
beer, but by the time you were tossing your salad all over the bar, you
were well and truly *monstered*."

"Well," he muttered, with an embarrassed cough, "be that as it
may . . . Only Renthrette knows, I think, and I'd prefer it if . . . you
know."

"Say no more," I agreed chummily. "Silent Will, at your service.
Not a word. Water . . . or, in this case, *beer*, under the bridge."

He gave me a doubtful, sidelong glance and we went to the market, or at least I went and Garnet sort of tagged along.

"So which are the stalls we are supposed to be watching?" I
asked.

"One of them hasn't set up today, but that one over there," he
nodded, "the one with the crates in front of it, belongs to Caspian
Joseph. Don't look, though. It's too obvious."

"Right," I said, "I'll sneak up and buy something."

I strolled nonchalantly over to Caspian Joseph's stand and began to paw things over without looking up. It was mainly jewelry:
silver brooches set with semiprecious bits of stone. Most of it was
glitzy, obvious stuff. In other words, junk. Still, I've seen worse. Come
to that, I've sold worse.

"Can I help you, sir?" said a voice.

"Just looking, thanks."

He was a burly man of about fifty with a blondish beard streaked
with gold and full, flushed cheeks covered with tiny blood vessels fine
as cobwebs.

"Something for your wife, perhaps."

"I'm not married." I smiled.

"Girlfriend?"

"Kind of," I said.

"What about a bracelet set with turquoise or amethyst?"

"I don't think so, thanks."

"A necklace, perhaps?" he suggested. "I can do you a good dis-
count on one of these. Ironwall silver and imported Thrusian jet. A
lovely piece. A nice contrast. What color are the lady's eyes?"

"Blue," I said, wondering for a moment if they were.

"Then the jet is too dark. A brooch with a tiger's-eye pin? Or
one of these silver snakes with turquoise eyes? Isn't that lovely?"

"Yes," I said, concealing my distaste, "but no thanks."

"Earrings are always a nice gift. We have a good selection covering a wide price range. Would you care to see some?"

"No, really. I'm just looking," I said, flustered by his pushiness.

"What about a pendant? We have some just in."

"Sorry?"

"A pendant. Like this one with the blue sun disk. A very unusual
piece. The sapphire is flawed but genuine. I could make a very good
price for you. Sir?"

"Yes, all right," I said quickly. My throat felt dry.

⁂

"You're sure?" said Mithos.

"I'm positive," I assured him.

"Not just similar?"

"No, this is it. I got a good look at it. He was on his way out of
Ironwall as we arrived. I thought of him when we were at that all-
you-can-drink blood ritual. The man who took us said something
about the victims of the attack. Silver traders. I bet it was the wagon
we passed. The merchant was wearing this."

"So now what?" asked Garnet.

"We have our evidence linking Caspian Joseph to the raiders," I
said.

"It's not enough to bring the duke down on them," said Mithos,
"and I doubt that arresting him would do more than show our hand.
He may not even know anything. We're better off watching Joseph
and tailing anyone he has contact with. That way he could lead us to
the next rung in the ladder. We have to get to whoever is controlling
the raiders and where they are. At least we can stop watching the
other house."

Garnet—who thought this plan didn't involve anywhere near
enough axes—frowned, but the rest of us agreed.

"And the duke?" asked Orgos.

"Let's keep this to ourselves for a while," said Lisha. I gave her a
swift look, but her face said nothing.

"You don't trust him?" Renthrette ventured.

"I'm just not clear on a couple of things. Like how the raiders
knew we were in the Sherwood last night."

"Those guys at the bar heard us talking," I said.

"Perhaps."

I gave Renthrette the pendant, as a peace offering for getting her brother wasted. I still didn't think it was my fault that he couldn't handle his beer, but it seemed the diplomatic solution. I never saw her wear it.

I couldn't sleep that night and volunteered to watch the Joseph house. Renthrette walked me down to show me the best spot. I suggested she let me put my arm round her so that we would look like a normal couple, but she was having none of it. It was a warm evening and she wore her sleeveless bottle-green dress with the narrow waist and lowish front. I told her that she looked good in it, and while she shrugged it off with a knowing smile, she didn't actually threaten me.

As soon as we got to the little hawthorn hedge that was to be my lookout spot for the evening, she left me. I lay on my stomach and wondered what it would have been like if she'd stayed. Pretty much the same, probably.

The rear door into the yard, wide enough to get a wagon through, was ajar. The sun hadn't quite disappeared, so there was enough light to see by. I would just look. No more.

I ran softly over to the perimeter wall and squashed myself flat against it. There was no sign of life, so I inched along to the doors and peered in.

There was a courtyard and a row of sheds joined to the back of the house. Four big men, stripped to the waist, were pulling something out: a large high-sided wagon. A moment later, grunting and sweating, they brought out two more. The bearded man who had served me at the stall, probably Caspian himself, was supervising the loading of the wagons with crates and boxes from the house.

I ran into the street and across town as if there was an army after me, which, in the circumstances, wasn't out of the question.

I didn't stop till I reached the Bricklayer's Arms and blundered in shouting to the others.

"They're moving out!"

"Positive?" said Mithos, leaping to his feet. They were all sitting downstairs, having a last drink before bed.

"Yes, they're packing up to leave."

"When?"

"You people never stop asking questions till you find one I can't answer. I don't know," I said. "It will take some time to get those wagons loaded. They probably won't go until morning, but I could be wrong. It has, as I don't need to tell you, been known to happen."

Obviously we had to follow them, but that wasn't going to be easy. Big wagons like that needed major roads, and that meant long open stretches where anyone following would be ridiculously obvious. We couldn't guess where they were heading and they could leave the road at any point and vanish, leaving few or no tracks in the hard summer ground.

Garnet took a horse and rode down to the house, ready to report back if they moved off.

"We need a trail," said Lisha.

"I'll give them some bread crumbs," I muttered.

"Mithos," Lisha continued, ignoring me. "Do you still have the triggers we used to set the crossbow traps in the Hide?"

"In the green trunk."

He went upstairs, and returned with a device the size of his fist, a collection of gears and springs fitted to a brass plate. Lisha took it in her hand and pushed a cog round carefully. On the fourth complete rotation a tiny hook snapped back and then closed up again.

"If we could add some gear wheels to the axle of one of the wagons, we could adjust this so it would click over every half-mile or so."

"Doing what?" I asked.

"It could release a stopper or plug or something. Paint, perhaps. Then it would leave a spot on the road each time it clicked over."

"Paint is too obvious," said Orgos. "What about chalk dust?"

"Can you do it?" said Lisha.

"I need the parts," said Orgos, turning the wheel. "There's a clockmaker's in the next street. They should be glad of the chance to sidestep the trade tax."

"Hang on," I said suddenly. "How are we going to get at the wagon?"

"Not sure," said Lisha. "We'll meet in the street outside the house. Make your way there as indirectly as you can. Will, you get the chalk."

"What? Where from? It's the middle of the night. Where am I going to get chalk dust at this time?"

"I don't know," she answered. "But I'm sure you'll think of something."

✦

Great. It was midnight and I was out looking for chalk dust. Who works with chalk? Artists? Circus weight lifters? I didn't know many of those. I had some vague idea it might be used in metal casting, but I wasn't sure. Then it hit me.

Bread crumbs.

Not far from the Bricklayer's Arms was a block of buildings hung with the aroma of fresh bread and pastry. At the far end, where the run-down houses leaned erratically and the roads were potholed and overgrown, was the house I had entered with Orgos, the first of the three Joseph houses to have been crossed off our list. I could hear running water not too far away: a stream. With the bakeries all clustered in this area it seemed safe to assume there'd be a mill.

There was. I ran across a rickety wooden bridge, and rapped on the door.

"What is it?" said a floury middle-aged man in overalls. His arms were thick and powerful and a cloud of white hung about him, stirring as he moved.

"I want to buy some chalk dust."

"Are you trying to be funny, pal? I ought to punch your face in. And if you're from the union or the food marketing committee, I want to see some papers. I'm saying nothing until I do."

"I'm not," I assured him calmly. "I just want some chalk dust and I want it now."

"You've got a cheek coming round here—"

I held out six silver pieces and he shut up as if thumped with half a brick. He gave me a doubtful look, returned his gaze to the coins, and said, "How much do you want?"

I gestured with my hands, showing an area a couple of feet square.

"That's all?"

"That's all."

"Wait here."

In a moment the exchange was complete.

"That ought to be plenty," he said. "Half of one part chalk to one and a half parts flour. More than that and the bread'll taste like powdered rocks."

"Thanks," I said.

⁓✼⁓

Strolling back into the inn's stable yard ten minutes later, I looked up and saw a face peering through the curtains of one of the guest rooms' leaded windows. I had seen him in the bar the night before and had had the idea that he was too obviously doing nothing. He was in his late thirties, a lean, sinewy man with a pink complexion and hazel eyes. He was smoking a long-stemmed clay pipe and looking fixedly into space. I remembered the pipe, and was sure I had seen him before coming to Hopetown. Across a barroom back in Shale? His tobacco, I remembered, was strong with a curious flowery scent. He stood at the window looking down at me, the slim white pipe balanced between his fingers. Just a traveler preparing for bed? Perhaps.

⁓✼⁓

"All right," said Lisha, "here's the plan."

We had taken our food up to her room and I had been busily eating as she and Mithos whispered with Orgos. Garnet was standing by the door, ax in hand. Renthrette inexplicably offered me a bite of her apple.

We turned to Lisha and she rolled the map out for the hundredth time.

"If they know we're following those wagons, we are in trouble. We have to make it look like we're still here."

"We must also be especially alert tonight," added Mithos grimly. "They know where we are and want us dead."

There was a thoughtful silence, and then Lisha said, "That would actually be quite convenient."

"Of course," I agreed, deadpan, "I mean, still being alive next week would simply *wreck* my schedule."

"If they attack us and we can convince them we didn't survive . . . " Lisha mused.

". . . it could buy us some time," Mithos finished.

"That will depend on their method of assassination," said Orgos like a man choosing between fish or chicken.

"Someone will have to watch the Joseph house," said Mithos. "And get that chalk device fitted to one of their wagons."

"Garnet and I will do it," said Renthrette quickly. She was sick of waiting around while People Less Qualified (me) got to do stuff.

Mithos looked to Lisha, and there was a pregnant pause before she nodded. "Just be careful," she said.

Garnet glanced at his sister and both of them grinned broadly. So this was how you cheered them up: offer them the kind of task any sane person would give their right arm to avoid.

"Can we take Tarsha?" Renthrette asked, trying in vain to stifle her excitement.

"No," said Mithos firmly. "If anything will get you noticed, it's that damned horse."

Renthrette would have said more but Garnet gestured suddenly for silence. He tipped his head to the door. A moment later came the sound of careful footsteps coming towards us in the corridor outside, then a knock.

Garnet stepped behind the door, his ax drawn. I grabbed my crossbow but hadn't had time to cock it when Mithos called, "Come in!"

The door creaked open, admitting the inn's serving boy with a large jug.

"More beer," he gasped, struggling to find a place where he might set it down. "It's from the landlord. On the house."

"Thank you," said Mithos as the boy left.

"That was very civil of him," I said, refilling my mug.

"Well," said Orgos, taking my beer before I could take a sip, "now we know how they plan to get to us."

"Hey, get your own—" I began.

"Have you seen anyone give anything away in this town?" said Orgos. He took the jug and poured the beer into an empty chamber pot in one smooth motion. Then he put his hand into the jug, scooped out a thin smear of grainy sediment, and tasted it gingerly.

"Not poison, but they'll be expecting us to get a very good night's sleep this evening," he concluded, adding, "They're going to be *so* disappointed."

The Assassins

We slept two to a room as before, or rather, we sat up all night two to a room. I was with Orgos. Renthrette and Garnet had slipped out as soon as it got dark and were waiting for the Joseph wagons to move. The rest of us were to stay where we were and wait to be assassinated.

Orgos sat in the corner, one sword across his lap. He had been absently polishing it but had begun to doze a little. I was wide awake, so I let him sleep and watched for both of us. We had a single oil lamp turned so low that you could see no more than shadows. I thought of the dark-eyed assassin who had shot at us in the bar and wondered if it would be him slinking in to finish the job he botched last time. Then I thought they might torch the whole building as they had fired the Sherwood, but that was a noisy and unreliable means of assault, even if we were supposed to be in a drugged stupor. I wondered why they hadn't just poisoned the beer they'd sent up, but I suppose we had been there long enough for people to know that I was the only one who drank beer in any quantity and at least two of the party never touched the stuff (unless I was educating one of them in the delights of getting totally hammered). Time passed and Orgos began to snore softly. I began to think we had overestimated our peril.

Fat chance.

At about two o'clock, when the night was darkest, I was staring blankly into the middle distance when the dark frame of the door seemed to blur. I blinked. A thin mist was gathering in the center of the room.

Staring at it, I poked Orgos. He grunted and continued to snore.

It was getting colder and the mist seemed to be thickening.

"Orgos!" I hissed, turning the lamp up and reaching for one of his swords, the one with the crystal in the hilt.

I shook him again and this time his eyelids fluttered and opened, then tightened in confusion. The fog, which stood in a narrow, six-foot column in the center of the room, was no longer merely thick; it looked as if you could touch it. There was even some color in the greyness, as if the shape was becoming solid. A moment later the mist had coalesced further and it was now unmistakably a man, a man in the full helm and scarlet cloak of the raiders.

Orgos snatched up his other sword and leapt to his feet as the mist seemed to blow away, leaving the raider—now solidly present—close enough for us to see the pale stone set between the eyes of his helm. For an uncanny moment we just stood there, and then his hands moved, and for the first time I noticed that he seemed to have no scyax or weapon of any kind.

He was holding only a small wooden box. His first and only motion was to flip the lid open and dump its contents onto the floor, where it collected in three liquid puddles.

I didn't know what he was doing, but I was sure I had to stop him. I held up Orgos's sword and focused my mind on bringing out that flash of light and power from the crystal.

Nothing happened.

By the time Orgos had pushed past me and crossed the room with his sword poised to strike, the mist was already gathering about the raider. Orgos swung his sword, but it passed through what was now only a column of smoke which blew away in the wind of the sword stroke.

"What the hell was that?" I shouted.

And then the lamplight picked up what I had taken to be the dark fluid which the raider had tipped out of his box, and I could see that it wasn't fluid at all. It was legs: thin, spindly, and covered with short bristling hair, tentatively reaching and feeling their way around.

Spiders.

Now, spiders have never bothered me particularly, and although these were bigger than most, at five or six inches across, I can honestly say that my first sensation was one of relief. Given the strangeness of what had just happened—the mist, the menace of the raiders—spiders seemed like the soft option. I was wearing boots and would make short work of these three little assassins with a lot less trouble than I would a single crossbowman. I turned to Orgos and found him frozen to the spot with terror, his eyes wide.

So Orgos was an arachnophobe! Perfect, I thought. Time to show a little courage of my own.

I grinned at him but he was staring at the floor. When I took a step towards him, he raised a hand to stop me and hissed, "Yellow wolf spiders!"

I selected one and raised my boot.

"Piece of cake," I muttered sotto voce.

Then it jumped.

As I've said, spiders, even big hairy ones, don't really bother me. When those spiders launch themselves at your face, however, the matter takes on an altogether different complexion.

I threw myself back, shutting my mouth as the spider hit me for fear of it getting inside. For a fraction of a second I felt its body, soft and warmish, those thin, clawed legs struggling for purchase on my face. Then Orgos was sweeping the thing to the ground with his hand and finishing it off.

I backed away, stunned into inaction as Orgos expertly and stealthily lanced another with his sword and deflected the third as it jumped at him. It fell by the shuttered window and burst with a soft plopping sound.

"Oh my God!" I gasped, panic and revulsion overcoming any pretense at courage. "What the hell are those? Those fangs were an inch long. And what kind of spider jumps at your head when you go near it?!"

He approached me, examined my face, and then became quite still, staring at his right hand. He moved it into the lamplight and frowned.

There was a thin cut just above his knuckles.

"Yellow wolf spiders," he said again, quietly, and with a resignation I didn't like.

"One bit you?" I whispered.

"Let's hope not," he said in a voice no more than a breath. "If we'd been asleep, we wouldn't have had a chance. Assassins in the Thrusian marsh villages use these things all the time. They are extremely reliable killers."

I just looked at him. He smiled, but it was a small, grim kind of smile.

"But . . . I mean, you're going to be all right, aren't you?" I said.

"I really don't know," he said.

"Of course you will," I said, with a breeziness I didn't really feel. "You're Mr. Adventurer, the battle-hardened weapon master. You've got a magic sword, for God's sake. Supposedly. You can't get killed by a spider! What kind of story would that make?"

"The real-life kind," he said, and there was no smile on his face now. "Wait here. I have to speak to Lisha."

I stared at him as he left, momentarily lost for words. There was a chill panic in the pit of my stomach and a desperate voice in my head.

No. He can't die. Not Orgos. He's . . .

What? My friend? I don't think the possibility had occurred to me before now.

It seemed he was gone for hours. When he crept back in, I stood up.

"Well?" I said.

"Well, what?"

"Are you going to be all right?"

"I don't know," he said. "It looks like a bite, but it isn't deep, so the venom might not have got into my system. Lisha cleaned it up and . . . We'll see."

He offered me a small glass bottle and said, "Drink this."

I uncorked it and smelled the contents.

"Will it help?" I asked.

"If you were bitten and we didn't notice? No. Drink it anyway."

I did so and it went down warm with a sweet, citrusy aftertaste.

"Now lie down and wait," he breathed.

"But what if that *is* a bite?" I hissed back, gesturing to his hand.

"We'll know soon enough," he sighed, "or, at least, you will. In the meantime, you can give me my sword back."

I did. The thing was useless anyway.

"You know, Orgos," I began, unsure of where the sentence would end up, but sure I had to say something, "when I first met you guys, I felt totally . . . I mean, I think that you have—"

"Tell me tomorrow," he said.

He glanced at me and the smile was back, a little wan, maybe even sad, but there nonetheless.

"All right," I said. "I'll tell you tomorrow, then."

I think, even at the time, I knew that that wasn't going to happen.

SCENE XLI

Rest in Peace

It was dark. I woke strangely, my senses seeming to revive one at a time. I felt numb throughout my body, and though I tried to move, it was as if my muscles were still asleep. I was lying on my back, arms formally by my side. It was an unnerving feeling, lying stiff in the blackness, listening to my heart quicken. I tried flexing each part—legs, shoulders, chest, straining against whatever invisible bond kept them so uncannily still—but nothing happened.

I'm dead, I thought. *My body has shut down, and only my mind is still alive. Those hairy little bastards got me after all.*

But then I could feel something near my fingertips: my shirt fabric. In a moment or two I could move my hands and wiggle my toes, and within another agonizing half-minute, life spread back up from my extremities and my body finally awoke.

I rolled to the right, or rather began to, and found I couldn't. There was some kind of wall against my side. It smelled of pine. I rolled the other way with the same result. Panic seized me as, trying to sit up, I found the same solid restraint immediately above me. I was in a box.

Not just any box, though.

I clawed desperately at the wood with my fingernails as the awfully familiar shape of the thing registered: a coffin.

So I was either dead and having some kind of ghostly moment of consciousness, or someone had thought I was dead and I soon would be.

It was bloody typical that I should die, in this miserable fashion, through someone else's stupidity. I drew up my forearms and attempted to bang on the underside of the lid, knowing immediately that it was a complete waste of time. I probably had about eighty cubic feet of dirt weighing down on me, slowly splintering the timber till the rats and worms got through.

Let's hope I'm dead by then, I thought. This body might not be up to much, but I didn't want to stand (or rather lie) by as it got stripped down (an eye here, a kidney there) by vermin even lower than I had been in life. I pushed at the lid again.

And against all the odds, it moved. The lid lifted perceptibly and a crack of light appeared at its edge. I gasped away my terror-stricken panic and pushed hard. It splintered and tore free. Laughing with relief and shielding my eyes, I sat up.

I was in the back of the wagon and we were moving. There were five other coffins, neatly stacked and completely filling the wagon.

Now, it could have been that morbid obsession that sometimes draws us to glimpses of death, or it could have been feelings for my comrades that I had not really admitted, but I grabbed a conveniently positioned crowbar and began to jimmy the sides of the nearest coffin.

Burning with a dreadful anticipation, I freed the lid and pushed it aside. Inside was Orgos. Any hopes that he had been placed here prematurely crumbled as I touched his cheek. He was stiff, unresponsive, and cold as the grave.

I studied his still, lifeless face and felt a sense of loss and failure. Orgos was dead, and the knowledge that he had taken the bite to save my hide made it worse.

"Afternoon, Will," said a voice from the front of the wagon.

I turned to find a man smiling at me. His face was grubby and his clothes hung in rags, but there was something about the voice . . .

"Mithos?" I said.

"Who else?" he remarked. "So you hatched by yourself?"

"Orgos . . ." I faltered.

"Within the hour, I expect," said Mithos, turning back to the road.

"What? You're taking all this resurrection pretty damned calmly."

He gave me one of those what-is-your-mental-inadequacy looks of his.

I crawled into the front.

"So Orgos *isn't* dead?" I said. "Is this magic as well? Like the sword and the raiders who come in the mist and . . ."

He gave me that look again, confused but suspicious at the same time, as if he thought I was being stupid on purpose.

"Orgos isn't dead," he said, returning his gaze to the road.

"That's good," I replied, totally bewildered.

"Yes," he agreed. After a moment he added, "Why would he be dead?"

I wondered which of us was the imbecile. It was usually me, but it seemed time to make that nice and clear one more time.

"Why would he be dead?" I repeated. "Well, when people get bitten by lethal spiders to which there is no known antidote, and shortly afterwards they stop breathing, go very stiff and cold, and people put them in coffins, that tends to be the first thing I think of. Stupid, probably, but there it is."

"He didn't tell you about the drink Lisha gave you?"

"What about it?"

Then there came one of those rare remember-it-for-prosperity moments: Mithos laughed. It wasn't a guffaw or a full and throaty chuckle, but it was there, if brief. Not a smile, a laugh.

"It seems Orgos got the edge on you for once," he said.

It turned out that Lisha brewed a species of potion for just such eventualities. It slowed the heart rate, shallowed the breathing, and induced a slumber that resembled death to all but the most thorough examination. Renthrette and Garnet had slipped away to follow the wagons. Lisha, Orgos, and I had been carried about publicly, to make people think that the raiders' attack had been a success. It had all gone according to plan, except that no one had told me that there *was* a plan.

"We're a day behind them," said Mithos, "but the chalk device is working well. I think Renthrette took a leaf out of your book, Will."

"My book?"

"She did something *theatrical*: distracted the driver while Garnet got under the wagon to fit the mechanism."

"Distracted?" I repeated vaguely. "How?"

"I don't know," he said. "She said something about *exploiting her femininity*, whatever that means."

What *did* that mean? Selling fruit in a low-cut bodice? Hitching up her skirts and posing as a low-rent hooker? Doing exotic gypsy dances in the street with little cymbals on her fingers and tassels attached to her . . .

"You can start opening those coffins, if you like," said Mithos.

I came back to reality, such as it was, and did so. Lisha lay quiet and peaceful in her small coffin, a strand of her long black hair across her face. I brushed it aside and looked at her. This deathlike trance didn't look as bad on her as it did on the usually more animated features of Orgos. She looked as if she might open her eyes at any second and go about her business with a small nod of acknowledgment to me for not getting them all killed somehow. I was beginning to understand Garnet's reverence for her. How could someone look so insignificant and make you feel so small and transparent?

I had to shift the top coffins to open those stacked underneath, which I couldn't possibly have done except that Orgos had woken up. He looked dazed, but after stretching his broad shoulders he saw me and grinned.

"I guess you forgot to mention that we would all be sleeping for a while," I said reproachfully.

"Guess so," he said. "Help me up."

I took his hand, and as he pulled himself upright he sort of half embraced me and slapped me on the back.

"Good to be alive," he said, checking the slender cut on his arm.

I nodded. The things I had felt like saying before now seemed embarrassing and unnecessary, so I just said, "Make yourself useful and help me get these open."

One of the coffins contained food and equipment, and the last two contained a pair of massive crossbows with slides that looked like they'd need a team of horses to draw them. They could probably skewer four men and their mounts at a hundred yards. I whistled, and Mithos called from the front, "They may help to even the odds a little if the raiders attack. The man who makes them called them scorpions."

They'd pack one hell of a sting.

I said nothing as I climbed back through, one of the massive, brutal-looking bolts held loosely in my fingers. I wondered what it would feel like to be on the receiving end of one of those. No worse than being killed any other way, no doubt. Better than some, probably.

"I want you to take charge of them, Will," said Mithos. "When we stop for lunch you can set one up and familiarize yourself with how it works."

"So now we blast our enemy out of the saddle from a hundred paces?" said Orgos with a scowl.

"The raiders aren't going to line up and fight you in single combat," said Mithos flatly.

"And their lack of honor means that we resort to . . . these?" Orgos demanded, with a nod at the colossal crossbows.

"Absolutely," said Mithos.

Orgos scowled again and started polishing the blades of his swords, as if to make a point.

I was with Mithos on this one.

Still, my feelings were mixed. The crossbows (an inadequate word for those great, clanking death throwers) made me feel powerful, but what happened when the enemy came in close? What chance did I have face-to-face against men who had to be killed with machines like these? And what of Mithos's new faith in me? Will the missile man? Bill the linchpin, cornerstone of the outfit? Someone to be relied on when the enemy charged? Suddenly I saw why they were all so earnest. It wasn't about honor and virtue at all. They just couldn't bear the thought of screwing up and having the deaths of their friends on their consciences. I looked at the scorpion crossbows and felt a gathering knot of cold somewhere between my stomach and my groin.

"The chalk marks are too close together," Mithos said, looking at a pale blotch on the road. "I hope there's enough dust."

"Any theories?"

"About where they're going? We're heading north. I'd say Verneytha. Possibly the capital itself."

"Well, at least we're ready for the raiders now," I said.

"The crossbows?" asked Mithos.

"No," I replied, "the coffins. One each."

The Farmhouse by the Woods

Ten miles south of Verneytha, the chalk vanished. We had lost them. But only for a moment. Garnet and Renthrette had re-traced our path, and now they came cantering back from behind glowing with excitement.

"They left the road a quarter of a mile back," said Garnet. "We picked up their trail a couple of hundred yards after the last chalk mark."

We doubled back to where a narrow dirt track trailed off to the west through an orchard of small apple trees.

"We didn't want to risk following the wagon without you," said Garnet, proud of such superhuman restraint.

"It goes to a farmhouse," said Renthrette. "There's nothing else there."

"Excellent," said Lisha, and they grinned at each other as if she'd tossed them a bone to gnaw on. "Plan?"

"We get a closer look," said Mithos.

It had started to rain, and the early-evening sky was heavy with dark clouds. We had concealed the wagon and horses in a grove of trees close to the road, and then moved cautiously through the orchard in silence.

The farmhouse was a rambling sprawl of ramshackle buildings gathered around a courtyard that housed a few chickens. The wagons we had pursued from Hopetown were there, their sides folded down, empty. There was no sign of life. We lay in the long, wet grass at the edge of the orchard and watched.

I was just starting to get stiff from the cold when a man in a white linen tunic emerged from the main house and walked around the perimeter, looking about him. It was Caspian Joseph, the man who sold me the pendant. He completed his circuit of the buildings and went back inside, apparently satisfied.

"Not much of a patrol," said Garnet.

"I don't think it was a patrol," said Lisha. "Something is about to happen."

And, right on cue, eight raiders emerged from the house in full armor.

I reached for my crossbow, but Orgos stilled me with a touch.

"They aren't coming for us," he whispered.

He was right. The raiders came out carrying two coffinlike boxes, walked around the pigpen, and moved away from us, towards . . . what?

"What's over there?" I asked.

"Nothing," said Renthrette. "Fields, orchards, the edge of the Iruni Wood."

What was going on?

Caspian Joseph had followed them out, but once they got a little ways from the farm buildings, he turned back towards the wagons. The rain was falling more heavily now, and there was a rumble of thunder that lasted several seconds.

"Now is our chance," said Mithos.

"For what?" I asked, fairly sure I wouldn't like the answer.

"To look in the house," he said. "I'm betting he's alone. We can probably get in and look around without him seeing us. If he spots us, we can take care of him."

"And the raiders?" said Orgos, as if all was perfectly reasonable thus far.

"Orgos and I will follow them," said Lisha.

Mithos and the siblings clearly had the better deal, though I doubt they saw it that way.

"If we aren't back by morning," she added, "we'll meet in Harvest at the governor's palace. Will, you're with us."

⁂

So while the others set to investigating the house, I went trekking through the rain with Orgos and Lisha to see what grim little picnic the raiders were on. I was on strict instructions to keep my distance and not "engage" the enemy. As if I needed telling.

The storm had begun with gusto now, and we probably could

have walked right behind the raiders and they wouldn't have known we were there, but we went from tree to tree and ditch to ditch to be on the safe side. In fact, it was the first time since the mission had begun where I felt a kind of thrill: They didn't know we were here, so we had the upper hand. Of course, if they suddenly turned and wheeled those scyaxes of theirs up to fight, that would change very quickly. We had had enough difficulty fighting them on even terms. With three of us against eight of them (assuming that the coffins didn't spring open and release another couple of zombie raiders to make it a round ten), we wouldn't have a chance.

Renthrette had been right. The edge of the Iruni Wood, which we had seen from the Shale side that night in the burning village, loomed sudden and black out of the storm. The raiders went in.

I faltered, but Lisha, moving close to the ground like an animal, her spear clasped in both hands, kept going. Orgos drew his sword and gave me a nod of something I took to be encouragement. I followed.

It was better in the woods. There was more cover and less light. But I had barely had the chance to acknowledge this when muffled voices came through the pattering rain: They had stopped.

Lisha raised a warning hand and Orgos fanned right. She nodded to me, and I, cautiously, moved left, unsure of what I was doing, certain that the snapping twigs under my feet would bring those crimson-cloaked monsters screaming out of the rain.

We inched forward and the light changed subtly. Somewhere up ahead there was a break in the trees. A few more yards and we saw it: a clearing like a great hole in the forest. In the center was a circle of rough-hewn stones, each a little larger than a man. I hesitated. The place felt odd—dangerous—and not just because the raiders were here. I peered round a great oak into the clearing. In the middle was another rock, different from the others, pale and lustrous so that it seemed to glow slightly in the odd light of the storm.

The raiders entered the circle, several of them crouching by the coffins they had carried. They were opening them.

I turned to stare at Lisha, consumed with certainty that something bad was going on, something strange that I didn't want to see or be a part of, something that would make all that talk of magic swords look like very small potatoes indeed. I could barely see her through the gathering darkness and lashing rain. She caught my gaze and pointed. She wanted me to get closer to the stones. I swallowed hard and chose the biggest.

The raiders were busy with their coffins, so none of them was looking my way. There was a flash of lightning, followed by a lengthy roar of thunder. It was now or never. I scampered through the wet bracken and flattened myself as quietly as I could against one of the great half-sculpted stones.

The raiders opened the coffins and lifted out a pair of corpses, both dressed in scarlet and bronze. These they dragged over to a pair of the standing stones only a few yards to my left, and propped them up in sitting positions. I stayed low and watched as the raiders gathered in a tight circle around that central milky boulder.

And then I had an idea.

Moving as quickly as I could, I slid over to the next stone, paused, then moved to the next, and the next. In a matter of seconds I was hiding by one of the great monoliths against which a dead raider lay. I didn't think about Lisha or Orgos, or pleasing the party, or risking my life. I just had an idea and I was suddenly overwhelmed by what I can only describe, albeit inadequately, as curiosity. There was something I needed to know, and the presence of the raiders wasn't going to stop me from finding out.

It wasn't like they were going to see me anyway. It was dark, and the rain was coming down in sheets, and the wind was howling, and they were all wearing those closed helms with tiny eye slits and standing in a little huddle thirty yards away with their backs to me. I could just look quickly and then get away. Just a peep. Two seconds. Tops.

I scrambled round the stone and stared at the dead raider's bronze face. The stone between his eyes was just like the others I had seen, and it had the opaline pallor of the rock in the center of the circle. I thought I heard voices from the raiders and glanced over my shoulder. Their voices rose in unison and sounded rhythmic: a chant.

Whatever they were going to do with this raider corpse, it would involve that crystal in his helm. I was sure of it. It was set right into the metal, so I couldn't pry it out. Instead, I fumbled at the chin strap and tugged the helm off. The raider's eyes were open but sightless, and there was blood on his chin, but otherwise he looked quite ordinary and quite dead.

I bolted, stepping quickly back round the standing stone and crouching, feeling my chest heave and my pulse race. Real evidence, at last. The mystery of the raiders was inextricably bound to the crystals in their helms. That was why the only raider corpse we had seen before today was one that had been beheaded and taken by those ritualists in Ironwall. The stone in the helm had power, the way Orgos's sword had power, though what it did, I wasn't sure.

Then the chanting from the center of the darkened circle rose suddenly above the storm and ended with a shout. There was a crack of something that might have been thunder, but the pale light that accompanied it wasn't lightning. For a second it was bright as day and the standing stone at my back threw a long, hard shadow; then it was dark again. I didn't notice the mist for a second, but when I did, all my curiosity and triumph evaporated in the old panic. The raiders were coming! They were going to materialize in front of me and I was sitting here with one of their helms in my hand. . . .

I fumbled for my sword, still clutching the helm, but then I saw that the stone in its forehead was glowing softly. As it glowed, the mist grew denser. And I finally understood what the helm did. The mist wasn't bringing a raider to me, it was gathering around the helm in my hands. It was taking me with it.

SCENE XLIII

One of Them

For a second the greyness of the mist was complete. Then it began to thin and I instantly knew that I was not where I had been. There was no rain. There was a glow, as of torchlight, and I could see great stone walls and arches. I was inside some vaulted chamber that had no windows and smelled strongly of horses. It was hot and stuffy. And there were raiders everywhere.

There must have been fifty of them. They were walking in pairs, some carrying boxes and weapons, some dragging corpses. They were all in full armor and looked like they were getting ready for something important. The mist was still clearing about me. Before it blew away altogether, I did the only thing I could think to do and jammed the raider's helmet on my head. Instantly the world got a little darker, narrower, and more claustrophobic as I peered at it from inside the helm.

I was standing in one of a series of arched alcoves around the wall of a huge circular room. To one side was a stack of scyaxes, to the other a pile of folded crimson cloaks. I grabbed one of each, threw the cloak over my shoulders, and hoped it would do. It was stuffy and dry in there and I could feel the sweat breaking out all over me. On the other side of the room, I could see a handful of raiders stepping out of similar alcoves and guessed they were the ones who had traveled with me from the stone circle in the Iruni Wood. Two of them started dragging one of the corpses from the circle. The other corpse, minus his helm, was probably still there. I had taken his place.

The other raiders walked away. Only two were to do the job of funeral detail and they hadn't come for me yet. I watched, thinking fast. If I played dead well enough, I might yet get out alive.

I slumped down and kept very still, watching through my helm as the soldiers shouldered the corpse onto a table beside a pair of small metal doors. They removed his helm, cloak, and body armor, working quickly and methodically, as if they had done this many times before. When he was left wearing nothing but the light blood-stained clothes he wore under his armor, one of them took a long steel hook and used it to open the metal doors. As soon as the doors were opened I could see what they were doing. My heart sank.

It was a furnace. The chamber was hot and stuffy because they cremated their dead down here. They just used the same magic that allowed them to transport themselves into a fight to spirit any dead away to where they could be privately and absolutely disposed of.

And if I played dead much longer, they'd be sticking me in there to burn me with the others.

I got to my feet, checking that the funeral detail wasn't coming for me yet, then moved quickly, looking for a way out, walking with what I hoped looked like a sense of purpose. It would only be a matter of time before they realized they were missing a dead body.

There were two stone staircases going up the sides of the chamber. I made for the left one, knowing that whatever was upstairs had to be better than this. I was halfway up when another piece of the puzzle fell into place.

Looking down, I could see that the floor of the great chamber was a single vast stone, pale and lustrous like quartz. It was the same as the rock in the stone circle by the farmhouse, the same as the crystals in the raiders' helms. Whatever this place was, it had been built on an outcrop of that same rock. I stood there, staring at it.

"Get down there," said a commanding voice at my elbow. It was a raider: an officer, judging by the lateral crest on his helm. "You're blocking the stairs. We're ready to move."

I mumbled and stepped aside to let him pass, but he wasn't to be sidestepped.

"I said get down there," he growled. I wondered if I could come up with something that would get me up and out, but then I saw something that changed my mind.

Coming through the heavy oak door at the top of the stairs was the raider with the staff and the great horned helm. He moved slowly, and if the raiders always moved like cogs in a great machine, he was something different, something earthy and terrible, something animal but saturated with dark purpose. Immediately I knew that he was the one who worked whatever magic moved the raiders from place to place. Even at this distance I could feel his strangeness and the power that seemed to come off him like an odor. I wasn't about to go up to meet him.

The officer who was ordering me to go down sensed his presence and fell silent as if unnerved. Hugging the cloak about me, I hurried down. He followed at my heels, and right behind us came the magic worker in his horned helm, breathing power and malice.

"Get your horse and weapons," said the officer, and then turned away quickly, as if he was as anxious as I was to get away from the figure behind him.

Suddenly the raiders seemed to be everywhere, hemming me in, moving as a unit. With no other options, I moved with them, down a passage to a great curved corridor that circled the chamber we had just come from. In fact, it wasn't a corridor so much as a long narrow room where the smell I had picked up before became almost overwhelming. It was a stable.

The raiders all seemed to know where they were going, and the moment I hesitated I was jostled until I got into the line. We kept moving as we filed past dozens of gigantic horses, all barded with leather and ring mail and cloaked in scarlet. Each raider opened the door to one of the stalls, seized the bridle of his mount, and waited. I had no choice but to do the same. Maybe we would lead our horses outside and I could slip away as soon as I had figured out where I was.

Then a sound went through me like thin steel, a high, wailing cry from the circular chamber, a keening that contained words I couldn't catch. There was a great roar, as of thunder, a flash of white light that bounced off the walls and made the horses start and whinny. As I tried to calm mine down, I saw the mist begin to gather around both of us and knew only that whatever nightmare I had stepped into was about to get worse.

SCENE XLIV

The Raid

The mist had barely begun to clear when I felt the rain. It felt cool and refreshing after the stifling closeness of the stables, and it immediately made me think I was back where I had been. As the thin fog blew away I looked about me for the stone circle, then realized that I was also looking for Lisha and Orgos, desperately hoping that they would not be there when fifty crimson raiders appeared out of the air before them.

They weren't there. But then, neither were the stones.

In the darkness, I could barely see the vast ring of raiders, though I heard them mount their horses as one. We were not in the Iruni Wood, but more than that I couldn't say. The ground around us was open, the grass short as if it had been heavily grazed. A field, then. There were trees, but they were some way off, and the rain was lighter than it had been in the stone circle. If it was the same storm, then I could be south of the Iruni Wood, I thought, only a mile or two from that torched village where we had first encountered the raiders. If I made for the forest and headed north, I might find the farmhouse and the others.

But the raiders were already moving off, silent and purposeful as ever, and I knew that riding away would get me nothing more than a red-flighted arrow in my back. I clambered unprofessionally up onto my colossal horse, ignored the glance of the nearest raider as I swore my way into the saddle, and moved with them, trying to contain my dread at what might happen next.

As an actor I was used to noticing how people moved, and it suddenly occurred to me that even in the low light of the evening I didn't look remotely like a crimson raider. I didn't have the stature, or the physical confidence, and I was obviously terrified of my horse. I needed to get out of this situation before it got me killed.

Suddenly the column came to a halt and the officer up front

gestured as another lit a torch. The column became a broad line facing forward, facing—more importantly—a village.

My horse seemed to know what to do, and moved into the line
with the rest, but that didn't make me feel any better. Riding through
the downs between Adsine and Seaholme, we had passed half a dozen
villages just like this, and they were largely the same: small, poor, and
totally undefended. This was going to be a massacre, and I was going
to be part of it.

You have to do something.

Like what?

*Tell the raiders that butchering villagers is immoral. Tell them
that the village is hiding an army.*

Right. More arrows in my back.

I had no solution, no plan; but waiting for the order, waiting to
participate in the raiders' slow, methodical advance and the slaughter that would follow, was too much. The bronze helm felt like a vise
on my head. I couldn't breathe. I wanted to scream.

Instead, I put my heels to the flanks of my mount and charged
forward alone.

I really don't know what I was trying to do, but some dark and
stupid part of my brain had said that if I could get into the village
only a few seconds before the army smashed its way in, then some of
the villagers might fight back. They couldn't win, but maybe they
would get enough time for a few to escape. . . .

The massive horse thundered erratically toward the dark buildings and I clung on for dear life, shouting muffled warnings and curses
at the top of my terrified lungs.

Behind me, there was silence. My sudden assault had caught
them off-guard, and I could imagine the horses shifting and rearing
as their riders tried to figure out what was happening and what they
were supposed to do. They would be after me in a moment, but I had
a few seconds. . . .

An arrow flew out of the night from behind me and scudded
past my right shoulder.

I reined my horse towards the central street and tore the helm
from my head so that my screams would be heard. I saw a face at a
window, small and wide-eyed, and a lamp lit in a house farther down
the road. A door to what might have been a tavern creaked open a few
inches and I felt eyes on me.

"Raiders!" I shouted. "Crimson raiders! They are coming. Get up! Defend yourselves!"

I turned in the silence and looked back to where the dark line of cavalry were lighting their torches and their arrows. My horse, sensing my unease, reared, and I almost fell off into the wet street. More lights were coming on, more doors and windows cracking warily. And then, with a rumble of hooves, the raiders spread themselves into a wide arc and began their slow and brutal approach.

Someone shouted a question from a window, but I couldn't tell what they were saying so I just went on screaming the same thing over and over. A few men stumbled sleepily into the street, fumbling with bows and spears, mattocks and hoes. Then there were families with children, wide-eyed and crying, huddled in doorways, watchful and uncertain.

I turned back to the raiders, half hoping that this tiny alarm would deter their attack, but they were not so easily put off. They were coming closer, still slow but just as assured. My little diversion had done nothing. Then their burning arrows were loosed, and with a rush of wind like a great, vengeful sigh, thatch and timber caught fire all over the village. The crying and panic and the hopeless pleading for mercy swelled almost immediately, and it was clear that there would be no fighting from the villagers. I looked back to where the raiders waited, poised for their final assault, and you really couldn't blame them. Even running seemed futile.

But I remembered the torched village in Shale and how the horse tracks didn't go beyond the main street. They appeared, they destroyed, and then they disappeared. They didn't wait around to be seen, and they didn't hunt for survivors beyond the village limits. If I could get out and into the woods, I might have a chance. What else could I do?

I checked behind me and saw a door open in one of the houses about twenty yards away. A girl came out, maybe ten years old, brown shoulder-length hair and eyes like dinner plates. Holding her hand was a little boy. The raiders were coming and they had nowhere to go. I didn't have time to go back for them. I couldn't carry them anyway. And they'd be dead before I got there. Then I'd be dead too. I really didn't have time to go back for them.

I went back for them.

I turned my horse as well as I have ever turned a horse, though that isn't saying much, and set it cantering down the street towards them. Beyond them I could see where the raiders were pouring into the village. Some of them were dismounting and entering the houses.

"Give me your hands," I called to the children. They didn't scream. They stared. "Climb up," I insisted. "I won't hurt you."

They backed hurriedly inside.

Go, I thought. *You tried. You have to get out of here now.*

Shooting a desperate look back towards the raiders and hissing terrified, exasperated curses under my breath, I dismounted and followed the kids inside.

"Where are your parents?" I demanded. More silent staring. I took the helm off with an oath and tried again. "Are you alone? Quickly!"

"In the next room," said the girl.

"Your parents?"

"And granddad," she said. "And uncle . . ."

"I can't take them all. Only you. Quick."

I held out my hand, but the boy huddled up to the girl and began to sob.

"We can't leave them," said the girl.

I stared at her, disbelieving. She was tiny, and she was at least as scared as I was, but she wasn't about to change her mind.

"Get them," I hissed, watching the door behind me. "Get them all. Quickly."

The little boy ran into the next room, where there was a great deal of shouting and banging, but the girl stayed where she was, looking at me.

"What is your name?" she asked.

"What?"

"My name is Maia," she said. Her eyes were still wide, but her face showed no distress, more curiosity and a hint of defiance. "What's yours?"

"Will," I said, checking behind me.

"Hello, Will."

"Listen, Maia," I said, "you are going to have to help get these people out of the village. Is there a back door?"

"Outhouse," she said, pointing to a door in the far wall.

"Good," I said. "Make for the outhouse, but keep going. Just run. As far from the houses as you can get."

"What about the others?"

"Others?" I said.

"In the other houses?"

"We don't have time," I said.

"I could go," said the girl. "I know how to get into Rafe's house next door. And Mr. and Mrs. Delways's."

"There isn't time," I said again, turning back to the door.

"I can do it," she said. And before I could say another word, she was going out the back way, scampering like a rabbit.

Her father came in, pointing a heavy crossbow at me. Behind him a family of faces crowded the doorway. He was a big man with the body and skin of a man who worked outdoors.

"Go out the back way and get clear of the village," I said.

The father watched me as the little boy led his mother to the back door, his crossbow trained on me. Then suddenly he wheeled the crossbow toward the door, shooting quickly; too quickly.

I heard the bolt slam into the doorframe, and turned to see a raider already in the room, scyax swinging. The unarmed villagers shrank back towards the back door. Only I could stop him from killing them all.

I don't think he expected a fight, and my crimson cloak had him momentarily confused, so my quick lunge caught him off-guard. He parried unevenly, suddenly too big for the room, as I shifted and cut like a gnat harassing a cow. But it only took a second for him to regain his composure, and then I was the one stumbling backwards, batting unsteadily at his blade as he closed on me. It would be only another moment now.

I was still clutching the bronze helm. With all my strength I hurled it at his head. It clanged against his own like a bell, and for a second he swayed as if concussed. I seized the moment, stepping sideways as he cut blindly, stabbing low and hard. He stepped backwards and sort of shrank, crumpling as if the wound had let all the air out of his body. If he wasn't dead when he hit the floor, it happened very shortly thereafter.

For a moment I just stood there, breathing hard, feeling my arms shake and the furious, hot, and horrified blood singing in my ears. Then the cries of the boy brought me back, joined with the shouts and wails of the others.

"Quiet!" I said. "They'll hear you and they'll come looking for you. Go that way and follow Maia."

They had to go now, or they would never get out. Outside I could hear the fires getting closer, and there were shouts of command as the raiders moved through the village. I peered out through the doorway, then stepped quickly into the street. Taking my horse by its bridle, I led it quickly round the back. I could still make the woods. . . .

"Will?" It was the little girl. I nearly kept going, but I just couldn't. I turned and looked at her. "Should we follow you?" she said.

I looked at her and the huddle of terrified villagers behind her, so surprised by her trust that I forgot my own desire to get away.

"Yes," I said.

And they did.

It was a noisy, messy, and disorderly affair, but they followed. Behind a large timber building farther down the street there were more, maybe ten or twelve, waiting for guidance and some magical path to safety.

"These are our neighbors," said Maia simply. "They need to come too."

I stared at them.

"Right," I said. "Come on."

And I led them.

It was getting darker, and that was all to the good, because back here on the track behind the houses there was only a scattering of barns and workshops, and a series of low, erratic hedges between the fields and cart tracks. There would be almost nothing in the way of cover till we reached the edge of the forest a very long mile to the north.

We moved quickly, but part of the village was already well ablaze. The sky was orange, flecks of burning tinder swirling and sparking in the heavy smoke, but there was no sign of the raiders, and I was fairly sure that I had killed the only one who could have seen us go. And besides, there was no reason for them to expand their hunt beyond the village. That wasn't their way.

Except, of course, that there *was* a reason this time. Me. The raiders might have torched a dozen or more villages over the last few months, but this was the first time one of their number, one who had appeared with them out of the fog, had charged ahead of the attack and tried to sabotage the assault. They had lost me in the chaos of the battle—if you can call the slaughter that was going on a hundred yards behind me a battle—but I might just have done enough to make them curious about me. A bunch of random villagers, they couldn't care less about, but one of their own undermining their murderous labors? A very different story. They would come after me. After us.

SCENE XLV

Flight

It wasn't just Maia's family I had to worry about. Once we had been joined by her neighbors, another family from the last house on the street, and a straggling handful who had just been milling about, there were about twenty-five of them, mostly children. There were three who looked like they might die of old age before we reached the forest, and a handful of women, one of whom was shrieking with grief and terror. Maia's mother—a woman with a hard, tear-streaked face—took the woman's hand, but she just got louder. Her husband had been killed in front of her, and one of her children was missing. There really wasn't much you could say, but her screaming was like a beacon in the night, telling the raiders exactly where we were.

There were only four men who looked capable of putting up a fight should the raiders catch up with us, and, apart from Maia's father, who still cradled the crossbow, they boasted no more than kitchen knives and a pitchfork, weapons-wise. I was the only one on a horse, and all that seemed to do was make us conspicuous. I dismounted, gave the reins to Maia, and told her to lead the women and children along the track towards the woods. Once they reached the last farmhouse, they were to get off the path and make for the tree line. I called Maia's father over, and gathered the other three men at the back of the slow, wailing column.

We were hidden behind the houses of the main street, many of which were burning. I could hear that there was some fighting going on at the far end, but it was only a token resistance, and the raiders would be on us soon enough.

"When the raiders come," I said, "they'll have to go through us."

The men nodded, and I found myself listening to my voice as if it had come from someone else: someone like Orgos or Mithos who knew what he was doing and had organized tactical retreats like this dozens of time. I pictured the Cresdon audiences gazing up at me in this new and unlikely role and almost smiled.

One of the men was only a teenager with a blond wisp of a beard. His eyes looked scared. Maia's father, a burly man whose name was Grath, put a heavy hand on his shoulder as if to pass a little courage his way, and then started walking backwards behind the women, his eyes on the village's blazing silhouettes. I cocked my crossbow and tried to stay low, scuttling backwards like a crab.

The first horseman appeared behind a sprawl of low buildings with chimneys that I took to be a smithy. He had a torch, or I would not have seen him. Another joined him, flashing blackly into view as his horse cantered past a wall of flame. Then another. They were looking for me; I could feel it. They seemed to talk and then wheeled to face me, peering into the darkness.

We were a good 150 yards away and we had no torches or lanterns. There was a hawthorn hedge slanting across a field between us and them, not enough to obscure us completely, but enough to demand rather more of their eyes. We might have made it, had it not been for the crying of the bereaved.

The raiders caught their keening on the wind and their attitude shifted, grew tense and alert, like dogs. Then they began to move. They approached slowly at first, but you could feel their pace increasing with their certainty. Yes, there were people out there running away, and yes, they could reach them and kill them.

But there were still only three of them.

"Keep moving," I called to the column of refugees as they trudged along the track towards the trees. "They are coming."

The cries of grief slipped into a higher, more panicked register.

"Grath," I said to Maia's father, "hold the middle of the path." I pushed into the hedge on one side and gestured for the kid with the crossbow to do the same on the other side.

There wasn't time to think, and that was probably just as well. In a moment the three horsemen would be upon us.

Our two crossbows seemed to shoot simultaneously, but I couldn't see what happened. One of the horses snorted and reared, and his rider crashed to the ground. I drew my sword and tried to block the downward slash of one of the other raiders' scyaxes, but the force of the thing was too much for me and I fell to the road, those great hooves stamping around me. The kid was grappling with the fallen raider, rolling on the ground and grunting with pain and anger. Grath was using a pitchfork to stab and parry at the third horseman. Then his pitchfork fell to the road, and Grath slumped back, kicked hard in the stomach by the raider's great chestnut mount, and I looked up to find a bronze face looming over me.

I struggled to my knees to block his scyax with my sword, but my strength had gone, and his blow put me on my back again. The raider stooped low in the saddle and raised the scyax above his head to strike. I looked over at Grath, but he was lying where he had fallen, and the kid was still locked in battle with the other raider. He might win, but it would take about five seconds too long.

So, I thought, with sudden clarity, *this is it.*

I tried not to shut my eyes.

And then there was silence. Real silence. The silence of a shocked, spellbound audience, when you can't even hear the creak of the stage or the crunching of nuts in the pit because everyone, every living soul in the place, is momentarily still.

Then there was a swish of air, a thud, and the raider above me rocked quietly out of his saddle, the pitchfork embedded in his chest. I rolled and looked for Grath, trying to gasp out my thanks, but Grath was still lying on the road, winded and groaning. Maia's mother stood in the center of the lane, slender and pale, her eyes streaming, her right hand still raised and open.

The third raider reined his horse to a stuttering halt and turned back to the village. He wasn't about to take us on alone, and he would return with more, but for a moment, it was over.

As Maia's mother crumpled to the road, giving way completely to her grief and horror, I realized something. Until now, our mission had been about obligation, a way to make some money and stay alive. The only emotion my duties had instilled in me so far had been fear. Now there was something else: outrage. I didn't know that I could do anything to stop the raiders, but the party was the only force I had encountered so far that might even come close. I needed to get back to them.

So we kept moving. We took the two horses and the raiders' weapons. In three more minutes we were off the lane and in the lee of the Iruni Wood. I stayed at the back, watching, but they didn't come after us. Not this time.

❧

We walked through the woods for about an hour, and then, when exhaustion was starting to get the better of the older villagers and the smallest children, we stopped and slept as best we could in the rain. When we rose at first light we had no food or water, and the villagers had nowhere to go. I wanted to press north towards Verneytha, but if we stayed in the forest, we would eventually get dangerously close to that stone circle, and that was not a chance I was prepared to take. After a couple of hours of walking through the trees, we pulled east and were out of the woods altogether by lunchtime. Not that we had any lunch, of course. But it had stopped raining, and that was something.

As we walked, I tried to make sense of what I had learned in the last day or so. It was odd, but the villagers treated me like a soldier who knew what he was doing, so I started thinking in those terms: Will the specialist, the tactician, the man with secret knowledge about the raiders and their methods.

I thought about the maps we had looked over in Adsine, the ones showing the location of the raider attacks. I now knew how they got from place to place unseen, and I had started to wonder if there was a range limit to the power that moved them, or if they could appear only in certain places. Clearly the pale rock in that underground chamber was the source of their power. A smaller version of the same opalescent crystal had been in the center of the Iruni stone circle, and the fact that the raiders had walked there with their coffins suggested that they couldn't just vanish and reappear anywhere. But when the raiders had massed to assault the village, I had seen no such stone circle where we had appeared, nor had there been anything similar near the road when they attacked the coal wagons.

That scary raider with the horned helm was also a factor. He had been with them when they assaulted the convoy, and had seemed to move us from the circular cavern to the village, but the raiders at the stone circle had not required his presence to take them to the stables. Unless they could call on him, somehow, from the stone circle. Perhaps he could then bring them to the underground chamber.

That made a kind of sense, and would suggest that all the other stones (including the ones in the helms themselves) were receptors: it was the crystalline base of that underground chamber that did the work. Surely, that was it.

The attacks, as I recalled, were clustered in the central downs, ten or twelve miles south of Verneytha, in the borderlands of Shale and Greycoast. Some had been farther west, around Adsine, and some had been along the shores to the south. Ironwall, which was the easternmost city, had never been attacked, though the roads linking it to Seaholme to the southwest and Hopetown to the northwest had. Could it be that Ironwall was too far from the underground chamber? Or maybe the lack of attacks close to the city was just a way of pointing suspicion elsewhere. The raiders could be nestled snugly under Duke Raymon's palace for all I knew.

There was the Razor's now-ransacked keep, of course, right in the middle of it all. And we hadn't searched the place for a chamber in the bowels of the castle. But if the raiders could materialize in the keep itself, why appear in the woods outside to attack the place?

My mood worsened as the slow march progressed. We needed food, supplies, and a clear sense of where we were going. I figured that the rest of the party, after examining the farmhouse by the stone circle and giving up on my returning, would make for Verneytha's capital city, Harvest, and check in with Treylen, the governor. I should try to meet them there, I decided. I mentioned this to Grath and he passed it along as if everyone was invited. They seemed to think this as good an option as any and trailed after me like I knew what I was doing. It was all fairly bizarre, frankly, though not comically so.

Part of me wanted to just ride off. Even as poor a horseman as I was, I would reach Harvest in about a third of the time if I hadn't been dragging this string of starving refugees. But I couldn't leave them.

The families stuck together and enfolded the orphaned and lost to their collective bosom. I walked my horse slowly along, not talking to anyone and avoiding their eyes, keeping my distance in every way possible. The woman who had lost her child had found him alive and well just outside the village, but she then had to explain that he would never see his father again. They seemed lost and desperate, infected by terror like it was a disease. Of course I couldn't leave them.

By midafternoon we reached a scattered hamlet with a mill and a rustic tavern, and it was like finding an oasis after weeks in the desert. The kids shrieked with delight and danced, jumping into the stream, while the adults hugged each other and cheered and wept. I went inside and bartered with the tavern owner for bread and cheese and a few draughts of ale.

A few of the villagers stayed at the inn, but most, including Maia's family and the teenaged kid with the crossbow, who seemed to have aged about ten years since I first met him, stayed with me. We bought a broken-down cart and a couple of horses to pull it, or, rather, I bought it and the others threw in the few coppers they had left. We covered a few more miles, but it was painfully slow, and once it got dark we had to stop and make camp. Again, I kept myself to myself and slept fitfully, getting up several times to make sure there was no sign of the raiders. Everyone was still treating me like some kind of military expert and savior, and though I could play the part well enough, it was exhausting and terrifying. If the raiders caught up with us . . .

I couldn't wait to meet up with the party, if only to hand off the responsibility for these people to someone who would know what to do with it.

The next day we reached Verneytha. It was all I had heard and more. Golden wheat fields spread to the left, and dairy herds, plump and shiny, grazed on the right. We were stopped by a unit of Verneytha's light cavalry and asked about our destination. Everyone looked at me, so I did the talking.

The soldiers were armed with lances and wore light brass-scaled hauberks. Capes of green silk fluttered in the sun behind them. I explained very briefly the history of my sad little entourage, but you could tell that the officer didn't really care one way or the other. I told him who I was anyway, made it sound like Governor Weasel and I had been in short pants together, and told him we would need a military escort to the city.

The officer's attitude changed as soon as I mentioned Edwyn Treylen, becoming more helpful and attentive. I asked what they were doing, riding around like this, wondered even if they had been looking for me. It was standard procedure, they said: fast, mobile policing. It gave the governor eyes all over the state. I asked him what the crime rate was like, and he gave me a blank look, like I'd asked him which part of the moon served the best beer. There was no crime, he said, slightly offended, committed by Verneytha subjects; there were only "malefactors from abroad." Recently the raiders had taken to hitting patrols like his, he said. Three units had been lost in as many weeks. Now speed was also safety. In fact, if I would saddle up and ride with them, we could get back to Harvest and the rest of the party in no time.

"What about them?" I asked, nodding at the villagers.

"They've come this far without an armed escort, and through much more dangerous country," said the officer.

I stared at him, then said simply, "No. You watch them all the way to the city, or the governor will hear about it."

He agreed readily enough, though I don't think he really got it.

I took Maia and her parents aside. "I have to go on ahead," I said. The little girl's face fell and she clutched my hand, small and tight. "I'll let the governor know you're coming," I said, a little too lightly, avoiding those vast brown eyes. "You'll be looked after when you get there. You'll be safe."

Would they really? I didn't know. If the raiders could smash one of Verneytha's mounted patrols, they could get to the villagers easily enough; I just hoped they saw no reason to bother. As for what Edwyn Treylen would make of these poor and exhausted refugees, I couldn't say, and preferred not to speculate. But the place looked like it could use still more field laborers, and that couldn't be too bad a life, could it? I watched the farmhands as they worked by the road, their eyes cast down as if to look at us would be the height of rudeness, and I had an odd sinking feeling. For all its wealth and fertility, Verneytha might not be the paradise I had hoped. The laborers all had something of a haunted look and couldn't wait to get back to their vegetable picking, staring intently at the ground; it was as if they were afraid, but it was a muted, familiar fear. A legion of raiders in full armor could have ridden right by them and I don't think they would have seen them, unless they were dressed as asparagus.

Harvest

Orgos hugged me. It was a bit like being strapped into some kind of torture device, but he grinned broadly and said he was relieved to see me. Even Lisha and Mithos smiled and said they had been worried about me as if I was something they had lost and thought they wouldn't get back, like, I don't know, a dog or something. It was strange, but I grinned back. There was an odd sense of familiarity, if not of actual family. Garnet shook my hand as if we had never met before, and said it was good to see me.

"You brought all those people?" said Renthrette. "You got them out of a village when the raiders attacked and brought them to Verneytha *by yourself?*"

I had a feeling this was going to come up and I had been dreading it. I didn't know how she had heard the story, but word seemed to have reached the city before I did.

"Well, yes," I said, feeling stupid. "I didn't know what else to do with them, and they had nowhere to go that was even slightly safe, so . . ." My voice trailed off. It was a dangerous and moronic thing to have done, and I was sure it would get us into still more trouble with the rat-faced governor. I waited for the verbal onslaught, studying my beer, which—though better than anything we'd had in Shale—didn't really deserve the attention.

The more I thought about the whole thing—I thought of it as "the Rescue Scene"—the more theatrical it had seemed. It was like one of those actor's nightmares when you walk out on stage quite confidently and then realize you don't know your lines. In fact, you don't even know what play you are in. Usually in this dream, my attempts to keep the story going onstage are so witless that at some point someone stands up and shouts "You're not an actor!" Then everything ends in pandemonium, misery, and humiliation. But in the miniplay that was my nightmarish encounter with the raiders, something odd had happened. The audience hadn't recognized me as some comic buffoon who couldn't do anything but pratfalls and one-liners, and so they had assumed I could play the hero. Their assumption (well, Maia's at least) had somehow made it true.

Renthrette was still watching me. "That was . . ." She thought about what exactly it was, everyone else waiting to hear her decision. "Brave," she ended lamely.

I studied her quickly, looking for the sarcasm, but it wasn't there, and neither of us seemed to know what to say next or where to look. It was as if a trout that had been flopping on the riverbank had been picked up carefully by a cat and dropped back into the water.

I gaped, fishlike. No one spoke for a long time, and then Orgos started making cracks about my selflessness and heroism, everyone laughed, and we got back to our beer and a lighter mood. But, even as Garnet clapped me on the back and said he was ready to try another pint of lager, Renthrette watched me, wary, as if expecting to be somehow caught out and humiliated by whatever I did next. I suppose I watched her the same way. Brave? No. I hadn't been brave. There had been no decision, no knowing risk of my life, and you couldn't be brave without knowing it, could you? The house had assumed I knew the role, and so I did. Had Renthrette been in the audience, I might have fallen back on wisecracks and the kind of incompetence that would have gotten them all killed, but that's life in the theatre for you. If your audience doesn't believe in you, you can't believe in yourself.

⚜

I told them the whole story, all about the stone circle, the helms with the crystals set into the bronze, the massive circular chamber with its stable and its horned priest, the attack on the village, and all my musings about where that cavern might be and how it worked. Orgos watched me closely as I spoke of the crystal, and I tried not to look at the pommel of his sword. He smiled as if he were pleased with me. I looked at Garnet as I talked so I wouldn't have to deal with it. After I had told them everything, we went to see the ratty governor.

The governor's palace was a curious construction. It sat in the center of Harvest, a tower made from more glass than I had ever seen. We were led inside by a guard and ascended a spiral staircase up the center of the tower.

Its outer walls were lined with rooms where scribes wrote, treasurers calculated, and traders met. All were clearly visible as we passed by since the rooms were backlit by the huge windows, but there was almost no sound in the tower and no one responded as we passed their doors. The guard noted our curiosity and grinned. It was an odd grin: a little smug and knowing, but with an edge which resembled that hunted look I had seen in the faces of the field hands.

"They can't see you," he said. "Special glass. We can see in, but they can't see out."

At the top, in a sparse, aggressively functional chamber lined with windows, scribbled Governor Treylen. There was something furtive about his long hands and yellowing nails as they flashed among his papers, and I couldn't shake the wary distrust I felt when his black, shiny eyes flicked onto mine. He nodded us into chairs and consulted a clock, assessing how much time he could spare us.

"You are later than I expected," he said, fixing his beady gaze on Mithos. "I thought we would be getting more regular progress reports for our money, particularly since the attacks seem to have increased in daring. You had better have good tidings."

I told him everything, and he listened, clenching and flexing his bony, spider-leg fingers, fixing me with a glassy stare.

"So the raiders can appear and disappear by magic?" he said as I finished.

"I'm not sure that it's magic," I said, faltering. "I mean, it's something to do with those rocks and . . . I can't think of another word for it, though. Yes, they're using magic."

"I have lost thirty-two wagons since you took this job," he said, his thin lips pulling back from his long yellow teeth. He was smiling, but it was a smile that held no joy or amusement, unless it was at our expense. I wasn't sure what I had expected, but disbelieving contempt hadn't been high on the list.

"Three villages have been destroyed," he went on evenly, "their wheat fired, their hands slain, and their ploughs destroyed. In one attack alone I lost two hundred head of cattle, sixty pigs, and a hundred and fifty sheep, roasted alive as they waited for market. A forty-man cavalry unit was wiped out as they gave chase, and a total of fifty-five other Verneytha soldiers have been killed while acting as escorts or patrols. This report of yours with its fanciful tales of stone circles and disappearing raiders does little to restore my confidence in your abilities. If I'd wanted children's stories—"

"You wanted to know the truth," I said, "and I've told it to you. If you want to fight the raiders, I suggest you pay more attention to what I'm telling you."

Mithos gave me a quick look, but I had no intention of saying any more, so I shut up and waited to crush whatever the governor said next: improvised dialogue, I could do.

"Ah, Mr. Will Hawthorne," said the governor in his smuggest, oiliest tone. "Yes. The party's mouth. The party's braggart and fool. The last time we met, you had to throw yourself on Raymon's mercy to avoid a particularly unpleasant and degrading death, earned by your inability to keep your tongue in check. Of course, talk is what you do, isn't it?" he said, gazing thoughtfully at me. "We thought we had hired soldiers and investigators, but if the rumors are true, you are no more than an *actor*! A storyteller. No wonder your lies come so fluently. What sewer did you crawl out of, Mr. Hawthorne?"

"If I'm a sewer rat, I should fit right in here," I returned. "I might even run for public office."

There was a long silence. The governor just sat there and looked at me until I felt embarrassed and flushed.

"Step this way, Mr. Hawthorne," he said suddenly. "Come; don't be afraid, I shall not hurt you. That is not our way here."

He had risen from his seat and stepped back a few feet behind the desk. I glanced at the others uncomfortably. There was something cold and collected about his manner that filled me with panic. He crooked a long, pale index finger and oozed, "Come, William, I have something to show you."

With a swift movement he kicked open the cover of a circular, well-like hole in the floor.

"Come," he repeated, and his voice was disarmingly gentle. "The rest of you stay exactly where you are. There are guards watching you everywhere."

I couldn't see any, but there were windows everywhere, and I didn't doubt him for a second.

He stepped into the hole and began to descend a spiral staircase, while looking up at me and grinning. His fingers clutched my wrist and pulled me down quickly after him. I recoiled from the strong, fibrous fingers, stumbling down after him until we reached a wooden scaffold from which four evenly positioned staircases descended. Each wound down in a spiral and each was surrounded, all the way down so far as I could see, by softly lit rooms: cells.

"You see, Mr. Hawthorne," he whispered, "there are no torture chambers or disemboweling knives here such as you would have experienced in Greycoast. No rack, branding irons, or manacles."

He said each word with relish as if imagining them in use. The hair on my neck rose and for a second I thought he was quite mad.

"But there are no criminals, either," he said. "All due to potentially continual surveillance. The people never know *when* they're being watched, so they have to behave as if they always are. And not only our prisons have glass walls. Offices. Schools. Markets. Brothels. Everyone monitored. All monitors monitored in turn. Field laborers paid to watch each other. It's a self-policing society, Mr. Hawthorne. A perfect economy made secure by a myriad interconnected eyes and ears. A society where the police are in here"—he smiled, tapping his temple—"so it becomes impossible to even *think* criminally. You are never alone in Verneytha. Never.

"So you see, Mr. Hawthorne, how careful you have to be when you enter a new land. Perhaps you hated Greycoast's dungeons, but believe me, for a free man like yourself, there is nothing more terrible than continual surveillance. Nothing. In time you would yearn for the rack and the gallows, Mr. Hawthorne. You would plead for a torturer to let you pay your penalty and cover those awful, lidless eyes that watch you day and night. A few months in my cells, and you would never know what it was to be alone again. Even when no one was there you would feel them, watching, listening. Controlled madness, Mr. Hawthorne. Regulated insanity for the good of the state. Go and tell your stories about *that*, and leave the magic for the children and the very, very stupid."

He gave me a long, hard look and then snapped, "Upstairs! Quickly!"

I stumbled blindly back up the spiral. The others stared at me when I emerged. I must have looked pretty haggard.

"Now leave me," snarled the governor, his tone suddenly harsh. "I will summon you after I have decided what is to become of you."

"We are staying—" offered Mithos.

"I know where you are staying, you idiots. Now get out."

I tried to tell the others what I had seen in the tower but I couldn't convey its awfulness. Garnet had just looked bemused and shrugged it off as something that "didn't sound too bad." He told rival tales of dismemberment in Thrusia that once would have made me sick. But he understood with his gut what he didn't grasp with his conscious mind. He developed a new irritation at the way people watched us pass. We all did. Even at night, from time to time, lying there in the darkness of your bed, you thought you could feel the eyes.

❧

It was impossible to tell who was in the pay of the governor, so we locked ourselves in our tavern room and tried to decide what we were supposed to do next. To my mind it was clear: "We've got to split up and spread out. We can't move around Verneytha as it stands. It's a waste of time. There are people watching everywhere I look. When I go to the bathroom I feel like I'm playing to a capacity crowd."

"Will's right," said Lisha. "We should leave quickly, before the governor decides he wants us to stay in one of his little windowed prisons."

"But where do we go?" said Garnet to himself.

"God, this is a mess," said Mithos. Since the meeting with the governor, he had grown dour and unapproachable. "They've probably been watching us since we left Adsine. What a bunch of amateurs we must look like! We do have to leave, but I'm coming back, and they won't see me this time. Will, check the corridor."

We were all getting a little paranoid. I stood outside, eyes skinned for anyone who could be a spy. There was no one about, so this was one conversation the enemy wouldn't hear. Come to think of it, neither would I. That was bloody typical of them. They would send me into the line to prove what an integral member of the party I was, but when it came to making decisions, good old integral Will had to check the corridor.

Garnet flung the door open suddenly, and it was obvious that he was unhappy with whatever had been decided.

"Come in, Will," he sighed.

SCENE XLVII

Alone at Last

It was noon. The sun was high and the air still and humid. The wagon felt slow and conspicuous, trundling along like a very large beetle, but I had left Harvest two days ago, had just crossed the border between Verneytha and Shale, and hadn't so much as glimpsed a crimson cloak. Indeed, I hoped to catch sight of Adsine before sundown. Recently, sundown had become a big deal with me: it reminded me that another day had passed and I was still alive.

They had sent me ahead with the wagon figuring that the safest place for me to be was Shale, beyond the jurisdiction of Verneytha and Greycoast, whose leaders considered me a slightly less welcome visitor than, say, some unpleasant disease that made all your gristly bits fall off. This suited me just fine, because things were getting too grim by half for me to want to stay with the others. So far I'd been lucky and we'd survived all my cock-ups, but it was only a matter of time before something I did got Orgos stabbed or Garnet shot off his horse. The more I had come to like them, the more difficult it was to be Will the Weak Link. I moaned to Orgos that they were treating me like a child, sending me out of harm's way and all, but secretly I was relieved.

Lisha was to ride south to the villages that had borne the brunt of the attacks. Garnet would ride Tarsha part of the way with her and then return to Hopetown and Ironwall. There he would fume and complain by himself about how little action he was getting while reinvestigating the Razor's keep. Orgos was going back to Caspian Joseph's warehouse by the Iruni Wood, the closest thing to progress we'd achieved so far, even if it was still a bit of a dead end. The house was indeed where the raiders had been hiding their loot, but it wasn't the operations base we had hoped for. Orgos was to go back, skulk through the orchard, peer through windows, and generally creep about (in an honorable way, of course) in the ludicrous hope that someone would tell him, in passing, like, who the raiders were, where they lived, and so on. He was expressly ordered not to try to re-create my little jaunt via the stone circle.

Mithos had moved out of Harvest but he would be back with a different name and face to learn what he could about Verneytha without Treylen's spies monitoring him. It seemed to me that he was the only one doing anything useful. It seemed that way to Garnet also, who complained loudly about being gotten out of harm's way. But in one week, barring significant events (which I felt we could rule out), we would all meet again in the Adsine keep.

I was glad to be out from under Verneytha's watchful gaze. Though I had been there only a couple of days, I still found myself looking over my shoulder to see who was taking notes on the way I ordered a beer. It would wear off in time, no doubt, but at the moment I was as jumpy as a gazelle in lion country. Still, I was away from both Duke Raymon and Governor Treylen, there was no sign of the raiders, and Renthrette was currently asleep in the back of the wagon.

Realized that she wasn't accounted for, had you? She hadn't been much fun so far, to tell you the truth. Like her brother, she felt she was being protected, and that we had seen all that needed to be seen in Shale. Lisha corrected her, reminding us about the catacombs near Ugokan to the north of Adsine, which we had been told about when we first arrived. It was probably a blind alley, but we were used to those by now. After we had snooped around the deserted caves for a while, we were to meet with the count in Adsine and be the party's goodwill ambassadors, hopefully countering whatever tales of our incompetence had found their way over the border.

I slid the hatch open and peered into the back. Renthrette was curled up on a sheepskin rug, her sun-touched hair carelessly strewn across the pillow—though she'd tie it back as soon as she woke lest I thought she was making herself look good for my sake. Her brow was creased into a frown. Above her, one of the scorpion bolt throwers was set up on its tripod. If we were attacked, it might prove essential. Then all I had to do was turn the winch a few dozen times, find the groove, put a bolt in, take the safety off, turn it round, aim, miss, and hope the raiders laughed themselves to death. Still, this little study in futility was, they assured me, a gesture of defiance and therefore valuable. So calling them names ought to help too.

By late afternoon we had reached the village of Ugokan, where we saw little more than a few shells of timber and stone: no people were left. A handful of children had gone missing in the ancient caves and the search party never made it out. Other villagers vanished after that, and finally the rest just packed up and left. A century ago, said local stories, the caves had sheltered an army that had ravaged the entire region. We were about to see what they sheltered now.

Renthrette was always irritable when she woke up. She particularly didn't like to see my face as soon as she opened her eyes, since it reminded her that she had been sent off on a wild-goose chase with the apprentice, especially since we had already decided there was nothing in the catacombs but ghost stories. They were just too far west to be a useful base for the raiders. In any case, turning this pointless excursion into a romantic trip was going to be tough. Maybe I could set up a candlelit dinner in the caves and get the fruit bats to serenade us. Or maybe it would be so hot inside that we'd have to strip down to the bare essentials and we'd be rolling on the ground before you could say "Wake up, Hawthorne, you pathetic loser."

We had left the fertile ground back in Verneytha and the earth had been getting steadily more dusty and worthless ever since. As we passed through the empty village, sand swirled in our faces, and there in a group of smooth, yellowish rocks was the opening to the caves.

"At least it's shady," I said as we approached. Renthrette sighed. We had shared a room in an inn the previous evening and that had been one of my life's more major anticlimaxes. She had "kept watch" (on me) from midnight till dawn, intending to sleep in the wagon today. Now she was tired and sulky.

"After you." I smiled as we neared the entrance.

"Please," she muttered, pushing past me into the cave, adding, "Light?"

That was a request of sorts, so I struck my flint against the wall and onto an oil-soaked rag. From that she lit her lantern, and we advanced.

The cavern was large and smooth-sided. It looked like a natural formation, but I couldn't be sure. The rock was pale.

There was only one way through and we took it, feeling the air chill as we pressed on. She shivered and I tossed her a blanket.

"Thank you," she said distantly, wrapping it around her shoulders, listening. Somewhere in the tunnels beyond, water was dripping. We followed it. I wondered if we should have been unraveling a ball of string behind us, but it was too late now. I hoped that Renthrette knew where she was going, because I hadn't been paying much attention.

The path, such as it was, descended slowly until the walls were cream-colored. Running water had cut little rivulets and channels into the floor, but there were hard angles down here unlike anything at the entrance: these passages were man-made. We passed small chambers cut into the rock, each bare as if it had been brushed clean. After another hundred yards or so, we came upon the first cache of bodies.

They were adults and they had been down here some time, but were far from completely decayed. The smell was bad, though not as bad as you might expect. Fungus grew on their faces, and in places where their flesh had gone, their rat-nibbled bones showed through. I didn't look too closely. Renthrette did, but I sensed that it was for my benefit, to show what a strong stomach she had. As if I needed to be shown that.

The bodies obviously belonged to the search party who had gone looking for the missing children. What bewildered me was how they had died.

"They seem to be holding their throats or covering their faces," said Renthrette. "I can't see any wounds or broken bones. You think this could be part of the chamber you were in when you were with the raiders?"

We hadn't spoken for a while and her voice echoed in the confined space so suddenly that I looked around me uncertainly, as if afraid of offending someone. "No," I whispered. "That was a building. This is quite different."

We moved on, stepping through a doorway into a cavern. It was huge, and vaulted like a temple. Renthrette held up her lantern, and as the light splashed across the floor, we froze. On the far side of the cave were four seated figures, armored with bronze and cloaked in scarlet. They were facing us.

The Secret of the Caves

I gasped and turned to flee, pulling Renthrette after me. I blundered against the wall but managed to stay upright, and began stumbling back the way we had come, blinded by terror and sudden claustrophobia. I had barely gotten out of the corridor when a strong hand seized my wrist and pulled me sharply backwards. The shock felt like it would tear my arm out of its socket. Stopped in my tracks, I twisted round to face my captor.

A lantern shone in my face and Renthrette whispered, "Get back in there."

I stared at her in amazement as she walked back down the stone corridor and into the great chamber.

"You want to take them on by ourselves?" I hissed. "Good luck."

"I think even you could handle this fight," she answered without looking back.

She strode away, not even trying to be quiet. I waited where I was, considering her composure and the sudden darkness. (She had, of course, taken the lantern with her.) As I started cautiously after her, she called back, her voice booming from wall to wall, "They're dead, Will. See for yourself!"

She was right. The raiders were sitting against the wall, their weapons on the floor in front of them, their hands and faces leathery. Across the cavern lay several more. All dead.

"What the hell is this?" I whispered.

Renthrette adjusted the flame of her lantern and we got a better look at the cavern. We saw a dozen bedrolls and as many cloaks and weapons strewn about, but no sign of a struggle. I walked over to the back of the cavern and found a well shaft, almost brimming with dark water. Behind it was another dead raider, his helm in his hands and a twisted look on his desiccated face. I sat on the edge of the well and looked at him. They could not have been dead more than a couple of weeks, perhaps only days.

"The enemy has been tracking our movements since we showed up," said Renthrette. "They knew we were bound to come here at some point."

"You think this was a trap?" I said. "For us?"

I looked around some more, considering the damp stone of the walls as it picked up the light and glowed pale as opal. The entire cave sparkled softly with that same crystalline rock.

Well, at least you know how they got here.

Which meant that more raiders could appear here any second, taking the places of their comrades who had been killed.

"Renthrette!" I said. "I don't think we should be here."

She was crouching by the four seated corpses, and looked in my direction when I spoke. I was going to say more but then I heard a sound somewhere below me: it was a glugging sound, thick and liquid. I snatched the lantern and peered into the waters of the well. There was a moment of near-silence, the soft dripping of water resonating through the caves and tunnels, and then it came again, this time resembling a gurgling, bubbling sound that I could feel vibrating through my stomach. The water stirred, as if it was beginning to boil.

Something was coming up.

I leapt to my feet and ran, shouting, "Get out! There's something in the well!"

I hit the opposite wall as the water sloshed over the rim and splashed onto the floor. I turned and saw, or half saw, the faint haze of an almost colorless cloud breaking from a bubble in the water.

"Gas!"

We ran.

We ran out and up, back the way we had come. With each step I fought my dread of the tightening of my lungs, a dry, sickening drowning feeling. . . . I stumbled and fell more than once. I held my breath until I could go no farther and had to gasp the thin cavern air, terrified of sensing some scent or flavor that would mean death. I was at Renthrette's heels all the way, heedlessly bashing my knees against the stone until we burst from the caverns into the afternoon light. I've never run so hard or so fast in my life.

We threw ourselves into the dust and drank the air, wheezing and laughing at our escape. She sort of half embraced me in her joy, and I hung on until her desire to break away became unavoidable.

"Just some kind of gas," she said, amazed.

But there was no "just" about it. I thought of those doubled-up corpses inside; we had survived where the raiders hadn't. They weren't invulnerable. They weren't unbeatable. We *weren't* destined to lose every time we saw them. I grinned at Renthrette and she grinned back, without distaste or suspicion. It was about time.

※

We readied the wagon and made for Adsine, pushing the horses as hard as we dared in the heat. Renthrette was as matey now as she had ever been, and I tried to think of a way to capitalize on her good humor. It wasn't that she was never civil to me, but actual pleasantness tended to be the kind of thing you record in a ledger, like a lunar eclipse or the birth of a two-headed cow.

"It was a good thing you saw that gas," she said with a disarming smile as we rolled into the afternoon.

"I heard it first, gurgling down there like the witch's cauldron in a children's story."

"I don't really know any stories," she answered. "Once our waiting woman—"

"Hold it! You had servants?"

"A couple," she replied.

"Tough life," I muttered.

"One of them was my old wet nurse," she explained, ignoring me. "She was once caught telling us stories and was replaced. My father said that such fantasies were corrupting nonsense."

"I've heard that before," I sighed. "For a while back in Cresdon I was held personally responsible for the collapse of morality and religion all over the region. I wish I had been. Maybe you saw some of my plays," I ventured hopefully.

"I've never been in a theatre," she said.

"Never? You're joking! Never?"

"Did I miss something?"

"Theatre is where the world makes sense!" I exclaimed. "It's where we admit the roles we play daily, where we confess our love of intelligence and evil. It's where . . . You aren't listening, are you?"

"What?" she said suddenly. "Oh, I'm sorry, Will. I was trying to remember Nurse's story."

"Don't worry, I'm used to it."

"It was something about a girl, and a dragon who was so lonely that he wept constantly—"

"And his tears flowed down the mountains and threatened to drown the village," I said hurriedly. "Yes, I know it. But it was a boy, not a girl."

"In mine it was a girl," she said.

"Whatever."

She paused for a long, thoughtful moment and then, with what I took to be courage, looked at me and said, "I don't remember how it ended. The story, I mean."

It was a request, of sorts.

"Well, as you'd expect, I suppose," I said. "The little girl has to save the village, so she goes up into the mountains and petitions the dragon to stop crying. At first the dragon is angry and he weeps tears of rage so that the waters rise to the windowsills of the houses below and the villagers have to go upstairs. Then the little girl tells him about her family and how they are in danger, and the dragon cries tears of sadness so that the waters rise to the door lintels and the villagers have to climb onto their roofs. Then the little girl, realizing that the dragon is merely lonely, offers to befriend it, and the tears stop. The waters subside and they all live happily ever after. The end. Not much of a story really."

"I like it," she said without taking her eyes from the road ahead.

"I suppose it has a certain charm," I confessed, watching her.

She was staring ahead so as not to show me her face but I caught her rubbing her eyes before she turned and smiled at me. "Thank you," she said.

❧

In three hours Adsine lay below us, its keep on the hill by the river. To the east were the stables, which were Shale's last economic asset. Then there were woods, and the Wardsfall, which snaked gradually south and east to Greycoast. As soon as we got there I would have to go back to playing ambassador and soldier to the count and his entourage. Part of me would much rather stay on the wagon with Renthrette. I could do without the raider corpses and running through dark tunnels with gas clouds at our heels, but the trip had been pleasant in some ways. I wasn't sure what it was about her I liked, if "liked" was the word, and she sometimes got right on my nerves, but . . .

There isn't an easy end to that sentence, is there?

Renthrette smiled and I guessed she sensed my mixed feelings about reaching Adsine. As the sun sank, red and clear, we crossed the bridge and gave our names to the guard at the gate of the keep.

There it goes again, I thought, watching the sun go down. *I'm still alive. Kind of miserable, admittedly, but alive.*

For a brief, unreadable moment, Renthrette slipped her arm about me and squeezed me to her side. I jumped slightly, taken by surprise. She smiled, and murmured, "Cheer up, Will."

I gave her a blank look and waited for the punch line. Then the guard returned and, as he led the horses by the bridle, she released me. The moment, whatever it had been, evaporated.

SCENE XLIX

Adsine Again

I got my old room back. There was my bath and my bed as before, and I found myself wondering what had happened to the dreams of wealth and glory I had contemplated on my first night here. Renthrette was next door. Chancellor Dathel, still in his black robes of office, left us with instructions to join the count for dinner in an hour. Everything was as it had been, the downstairs bustling with bored infantry and cavalrymen with nothing to do but exercise, tend their equally bored horses in the courtyard stables, and flirt with the maids. It was reassuring to know that their castle duties gave most of them solid alibis for the major raider attacks. It made me feel safer.

I had a bath, dressed slowly, and wandered round the second floor. Over by the south wall I came upon a tiny library, not much larger than my bedroom. To keep my mind off Renthrette I browsed some collections of old plays, many of which I already knew. It struck me that I hadn't seen a single theatre in any of the three lands. It was a shame; these people could use one. I pulled out a volume of local folktales and flicked through it for ten minutes or so, wondering if I could learn more about the spectral army from two and half centuries ago, while trying to convince myself that dinner would be an improvement on last time.

It wasn't. If anything, it was worse. The continued activities of the raiders were having telling effects on Shale. Even Arlest, as he told us apologetically, could not afford to pay what his neighbor countries were demanding for basic foodstuffs. The count was, as before, subdued and strained, wearing a plain robe belted with rope and a simple copper circlet on his head. Renthrette smiled at him encouragingly, but he looked sad and tired. Something in his wife's eyes suggested a concern for his health. He was getting slimmer all the time, as if he was an image of the land he governed.

Renthrette related our escape in the caverns and his eyes filled with concern, so that I nearly told her to drop it and spare him the anxiety.

"Do you feel you have made progress?" he asked, not looking hopeful.

I instantly thought of that hellish journey to Ironwall with burning coal wagons and bleeding boys and hoped to God that we wouldn't have to talk about that. Words make you live it all again.

"There are certain possible solutions which we have pursued," said Renthrette, "and managed to cross off."

The count nodded thoughtfully and asked, "And have you any ideas as to the whereabouts of the raiders?"

"Again, it is more a question of where they are not," she answered. "We have narrowed the range of possibilities."

I took the opportunity to lead the conversation away on a random stream of subjects from the weather to the state of our horses (about which I knew nothing). I talked for about three minutes and no one said anything, just drank their thin soup and dipped their chalky bread in it, for, as I can be sparkling in conversation when I want to be, so I can be downright tedious. Too many things from the past few days couldn't be spoken of, and not merely for security reasons. I wasn't about to go through it all again, nor was I to deprive the dead of their dignity by telling the horror of their ends.

I figured I'd bore the count and his wife to their beds instead: "I saw some trees outside that reminded me of some back home. Can't remember the name, but they have a sort of smooth bark with pointed leaves that go red in the autumn. Sort of red, but darker. Brown, perhaps, is closer. A reddish brown. Or, rather, a brownish red. You know the kind I mean? Pretty, as trees go. Well anyway, we used to have one right outside my house. When I was a child, I used to climb it. I remember every night at about six o'clock, my mother used to come out looking for us. My mother was a smallish woman who made shoes. When I say 'smallish' I mean about my height. Probably a few inches less. Not *short*, exactly, but kind of *small*. The shoes she made were a sort of brown a bit like the tree, but not exactly brown. . . ."

And so on.

No one could stand too much of that for long. The countess suppressed a yawn and I wound the thing up as anticlimactically as I could. They smiled politely and tried to figure out ways to escape before I started on another topic.

We retired for a drink before bed. I was exhausted, but Renthrette, having slept most of the day, seemed to want to talk for once. My blithering over dinner had ensured that no one would want to sit with us into the small hours, so we were alone.

She was wearing her bottle-green dress again and had her hair down. Her skin had lost the pinkish burn it had developed when we first crossed the Hrof wastes, softening into a tan that showed off the blue of her eyes. I thought about mentioning this, but didn't. I poured her some wine and sat on a beer barrel behind the counter.

I found myself drinking and talking aimlessly about acting in Cresdon and running from Rufus.

To my astonishment, she started laughing. "What were you talking about tonight at dinner?" she said. "Something about a tree you used to climb. What was all that about?"

"I just didn't want to talk about what we've been doing," I mumbled. "I'm getting tired of rehashing it all."

"I think I know what you mean," she said gravely.

I looked at her sharply. There was no sarcasm. She was looking at the threadbare carpet and cradling her half-empty wineglass.

"It's just, I don't know," I said quickly, "kind of painful to have to keep thinking about, you know—"

"The convoy," she said.

"I suppose so, yes," I sighed. "And the visit to the Razor's keep, and the attack on the village. Both attacks. Both villages. It seems that all I've done over the last couple of weeks is watch people die."

"I know," she said softly. I watched for the usual mask of steel to slip over her face, but it didn't. She just looked at me sadly, and something passed soundlessly between us, as if we had come out of a play together, a tragedy, and didn't need to talk about it.

"Was there a tree, Will?"

"What?"

"Was there a tree where you grew up, like in your story?"

I thought about what I should say. I could tell her about all the trees she could ever wish to hear about. I could pour out nostalgia, paint a picture with words of a happier time for Will Hawthorne, and she would pity me and take me in her arms.

"No," I said. "There was no tree. I made it up."

She looked at me for a long time, until I could stand it no more and looked away. Without warning, she kissed me quickly on the cheek and stood up. "Good night, Will," she said.

She was gone before I was able to reply, closing the door as she slipped through it. It was the kind of kiss you might bestow on a nine-year-old or a pet rabbit, but genuine for all that. I poured myself another drink and replayed it all in my head.

≈✖≈

Almost twenty-four hours later I was back there again. The bar storeroom was piled high with beer barrels (apparently the only thing they had in good supply) but I thought wine made me look classier, so I opened the only bottle there as Renthrette arrived. We hadn't seen each other all day and her manner was deliberately casual. She hadn't forgotten the previous evening, but didn't want to dwell on it. Not that there was much to dwell on.

She had a message from her beloved brother. The raiders had made no attacks for a week now, the longest respite since they had begun.

"That's great news!" I exclaimed. "We must have whittled them down bit by bit. A casualty here, a casualty there. The ones who were poisoned in the caves must have been the last."

"No," she said. "They weren't. You know there are dozens, possibly hundreds of them left. They are lying low. Perhaps one of the party has got close to finding them and they daren't move. Perhaps they are preparing for a bigger attack than any so far."

Sometimes I wish people would just take things at surface value. Analysis is a great complicator of existence.

Naturally, she was right again. Word came from Orgos in Greycoast within the hour that a number of raider units, totaling perhaps 160 men, maybe more, seemed to be coming together in northern Greycoast. They had been seen by Verneytha border patrols but they had, curiously, not vanished, continuing to move slowly, quietly, and without making further attacks.

I was aghast.

"A hundred and sixty or more!" I exclaimed. "Hell's teeth, that's more than we *ever* thought there were! Still, no match for the six of us, eh?" I added. We had obviously made a real dent in their operations.

"Why are they suddenly being so obvious?" Renthrette mused aloud.

"Like you said, something's happening."

"And we are stuck here," she said miserably.

"Good," I said sulkily.

"Don't you feel we should be there with the party? They will gather together, all of them. We should go."

"And die as one big happy family. What a treat."

"We're achieving nothing here," she said, getting up impatiently. I gave her a suggestive glance and said, rather stupidly, "That depends on what you're trying to achieve."

She shot me a pointed look as if what I had meant vaguely romantically had sounded merely lecherous.

"That didn't come out right," I said, too frustrated to put my heart into sounding apologetic. I poured myself a glass of wine and looked at the floor, instantly recognizing it as Square One.

"Is that wise?" she said frostily, regarding the wineglass as an elderly schoolteacher might.

"Very," I said, drinking deeply. "I need to relax more. In fact," I added, tipping the dregs of the bottle down in one gulp, "I'm going to get some more."

"I don't think that's a good idea—" she began.

"I'm not interested in your ideas," I said quickly.

"You can't—" she began.

"Watch and learn. This is called 'The Hawthorne Guide to Staying Alive.' Step one: When five of your friends suggest that you fight a hundred and sixty trained killers, go home immediately."

I walked out of the room and down the corridor, passing the count's rooms and the long, straight wall with the tapestry, Renthrette running at my heels.

"Step two . . . ," I continued, descending the stairs and ignoring her spluttered attempts to interrupt, "spend the rest of your life sitting in a bar, drinking lots of beer, playing cards, and picking up women."

On the ground floor she caught hold of me and thrust me against the wall in a move worthy of her brother.

"Now, you listen to me," she began. "We saved your neck—"

I'd heard this all before and turned away with disinterest. The barrack doors were open and over her shoulder I could see in and across the bunks of resting cavalrymen to the windows on the other side.

Windows, I thought. *On the other side. . . .*

Suddenly something hit me like a falling buffalo. I said the word aloud to Renthrette.

"What?" she asked.

"Windows, look."

"So?"

"Come upstairs."

I half dragged her up, past the second story, where we had been drinking, and on to the next, where a heavy oak door took us out onto the battlements. Still running, I led her to the front of the building, blinking against a light rain and what was probably a breeze on ground level, but felt like a gale up here.

"What?" she demanded irritably as we reached the forward-facing parapet. I spun her to look back across the top of the keep. The wind picked up suddenly and I had to shout. "Look at the shape of the building," I said. "The foundation is cross-shaped. Each level is the same size and shape. On the ground floor the crosspiece is the cavalry quarters, one room on the west side and one on the east. On the top floor the crosspiece is more battlements. But where's the crosspiece on the middle floor, the floor where our rooms are, the floor where the count lives?"

"I don't follow."

"Why are there windows on the middle story at the front and the back but none on the sides?" I said. "The cavalry barracks on the ground floor house two hundred men. There must be rooms of the same size directly above them that we've never even seen! There are probably doors behind those tapestries. God, Renthrette," I exclaimed with sudden and heart-stopping fear, "we've found the raiders. They were here all the time."

SCENE L

❧

Implications

N o," said Renthrette.

She had said that a lot in the last half hour.

"Yes," I said. "It all makes sense."

"It makes no sense at all," she said. "Why would Arlest shelter the raiders here? It's crazy, and we have no evidence except for some *idea*."

I told her that investigation was too risky but, like her brother, she thought theories were for sissies. We walked along the long corridors that led to our rooms wondering if those moth-eaten tapestries concealed doors, but we were always under the casual watch of the guards. We thought, very briefly, about going to the chancellor or to the countess, or even to Arlest himself, but that was clearly hopeful to the point of stupidity. We had to presume they were all involved. That left us with a puzzle: How might we get a look in those rooms?

An hour later the puzzle had changed. How had Renthrette convinced me to stand guard while she climbed a rope from the battlements down the side of the keep? We were back on the roof, where the troops were few and not so much casual as dormant. One of them asked me where my "lady friend" had got to and went off chuckling, convinced that she'd dumped me for some burly soldier. Nothing so mundane; she was swinging at the end of a rope, trying to force the second-story shutters with a throwing dagger. Naturally.

But then she was calling me to climb down after her, and I had other things to worry about. I'm not fond of climbing; factor in a howling wind and a rain-slicked rope, and you might understand why it took me three hellish minutes to inch down to the shuttered window where Renthrette was waiting for me. Then she was muttering about my incompetence and pulling me in with the kind of rough, physical manhandling that always sounds like it should be exciting, but is usually just embarrassing.

Inside was exactly what we had expected: one of two large dormitories identical to the cavalry barracks below. The room was deserted, but there were footlockers full of red-flighted arrows and scarlet cloaks hanging from racks around the walls. At one end of the room was a heavy door. I felt we'd seen enough, but Renthrette tried it anyway.

Behind it was a stone staircase.

We inched down the stairs. They went not to the ground floor, but to a familiar round chamber in the basement, its floor glowing with the soft, white luminescence of the Ugokan caves and the Iruni stone circle. I stood on the steps and looked at it, as if I had seen it only in nightmares before. There was, thank God, no sign of the raiders, but the place alone gave me the creeps. Renthrette felt it too. She gazed wide-eyed at the room and then looked back to me. "It's just as you described it," she said.

"You didn't believe me?" I asked, momentarily incredulous.

"Of course I did," she said, "but, you know . . . You're the storyteller, right? I thought perhaps you had embroidered it a little. Made it more dramatic."

"You want drama?" I said petulantly. "Try filling the place with raiders. That part was true too."

She gave me a slightly pained look. "Right," she said. "Sorry."

All I wanted to do right now was get out of this awful place: not just the room, or the secret barracks, but the castle itself. For once, she seemed to agree. We retraced our steps, climbed back up the rope to the roof, and returned to our rooms, badly rattled but apparently undetected.

❧

It was difficult to decide where our discovery left us, other than with the sense that we should have thought of this weeks ago. There had been clues that we had managed to miss completely, like the fact that we'd been served conspicuously watered ale while the bar was piled high with beer barrels for its less public inhabitants. Or the prohibitively expensive horses at the huge ranch by the river, which was obviously just a big stable for the raiders who were on the ale over at Count Arlest's House of Hell. What was more difficult to figure out was what we were supposed to do with our discovery.

One thing we did learn, for what it was worth, was that although

the long corridors did have concealed doors into the raiders' quarters, the raiders themselves almost certainly never used them. The
raiders moved between their barracks and the great circular chamber in the basement, which could put them anywhere in the area.
They could come and go without ever setting foot in a public area
inside or outside the keep. It was tough to swallow the idea that the
servants, the regular army, the count, his pale wife, and the rest of
the castle were unaware of the presence of two hundred armed men,
but it *was* possible.

"Well, now we know," said Renthrette with a satisfied smile, as
if she'd figured it all out for herself. This annoyed me, as it had been
my flash of genius, but it was typical of Renthrette and Garnet. You
only make progress by *doing* things. Ideas are worthless. What really
moves things along is hefting your ax at somebody or swinging from
the walls like some lesser primate. I might as well give up on the
smooth, witty banter and just toss her a piece of fruit from time to
time.

But not everything was falling neatly into place. The attack on
Arlest, which we'd witnessed when we first arrived, was a round peg
for our square holes. I was tempted to see the count as innocent and
the attack as genuine, while Renthrette thought they were all guilty
as hell and the attack had been purely for our benefit. That men had
died in the course of laying this false trail only convinced her of its
spuriousness.

I considered the spectral army that had ravaged the region 250
years ago. After the dust had settled, three new capital cities had
been built, and one of them had been Adsine. The keep was as old as
the town. Someone had known what that opaline rock could be used
for and they had built it into the basement of the fortress. Had those
who had lived here ever since forgotten about the spectral army, or
had they always known what that stone could do, and Arlest (or
whoever was responsible) was merely the first to use it since? And if
so, why now?

As ever, the more I learned, the less I understood. The only thing
I knew for certain was that we had to get out, and we had to do so
quickly and without rousing suspicion. I figured we should just fill
our saddlebags and take a couple of fast horses. Renthrette argued
that the contents of the wagon were too potentially useful in what
might yet transpire.

Right. We needed that wagon like we needed cobras in our underwear. I told her it was slow and obvious. She said we weren't supposed to look like we were running away and that if we did, no matter how fast our horses were, they would get us. I suspected they would "get us" whatever we did, but she was sick of hearing me say that, so I shut up and let her play party leader, grudgingly grateful for her not pointing out that I could no more handle a fast horse than I could beat my arms and fly back to Cresdon.

It was a curious thing, but considering that we'd solved the main part of the mystery, I couldn't help feeling that it made little difference. After all, knowing where the raiders came from didn't make them disappear. What were we supposed to do, shout "We know where you live!" and figure they'd go away out of sheer embarrassment?

Renthrette was all business, only interested in the job at hand. Whatever minuscule spark there had been between us had given up the ghost as soon as adventuring had reared its ironclad head. Her face was all steely again and she had gone back to double-checking our equipment and polishing her sword. I was just an extra, a walk-on who announces the arrival of the mad duke and then goes off into the wings and is forgotten. In my plays I'd always tried to give my walk-ons a bit of something special: some pithy philosophy or wry political humor. I got *Enter Messenger. Messenger gives letter to the warrior queen. Exit Messenger.* Renthrette had her script memorized and was ready to hold center stage for a good while to come.

Then, while I was laboriously pursuing this metaphor through my head and she was carefully checking the links of her mail shirt one by one, she said, "You'd better think up something to tell the count so that he won't suspect anything."

Great. So she's in control but I have to think us out of this fortress.

"Such as?" I said testily.

"You're the storyteller," she answered, without looking up.

❧

I thought through all the lies that had helped me out of tight corners before: the sudden death of an aged aunt, the news that my house was on fire or that my wife had just had twins. I was a good liar and could deliver all the usual one-liners with a straight face: "What a delightful baby," "You can count on me," "I only play cards for fun," "I wouldn't dream of such a thing, Officer," and of course, "Your *wife*? I had no idea. . . ." Still, this time my back was really up against the wall and the old chestnuts wouldn't help. As a rule, however, I don't worry about plausibility when I lie, I just state the case and adamantly say that it is so until the opposition begins to waver and confesses that he was too drunk to recall, exactly. . . . I went to think amongst the ancient volumes of the tiny library on the second floor.

❧

Renthrette and I saw Arlest immediately before dinner and announced our intention to leave as soon as we had eaten, hoping to travel a few hours before stopping for the night. She thought this was too sudden, but what we had learnt had radically altered my perspective on the place and the people in it, and it was becoming increasingly difficult to imagine speaking to Arlest at all without freezing up. The castle seemed still darker and colder, with longer, more eerily silent corridors and more guards than seemed necessary. The chancellor struck me as calculating and the pale, silent countess was positively sinister. It had become a place of strange shadows and howling winds: a castle of ghosts and vampires. Only Arlest himself remained oddly unblemished. I still couldn't quite cast him as the villain, plotting and laughing up his sleeve as he ensnared his victims. I had seen too much death and misery to be able to pin it all on this weary, mild-mannered old man.

"Why the change of plan?" he asked with guileless interest.

"Well, sir," I began.

"You needn't call me sir, Will, you know that." He smiled.

"Right," I said, a little uncomfortably. "Well, we are moving off because we have vital information to pass on to our friends who are currently monitoring the movements of the raiders in northern Greycoast."

I felt Renthrette shift anxiously. We hadn't discussed my story.

"Information?" he said. "What information?"

"I know where the raiders come from," I said.

Again Renthrette moved, fractionally. They were both still and tense, waiting to hear what I had to say. I swallowed hard to steady my nerves. "They come from the lost kingdom of Bangladeia across the sea."

I paused for effect and the count sat down slowly, as did Renthrette. I doubted either had heard of Bangladeia, and both, for quite different reasons, were about to start doubting my sanity.

"Over two hundred years ago," I went on earnestly, "the people of Bangladeia were beset by a terrible calamity which the books of your library here describe as a dragon."

"A dragon?" said Renthrette, a little too dryly.

"Probably a poetic description," I added with the indulgent smile of a teacher imparting knowledge, "for something far more mundane. A drought or famine, for example. The small kingdom of Bangladeia was unable to support itself, and many of its people died. From the dregs of their civilization they formed an army and set to wandering from place to place, taking from others what they could not grow or produce for themselves. Somewhere along the line, it seems," I went on, quite reasonably, "they met Relthor the Necromantic Sage of the Western Mountains, and through him they traded their souls for life. After a hundred and eighty years of wandering, they have found their way to your lands. The warriors are vampires. We must completely re-think our approach, since I am in no doubt that we are facing the ranks of the Undead, who dwell in the darkness of centuries and survive by drinking the blood of their victims."

There was a long silence and they both looked at me with wide eyes.

"You think the raiders are vampires?" said the count, cautiously.

"Certainly," I replied with becoming gravity. "And have been for a hundred and eighty years. They turn into bats between attacks."

Renthrette's mouth was moving, but no sound was coming out.

"So you'll want to borrow some good horses," said Arlest with a sort of resigned bewilderment. I couldn't say if he was disappointed or just caught completely off-guard.

Renthrette found her voice and cleared her throat before saying slowly, "We are in no great hurry. Will has been working very hard over the last few days and is—" She paused for thought. "—rather *tired*. I will drive the wagon back to Greycoast and he can rest in the back."

Now she was getting the hang of it. The two of them exchanged knowing glances, and Arlest nodded thoughtfully.

"I'll provide some blankets," he said kindly.

"That would be helpful," I said, "and we will want as much garlic as you can get hold of."

The count nodded slowly, his eyes wary. I tapped my finger on the side of my nose significantly and sidled over to the bar. I poured myself a very large glass of wine, downing it hurriedly as I muttered about sunlight and wooden stakes. Meanwhile, Renthrette and the count talked in concerned tones.

Fine. I get to be scapegoat again, but if it gets us out of this for-tified charnel house in one piece, I'll take it.

The rest of the dinner party arrived as I was conspicuously down-ing a third cup of wine, and they were informed of our decision to leave, along with a version of the reason. Nobody said too much about Bangladeia and its blood-swilling geriatrics. Renthrette didn't speak to me until dinner was over, though she gave me a couple of long, blank looks while I was talking earnestly about vampire battle tactics and plotting the positions of certain ghoul units with pieces of cheese and cured ham. It was a quiet meal.

⚜

A couple of hours later we were on the road and Renthrette was driving. Once out of Adsine's rutted and smelly streets I came up front and sat beside her. She turned a stony face on me and said, "What exactly were you trying to do, Will? Get us killed?"

"We were quite safe," I answered cheerfully.

"I have never heard such rubbish in all my life," she said, clutch-ing her face in both hands for a moment. "I couldn't believe my ears."

"You told me to come up with a story. I did."

"How could you come up with something so absurd? All that Bankle-whatever-it-was rubbish—"

"Bangladeia," I inserted.

"Whatever," she snapped back at me. "If I hadn't suggested you were going mad, he would have smelled a rat so fast that our heads would be on the block by now."

"You're a lousy judge of human nature."

"What's that supposed to mean?"

"It means," I said, "that so far they haven't given us credit for discovering anything. They must believe that we'd fall for something utterly preposterous or they wouldn't have invited us to share a cas-tle with the raiders, would they? If Arlest really is responsible, then he brought us in on the assumption that we were too stupid to figure out the truth. They are dying for a chance to laugh at our stupidity, so I gave it to them, and they went for it. Hook, line, and sinker. You don't have to be plausible. Just give them what makes them feel good about themselves."

"Well, it seemed dangerous to me," she said, a little less emphatically.

"A serious excuse would have made them analyze it seriously. In our position, our greatest strength is our ineptitude."

She thought for a moment and said, "How on earth did you dream up all that garbage?" she said.

I couldn't tell if this was supposed to be praise, but I took it as such.

"Actually," I said humbly, "most of it is from a legend I came upon in the library. As I said, it's probably a reworking of that ghost army story. If you see it as just a small, ruined country trying to win itself some profits by force, then it seems kind of similar to Shale's current position."

"So you were deliberately sailing close to the wind."

"If you have to sail at all, you may as well get a thrill out of it."

"But," she said, coming back to the matter in hand with a jolt, "the raiders have attacked villages and convoys in Shale as well as elsewhere."

"True. But, as you said, they also seem to have staged an attack on Arlest in which their own people got killed. Maybe they wanted to divert suspicion, or thin out the population a bit. You know, make resources go further."

"That's appalling."

"Yes," I agreed. "It is."

❧

As the sun got low behind us I turned over the question as to why Arlest had let us go. Though it was tempting, I couldn't quite resign myself to the idea that—if it *was* him holding the reins of the raiders—he had believed us so completely that he no longer considered us a danger. That seemed far too casual for so meticulous an operation, even considering what a wooden sword our knowledge was. Someone in that room, maybe several or all of them, knew that our discovery of those barracks had always been a danger. That they took our departure so calmly bothered me and made me wonder for

a moment exactly who it was who had been deceived. I felt the explanation in my bowels rather than in my head. They were about to
do something that would make our suspicions and discoveries worthless: something conclusive.

It was getting too dark to go on, rather like this narrative. We
would soon have to camp or stay in an inn. I told Renthrette that I was
worried. For once she didn't seem to want solid reasons. I wondered if
she felt it too, that sense of brooding heaviness, like the air before a
storm. I was glad when we came upon an inn and the chance for a beer
and a night's sleep. Renthrette suggested that we get up early and—if
we could buy or rent them from the innkeeper—yoke two extra horses
to the wagon. That way we might be over the Greycoast border by
noon the following day.

Nothing of a remotely personal nature happened.

SCENE LI

A Decision

By the evening of the second day we were only ten miles from the road between Ironwall and Hopetown and we had worked our four horses till they staggered and snorted with resentment. I patted one on the neck and it tried to bite my hand off. I sat, gazing out of the back of the wagon, and wondered vaguely what I was supposed to do if the raiders appeared. Wave? Make one last move on Renthrette? It would have to be a quick one.

The track rolled through the Proxintar Downs until the Iruni Wood was small behind us. Atop each rise we looked for horsemen, and on one of the highest of the hills we could see the distant citadel of Ironwall to the southeast as the sun set. Even from this distance, it was impressive. We would make for it at first light and hope to find some of our company there, alive and well, though who knows what trouble they could have gotten themselves into by now.

I made a small fire by the wagon while a little light remained and put a billy of vegetables and water on it. Renthrette tended the horses, whispering secretly to them. We ate, and the meal was hot, but nothing more. It wouldn't feed my soul, but it might sustain my body until the raiders had other plans for it.

For once she did not shrink away when I sat close to her, but her mind was elsewhere and I didn't pursue the advantage. After a while, when her total lack of interest had started to infect me, I went to sleep under the wagon. I think she was grateful.

It was just becoming light when I heard my name called by a strong male voice. I jumped, bashed my head on the front axle, and rolled out, instinctively moving away from the caller. With the wagon between me and him I had time to cock my crossbow before I peered round the side. My first thought was that the raiders had come, and my second was that Renthrette was nowhere in sight. The Downs boasted little in the way of cover, and though she could have been hiding somewhere nearby, I doubted it. I heard voices out there and swallowed hard. Not for the first time, I thought my number was up. And I wouldn't get to use all those great speeches I'd memorized. It was the actor's nightmare, dying alone, poised to give the best performance of his career to an empty house.

"I'll show them what Will Hawthorne is made of," I muttered to myself, almost immediately regretting my choice of words. I dived out from behind the wagon, grunting as I hit the ground and shooting the crossbow towards the approaching people. The bolt whistled wildly off into the air and they ducked as it soared harmlessly overhead.

"It's a good thing you still can't shoot," called a large black man. "If that had come near me, I'd have been really irritated."

"Orgos!" I shouted. "Lisha! Where have you been?"

I ran towards them shouting random insults at the top of my lungs. And then I saw that they weren't alone. With them, brandishing makeshift weapons that looked suspiciously like farming implements, were Maia, her parents, and the other villagers. Lisha had gathered more from the surrounding area, so that there were forty or fifty of them, probably all homeless and destitute, all looking for a cause around which to rally.

They were pleased to see me, and I got the distinct impression that even those villagers I had never met had heard things—good things—about me from the others. It was like being back on the stage in Cresdon.

"Hello, Will," said Maia. She smiled a little but her eyes were as big and serious as ever. Recent events seemed to have aged her, and when she gravely put out her tiny hand to shake mine, it didn't seem inappropriate. I said hello and chatted to the ones I recognized, though it was an odd dynamic, since we had been through fire and death together but knew nothing of each other. Most of them were no more than faces from a dream and I couldn't think of anything to say to them. But they smiled and shook my hand or slapped me on the shoulder as if genuinely glad to see me; as if, in fact, they thought my presence would somehow help. They were all armed, even the children, and suddenly my heart sank, because this could mean nothing but torment and death.

"Will somebody tell me what's going on?" I said.

"The raiders are out in force and moving this way," said Orgos. "A lot has happened since last we spoke. Renthrette has told us of what you have discovered and we have the highest regard for you—"

"Save it," I said, pretending not to care.

Orgos nodded and grinned before continuing his story. "When the raiders appeared in force on the Verneytha border a week ago, Mithos went to see the governor. Treylen authorized Mithos to take control of what troops were available, some two hundred light cavalry. We got word to Hopetown, where Garnet met with Duke Raymon. As the raiders moved out onto the moors of northern Greycoast, Mithos took command of the Verneytha cavalry and began to press them south. No blows have yet been struck, but we hope to join our small force with the armies of Hopetown and Ironwall to effect a pincer movement, trapping the raiders on the plains before the citadel. It will be a bloody encounter, but one which will end the threat of the raiders. We'll need you to help organize our forces."

I looked at them standing there, so brave and noble, and wondered if they'd forgotten the way the raiders had mauled us when we had crawled up from the coast with our cargo of coal. For a second I could smell the battle, see it, hear it, feel the sweat on my back and the blood in my eyes. I saw the raiders as I had first seen them in the flame and smoke of a sacked village, their lances lowered and bronze faces impassive. I pictured that crimson machine materializing out of the fog, biting through the untutored ranks of our boy soldiers and farmers, and my heart bled for them.

But most of all, it bled for me.

"I'm sorry, Orgos," I said. "This is as far as I go."

SCENE LII

A Different Road

Well, do you blame me? Really? It was—had always been—hopeless. But calling Mithos's name wouldn't help now, and we weren't facing a handful of them, stuck in the tight spiral of a lighthouse. We were facing an army, hundreds of them, appearing out of the mist on top of us. I knew what they were capable of (in every sense of that phrase) and no talk of principle could make a silk purse out of this particular sow's ear. It would be a rout, and I would have no part in it.

I'm not sure when I made the decision to leave, though the possibility had been there since I first met them and had never completely gone away, even when things seemed to have been going well. But lately things hadn't been going well and I had nearly wound up dead too many times. The idea that all those encounters had been mere rehearsals for the grand show itself was just too horrible. I couldn't survive anything worse than I had already been through, and neither could they. Riding into certain death might be what they lived for. Not me.

Orgos was furious, of course, and my attempts to persuade him to come with me, to persuade all of them to quit now while they still could, just made him madder. Renthrette stared at me, her face flushed as if I'd slapped her very hard. As Lisha was saying that she understood my position and that I had more than repaid them for getting me out of Cresdon, she walked away and started messing around with her horse's bridle, without looking back.

"You'll need some expenses to get out of Shale," said Lisha, handing me a small purse.

"I don't need your money," I said, suddenly feeling defensive.

"You earned it," she said. "Though I wish you would reconsider."

"You too," I said. "And I'm no use to you anyway."

She started to say something, but I waved it away. "You know what the odds are in this battle you're walking into?" I said.

"Yes," she answered. "But I know that without us, these people, Maia and the others you saved, have no chance at all. We have to try. Even if we can't win, it is important to stand up to an enemy like this. I know you don't think that ideas like that serve a purpose, but sometimes even destruction is better than compromise."

"No," I said. "I don't believe that. There are battles elsewhere you could win, causes you could champion. Why throw yourselves away in something so obviously futile?"

"Because this is where we are now," she said firmly. "This is the injustice we are confronted with, and no fight is wholly futile."

There was nothing to say to this. Orgos had been fuming up and down the makeshift campsite, but his anger had burned out. When I finally sidled up to him he just listened gravely and then smiled a sad, distant smile. "I had hoped you would ride into battle beside me," he said.

"You'll do better without me," I said honestly. "It's pointless to say otherwise, and it's pointless to ask you to be careful and not take risks unnecessarily, but . . . Look after yourselves. Please."

Lisha shook my hand and wished me well. Orgos clamped me to his chest and then, before releasing me, stared hard into my face.

"You're a good man, Orgos," I said, really believing it for the first time.

"So are you, Will," he said. It was a kind of entreaty. I smiled and shook my head sadly, and walked away. I wasn't a good man. I never had been. But I was a survivor, and that had to be worth something, to me if not to anybody else.

As I climbed into the saddle of my mare, I turned to look back at Renthrette. But I couldn't place her among the crowd, and after a moment feeling foolish and indecisive as the villagers watched me, I rode away.

❧

I figured I'd head west, mainly because it would be the shortest way out of the region, but also because it would take me back towards Stavis, which was at least familiar. I doubted I'd dare risk returning to Cresdon, even if I could find passage across the Hrof, but Stavis would serve as a place where I could gather my thoughts and look for options. Surely the Empire would have forgotten Will Hawthorne by now?

The downside of heading west was crossing Shale. Since I really didn't want to ever lay eyes on the Adsine keep again, I figured I'd head north for a little ways, skirt the city, and then dip south and west again, wending my slow way across the two hundred miles of Targev coastline we had glimpsed from the deck of the *Cormorant*. Two hundred miles was a long way, but since I had no real destination in mind, it didn't matter so much. Maybe I'd find a town with a little theatre or a pub where I could pull pints for a while.

I had the whole day ahead of me and, with luck, I'd be out of Shale territory before I had to stop for the night. The light rain that had been hanging around the area like a pathetic friend you couldn't get rid of finally pushed off, and even the scraggy hills and tussocky fields looked almost beautiful enough to put the past weeks out of my mind. By midmorning I had started cutting north. I trotted on, right through lunch, until Adsine was behind me and I was only a few hours from the edge of Shale. I ate in the saddle wondering how mobile I'd be the following day after all this riding. It was still light, and I could see the sea. After another hour or so I passed through a tiny hamlet and dismounted to ask how far it was to the border.

"The Shale border?" replied an old woman with a basket of pears on her back. "You passed it about a mile back. You're in Targev now."

I nearly kissed her, but reason won out (she was seventy-five if she was a day) and I opted to celebrate my departure from the life of an adventurer by booking a room in the local inn and washing down the best supper on offer with a few pints of strong brown ale. I was still too close to Shale to expect a real feast, but I booked into the imaginatively titled Red Lion with a light heart and a sense of real escape, and not just from the raiders. It was the entire world I had gotten away from, that universe where wrongs have to be righted at tremendous personal risk and no one ever gets a decent meal or curls up with a warm body beside them. I ordered two pints, then, as soon as I got my platter of potatoes and roast pork—studded with rosemary and lined with a perfect ribbon of soft fat and crunchy skin— asked for a third.

There was no one else staying at the Red Lion. The landlord said that traffic on the road to Shale had completely dried up since the raiders had become a feature in the region. He wanted me to swap theories and speculations about who they were and what they were after, but I wouldn't be drawn.

"Just passing through," I said. "Can't say I've heard much about them."

He would have told me all he knew (most of it rubbish) but the journey and my first decent meal in weeks had exhausted me, and I could honestly tell him that I was ready for bed. It was one of those rare nights when, proverbially, I really was out as soon as my head hit the pillow, and my sleep was deep and dreamless.

I was woken by the sound of movement and voices downstairs. I wandered unsteadily down, still bleary-eyed, conscious that the sun was barely up. The landlord was talking to a tall man in a long grey traveling cloak dripping with the rain that had apparently returned. It was his boots that were making all the noise on the wooden floor. The landlord spotted me and made an apologetic face.

"Let me just deal with this gentleman, and then I'll start breakfast," he said.

I settled at a table and gave myself over to waking up properly as they haggled over the price of meat and bread. I peered out of one of the leaded windows into the courtyard, where four or five men were tethering horses and stretching as if they'd been on the road a while already. They all wore the same rain-spotted grey cloaks. The exact same cloak. I sat up, needled with a familiar anxiety, and at that moment, one of them came into the bar, stamping and shrugging off his wet clothes.

My first thought was that they were raiders and the grey cloaks were their version of being incognito. But the cloaks were clearly a uniform, one that fit neither the raiders nor any of the troops we had seen before. Shale soldiers wore black, Greycoast blue and silver, Verneytha green and copper. So who were these guys, and where had they come from? Maybe they were some neutral party from the north who could be persuaded to go and bail Orgos and co. out of the death trap they had thrown themselves into. . . .

As these hopeful thoughts circulated vaguely in my head, three things struck me almost simultaneously, appearing raiderlike out of the mist and driving all optimism into a screaming retreat. First, the prices being quoted by the landlord were astronomical if there were only five or six of them looking for a few loaves and a joint of pork.

Second, the strangers all had the sort of fluid, powerful bearing that comes from training, exercise, and discipline. And last (but worst of all) was the fact—revealed unmistakably as the newcomer turned from hanging up his dripping cloak—that they wore shortswords and steel grey armor over white linen tunics emblazoned with a blue diamond.

I moved as quickly as I could to the door and looked out beyond the courtyard to where a hundred Empire troops, bristling with spears, their horses steaming, were sheltering from the rain, hoping to grab some fresh provisions for their journey east. They had found me after all.

But of course, they hadn't come for me. You didn't send a hundred battle-hardened Empire troops (and who knew how many more right behind them) all the way from Stavis after a minor fugitive. So what were they doing?

It seemed obvious. They had heard of the escalating problems in Shale, Verneytha, and Greycoast, and were moving east to capitalize on the slaughter. They would wait for the crippled victors to emerge, broken and bleeding, and they would roll right over them before they could take a breath, conquering all three lands in a handful of minor skirmishes. And if Orgos, Renthrette, and the rest survived the raiders, they would be wiped out in the conquest that followed.

It was as if one of the soldiers—it no longer seemed to matter much whether they wore red or white—had pushed the tip of his spear into my bowels and leaned on it, so the cold hard truth passed through my body, bringing pain and horror and delirium. You hear of people having their lives pass before their eyes in moments of danger. I had thought the experience would be kind of interesting, if not, in my case, terribly impressive. But now—a moment as full of dread and danger as any I had experienced in the dreadful and dangerous weeks that had just passed—I saw not my life, but other people's deaths. Suddenly I saw—as in a dream, but with absolute clarity—Orgos's body cut down and bleeding in the thick of the fight. I saw Garnet unhorsed and lifeless. I heard Lisha scream for the first and last time. I saw Mithos outnumbered and weakening as he flailed and parried. I saw Renthrette facedown in the mud of battle, her hair stained with blood and filth as the victorious Empire tramped past.

God alone knew what I could do to stop such visions from becoming reality, but I had to try.

Back on the Horse

I rode as fast and as hard as I have ever done, and while that isn't saying all that much, I covered a lot of ground and was well inside Shale territory by lunchtime. I had to assume that the Empire would march on the surviving armies as soon as they could be removed from each other's throats. That meant they would head for the plains outside Ironwall, where Mithos was pushing the raiders towards Garnet and Orgos with whatever armies Greycoast and Verneytha could muster. It would take me several hours of steady riding just to get in sight of the citadel, and that was if I rode as the crow flies. But the crow flew straight through Adsine, under the very eaves of the keep that housed the raiders. I told myself that with the mystical transportation methods open to them, the raiders were unlikely to be trotting through the streets of Adsine, especially if the ordinary people of Shale didn't know that the raiders were their neighbors and brothers, but it was impossible to be sure. I bent low in the saddle, pulled my cloak over my head to shelter me from rain and prying eyes, and spurred my horse towards Adsine.

I figured I had two choices as I entered Adsine and felt the keep watching blankly from the high ground in the center of the town: I could either charge through the streets as quickly as I could (fast but conspicuous); or I could walk my horse in a nonchalant fashion, blending in nicely and taking about a decade to cover four hundred yards. In the end, I followed both impulses, entering the city slowly and inconspicuously and then, when I glimpsed the first stray Shale trooper in his black-and-silver armor, bolting with panic and charging out of town as if the hosts of hell were at my heels. Remarkably, then, I managed to be both slow and conspicuous, once more demonstrating exactly why I wasn't cut out for this kind of life at all.

I didn't slow down till Adsine was a good half hour behind me, and I spent that half hour glancing backwards in search of pursuing horsemen. Knowing that those horsemen could be wearing black, red, *or* white and it would be equally bad news for Will the Hopeless Fugitive wasn't encouraging, but I saw no traffic on the road at all until I reached the Proxintar Downs. There the road was clogged with bullock carts as a convoy of farmers and miners tried to get out of Ironwall before the approaching storm. Part of me wanted to warn them of the perils that awaited them as they headed west, but I doubted that my various enemies would bother with the likes of them, and I resented their abandoning of my friends. The fact that I had also abandoned my friends twenty-four hours ago was conveniently clouded by my sense of heroic purpose. I was a warrior returning to save the day, bringing crucial information and a keen eye with a crossbow, putting my life on the line for my friends. Well, kind of.

To be honest, my newfound heroism was due at least in part to a plan I had been forming in my head. If I could get to the party in time to explain the situation as I saw it, we would have the upper hand. We could hit the raiders hard and fast while our force still outnumbered theirs, then we could take the remains of our army into Ironwall and sit out the Empire's assault. Those Diamond soldiers were looking for an easy victory, not a lengthy siege of the most secure citadel in the region. If we could get inside as soon as the first battle was over, they would probably just trek back to Stavis with their tails between their legs. People are fond of saying that knowledge is power. This time it might actually be true: knowing that the Empire was on its way might be all we would need to turn them back.

The sun was at my back and turning a deep red by the time the massive citadel came into view across the plains before me. I put my heels to my horse's flanks and reached the guardhouse moments before they were due to lower that massive portcullis for the night. Indeed, they started its immeasurably slow and clanking descent as soon as I was in, and even though it took ten minutes to close completely, it was the most comforting sound I've ever heard in my life. I went up onto the walls before I sought out the party and gave a last look westwards to see if any of our enemies were coming.

SCENE LIV

The Gathering

The party greeted me pretty much as you would expect, Lisha with a small-but-genuine smile, Orgos with loud whoops and hugs and "I told you so"s to anyone who would listen, Garnet with a nod that said I had surprised him in a good way (for once) and a matey thump on the shoulder that nearly sent me sprawling. Renthrette just watched me in a sideways kind of manner, like someone keeping an eye on a dog that was likable enough but wasn't to be trusted. Fair enough, I suppose.

I told them about the approaching Empire army and they exchanged thoughtful glances as they weighed my strategic advice and found it, somewhat surprisingly, to be sound. But as Lisha talked tactics, Orgos sharpened his swords, and Garnet muttered excitedly about having a go at the Empire once the raiders had been "eliminated," Renthrette continued to watch me like I had just regurgitated an entire goat that had then wandered off bleating. In short, whatever trust she had placed in me between the Ugokan caves and our retreat from Adsine had evaporated with my running away, and my heroic return had only served to make her more suspicious. I opted, as is my wont, for a flirtatious playfulness designed to defuse the situation.

"You didn't think I'd come back," I said with a sly grin, the moment I caught her alone.

"Why would I?" she said, her eyes on the straps of some ring mail she was adjusting. "You ran away to avoid a battle."

"And I came back to take part in two," I inserted deftly. "Doesn't that tell you something about who I am?"

"Right now," she said, "all I want to know about you is whether or not you told the Empire how to find us."

I had been prepared to fake a hurt surprise, but this was a lower blow than I had expected and my shock was genuine.

"You thought I'd turn you in?" I said.

"Did you?" she asked, and she was looking at me now, her eyes hard and cold and perfectly serious. I was aghast.

"If I had, would I have come back and warned you the Empire was on its way?"

She was silent and for a second I thought I had her, that she'd melt into apologies and confessions of how relieved she was to see me again.

"How could anyone figure out the way your mind might work?" she said.

That could, I suppose, have been a kind of compliment, but I doubted it. "Fine," I said with dignity. "Fine."

I was on the point of storming out when Garnet burst in.

"They're coming," he said. He seemed quite pleased.

⁕

The "they," it turned out, were the raiders. Mithos and the governor of Verneytha were pushing them south onto the planes before Iron-wall. A few days ago I wouldn't have believed the palpable good humor that the Greycoast soldiers exuded at the prospect of facing the raiders, but things had changed, and memories, it seemed, were short. The raiders were charging into *our* trap like sparrows flying full tilt at a pane of glass. Well, maybe not sparrows. More like a kind of buzzard. But our window was made of two hundred Greycoast infantry, forty cavalry, and a contingent of about fifty homeless villagers. In time, the buzzard would claw its way through, but with three hundred men at its heels, time was what it didn't have. Then we could get inside Ironwall and close up the citadel while the Empire sat outside, mulled their options, and finally went home. We were headed into our final battle, and the relief that that idea brought drowned any fear for what would happen while the window cracked.

I watched the villagers going through some basic training moves outside the city walls and then hurried up to the white buildings surrounding the duke's palace. I met Garnet and forty cavalry from the Hopetown garrison, all humming with enthusiasm. Garnet was earnestly tightening the straps of his horned helm while Tarsha steamed quietly in the shadows. I was talking to him when Renthrette passed, scowling and looking away, ignoring Garnet as he called after her. He gave me an odd look, guessing that this had something to do with me. I gave him an awkward combination of nods, shrugs, and smiles all stacked precariously on top of each other, in an attempt to convey a sort of noncommittal goodwill. He returned a similar sequence and, thus sidestepping any recognizable species of communication, we parted, trying to figure out what the hell all *that* had been about. As I walked up to the palace I reflected that if meeting my friends was this strange, encountering His Pompous Immensity, the duke of Greycoast, was likely to be very bizarre indeed.

He was waiting for us in the uppermost marketplace, reviewing the citadel garrison with the rest of the party, save Mithos and Garnet. A buzz of excitement hung about the soldiers as they readied themselves. He stood scowling and shooting petulant orders at the squire who was trying to spoon him into large pieces of plate armor. Hearing us approach, he turned, sloshing and quivering like a rich dessert. He sort of smiled at us through his thick reddish beard like he had somehow been vindicated about our uselessness, and when he spoke, his civility was tempered with superiority and disdain. "I am gratified that you have come to lend assistance," he said. "I'm *sure* it will make a difference."

He gave me a long, cold look and I returned it blankly. I wasn't sure exactly why I was there, but it certainly wasn't to please him.

"Orgos," he said, "I want you to lead B Company."

He gestured behind him to a block of a hundred infantrymen. He went on, his manner declamatory, his heavy pinkish hands cutting the air like ax blades cleverly fashioned out of chopped pork. In his armor he looked hulkingly powerful and slightly ridiculous. He couldn't turn his head without swiveling his entire body, and his arms stuck out short and awkward like the forelegs of a kangaroo.

"Form a barrier at right angles to the citadel gate," he said to Orgos. "The enemy will come right at you. As they close in, I will send A Company out of the city, joining your force and striking the enemy in the flank simultaneously."

"That will leave you no reinforcements in the citadel," said Lisha. The duke glanced down at her as if he had forgotten she was there. His face crinkled into an avuncular smile. A bead of thick spittle stuck to his lower lip, and his voice was moist and thick.

"Well, my dear," he said, "we have a very dangerous enemy which needs to be destroyed quickly before it can damage us. If we hold anything back from the first clash, we may lose our advantage in the field, and a few reinforcements will never win the day back for us. We must hit them hard, putting all we have into a single counterthrust."

Don't you worry your pretty little head about it, in other words.

"And you'll be leading them into battle, will you?" I said, absolutely incapable of keeping my mouth shut.

"I shall be with them when they charge—" Raymon began.

"What does that mean," I said, " 'be with them'? Will you be *leading* them or not?"

"Not leading them, exactly," he said, as if it was a minor distinction. "But I will be there until they charge and, depending—"

"On whether there's any risk involved whatsoever," I interrupted him, "yes, I think I get the picture. You'll ride around in your armor and be ready with the waves and the patriotic victory speeches—"

"I don't think you, of all people, are in any position—"

"Probably not," I agreed hastily, wondering—not for the first time—what I was trying to achieve. "But you know what? There'd be no raiders without people like you. Remember that."

I don't really know why I said it and I was far from clear what I'd meant, but it felt true and I was glad I had put it out there for him to think about. He didn't, of course. He gave me a long, bewildered look, and then the squire tugged the strap of his breastplate too tight, and, with a snort of irritation, he turned on the armorer, barking indignation.

As they started hoisting the duke astride his stallion, a messenger arrived to speak to him. Though the horse was larger than the duke (a little) it looked like it might collapse under his weight at any moment, struggling as it was like an ant with a grapefruit. He looked, I was pleased to note, quite absurd, and everyone knew it. One of the soldiers looked deliberately away and smirked at his friend. Maybe that's what did it. I had wondered about telling him of the hidden rooms in the Adsine keep and flaunting the fact that it had been me who found them, but he wasn't worth trying to impress. The identities of the raiders didn't matter now anyway. We'd go over all that after they had been vanquished.

The duke gave a single bark of laughter and set his horse to a laborious and unstable-looking trot, his face rosy and enthusiastic.

"The raiders are in sight," he announced, his stallion wheezing like an octogenarian pipe smoker on a twelve-mile hike. "They are coming this way with the Verneytha cavalry at their heels."

"I hope Mithos keeps his distance," said Orgos. "If the raiders turn on him, he will never hold out."

"Mithos knows the situation," Lisha replied. "He will hold back until we are ready to engage them."

"I must get that wagon set up," I said to Orgos.

The air was heavy with an oddly joyous anticipation, and I saw how battle could be thrilling when you knew you were going to win. It was like watching a play you've seen before and enjoying not *what* happens but *how* it happens, suspending your knowledge of the ending in your head so you can relish it even more. And, like a lot of plays, it was about revenge, and few things feel better than that.

Orgos nodded briefly and clasped my shoulder. "Be careful out there," he said.

"Oh, I will," I assured him. "And you too."

"Good-bye, Will," he said. As he walked away I wondered why that sounded so final, but I was armored with optimism three inches thick and the thought glanced off like a spent arrow.

The Enemy

The gatehouse was a mass of soldiers waiting for their orders. The drawbridge was down and the portcullis hung on its chains high above us. Since it took an age to lower the thing and we would be sending soldiers out right up to the moment when the raiders hit us, it would probably stay open all day. I watched Renthrette and Lisha organizing a line of spears and crossbows. It was all oddly familiar, but this time the sun was high, the air was clear, and we outnumbered the enemy two to one.

I moved around the wagon, freeing the bolts and folding the sides down halfway. I clamped the axles and began to assemble the massive crossbows. After that I slipped my head into my mail shirt, felt its coolness and weight through the soft leather beneath. All around me the village irregulars prepared themselves to meet the crimson raiders once more, the sun shining on their makeshift armor and newly ground ax bits. I belted my sword about my waist and laid a shield on the wagon floor as if I was a hero who knew what he was doing.

Renthrette was already armored and ready, though she had yet to put on her helm. I watched her dig her heels into the sides of her horse and shout at the swelling and straightening line of boar spears and homemade pikes; then she turned suddenly and looked north. I stood up and could just make out a dust cloud, broad and low on the horizon. Trumpets sounded from the citadel turrets and a cry of wild joy went up around me like when the dogs see the bear.

From the gatehouse came the first hundred of the Greycoast infantry, Orgos mounted on a white charger at their head. He wore a tunic of russet linen with dark leather armor, waxed and overlaid with rings of steel. A helmet of iron and boars' tusks covered his head and the nape of his neck, topped with a black horsehair plume that trailed to his shoulders. Apart from the angular cheek guards, his face was exposed. While I felt like a hero but looked like an idiot in armor that didn't fit—a fish out of water of the duke-of-Greycoast-on-a-horse variety—Orgos was the real thing, and looked the part. He crossed our lines and nodded briefly to us, a nod of confidence and dignity. The men around me watched him and you could feel the way his presence lifted their hearts. I fiddled with my crossbows.

In the mouth of the gatehouse I could see the first ranks of A Company waiting, pressed to the walls to allow Garnet and his Hopetown cavalry to exit the city and veer towards us. They wore silver scale armor and chromed helmets with short blue capes like the men who had escorted us from Seaholme, but they looked confident and professional. Their hooves clattered over the bridge, and an appreciative shout went up from the Greycoast soldiers. Garnet, sitting pale at their head in grey mail and a horned helm, adjusted his shield and gestured to the riders with his battle-ax. They wheeled in front of the wagon, then formed a block at the corner of the citadel facing towards the center of the plains. Garnet also looked the part, calm and impressive astride that bloody immense horse. I scowled and wondered why I was the only one who looked like he'd walked out onto the stage by accident. Whatever I thought about the coming encounter, I still felt like a sham. Even the bloody villagers looked like they knew what they were doing, and most of them were armed with gardening implements.

The dust cloud was coming, but I figured we had a few minutes yet, more if they slowed their approach. I lifted one of the crossbows onto its assembled tripod and bolted it into place, swinging it round and looking down its twin grooves like an expert. Renthrette was unhitching the horses from the front of the wagon and leading them away, and as I snapped the last bolt into place she looked up at me silently, shading her eyes with her hand.

"What?" I said. I couldn't see her face but I knew she was looking hard at me and thinking.

"Nothing." She shrugged. "Good luck, Will," she said, moving away.

I wanted to call her back, but had no idea what I would have said, and it would have spoiled this I'm-so-collected-and-efficient thing I was working on. She lowered her heavy iron helm onto her shoulders and her face was lost to me.

I was ready. The crossbows sat taut and deadly on their stands and I knelt behind them, consciously noting and re-noting where my personal weapons were so that I could seize them if necessary. The ranks had grown silent and expectant in the bright afternoon, all eyes towards the approaching riders. Orgos, still mounted, glanced over his shoulder to where the dust cloud had grown sharper and had sprouted men, distinct and shining in the sun. The sandy earth burst under their horses' hooves like breaking waves and they sailed towards us, motionless in their saddles, crimson cloaks now visible at their backs, their pennanted lances raised. They were slowing down.

Orgos called to his company and they lowered their spear heads in readiness for the charge. I snapped back the catches on the crossbows. In the gatehouse, the second company waited poised to rush the raiders as they came in close. Beyond the scarlet horsemen I could just make out the Verneytha cavalry pressing them towards us like the second half of a vise. Somewhere amongst them was Mithos. It occurred to me that he didn't know what we had discovered in the Adsine keep, let alone the news of the approaching Empire soldiers, but then neither did Greycoast or Verneytha. Like most of the things I could claim to have had a hand in, it didn't seem to matter much now. I saw them coming towards us and I thought it again: If we could withstand the initial impact of their charge, our flank and rear attacks should leave them powerless.

Then the raiders stopped altogether just outside the flight of our arrows. We waited in silence as the dust cloud drifted away. A minute later, ten or twelve of the duke's company came out to us.

"What's going on?" I demanded.

"Your wagon looks a bit vulnerable, so we've been sent to reinforce these farmers, or whatever they are," said a young corporal. He grinned and nodded towards the villagers bunched tightly around the wagon.

"Good," I said, reflecting that no unit that Orgos escorted would look "vulnerable," "but that wasn't what I meant. Why have they stopped?"

"The raiders?" He shrugged. "Beats me."

On the plains before us the raiders still appeared to be waiting, as if they wanted us to go to them. An arrow or two was loosed by some patriotic citizens on the citadel walls, but they fell hopelessly short. I was watching the raiders sit there as still and controlled as I had ever seen them when another shout went up: a long, pronounced hurrah that started in the citadel and spread throughout the Greycoast forces, even echoing down from the Verneytha cavalry. I turned to Lisha and the spear line in front of the wagon for an explanation, but only the handful of reinforcements seemed to know what was going on and laughed and cheered with the rest.

"Now what?" I shouted. At first they didn't hear, and I had to clamber onto the front of the wagon and tap the young officer on the shoulder.

"What are they shouting about?" I said, conscious of a laugh creeping into my own voice as I caught something of their mood. The corporal leaned forward and pointed westwards towards the Downs and the treetops of the border forests.

I turned and looked. There was a dark ribbon of men and banners: the black flags of a great army of horsemen steadily advancing towards us.

"Reinforcements," shouted the corporal.

"What?" I called back through the noise.

"We got word this morning," said the corporal, "Shale has sent its entire army to smash the raiders. Two hundred cavalry and over seven hundred foot soldiers."

I stared at him, suddenly cold.

But before I could say anything, there was another shout. A ripple went through our force, and the corporal's smile faded as he stared off to where men were pointing: not towards the raiders, or to the army from Shale, which was advancing from the west, but *behind* us, to the south.

I turned, feeling a sudden swell of dread, and found that the plains at our back were suddenly awash in a thick grey mist. A moment later, the mist was blowing away, and in its place was an army that looked as if it had sprung from the earth like corn. But this army was not wearing the crimson of the raiders.

They wore white.

In the sparkle of their silver helms I saw our certain destruction.

SCENE LVI

Desperate Times

I leapt down from the wagon and ran to where Renthrette and Lisha sat on their mounts with the villagers.

"It's the Empire!" I shouted, pointing wildly at the men who had appeared to the south. "Shale and the Empire! They've been working together all along."

Lisha was already driving her horse out of the throng, Renthrette quickly following. I didn't need to explain what was about to happen. The raiders and their Diamond Empire brothers, joining with the strength from Shale, would turn on the unsuspecting forces of Greycoast and Verneytha and wipe them out. In one fell swoop Shale would destroy its rivals according to whatever cozy terms Arlest had agreed on with the Empire, and our armies didn't even know it was coming. What had looked like a pair of manageable encounters had turned into one we could not hope to survive, let alone win.

Lisha jumped down from the saddle and shouted to Renthrette, "Tell Garnet! Tell everybody. Ride to the gatehouse and tell the duke, then Mithos. Stay close to the citadel and move quickly."

Without a word Renthrette kicked her heels into her horse's flanks and it lunged forward. Within seconds she had left Garnet shouting at his men and was galloping over the drawbridge into the gatehouse. The sound of cheering still echoed from the citadel and the Verneytha cavalry, but it was muted now, and there was confusion at the sudden appearance of these new soldiers clad in white. On my left, Orgos was addressing his troops, his voice uneven. He glanced round to the advancing black tide of horsemen that flowed towards us from the Downs, and south to the Empire cohorts who had appeared out of the fog and were now locked in a purposeful phalanx. We were surrounded.

The Greycoast soldiers shifted restlessly, scared and unsure what to believe. Some called out questions, wanting proof there was no time to give.

"What do we do?" I shouted to Lisha, all composure gone. Our two-to-one advantage had suddenly been inverted, and then some. "What can we do? We have to retreat into the citadel!"

"They'd be on us before we could get inside," she said. "And we'd never get that portcullis down in time to keep them out. We have to stop the three armies from joining forces. If we can keep them separate we may yet hold out, for a while."

She didn't sound hopeful.

"How?"

"Drive a wedge between the raiders and the Shale regular army. If we can catch them before they have ordered their ranks we'll have them at a disadvantage."

"Who with?" I asked, looking around desperately. "All we've got is forty mounted police and a few dozen villagers with pitchforks. The raiders will tear us apart!"

"Mithos will help," Lisha replied.

"How is he going to know?" I yelled back. It was supposed to be a rhetorical question. If our meager cavalry got stuck out there alone, it would be a bloodbath.

"He'll know," she said, and it was determination in her eyes, not hope. It was a doomed effort, but it was the best we had. She turned back to her horse and vaulted into the saddle, where she sat small and defiant, a triangular shield on her left arm and the elegant spear of silver and ebony in her right hand. She turned to Garnet and began speaking earnestly. For a second he glanced at his small force uncertainly, and then he looked back into her eyes and nodded.

I pointed to the horses Renthrette had moved away. "Get them yoked up to the wagon again," I yelled to a couple of the villagers. They couldn't have been older than fifteen, and I recognized one of them as a relative of Maia's.

Garnet was bringing his horsemen about him and joining them with the villagers. They looked pathetically few. For a moment I faltered and looked towards the citadel. I could run the distance to the gate in under a minute and they would have to shoot me down to stop me. I glanced up and saw Renthrette, her hair trailing from her closed helm, spurring her horse away from Ironwall and heading obliquely for the Verneytha cavalry. She was crouched low in the saddle, streaking arrowlike under the eyes of the enemy.

Lisha was now talking to the villagers. Grath was amongst them, a long boar spear in his hand and a crossbow across his back. One of the riders with him was a grey-haired man whose dark skin hung in wrinkles under his eyes, but the eyes themselves were bright and he held his long hafted wood ax grimly. Behind him was the teenaged kid who had wrestled with one of the raiders the night I had got them out of the village.

"We'll need that extra hundred infantry," I shouted to Lisha. "Somebody get the duke and A Company out of that gatehouse and drop the portcullis. They are wasted in there."

The boys had brought the horses over and were hurriedly hitching them up. Behind the spear line by the wagon were two men and a woman cradling heavy crossbows in their bare arms.

"You three," I shouted. "Get up here. One in the front, two in the back. We need a driver, someone without a mount."

One of the boys finished harnessing the horses and swung himself up into the front of the wagon. He was lithe and dark of skin and eyes.

"Can you drive this thing?" I asked uncertainly.

"As fast as it will go," he said with a grim smile. I nodded and turned to the handful of Greycoast regulars who had been sent to reinforce us.

"Corporal, get a couple of your spearmen up here. We might need them."

The corporal gave me a long, disbelieving look and said, "You can say that again. How many can you take?"

"No more than three."

It was already getting pretty crowded up there. I stood in the center, protected to the waist by the folded sides of the wagon, my arms gripping the two scorpion bolt throwers. On either side of me knelt a villager with a crossbow, the teenaged kid on my right, a powerful-looking woman on my left. Another crossbowman rode in the front next to the boy. A couple of axes and shields were passed up to them and they looked about as ready as they ever would be. We could only get two more aboard comfortably, so the Greycoast spearmen, with their silver hauberks and curved body-sized shields, clambered up into the back, one at the tail, one next to the woman. I glanced around and saw Lisha watching. Renthrette must have reached Mithos by now, unless she'd been cut off by the raiders.

Don't think about that.

Garnet appeared by the side of the wagon, looking down at me from Tarsha's back.

"Ready?" he said.

I glanced towards the advancing Shale horses.

"No," I whispered. "But let's go anyway."

Lisha called out, "Will, you go first. You'll need the lead time. Head directly between the fronts and attack whichever side gets closest to you. Don't get stuck between them or we'll never escape. Pull to one side and watch what Mithos does. Don't let them split our force, for God's sake. Do as much damage as you can and get out!"

I released the axle clamps, and the wagon rocked unsteadily. The spearmen held on to the sides and glanced at each other, suddenly confronted by the reality of what we were about to do. I looked at the boy in the driver's seat and said, "Did you get all that?"

He nodded. There was a momentary pause in which I took a deep breath.

"Go," I said.

SCENE LVII

Desperate Measures

With a shout and a whip crack to the horses, the wagon surged away from the Empire troops behind us. In the back I stumbled and hung on as we picked up speed. On our right sat the raiders, waiting, while on our left the massive banners of Shale grew steadily closer. Between them we went, as fast as the horses would take us, the noise of our heavy wheels filling our ears. The wind stung my eyes and great columns of dust and grit plumed out from the wagon's sides and rear. A few seconds later came a cry from behind us, and we turned to see our cavalry charging after us, gaining all the time.

Suddenly the raiders responded, recognizing the attack for what it was and turning their horses towards us. There was a moment's confusion, and then the scarlet wave was united and moving towards us again, kicking their steeds into a fast and heavy charge. We were already too close for them to use their bows, so they lowered their lance tips and aimed them at our hearts. Suddenly I could hear nothing but battle cries and the low, dragging roar of horse hooves on the hard ground.

On the left, the Shale cavalry, the two hundred who would fight from the saddle, broke into a full charge. There was no longer any doubt whose side they were on.

And we were going to get trapped between them and the raiders.

"Pull to the right!" I roared at the boy. "Cut across their front line."

With a sudden lurch the wagon swept round and across the path of the raiders. Our cavalry escort split, Lisha taking the irregulars with us, Garnet holding the Greycoast cavalry back. The raiders came on.

We scrambled to the opposite side of the wagon on our hands and knees as the floor kicked beneath us. When I stood up the enemy were less than a hundred yards away and closing fast on the wagon's side.

Wait, I thought. *Wait. . .*

"Shoot!" I shouted.

I squinted down the grooves of the right-hand crossbow and squeezed the trigger. The bolt appeared in the breast of a raider and threw him backwards and out of the saddle. On either side of me the other crossbows snapped, and I think another rider went down. They came closer, growing huge and distinct in just a few seconds. I shot again, moving so hurriedly and clumsily to the other crossbow that I didn't even see if I'd hit anything. The others were fumbling for their axes and spears now, waiting for them to get close enough. Twice more I shot into the sea of scarlet and bronze and twice more men fell, only to be replaced by more. They were too close now. It was with something like despair that I picked up my shield and drew my broadsword.

Then they were upon us, breaking against the half side of the open wagon like the immense, curling head of a wave hurling itself down onto an outcrop of rock. A lance tip stuck hard into the wagon timbers, cracking them apart with the force of the charge. I stepped back, horrified. The crossbowman at the front died instantly, thrust through with a lance. I threw myself forward and hacked at the raider's horse, but my blade slid off its leather barding. One of the Greycoast soldiers raised his spear like a javelin and pitched it into the throat of a horseman. The blood gushed down his breastplate and he lolled senseless from the saddle. As the spearman reached out to drag his weapon from the corpse, he was struck down by a lunge from another raider, an officer with a lateral crest across his faceless helm.

With a cry of outrage I attacked, bashing his lance aside with my shield and bringing my sword down hard across his head. The sound of battle was loud in my ears and I struck again, lashing out senselessly as the blade glanced off the hard bronze. Then, as he tried to turn his lance on me, he shifted and leaned to one side. My sword came down hard across his shoulder blade and I felt the edge bite through muscle and bone. This time there was no horror, only exultation, and I struck twice more before he fell.

A change came over the enemy. For a second they faltered at the loss of their officer, and it was in that second that Garnet brought his cavalry hard into their flank. Four or five of them went down before they knew where the attack was coming from, and on the other side of the wagon, the village fighters traded blows with an equally startled wing of the enemy. I don't think it had occurred to them that we would actually attack with so sorry a force.

The surprise didn't last. A moment later we were unable to move. One of the horses fastened to the wagon was dead. The boy cut it free, but we would be significantly slowed. The other Greycoast regular had received a lance tip in his leg and could do little more than defend himself with his oblong shield. The crossbow woman had died protecting the rear of the wagon with a wood ax. I saw her land several blows before she fell, and even after she was hit and dying she heaved her ax at her assailant and struck his thigh. They went down together. The splintered wagon was splashed all over with blood. All around me came the clash of weapons and the roar of voices meshed together in rage and defiance and pain.

When the charge began I saw Garnet briefly on the stamping and tossing warhorse, his ax high above his horned head. I had seen him bring it down hard, but after that he was swallowed by the chaos of the struggle and I couldn't say if he was alive or dead. I hadn't seen Lisha since we clashed with the raiders and I only knew that several of the villagers' horses had veered off free and riderless. With sudden, blinding conviction I saw that we could not survive. It was all I could do to keep my sword and shield tightly in my hands as I looked about me and saw only defeat.

The raiders boiled around our battered wooden platform, lunging with their lances, and all we could do was parry desperately with our shields and fall back to the opposite side of the wagon. I was pinned there, fending off the deadly lance tips with broad swings of my sword. My arms were shaking with exertion and frustrated rage. Then, as I looked for the black pennants of the Shale cavalry that was to be our utter destruction, I caught the green and brass of the Verneytha horsemen as they slammed into the back of the raiders.

It took a moment for the enemy to realize what had happened, and several of them were unhorsed by opportunist spear lunges as they twisted in their saddles to look behind them. One tore the helm from his head, as if unable to see properly, as he tried to face Mithos and his men. They were hemmed in and under attack from all sides. In the center of their force were raiders pressed together by their own horsemen, unable to push through to the enemy and fight. Horses reared in confusion, and at least one raider was thrown and trampled in the press. Before they could turn to fight the Verneytha cavalry, many had been thrust through by the green-pennanted spears.

Mithos had split his force, half of them assaulting the rear of the raiders, the other hundred forming a line facing the Shale cavalry, whose advance had already slowed. The raiders were trying to pull out, pushing hard through the thin wedge of villagers, swerving towards the citadel as they wrenched themselves free. By the time the raiders had freed themselves completely, pulling away from us and the Shale army, they must have lost sixty men and horses. Something like a hundred remained.

A roar of triumph went up from our infantry forces at this temporary respite. The Shale cavalry had slowed to nothing, but they were still a long way from where their infantry had dismounted. They stood uncertainly in their dark scale armor and black dragon-motif cloaks, trying to gauge what had happened.

Mithos appeared at the head of the Verneytha cavalry. His helm with its wire-wound dragon crest and fearsome mask was tipped back from his face. He found Garnet returning with his men, blood-streaked but exuberant, and called out to him, "Attack the Shale cavalry. Chase them to their lines, and watch for the raiders at our backs. Charge!"

As he bellowed that last word he pulled his helm down over his face and turned his steed. With a cry that rang from our force, the horsemen turned and followed. The hundred Verneytha horses that had stood between Shale and the raiders formed the first wave; the other hundred, augmented by the Hopetown garrison and the villagers, made a less ordered second. Right at the front, her sword aloft, was Renthrette.

I stood atop our crippled wagon and watched the Shale cavalry hesitate. They began to move forward, but the sight of our men crashing towards them broke their spirit. Officers shouted and the ordered ranks broke. Some met our charge head-on, some waited, and others fled back towards their infantry, our riders at their heels. Less than half of Shale's renowned cavalry made it back alive.

To the north, the remaining raiders watched us as we regrouped. They had started to attack from behind, but the Shale line had broken so suddenly that they had pulled back.

"Where are the others?" said the teenager, whose face was streaked with blood. "The ones in white."

I turned and squinted back to where they had been, but there was no sign of them. They had gone.

"There!" said the last of our blue-caped spearmen.

Out of the thin and blowing mist, the Empire troops appeared, right alongside their brother raiders only a few hundred yards away. We had kept the red force from joining with the black, but this was just as bad.

Orgos and Duke Raymon had brought their two companies together and marched them towards the center of the plain, where we might keep a block between the raiders and the rest of the Shale force. We set the wagon trundling towards them and the brief security they offered.

"Will," called Lisha, "over here."

I walked across, glad to leave the frightened soldiers to their own thoughts. A handful of women had spilled out of the citadel and one of them began to wail high and long. I saw her bent over one of the bodies, her face twisted and disfigured with grief and her cry floating through the air. I looked away quickly and tried to shut the sound out, but another voice began, joining her in abrasive harmony. The soldiers couldn't bear it. A ripple of unease was coursing up and down their ranks, a ripple you could see. I turned my back on the mourning women, slowly walking to where Lisha stood in front of the Greycoast infantry lines with the duke and the rest of the party.

"Now what do we do?" Garnet asked wearily.

"We weaken them some more," said Lisha. "Mithos, the Verneytha cavalry are fast. Can you get them close enough to throw their javelins?"

Mithos shook his head. "Only if you can keep Shale's archers focused elsewhere."

"We need a diversion," said Lisha.

Orgos nodded. "You'll get it," he said.

SCENE LVIII

Casualties

The green-caped cavalry wheeled off to the south as our infantry advanced slowly on the long, solid line of black shields of the Shale army. I forced myself to concentrate on reloading the crossbows.

A moment later the unearthly silence was broken by a distant swish that lasted a second or more. I looked up to see the air dark with arrows and our infantry standing under them, their body-sized shields locking swiftly together across the front and over the top at Orgos's order: a half-tortoise. I think they had waited until the first arrows were in flight before the formation shaped itself. The concave oblongs of timber, hide, and metal plates fitted together like the parts of a puzzle in a single movement that took less time to assemble than the arrows took to fall. I held my breath, heard the dull rattling stutter of the shafts striking home, and watched for holes appearing in the tortoise shell. Incredibly, I didn't see a single man go down.

Almost simultaneously, the Verneytha cavalry attacked the southern tip of Shale's infantry block. By the time the enemy saw them coming it looked like a full charge. Shale's foot soldiers, now dismounted and standing four or five deep, raised their spears to meet an attack that never came. Instead, there was a long, pronounced volley of javelins, after which the horses wheeled away. In seconds the maneuver was over and our forces were returning to the center. Shale lost a couple of dozen men, maybe more. But we were out of hit-and-run tactics.

The change in the tide came sooner than any of us expected. The Shale infantry saddled up once more and advanced across the plain towards us. This new movement held our attention until we heard the familiar drumming of horses' hooves to our rear. Turning, horror-struck, we found the raiders passing at speed between us and the citadel.

"Raise your shields," bellowed Orgos. It was too late. The arrows came pelting like heavy rain as the horsemen veered west towards the Shale line.

I think it was the randomness that was so appalling. In an instant our scenes of victory were bleeding and crying out around us. An infantryman in the front line called out for a surgeon over and over. Closer to me, a soldier screamed as his friend lowered him to the ground and tried to draw an arrow from his stomach. One of the village boys lay crumpled at my feet. I hadn't seen him fall and figured he had just fainted. I tried to lift him and found the arrow in his side.

Orgos's eyes flashed desperately about him and took in the damage. I watched the raiders ride away as they had done so many times before. As they crossed the plains, a shout of triumph rose up from the Shale force. We couldn't even give chase. There was nothing we could do, and the red, white, and black united. Their lines swelled and pressed towards us.

It's over.

I looked at Orgos, and his eyes were fixed on the approaching enemy, his nostrils flared and his lips parted slightly as his breathing came slow and even. For once there was no hope in his face. He looked too tired even for desperation. He felt my gaze upon him and turned towards me. As the enemy came at us, outnumbering us and bent on our utter demolition, I saw Orgos's values crumble and his better motives crushed beneath the raiders' brutal heel. It wasn't defeat that he couldn't stand, it was this heartless calculation, a calculation that had epitomized the raiders' operations since before we had even arrived. What could you believe in after this? They came towards us, and all his principles, all his honor and hope for human nature evaporated before them, dispelled by their stronger magic of greed and callousness. In a moment, his spirit was broken.

"Pull back!" shouted Lisha suddenly. There was a flicker of life in our frozen forces, and Orgos became himself again, or seemed to, though there was a deliberation in the effort that was unconvincing. I have rarely had a stronger sense of a man acting to keep the show moving.

The Greycoast infantry began a swift march towards the citadel. The duke roared at Lisha, "What the devil do you think you're doing?"

"Trying to save what's left of your army," she retorted, her anger suddenly apparent, "before it is destroyed."

"You don't have the authority . . ." began Raymon, his face red and sweating.

Mithos appeared beside Lisha, his horse steaming. "Do *you*?" he shouted back. "Will you make them stand against an enemy like that? Would you dare to try?"

He had a point, and the duke could see it. The troops were breaking into a full retreat and their ranks were beginning to strain. In seconds the lines would disintegrate altogether and we would be looking at a rout.

"Make for the citadel!" shouted Mithos. They did not need to be told twice.

And finally it all made sense.

I realized why the raiders had brought us here and kept us alive over the weeks of our investigation. We were tools, pawns in Shale's great chess game, and this was the moment we had been saved for. Under our auspices, the raiders had been tracked to this place. Here they had smashed the combined military strength of Greycoast and Verneytha. But there was more to it than that. They wanted the citadel.

Ironwall had been the first of the great fortresses in the area to be built, right after Vahlia had split into three territories. I had wondered why it had been built so far east, but now I knew why: It was out of range of Shale's magically shifting raiders. The early rulers of Greycoast had built the citadel just far enough away from Adsine that their old enemy could not appear within their walls, but that had been long ago, and much had been forgotten since. We, the party and I, had been part of Shale's larger plan to lure Ironwall's defenders out onto the plains where they could hit us hard and then chase us back inside. We couldn't get that portcullis down in time to stop them, and then they'd have it all.

"Get inside and lower the portcullis," I shouted. It was pointless, but we would make the enemy work for their prize.

What remained of our cavalry units arrived first, charging across the bridge and through the gatehouse. It was Garnet and Renthrette who appeared at the large square window in the central tower and who set the vast iron grate creaking its slow way down. But by the time I brought the wagon to the bridge, the portcullis was less than a quarter closed and barely seemed to be moving. Most of the infantry had already passed inside and were rushing up to the walls to hide or watch what happened next.

There was no point thinking about trying to defend the place with the front door open. I swung the wagon round to block the bridge as well as I could and released the horses, hoping vainly to slow the enemy down. Then I fled into the shade of the gatehouse. I could hear the slow, grinding chains of the portcullis, but a horseman could still enter with several feet of clearance.

The citadel was in chaos. There were men running all over in the green and blue uniforms of our allies. Women cried and fled. The duke sat alone on his horse a few yards inside the walls and looked hopelessly around him. I ran up the tower's tight spiral to where Garnet and Renthrette stood at the window and watched the approach of the enemy.

There were almost a thousand of them. At their head, surrounded by his raiders, was the one with the staff and the horned helm. Alongside him, on a chestnut warhorse and surrounded by a small escort in heavy armor and sable cloaks, was Arlest, count of Shale.

He looked ahead of him at the open gate. The copper circlet and hempen robe had been replaced by an ermine collar and a crown of gold that sparkled with precious stones. This was to be his day.

There was nothing to say or do as they rode closer and the portcullis ground slowly, too slowly, down. I watched the chains inching over their pulleys, but there seemed no way to speed them up. Perhaps, I thought desperately, if they cut the ropes or released the chains, just let it drop? . . . But it was just too heavy. Let it fall and its own weight would shatter it, leaving the gate open. There was nothing to be done. Around us the desperate citizens shouted pleas for mercy or ran for their homes. Then the raiders halted and dismounted. They would cross the bridge on foot, shields raised over their heads to protect them from arrows. Ironwall was defenseless and there was no need for them to take casualties now.

Arlest nodded and spoke to a grey-haired man in dark robes who stood at his horse's bridle: Chancellor Dathel. He passed along the count's command and the soldiers stepped onto the bridge, victorious and invulnerable, five abreast, their scyaxes in their hands and their bronze faces cold as ever before.

The bridge was no more than twenty yards long and the wagon was in the middle of it. There was no rail, so they had to negotiate it carefully, pushing the wagon to the right-hand side so that three of them could pass it abreast. As the first three approached the gate-

house, there was a sudden explosion of sound and a single white
horse charged from within, its rider giving a long, defiant battle cry
as he spurred his charger right at them and cut one of the raiders
down with one of the huge cutting swords he brandished.

It was Orgos.

As the second man raised his scyax, Orgos kicked him squarely in
the chest and brought his left-handed blade down hard across his
shoulders. With a cry the raider fell bleeding. As the third, clearly astonished by the sudden assault, swung his scyax wildly through the
air, Orgos led his pale steed straight at him. The raider stepped back,
lost his balance, and toppled backwards into the moat. By the time his
cloak had disappeared beneath the sluggish current, four more raiders
were squeezing past the wagon.

There was no shout of triumph from the citadel, for everyone
knew how short-lived this gesture of defiance must be. Against the
backdrop of the nine hundred men waiting to enter, Orgos, mounted
and alone on the bridge, was a strangely poignant sight as he shouted
his challenges and brandished his swords. Renthrette covered her
eyes and Garnet just stared as Orgos slid from the back of his scared
mount and sent it back into the city. He glanced behind him at the
lowering portcullis, and even he knew it was futile. He couldn't hope
to hold them off for the four or five minutes it would take to finish
closing the gate. I wanted to look away, but I couldn't.

The four raiders surrounded him and he held them at bay with
his swords, circling watchfully. One by one they lunged for him, and
each time he anticipated, parried, and cut. One came too close and
fell, slashed across the throat. The others closed in and he fought
them off like a caged bear tossing pit dogs aside with mighty jaws.

More of them came, pushing the wagon until it was half off the
bridge. Orgos spun the great swords about his wrists and dared
them to come to him, standing his ground and sweeping the blades
about him like an enchanter weaving magic.

But then the raider in the great horned helm called them back:
he was going to end this foolishness now. But even as I thought *he*,
something seemed wrong to me. I stared as the raider removed the
helm and shook out a head of long red hair. It was the countess.

Unmasked, she leaned in her saddle and muttered something to
her husband, who nodded and barked out a short command. Three
raiders readied their horses. Orgos looked again to the portcullis,

which was finally too low for a horse and rider to pass through. He laughed out loud at his token triumph, that great rolling laugh of his, his head back and his mouth open. They would be able to get in, but they would have to dismount; and that, I suppose, was the closest we would get to victory today. But the raiders were mounted and ready to take him on. I knew he had no hope of holding off a mounted charge, and from our curious balcony I could only watch, my hands to my face like a child who wants to cover his eyes but can't stop looking.

No.

Then they came at him. We loosed an arrow or two from the walls, but the horsemen were moving too quickly, surging forward, wavelike as ever. He parried one lance head and dodged the second, but the third was too much for him. It struck him hard in the waist, above his belt buckle, and the force of the charge carried him backwards towards the gatehouse. With an audible gasp he slumped to the ground, and a great quiet descended on the spectators.

"Advance on foot," called Arlest. "The gate is open."

There was a hard, almost metallic quality to his voice that I had never heard before, strident and determined. The riders returned to their ranks, leaving Orgos's body crumpled and motionless by the wagon.

And then, when things seemed as bad as they could get, the silence was broken by the distinct clanking of the gatehouse machinery in a different key.

"Someone is raising the portcullis!" said Garnet.

It was the duke, or, rather, a few desperate citizens acting on his orders.

"For certain considerations," the duke boomed from the tower, "we, the people of Ironwall, will bequeath our city to you in return for mercy. . . ."

In other words, he was going to use this pointless capitulation to barter for his own survival. The countess glanced at her husband and I thought I saw her smile, a short, brittle smile of amused contempt. I stared at her, at her husband, and at Raymon, who was speechifying from the tower. The sound of the gate ascending registered as one last insult to Orgos, who had died to keep it down.

It wasn't courage or principle, just a blinding anger that made me grasp the great rope that descended through the tower. I had no thoughts of dignity or honor as I slid down, only an irrational fury. We were dead anyway, and I didn't care anymore. After a lifetime doing all I could to stay alive and safe in the world, I was struck by the obvious: In a world like Arlest's, staying alive wasn't worth the effort.

Better to die telling him what I thought.

SCENE LIX

Realism

The vast iron grate, which had started its slow ascent, was high enough for me to pass through. I stooped towards Orgos, who lay still and bleeding, but only long enough to wrench his heavy sword from his fist. I would take it with me in tribute, I thought. As soon as I stepped through the gate and straightened up, I shot my tiny crossbow—the one Orgos had given me—at the closest raider and brandished his long sword with the yellow stone in its hilt at the man as he backed away uncertainly. The duke of Greycoast's pontificating surrender stuttered to a halt.

Moving purposefully between the corpses on the bridge, I advanced to where the wagon teetered on the edge, its front wheels already half submerged in the moat, hacking wildly at whomever I ran into. Despite the surprise attack, I barely managed to scratch them. One of them snorted softly as he stepped back off the bridge. It was an odd sound, and for a second I didn't realize what it was, but then it came again and spread amongst them: They were *laughing* at me.

That somehow brought me to my senses. I glanced at the sword in my hand, a sword that had always felt uncomfortable however much I'd practiced with it, and I slid it into my belt. I would keep it for my friend till they took it from me, but I couldn't wield it. Then I climbed into the tailgate of the wagon and, as the boards under my feet seesawed back to something like a horizontal plane, got behind the nearest scorpion crossbow and swung it round. Arlest was impatiently ordering more soldiers to clear the way. I felt for the trigger as he turned to look at me, sweat breaking out all over my body. Arlest's eyes met mine down the grooves of the huge crossbow, and for a second he seemed unnerved. But only for a second. Then there was nothing but scorn in his face.

"You're a murderer, Arlest," I said to him, my voice surprisingly calm. "A butcher."

"No, William," he said, almost calmly, "I am a soldier. A professional man of the world, while you are an emotional amateur. Not even that. You weren't even a fighter before you came here, were you?"

I said nothing, but stared at him, wondering what I was going to do. I had a crossbow trained on his heart. The portcullis still ground its way up. Time wasn't a factor to either side anymore. But it somehow seemed imperative to continue the conversation. He wouldn't listen, but there were things I needed to say anyway.

Arlest didn't seem to care what I did. He merely called insults at me across his troops. "Let's not play games, now. You are a coward, Will Hawthorne. My men told me how you hid behind a wagon when they attacked you on the road from Seaholme. We laughed about it. You are hiding again, even in this, your moment of glory. You're hiding behind those crossbows and your sense of righteous anger and bravery."

"Not bravery," I corrected him. "I am not a brave man. I am a realist, too. After all, look what happens to bravery," I said, gesturing to where Orgos lay. "He was the bravest, most valiant man I ever knew—"

"Don't sentimentalize the moment, Mr. Hawthorne," Arlest shouted back, his eyes fixed on mine, no trace of nervousness in them despite the scorpions aimed at him. "He was a mercenary. A hired killer."

"No, Arlest," I said, stifling any hint of emotion. "He was a great man, in his way. He was a man of principle. A man of honor. A friend. But that is, as you say, sentimental. There is no room in the world for friendship or principle or honor. That is why he's dead. I understand that now. Such things have no place in our world."

There was a glimmer of surprise in Arlest's eyes and I shrugged slightly, as if making a confession. I heard footsteps behind me and risked a glance.

Garnet was ducking under the portcullis. In front of him Renthrette was getting to her feet, an arrow in her bow and her helm tipped back so her face showed, pale and intense in its grief. Mithos and Lisha followed, tired and numb with sorrow, and crouched by Orgos's body. Behind them a crowd of ragged soldiers, citizens, and the remnants of the villagers stood watching through the gateway like prisoners in a dungeon, or the audience at some bizarre theatre. Their need to see what was happening out here had almost stifled their fear.

I turned back to Arlest and said, with his own condescension, "Fools like Orgos always fight back. They think it's noble."

There was a whisper of confusion behind me. Garnet, I think.

"This is fighting back?" Arlest laughed caustically, but he was laughing as much *with* me as at me. "Five of you and a corpse against a thousand? He won't be fighting back anymore, and neither will you. Any of you. The Orgoses of this world will always finish up dead on the bridge, while people like me, perhaps even Duke Raymon, will thrive."

"He's not dead," said Mithos quietly from the gate. "Almost, but not quite."

I did not dare turn to look, but I heard them move him. They rolled him under the portcullis and Mithos said to those on the other side, "Make him comfortable before he dies."

I looked at Arlest and he was utterly impassive, appraising me like one who has bought the best seats in the house and feels he has the right to criticize your performance.

"Perhaps I could join you," I began. "In return for sparing your life. One of the realist survivors."

"You?" he laughed, though there was definitely a note of curiosity in his disdain. "What about friendship and honor?"

"What about them?" I replied. "If those things really meant anything to me, I'd be charging you on a white stallion."

"Hawthorne!" called a voice from behind me, a voice charged with desperate anger. "You lying, cowardly snake." It was Garnet. I didn't turn.

"Let go of the crossbow," said Arlest, "and perhaps we can—"

"I'm not interested in *perhaps*," I remarked with a crooked smile, which he reflected at once. "I'm interested in a fast horse to get me out of here and some of the silver you now have so much of."

"What about your friends?"

"I can't save them," I said. "You have to kill them, as you will have to kill everyone in the city. You know that, and your men know that, and they accept it.

"Everyone," I continued with the same studied lack of concern, "every able-bodied man who might threaten your safety, any women who love those men, must die. And since you can't be sure that their children won't grow into rebels, angry at the rape and murder of their parents by your forces, you'll have to spit them on pikes too. Some would blanch at such an idea, but not you. It will be easy for you. After all, you've been doing it for months.

"Wiping out villages in Shale was your masterstroke," I said with an admiring smile. "Who would suspect a man would butcher his own people? Brilliant. Your men must be disciplined, but the real credit goes to you. How do you get a soldier to slice open his own neighbors, maybe even his own family? How many of your men's wives and girlfriends have had their heads and limbs hacked from them by their own comrades-in-arms? And all because you told them to!" I said, with the same note of amazed admiration. "This is your world now, Arlest. Orgos's world bleeds and dies with him. Yours is the world of might and expedient atrocity, and principles cannot hold out against it."

A curious ripple had been building amongst the ranks of the regular Shale soldiers. Perhaps it was because I knew they had played no part in the earlier raids, perhaps it was just because I could see their faces: in any case, it was them that I had been speaking to, not to the Empire troops. Certainly not to the bronze-masked raiders or to Arlest, the controlling monster.

He spoke hurriedly, then, conscious that something was happening around him. "This has wasted time enough. I see what you are trying to do, but, like your dead friend, you will achieve nothing." He looked past me at the gate, but there had been another ripple, and I saw in his face the knowledge that he should not have mentioned Orgos again.

"Orgos could not believe someone like you existed," I said. "Yet I doubt he would have shot you down, even now. He'd wait for you to attack and then he would respond on even terms." I smiled sadly. "He taught me many things, but I have something of your realism after all. Orgos would not cut you down, but I will."

I don't know if he didn't believe me or if he just wasn't listening. He muttered to the chancellor at his side and thirty soldiers came forward and assembled at the end of the bridge, bows poised and arrows in place. I thought of swinging the crossbows onto them and firing, but for once the leader needed to take responsibility for his orders. The chancellor spoke to the platoon commander and the archers drew back their bows and waited for the order.

Behind me, Mithos, Lisha, Renthrette, and Garnet stood shield-less, disdaining to flee or take cover. I looked along the faces of the archers, their eyes narrowed and their forearms tight with the strain.

Arlest's eyes met mine and held them. He smiled, a tiny rippling of the corners of his mouth and a spot of light in his eyes. Then he opened his mouth to give the word. On impulse—though what that impulse was, I couldn't really say—I put one hand to the hilt of Orgos's sword, which hung at my side.

I touched the pommel stone and, for once, I felt its power. I saw my purpose and its value with absolute clarity. There was a great flash of pale light that began at the sword and spread outwards like ripples on the surface of a pond. I felt the energy leave the sword, passing through me, but some of that energy came from me too, and the sensation was powerful and draining. As the wave of light passed over Dathel's poised archers, their eyes flickered, their taut arms re-laxed, and their arrows fell to the ground. They blinked in their confusion and I pulled the trigger.

Arlest pitched forward, blood spurting from his nose and mouth as he died. I wheeled the other crossbow, sighted, and shot the count-ess from her horse. There was no other movement or sound. Very slowly the archers relaxed their arms.

I wasn't sure what had happened, and I didn't care.

A long, disbelieving silence followed. I sat on the wagon and put my face in my hands for a moment as relief gave way to grief. I was suddenly too tired to stand, and all I wanted to do was go to sleep and wake up in Cresdon, playing cards with Orgos in a quiet tavern.

Then, out of the stillness, came footsteps. The chancellor had walked onto the bridge. His expression was stern and somehow weary, but he had barely opened his mouth to speak when a handful of the raiders charged him with their scyaxes drawn. In a fraction of a second he was surrounded by a group of Shale infantry in their black and silver, their shields locked about him and their spears turned out like the spines of a porcupine. The small cell of raiders attacked them, but they didn't last for more than a few seconds. When the skir-mish stopped, another dozen or so of the crimson raiders had been slain. The rest threw down their arms and plucked off their helms.

The monstrous machine suddenly had faces, many of them uncertain, embarrassed, or even ashamed. It was over.

The Empire troops seemed to recognize as much. They had no interest in taking on whoever would stand against them now that it was no longer clear who would come down on which side. I didn't notice when they started to move, but they withdrew as one, and by the time I started looking for them, they were a thousand yards away and riding west.

Curiously, it was *me* Chancellor Dathel addressed when he approached us. As ever, his tone was as dark and serious as his robes.

"On behalf of Shale, and as one now taking control of that county on the demise of Arlest the Second, I submit my land, army, and people to your control. I regret the destruction our land and leader have caused and I can only ask that our current surrender be taken into account in the trials that will inevitably follow. I can only say that I am extremely sorry."

Sorry?

I could think of nothing to say to that. I knew most of it was just political rhetoric, but I suppose that was the name of the game now. Raymon would have a field day. I only half believed Dathel: I would never know exactly what command he gave to those archers, but they had not shot even after the power of Orgos's sword had passed. Perhaps he had been disobeyed. Perhaps he had picked up a new mood in the ranks that he hadn't dared to contradict. I wondered if my words had made a difference and thought that they probably hadn't. Not in the long term, anyway; words never do.

"How much of what you said did you believe?" asked Renthrette, appearing suddenly at my elbow.

"My little speech?" I asked. "I'm not sure. Does it matter?"

She thought for a moment and then smiled very slightly, a smile so small and so sad that you had to be looking for it to notice it at all.

"I suppose not," she said.

⁓✤⁓

It was a comic situation, of course, and quite implausible, this sudden surrender by the obvious victors. If I'd seen it onstage or read it in a book I'd say it was fiction at its most ridiculous, though fiction has that privilege. But, oddly enough, I had known it would work. I knew the instant Arlest started to talk to me as I lined him up in the crossbow's grooves, because it was clear then that he didn't understand the game. He thought it was a debate, an attempt to sway his troops with logic. It had been no debate; it had been theatre.

Mithos gave the responsibility for disarming the Shale forces to Raymon, who was suddenly anxious to please. Then he slipped away with the rest of the party. He was going to find Orgos's body, and I was going with him.

The Curtain

Orgos lay in a dark, candlelit chamber that smelled of the wildflowers and incense on the table by his bed. Lisha had bandaged him and prepared a poultice. Some local wise woman had sung low incantations around the bed and anointed him with oils. Between them they had set his broken ribs and stopped the wound in his abdomen, but he had bled copiously, and they were unsure of what had been ruptured inside. It was unlikely that he would make it through the hour.

The bandages about his stomach were soaked through with blood, but that was somehow less disturbing than the greyish hue his whole body had developed, like a deep, inner pallor. From time to time his eyes opened slightly, but they were pale and sightless. Several times I found myself feeling desperately for his pulse, convinced that he was already dead.

The air was thick with the aroma of candle wax and petals. It was like a sanctuary or a crypt. I thought of the battle, of the pain in his face when the enemy had come at us in spite of our numbers. I thought of our flight to the citadel and his single-handed defense of the bridge, and suddenly I knew what I had to do.

Moving close to his bedside, I knelt beside him, took one of his large dark hands in mine, and began to talk.

I talked of honor and heroism. I told him what had happened after he was cut down by the raiders, how we had taken his position and held them off. I told of how the Shale soldiers had turned on their leaders and on the raiders themselves. I told him how we had thwarted the Empire, who was retreating back to Stavis even as we spoke. I told him everything and I thanked him for it. It was, after all, his victory.

I looked at his still face and his half-open eyes and, charged with emotion, I said, "So you *can't* die! We need you to champion the things you fought for and you can't do that on your back in some cemetery. You held off an army, damn it! There's too much for you to do here. You have to come back and finish the story."

His eyes closed for a second and their lids rippled. When he opened them again, he could see me. His mouth moved, but at first no words came out. Renthrette gave him water and he drank it, looking at me. He mouthed something that I couldn't catch and I had to lean in close while he tried again. "Will Hawthorne . . ." he gasped, "you talk too much."

I shrieked with joy as the others clustered around the bedside. Mithos looked at him and remarked, "I should have known Will could talk you round."

"He's better with words than he is with a sword," Orgos said softly.

"Tough to imagine," I said.

"Now that we have our swordsman back," said Lisha, "Will is welcome to stay our wordsman."

⁂

Words, like swords, have a way of getting people in and out of trouble. Morality was never my strong point, but I suddenly saw the attraction of being in the right and knowing it. Orgos always had, but for once this knowledge hadn't been enough and he had to be reminded. In this, I suppose, we were similar after all. A writer like myself doesn't pen plays just for the hell of it. There always has to be a sense that his audience, for the briefest moment and in some infinitesimal degree, are changed by what they hear onstage. It's the same for swordsmen: When the opposite of your values rides at you hacking and spearing, grinning through their bronze helms, you need a little more than principle to keep your hopes for humanity alive. Orgos had needed to see victory more than ever before. He needed to know he could change the world.

I suppose there is an arrogance there, but I could relate to it. The fighter and the writer struggle with the balance of absolute omnipotence and total impotence that are intrinsic to their media. It's that balance that keeps them on their toes. Yes, Orgos and I were more alike than I had ever suspected.

⁂

Orgos rose from his bed three days after the battle and within another week was recovered enough to walk around the citadel walls by himself. The bandages stayed on. During his recovery, Maia often came to sit beside him and hold his huge hands in hers. Maybe that did some good. He had become to her, and many of her friends and relatives, something of a hero—and by that I mean a real hero, not the actor I had been. I didn't resent this. It seemed only right and proper that the latest act of heroism should banish all previous acts from the audience's mind. I had been a hero because they had needed to see me as one. He was the genuine article.

Orgos and I spent a lot of time together and I noted in him a quietness that had been less evident before. It was a long time before I saw him polish and sharpen his swords again, and when he did, it was with a caution that verged on mistrust. When he grew sad or talked of the death and injury he had seen over the years, I would remind him of the battle on the bridge. Eventually the weariness and resignation left him and he grinned at me and said I'd been stupid to take them on by myself. Like he hadn't, right?

We had gotten lucky. It doesn't usually work like this, as we well knew, but for the moment, everything was on our side. We spent a few anxious days watching Greycoast's western border but the Empire never came back. I guess there were too many troops still intact for them to risk achieving by force what they had hoped to win by guile. We sat at the head table of a banquet of roast beef loins and exotic game birds and laughed with relief. We were cheered in the streets and people bought us drinks wherever we went. Women hung about me with glazed eyes. Gorgeous women. I was the conquering hero (one of them, anyway), and everyone wanted to know me. Funnily enough, I didn't want the attention so much, now that I had it. I spent a lot of time with the other party members and Renthrette smiled knowingly at both my offenses and my triumphs.

"I knew she'd appreciate me in the end," I lied.

"I don't know why I believe a word you say," Orgos laughed.

❦

Verneytha and Greycoast divided Shale between them. The Adsine keep and the Razor's fortified home became infantry forts that kept a watchful eye on the roads and borders. It took several weeks to divide up the goods and treasure from Caspian Joseph's warehouse, and the roads were continually dotted with heavy wagons of silks, silver, iron, and so on, all under cavalry escort en route to Ironwall.

Mithos and Lisha used the gratitude of the governor of Verneytha and duke of Greycoast to force their hands a little, and much of the revenue from the stolen goods was kept in a fund for retraining and housing the survivors from Shale and the villages hit hardest by the attacks. Shale's debts would be forgiven and its people would learn new skills, fitting comfortably into Greycoast's and Verneytha's economic success stories. That was the plan, at least. We had played our part and now we could only hope.

We never found out exactly who knew what within the government of Shale. There had been no vampire lord, no intrinsically evil force behind them, and I found myself in some sympathy with the land that had resorted to such desperate and unconscionable methods to get back on comparable economic footing with its rich and self-interested neighbors. That was, of course, the wrong way to think about it. Arlest and his Empire-supported raiders were the bad guys and had needed to be destroyed. It would have been easier if they had merely wanted to enslave the world, or if the victors had been a little more appealing. But Shale had lost and, in any future discussion of the matter, its people would turn into demons whether they had been so before or not. Alas, the victors write more than history books.

Dathel, chancellor of Shale, was taken off to be a guest of the glass tower in Harvest, where he would feel the eyes of the governor on him for the rest of his life. Greycoast took on the surviving raiders and the officers of the Shale regular army. Some were "educated" (tortured) and released. Others never came out or were executed, their heads displayed on the walls. As if there hadn't been enough blood spilled. We went to protest, but it was weeks since we had been instrumental in their capture, and our influence no longer extended into such "domestic affairs." It was time for us to leave.

We were paid double the original offer, a little reluctantly, by Governor Treylen of Verneytha, who thanked us for the revenue we had saved and the commerce which could begin again. We remained politely silent. Greycoast loaded a pair of wagons with our share of the bounty, which must have come close to four thousand silvers. I would have got into this business a lot sooner if I'd known this kind of money could be made legally. Or, do I mean "honestly," or something equally dubious?

I think both of the surviving local leaders were quietly glad to see us go so they could get back to their own squabbling and financial one-upmanship. Their farewell speeches had all the right words in them, but their eyes said that they were delighted to be back in control. We saddled up and headed west through colorful banners and cheering crowds of happy subjects, who no longer remembered searching through the corpse wagons for missing relatives or weeping from the battlements as the flowers of three lands were speared and hewn to pieces. That was the past and they had come through victorious, for which they thanked us and sang our praises.

From time to time I found myself inexplicably close to tears in the midst of the rejoicing and cheering faces, my mind full of blood and the dreadful, bellowing chaos of battle. Then it would pass and I would laugh and sing and play the hero again. We took our bows and smiled upon them as they fought to get close to the stage and shake our hands, but we avoided each other's eyes when we did so. I knew that this pageantry and carnival would not have been altered one iota by the death of Orgos, and that thought stayed with me like the cold steel of a blade against my skin.

～❈～

We rode out of the city, across the Downs, and into the forest, then farther west into what had been Shale. We avoided Adsine and went west into Targev, working our way back towards Stavis at our own pace. We rested for a few days when we came upon a nice inn that served decent food. When I asked Renthrette if we might go riding together one day, Garnet smiled.

Mithos and Lisha relaxed visibly, like a great weight had been lifted from their shoulders. I don't mean that they suddenly started doing stand-up comedy in the taverns; they just lost some of their sternness and distance. They smiled more at my attempts at humor, and didn't lecture me for telling some rustics that I was the king of Bangladeia, out with my vampiric warrior escort. It was all a far cry from my first meeting with them in a Cresdon pub, when they had shut me in a box and thrown insults at me. I thought of that time less and less these days.

The Eagle was distanced from me by more than miles, and I doubted I would go back, even if I could. Where exactly I *would* go, I couldn't say. We would reach Stavis soon. Then what? Lisha had asked if I wished to stay with them. I was flattered but remained evasive. I didn't know what I wanted. Like Orgos, I sometimes felt I'd seen enough blood for one lifetime; but also like him, I couldn't quite withdraw from it completely.

As we came close to Stavis one evening and the sun was setting low above the white buildings of the city, I knew I had to decide. Like most decisions, this one would be made on impulse and then stuck to until it had become the only conceivable course. We had stopped on a hillock with a view of the town sprawling down to the ocean. I looked at my companions one at a time, regarding them slowly and with care as they took in their destination. Orgos caught my eye and beamed. I smiled despite myself and looked from him to Renthrette, who rode pale and beautiful by my side, to the scarlet and bronze of the clouds that hung heavy over Stavis. Memories spiraled through my head, thoughts of the triumph, terror, and despair of the last months, and I found myself looking down the dark, featureless corridor of the life I had lived—or half lived—before I met them.

In a quiet voice touched with uncertainty, I said, "If you don't mind, I think I'll stay with you for a while."

A quiet smile spread through the group. Silently the wagon creaked into motion. I touched my heels to Tarsha's silky flanks and we moved off, through the dusk and into the city.

❧

THE END

ACKNOWLEDGMENTS

Special thanks to Liz Gorinsky and everyone at Tor, for pursuing this project so diligently, and—as ever—to my agent, Stacey Glick, without whom this would be just another stack of yellowing pages.

F
HA

Hartley, A. J.
   (Andrew James)

Act of Will.

DATE			

BAKER & TAYLOR